"Fast-paced... Grip[...] the
body of Gittings is [...] as
every move the e[...] gly
dangerous." [...]ew

"Carey is also a talented graphic novelist, and it shows:
The Felix Castor novels are splashed with color and
texture, their characters are larger than life (or death),
and the stories are, well...out of this world. Castor is a
remarkably believable character...and his cohorts, who
include a lovely succubus and a zombie, are not your
standard detective-thriller bit players...A wholly engaging blend of the detective and fantasy genres."

—*Booklist*

"Part urban fantasy thriller and part hard-boiled detective
novel...Carey has created a spooky world that begs interesting questions about life, death, and the ever after."

DaemonsBooks.com

"A dark but compelling book...Plus, Castor's point of view is a joy to read, with his sarcastic outlook and self-deprecating wit...For anyone who likes urban fantasy with a noir twist...And the very best news? This is the third book in the series so if you're coming to the series late, you'll have two more great books waiting to be read."
—**MyShelf.com**

"Readers expect [Castor's] adventures to be peppered with bons mots, lots of creatures of the formerly alive kind, and tsunamis of action, and this new outing won't disappoint...His 3-D extravaganza engages all the senses, then deftly holds the punch line until dead last. Readers seeking a leisurely summer read won't find it in this tale, which will have them staying up much too late for the pleasure of 'just one more chapter' before dousing the lights." —*Kirkus Reviews* **(starred review)**

"Strong subplots contribute satisfying depth and a sense of urgency to the mystery while readers familiar with the series will delight in Juliet's larger role and additional character building. If you haven't already discovered this fine series, run out; find a copy of *The Devil You Know* and start in; you won't be disappointed."
—**MonstersandCritics.com**

"Highly recommended for fans of dark urban fantasy."
—*Library Journal*

VICIOUS CIRCLE

"Felix offers a darkly droll take on the circumstances of his world, which is just as familiar, intricate, and morally tangled as our own."   —*Entertainment Weekly*

"[A] deftly crafted, can't-turn-the-page-fast-enough read. This book ratchets up the action, making it even more compelling than *The Devil You Know*."
                    —*Kirkus Reviews* (starred review)

"4½ Stars! Hugely entertaining...another wicked blend of supernatural mayhem and hard-boiled detective story...Smart dialogue, good pacing, and offbeat characters keep the pages turning."   —*RT Book Reviews*

"A fine supernatural thriller...Carey's imagined universe has some nice satiric touches."   —*Publishers Weekly*

"Carey's knack for detail draws you into this wicked world, and it becomes a feast for the senses."
                    —*Decatur Daily* (AL)

"A treat...Carey follows up his excellent debut with this even better sequel...Genre-bending at its best."
                    —*Booklist* (starred review)

Also by Mike Carey

The Devil You Know
Vicious Circle

DEAD MEN'S BOOTS

MIKE CAREY

GC

GRAND CENTRAL
PUBLISHING

NEW YORK   BOSTON

Copyright © 2009 by Mike Carey
All rights reserved. Except as permitted under the U.S. Copyright Act of 1976, no part of this publication may be reproduced, distributed, or transmitted in any form or by any means, or stored in a database or retrieval system, without the prior written permission of the publisher.

Originally published in Great Britain by Orbit in September 2007

Cover design by Dale Fiorillo and Don Puckey
Cover photo by Herman Estevez

Grand Central Publishing
Hachette Book Group
237 Park Avenue
New York, NY 10017
Visit our website at www.HachetteBookGroup.com

Grand Central Publishing is a division of Hachette Book Group, Inc.
The Grand Central Publishing name and logo is a trademark of Hachette Book Group, Inc.

Printed in the United States of America

First United States Hardcover edition: July 2009
First United States Mass Market edition: August 2010

10 9 8 7 6 5 4 3 2 1

ATTENTION CORPORATIONS AND ORGANIZATIONS:
Most HACHETTE BOOK GROUP books are available at quantity discounts with bulk purchase for educational, business, or sales promotional use. For information, please call or write:
Special Markets Department, Hachette Book Group
237 Park Avenue, New York, NY 10017
Telephone: 1-800-222-6747 Fax: 1-800-477-5925

To Charlotte Oria,
my transatlantic connection
for a quarter of a century,
with much love and gratitude

DEAD
MEN'S
BOOTS

~ One

I DON'T DO FUNERALS all that often, and when I do, I prefer to be either falling-down drunk or dosed up on some herbal fuzz-bomb like salvinorin to the point where I start to lose feeling from the feet on up, like a kind of rising damp of the central nervous system. Today I was as sober as a judge, and that was only the start of it. The cemetery was freezing cold—cold enough to chill me even through the Russian-army greatcoat I was wearing (I never fought, but poor bloody infantry is a state of mind). The sun was still locked up for winter, a gusty east wind was stropping itself sharp on my face, and guilt was working its slow way through my mind like a weighted cheese wire through a block of ice.

Ashes to ashes, the priest said, or at least that was what it boiled down to. His hair and his skin were ash-pale in the February cold. The pallbearers stepped forward just as the wind sprang up again, and the shroud on top of the coffin bellied like a sail. It was a short voyage, though:

Two steps brought them alongside the neat, rectangular hole in the ground, where they bent as one and laid the coffin down on a pair of canvas straps held in place by four burly sextons. Then the sextons stepped in from either side, in synchrony, and the coffin slid silently down into the ground.

Rest in peace, John Gittings. The mortal part of you, anyway; for the rest, it was going to be a case of wait-and-see. Maybe that was why John's widow, Carla, looked so strained and tense as she stood directly opposite me in her funereal finery. Her outfit incorporated a brooch made from a sweep of midnight-dark feathers, and staring at it made me momentarily imagine that I was looking down from a great height, the black of her dress becoming the black of an asphalt highway, the remains of a dead bird lying there like roadkill.

The priest started up again, the wind stealing his voice and distributing it piecemeal among us so that everyone got a beggar's share of the wisdom and consolation. Sunk in my own thoughts, which were fixed on mortality and resurrection to the exclusion of redemption, I looked around at the other mourners. It was a who's who of the London exorcist community: Reggie Tang, Therese O'Driscoll, and Greg Lockyear were there, representing the Thames Collective; Bourbon Bryant and his hatchet-faced new wife, Cath; Larry Tallowhill and Louise Beddows, Larry looking like a walking corpse himself with the white of his cheekbones showing through his skin like a flame through a paper lantern; Bill Schofield, known for reasons both complicated and obscene as Jonah; Ade Underwood, Sita Lovejoy, Michelle Mooney, all up from the beautiful South (Elephant and Castle, or thereabouts);

and among the also-rans, a very striking, very young woman with shoulder-length white-blond hair who kept staring at me all the way through the service. There was something both familiar and unsettling about her face, but I couldn't place it. That uncertainty did nothing to improve my mood, and neither did the absence of the one London exorcist I'd been hoping to see at this shindig. But then Juliet Salazar never did hold with cheap sentiment. In fact, she probably didn't have any to sell even at the market price.

Meanwhile, seeing as how this was a cemetery, the dead had turned up in considerable force. They clustered around us at a safe distance, sensing the power gathered here and what it could do to them, but so starved of sensation that they couldn't keep away. It was hard not to look at the sad multitude, even though looking at ghosts often makes them come in closer, as though your attention is a gradient they slide down toward you. There were dozens, if not hundreds, packed so closely together that they overlapped, thrusting their heads through one another's limbs and torsos to get a better look at us and maybe at the new kid on the block. The ghosts of the most recent vintage still carried the marks of their death on them in wasted flesh, oddly angled limbs, and in one case, a gaping chest hole that was almost certainly a bullet wound. The tenants of longer standing had either learned or forgotten enough to look more like themselves in life, or else they'd started to fade to the point where some of the more gruesome details had been lost or smudged over.

The priest seemed oblivious to his larger audience, which was probably a good thing: He looked old enough and frail enough that he might not weather the shock.

But people in my profession have the sight whether they like it or not, and it's not something you can turn on and off. At one point during the funeral oration, Bourbon Bryant reached into his pocket and half drew out the book of matches he always carried there—the particular tool he uses to get the whip hand on the invisible kingdoms, just as a tin whistle (Clarke Sweetone, key of D) is mine.

I put a hand on his arm and shook my head. "Not the time," I said tersely, speaking out of the corner of my mouth.

"I'll just torch one or two, Fix," he muttered back. "The rest will scatter like pigeons."

"I'll break your jaw if you do," I said equably. He shot me a surprised, affronted look, read my own expression accurately, and put away the matches.

Why hadn't I gotten drunk before coming here? Judging by the faces around me, I sure as hell wouldn't have been the only one. Exorcists often resort to booze to stifle their death perception, just as a lot of them use speed when they want to put a particular edge on it. But I'm careful about how I deploy my crutches. Today that would have felt like I was hiding from something specific I was ashamed to face, rather than just dulling unpleasant distractions. Bad precedent.

I defocused as far as I could, staring through the massed ranks of the dead toward the cemetery's high wrought-iron fence, which was topped with very un-Christian razor wire. No respite there, though; the Breath of Life protesters were pressed up against the bars like tourists at the zoo, shouting abuse at us that we were too far away to decipher. The Breathers, as we dismissively call them, are radical dead-rights extremists, and they view us ghost-breakers in much the same light in which staunch Catholics tend to see abortionists: You can always rely on them to break up the funeral of an exorcist if they get a tip-off that it's going down. Most likely, the priest or one of the sextons was a closet sympathizer and had sent the word down the line.

Things were starting to wind down now. Carla threw some earth into her husband's grave, and a few other people got in line to do the same. Then the sextons took over for the serious shoveling. Now that we'd made that ritualistic nod toward plowing the fields, we were free to scatter as soon as was decent. Carla's earlier plan for a post-funeral gathering at her house in Mill Hill had been canceled at the last moment for reasons that weren't entirely clear—and the service, which on the black-edged invitations had been set for three p.m., had been moved forward to one-thirty without explanation. Maybe that was why Juliet hadn't shown.

But just as I was congratulating myself on getting away easy, a shout from the main gates made me turn my head in that direction. There was a man there, running toward us at a flat-out sprint that sat oddly with his immaculately cut Italian suit. By and large, people don't wear Enzo Tovare to go jogging. All the muck sweat's not good for that delicate stitching.

This Johnny-come-lately looked pretty striking in other ways, too. His mid-brown hair was back-combed into an Errol Flynn–style college cut, and he had the Hollywood face to go with it—hard to get without plastic surgery or sterling-silver genes. He looked to be about thirty, but there was something in his face that read as either premature experience or some kind of innate calm and seriousness. He was old for his age, but he wore it pretty well.

He had a folded sheet of paper in his hand that he was holding up for our appreciation like Neville Chamberlain. That plus the sharp suit made it less likely that he was what I'd taken him to be at first: one of the Breath of Life guys trying to disrupt proceedings with a paint bomb or a noisemaker.

He slowed down as he got in among us, and I noticed as he passed me that he wasn't breathing hard despite the run. I wondered if he worked out in Italian linen, too.

"Mrs. Gittings," he said, offering the paper to Carla. "This is a warrant executed this morning by Judge Tilney at Hendon Magistrates' court. Will you please read it?"

Carla smacked the paper out of the man's hand so that he had to flail briefly to catch it again before it fell into the grave.

"Go away, Mr. Todd," she said coldly. "You've got no business being here. No business at all."

"I have to disagree," Italian-suit guy said politely enough, unfolding the paper and showing it to Carla. "You know what my business is, Mrs. Gittings, and you know why I couldn't just allow this to happen. What you're doing here is illegal. This warrant forbids you from burying the mortal remains of the late Jonathan Gittings, and it requires you to appear at—"

He ran out of steam very abruptly. He was looking into the grave, and he clearly registered the fact that it was already occupied and half full of earth. There was maybe a second when he seemed false-footed: all dressed up, writ in hand, and nowhere to go. Then he refolded his warrant and tucked it away in his breast pocket with a decisive motion, his expression somber.

"Obviously, I'm already too late," he said. "I was under the impression that this service was scheduled to start at three o'clock. I'm sure that was what I was told when I called the funeral parlor this morning. Perhaps there was a last-minute cancellation?" Carla flushed red, opened her mouth to speak, but Todd raised his hands in surrender. "I'm not going to try to interrupt a funeral that's already in progress—and I apologize for disturbing the solemnity of the occasion. If I'd been in time to stop the burial, it was my legal duty to do so. Now . . . I'll retire and consider the other avenues available to me. We'll talk again, Mrs. Gittings. And you can expect an exhumation order in the fullness of time."

Carla gave a short cry of pain, as if the words had physically wounded her. Then Reggie Tang—an unlikely Galahad—stepped in between her and the lawyer, fixing him with a look full of violent promise.

"Can I see your invitation, mate?" he demanded. At the same time I saw Reggie's deceptively scrawny-looking friend Greg Lockyear moving in behind Todd, looking to Reggie for his cue. I couldn't believe they were planning to lay some hurt on a lawyer in front of fifty witnesses, but the grim set of Reggie's face was impossible to misread. Like most of us, he knew John from way back, and like most of us, he'd teamed up with him a fair few times when there was nothing better on offer. That tended to be how it worked, and I guessed that maybe, like me, he was feeling some belated pangs of guilt that he'd only ever seen John as a last resort. So maybe beating up a man in a sharp suit seemed like an easy way to burn off some of the bad karma.

Stepping forward as much to my own surprise as any-one else's, I put a hand on Reggie's shoulder. He turned his glare on me, surprised and indignant to be interrupted when he was still warming up.

"Behave yourself, Reggie," I said. "You're doing no one a favor starting a fight here, least of all Carla."

We held each other's eyes for a moment longer, and I was half convinced he was going to take a swing at me. I took a step to the left to keep Greg Lockyear in view, because that way, at least, I wouldn't be fighting on two fronts; but the moment passed, and Reggie turned away with a disgusted shrug.

"Frigging parasites," he said. "Have it your way, Fix. But if he doesn't get the fuck out of here, I'm gonna put something through his face."

I gave Todd a look that asked him what he was waiting for. "Mrs. Gittings will be in touch," I said.

"I'm sure," he agreed. "But I really need to proceed with—"

"You need to pick your time. She'll be in touch. Leave it until then, eh?"

Todd looked at the grim faces ringing him and prob-ably did some calculations. He glanced around for Carla, but she'd stepped back into the supportive crowd and was being comforted by Cath and Therese. "I'm prepared to wait a day or so," he said, "out of respect. A day or so— no longer."

"Good plan," I agreed.

With a wry nod to me, Todd turned on his heel. He took the path back to the gate a lot more slowly and stayed in sight for the better part of a minute, further dampening the already tense mood.

We broke up by inches and ounces, swapping half-hearted conversation at the turning circle by the car park because nobody wanted to seem in an indecent hurry to escape. I said hello to Louise, whom I hadn't seen in a year or more, and we played the "ain't it awful" game, trading stories about the Breathers.

"They're running ambushes now," Louise said in her lugubrious Tyneside drawl, igniting a cigarette with a gold lighter shaped like a tiny revolver. "Picking us off. Can you believe it? Stu Langley got a call in the early hours of the morning. Some woman saying she'd just moved into a new house and there was a ghost in the bloody downstairs lavvy. He told her he'd come the next morning, but she started crying and pleading. Laying it on thicker and thicker, she was, and Stu's too polite to hang up on her. So in the end he got dressed and went out there. I'd have told her to hold it in or piss out the window.

"Anyway, he gets to this place out in Gypsy Hill somewhere, and look at that. There's a house with a for-sale sign up, exactly where she said it would be, and the front door's open. So he went on in, like a bloody idiot. Didn't stop to ask himself why there were no lights on, or why the sign still said for sale if this whinging old biddy had already moved in.

"There were four of them, with baseball bats. They laid into him so hard they put him in a coma. He lasted for a week, and then they turned the machine off. I'm telling you, Fix, they won't be happy until they've killed us all."

"Won't do them much good if they do," I observed, shaking my head as she offered me a drag on the cigarette. "Exorcism is in the human genome now. Probably always was, only it didn't show itself until there was something there to use it on. Killing us doesn't make the problem go away."

She blew smoke out of her nose, hard. "No, but beating the shit out of a few of us gives the rest of us something to think about."

Another knot of mourners walked past us, heading for their cars. One of them was the acid-blond girl, walking alongside two guys I didn't know, and she gave me another killing look as she passed.

"Any idea who that is?" I asked Louise, rolling my eyes to indicate who I meant without being too obvious about it.

"Which one?"

"The girl."

Louise expelled breath in a forced sigh, made a weary face. "Dana McClennan."

"McClennan?" Something inside me lurched and settled at an odd angle. "Any relation to the late, great Gabriel McClennan?"

"Daughter," said Louise. "And she's following on in the family tradition, Fix. Bigger arsehole than he was, if anything. When she found out Larry was HIV-positive, she backed off at a hundred miles an hour. You'd think he'd tried to give her a Frenchie or something. Or maybe she thinks you can catch it by talking about it, like my mum."

I didn't answer. The mention of Gabe McClennan's name had triggered a whole lot of very unpleasant memories, most of them dating from the night when I'd killed him. Okay, it was kind of by proxy: Actually, I just made it really easy for someone else to kill him. It wasn't like he left me much choice, either, since he was out for my blood; and the wolf I threw him to was one he'd brought to the party himself, so you could say what goes around comes around. Lots of great arguments to mix and match. None of them made me feel any better about it, though, and there was no way I'd ever be able to explain it to the wife and kid he'd left behind.

"So what's she doing here?" I asked.

"She came with Bourbon. I think he put the word out at the Oriflamme that John was going into the ground today—said he'd lay on cars for any exorcists who wanted to come along."

"She's a ghostbreaker?"

Louise shrugged. "That's what she's calling herself, yes. Following in her father's footsteps. I don't know if she's any good or not."

I took it on the chin, but it wasn't great news. If Gabe's daughter was in the same line of business as me now, and if she was operating in London, then we were going to keep running across each other's trail whether we liked it or not. Not a happy prospect. I watched Gabe's daughter down to the gates—saw her stop, her two escorts walking on without her, and exchange words with the Breathers on picket duty. Someone ought to have a word with her about that: It wasn't a great idea to encourage the lunatic fringe.

"How's the music going?" I asked in a ham-fisted effort to raise the mood. Louise played bass in a band that had had many more names than gigs. I had a vague feeling that their current nom de soundstage was something vaguely punk, like All-Star Wank, but it would be something different tomorrow.

"It's good," Louise said. "It's going good. We've got a new manager. He reckons he can get us in at the Spitz."

Larry Tallowhill came up alongside Louise at this point and slid an arm around her waist. "Felix Castor," he said with mock sternness. "Leave my fucking woman alone."

"Can I help it if I'm irresistible?" I asked. "How are the new drugs working?"

Larry shrugged expansively. "They're great," he said. "I'll live until something else kills me. Can't ask for more than that."

Larry was always amazingly upbeat about his condition, which was the result of the sort of arbitrary bad luck that would fill most people with rage or despair to the slopping-over-the-top, foaming-at-the-mouth point. He'd contracted HIV from a bite he got when he was trying to subdue a loup-garou—you might call it a werewolf, except that the animal component here was something leaner and longer-limbed and altogether stranger than that word suggests. It wasn't even a paying job; he just saw this monster chasing a bunch of kids across a Sainsbury's car park, and stepped in without even thinking about it. The thing was looking to feed, but it turned its attention to Larry as soon as it realized he was a threat, and like I said, it was sleek and fast and very, very mean. Larry took the damage, finished the job with one arm hanging off in strips, then walked a mile and a half to the hospital to get himself patched up. They did a great job: stabilized him, took the severed finger he'd brought with him and sewed it back on, stopped him from bleeding to death or getting tetanus, and eventually restored 95 percent of nervous function. About ten or eleven months later, he got the bad news.

For an exorcist, it all falls under the heading of

occupational hazard. There aren't very many of us who get to die of old age.

I changed the subject, which sooner or later was going to bring us around to the even more painful issue of how John Gittings had died—locked in the bathroom with the business end of a shotgun in his mouth. I'm not squeamish, but I'd been shying away from that particular image all afternoon.

"Business good?" I asked, falling back once more on the old conversational staples.

"It's great," Larry said. "Best it's ever been."

"Three bloody jobs all at once yesterday," Louise confirmed. "He's fast." She nodded at Larry. "You know how fast he is, but even he can't do three in a day. They get in the way of each other. The second's harder than the first, and the third's impossible. So I did the middle one, and of course, that was the one that turned out to be an absolute bastard. Old woman—very tough. Fought back, and I lost my lunch all over the client's carpet."

"Your breakfast," Larry corrected. "It was only eleven o'clock."

"My brunch. And this bloke—company director or something, lives in Regent Quarter—he says, 'I hope you're going to clean that up before you go.' And I would have done, too, but not after he said that. I hit him with the standard terms and conditions and walked out. Now he's saying he won't pay, but he sodding will. One way or another, he will."

As changes of subject go, it hadn't gotten us very far away from death. But that's exorcists' shoptalk for you.

After a few more pleasantries, Lou and Larry strolled away arm in arm, and I walked back over to the grave to say my goodbyes. Carla was now standing in deep conversation with the priest—maybe a little too deep for comfort. At any rate, she took the opportunity as I walked up to extricate herself, thank him, and disengage.

"I'm heading out," I said. "Take care of yourself, Carla. I'll be in touch, okay?" But she was holding something out to me, and the something turned out to be her car keys.

"Fix," she said apologetically, "could you drive me home? I really don't feel up to it. And there's something I want to ask you about."

I hesitated. They say misery loves company, but I'm the kind of misery who usually doesn't. On the other hand, I'd missed Bourbon's charabanc, and I needed a lift back into town. Maybe a half-second too late to look generous, I nodded and took the keys. "Thanks again, Father," Carla called over her shoulder. I glanced back. The priest was watching us as we walked away, the expression on his face slightly troubled.

"He asked me if I had any doubts," Carla said, catching the movement as I looked around. "Any bits of doctrine I wanted to talk over with him. Then, before I could get a word in, he was pumping me for clues."

"Men of the cloth are the worst," I agreed. "They don't approve, but they have to look. It's the same principle as the *News of the World*." That was slightly unfair, but it's something you come across a lot. People assume that we're sitting on a big secret: We have to be, because how could we do what we do without knowing how it's done? But it's not like that at all. Would you ask Steve Davis for an explanation of Brownian motion, or Torvill and Dean how ice crystals form? We've got a skill set, not the big book of answers.

Carla's car was the only one left in the car park: a big, roomy old Vectra GLS in a dark gray that showed off the splatter stains of old bird shit to good effect. I let Carla in—no central locking—and walked around to the driver's side, taking an appraising look at her in the process. She was calmer now that it was all over, but she looked a little tired and a little old. That wasn't surprising: Having someone you love commit suicide has to be one of the nastiest low blows life can throw at you. In other respects, she was still very much the woman I'd known back in the early nineties, before she'd ever met John—when she was a brassy, loud blonde I'd met at a poker session and almost gone to bed with, except that my fear of intimacy and her preference for older men had kicked in at about the same time and turned a promising fumble into an awkward conversation about micro-limit hold 'em. There's a line in a Yeats poem where he asks whether your imagination lingers longest on a woman you won or a woman you lost. While you're puzzling over that one, you can maybe give him an estimate on how long a piece of string is. If things had worked out differently, Carla and me could have gotten a whole Mrs. Robinson thing going, although even in those days, I was less of a Benjamin Braddock and more of a Ratso Rizzo.

I started the car and pulled away, noticing that the priest followed us with his sad eyes as we drove by. I sympathized up to a point. It couldn't be an easy way to earn a living these days.

We eased our way out between the pickets, collecting a fair share of abuse and ridicule along the way but no actual missiles or threats. Most of the people waving placards and chanting rhythmically were in their teens or early twenties. What did they know about death? They hadn't even gotten all that far with life yet.

The cemetery was all the way out in Waltham Abbey, and John and Carla lived—or rather, Carla still lived and John didn't anymore—on Aldermans Hill just outside of Southgate, in a flat over a dress shop. It was going to be a long haul, and the Vectra handled like a half-swamped raft. Turning in to the traffic, I remembered the half-bottle of metaxa in my inside pocket, fished it out one-handed, and passed it across to Carla. She took it without a word, unscrewed the lid, and downed a long swallow. It made her shudder; probably it made her eyes water, too, but there were plenty of other explanations available for why she rubbed the heel of her hand quickly across her face.

Looking in the rearview mirror, I noticed that we'd picked up a tail. I swore under my breath. It was one of the vans that the Breathers had arrived in—a big high-sided delivery truck that someone must have borrowed from work, deep blue and with the words BOWYER'S CLEANING SERVICES written in reverse script over the windscreen— because a good idea is a good idea, even if the emergency services think of it first. I didn't mention it to Carla: I just switched lanes whenever I could to make life harder for them. I was confident that I could lose them long before we got back into London.

"So what was all that shit with the lawyer?" I asked. It sounds tactless, put like that, but I've always found anger a good corrective to grief. Grief paralyzes you, where a good head of hacked-off biliousness keeps you moving right along, although it's not so great for making you look where you're going.

Carla shook her head, as though she didn't want to talk about it, and I was going to let it lie. But then she took a second pull on the brandy bottle, and away she went.

"John had always said he wanted to be buried at Waltham Abbey, next to his sister, Hailey," she muttered. "Always. She was the only person he ever loved, apart from me. But he wasn't himself, Fix. Not for months before he died. He wasn't anyone I recognized." She sighed deeply and a little raggedly. "There's a condition—EOA, it's called. Early-onset Alzheimer's. It got John's dad when he was only forty-eight, and by the time he turned fifty, he couldn't even dress himself. John was convinced that Hailey was starting to get it just before she died, and he was always terrified he was going to go the same way. He tried to make me promise once that I'd give him pills if it ever took him. If he ever got to the point where—you know, where there was nothing left of him. But I couldn't, and I told him I couldn't.

"Anyway, just because it *can* run in families doesn't mean it will. You don't know, do you? There's no point running halfway to meet trouble. But he'd have days when he couldn't move, hardly, for brooding about it. I tried to jolly him along when he was in one of those moods. Wait for him to pull out of it again, and then most times he'd say he was sorry he'd worried me, and that'd be that.

"But a couple of months before Christmas, he went through a bad time. He had a job on—something that was going to pay really well, but it seemed to prey on his mind a lot."

"What sort of job?" I asked, sounding a lot more casual than I felt. This was where my guilt was stemming from, in case you were wondering. I'd already heard a few hints about John's last big earner, and I had good reason to feel uneasy about it.

"He wouldn't say. But he put a grand in my hand, sometime back in November, it was, and told me to bank it—and he said there'd be more later. Well, you know how it is, Fix. Most of the time, no offense, you just work for rent money, don't you? Oh yeah, for young men, it's lovely. Two or three hundred quid for a couple of days' work, you're laughing. When you're a bit older, it gets to be different, and you never really have a chance to lay anything by. So I was over the moon for him, I really was. I said, 'What, is there a ghost in Buckingham Palace or something? Can we say we're by royal appointment now?' And he laughed and said something about East End royalty, but he wouldn't tell me what he meant.

"I think the truth was, whatever this job was all about, he didn't know if he could handle it. He called those two on the Collective—Reggie and that friend of his who never washes. But they wouldn't work with him anymore. They said he was too sloppy, and they wouldn't trust him if things went bad on a job."

She hesitated as if she thought I might want to jump in at this point and defend John's reputation, but I made no comment. Because if Reggie had said that, Reggie was right. John had never been the most focused of men, and he'd gotten worse as he got older. Having him at your back was far from reassuring: Generally, it just gave you one more thing to worry about.

But I didn't feel comfortable thinking those thoughts, because John hadn't called only Reggie. He'd called me, too, three times in the space of a week. The messages were still on my answerphone, since I never bother to wipe the tape. Three times I'd sat there and listened to him telling me he might have some work to put my way, and three times I hadn't even picked up because life's too short and you tend to avoid things that might make it shorter still.

Then I got a call from Bourbon, the de facto godfather of London's ghostbusters, with the news that John had kissed a loaded shotgun.

"Did he say who he was working for?" I asked Carla, crashing the gears as we turned onto the M25 sliproad. The blue van was still in back of us, but I wasn't worried; I hadn't even begun to fight.

Carla shook her head. "I asked him. He didn't want to talk about it. He just said it was big, and that when it was done, he'd be in the history books. 'One for the books,' he kept on saying. Something nobody's ever done before.

"And it changed him. He started to get really fretful and really paranoid about forgetting things. He'd make himself little notes—lists of names, lists of places—and he'd hide them all around the house. I'd open the tea caddy, and there'd be a bit of paper all folded up inside the lid. Just names. Then the next day he'd go around and collect them all up again. And burn them. For the first time ever, I started to think he might have been right all along. You know, about the Alzheimer's. I thought maybe the stress had brought it on or something."

She rubbed her eyes again. "It was a terrible time, Fix. I didn't know who to talk to about it. When Hailey was alive, I'd have called her over, and we'd have had it out with him all together. But I couldn't get near him. He started to fly off the handle whenever I even hinted that he was acting strangely. It got so I had to pretend everything was all right even when he was sneaking around like a spy in a film, picking up secret messages that he'd left for himself.

"Then one night he got into bed and started to talk about death. Said he thought his time would be coming soon, and he'd changed his mind about what kind of send-off he wanted. 'Forget about Waltham Abbey, Carla. You've got to cremate me.' Well, I didn't know what to say. What about Hailey? What about the plot he'd already paid for, right next to her? It was the disease talking. It wasn't him. So I did just what I did that time when he tried to make me promise to poison him. I kept shtumm. I didn't say a word. I wasn't going to make a promise that I didn't mean to keep.

"And then after he"—she saw the word looming, swerved away from it—"after he did it, I got this letter from a solicitor. Mr. Maynard Todd from some company with three names, and one of the names is him. He said John had come to him before he died and written a new will. Still left all his money to me, but he wanted to make sure he'd be burned instead of buried. Even picked out someplace over in the East End—Grace something. He'd put it all down in black and white. And he'd written a bit at the end about how he'd had to go to a stranger because he couldn't trust his own wife to do right by him."

"So what did you do?"

"Nothing," Carla said with bitter satisfaction. "I ignored it. I thought, Fuck it, let the bastard sue me. I'll do what my John wanted when he was still in his right mind. So I went ahead with the funeral, even though this Maynard Todd said he was going to stop me, and I moved the time from three back to one-thirty so he'd miss it and get there too late. Which he did." Her voice had been getting thicker, and now she burst into shuddering sobs. "But it doesn't matter anymore, Fix. I don't care what they do to John's body. I just want him to be at peace. Oh God, let him find some peace!"

There wasn't anything I could say to that, so I didn't try. I just concentrated on making life hideous for the driver of the blue van. The League Against Cruel Sports wouldn't approve, but if you know you're being tailed, there are all sorts of subtle torments and indignities you can inflict on the guy who's chasing you. By the time we'd reached the Stag Hill turnoff, I'd shaken him loose and relieved some of my own tensions in the process.

I drove on in silence, exiting the motorway and coaxing the uncooperative car through the congested streets of Cockfosters and Southgate. Meanwhile, Carla went through three handkerchiefs and most of what was left in the bottle.

When I pulled up at Aldermans Hill, she was more than half drunk. I parked in front of the costume shop, which was closed for Sunday, leaving the car on a double-yellow line because it seemed more important right then to get her back onto home turf and more or less settled.

The flat was on the first floor, up an external flight of steps with a dogleg. On the door frame there were a good half-dozen wards against the dead, ranging from a sprig of silver birch bound with white thread to a crudely drawn magic circle with the word *ekpiptein* written across it in Greek script. That translates as "bugger off until you're wanted, you bodiless bastards." Greek is a very concise language.

Carla fumbled with her keys, and I noticed that her hands were trembling. I was quite keen to get out of there now that I'd done my civic duty. I'm fuckall use as a shoulder to cry on.

"I'm sure he is," I said clumsily—and belatedly. "At peace, I mean. John was a good man, Carla. He didn't have any enemies in this world. You know I don't believe in heaven, but if anyone deserved—"

I stopped because she was looking at me with the sort of expression you give to dangerous madmen.

"No," she said bluntly. "He's not in heaven, Fix, or anywhere else. He's here. He's still here."

She turned the key and shoved the door open, but she made no move to go in. I stepped past her into the small hallway, smelling a slightly musty, unused smell, as though nobody had been there in a few days.

Three steps took me into the living room, and I stopped dead, if you'll pardon the expression, taking in a scene of devastation and ruin. Most of the furniture was overturned. The television lay in the corner like a poleaxed drunk, staring blindly up at the ceiling. Three deep dents scarred the screen, a fish-scale pattern of fracture marks spreading out from each one. Broken glass crunched under my feet.

And then a framed photo of John and Carla smiling, arm in arm, leaped up from the broken-legged dresser and shot through the air, spinning like a shuriken, to explode against the wall just inches from my head.

With a muttered oath, I dodged back around the corner and turned to stare at Carla in dazed disbelief. She gave me a curt nod, her face bitter and despairing.

Despite his faults, most of which I've already mentioned, John had always been a pretty easygoing sort of guy. But that was when he was alive.

In death, it was painfully obvious, he'd gone geist.

~ Two

SOME APOSTLE not noted for charm or tact once told an appreciative audience somewhere near the Sea of Galilee that the poor would always be with us. He could have said the same thing about the dead. Of course, back in Jesus's time, there were only maybe a hundred million people in the world, give or take, but even then they were heavily outnumbered by the part of the human race that was already lying in the ground. The exact ratio wobbles up and down as we ride the demographic roller coaster, but these days you could bet on twenty to one and probably not lose your money.

Twenty of them to one of us. Twenty ghosts for every man, woman, and child living on this planet. But that was an empty statistic until just before the turn of the second millennium. Until then most of the dead were content to stay where they'd been put. In the words of a million headstones, they were "only sleeping." Then, not too long ago, the alarm clock went off and they all sat up.

Okay, that's an exaggeration. Even now a whole lot of people die and stay dead—trek off across the undiscovered country, or dissolve into thin air, or go and sit at God's right hand in sinless white pajamas, or whatever. But a whole lot more don't: They wake up in the darkness of their own death, and they head back toward the light of the world they just left, which is the only direction they know. Most of the time they come back as a visual echo of their former selves, without substance, mass, or weight, and then we call them ghosts. Sometimes they burrow back into their own dead flesh and make it move; then we call them zombies. Occasionally, they invade an animal body, subdue the host mind by force majeure, and redecorate the flesh and bone so it looks more like what they used to remember seeing in the mirror. Then we call them werewolves or loup-garous, and if we're smart, we keep the fuck out of their way.

But here's the wonderful thing: In all their many forms, there were people like me who shouldered the live man's burden and came out fighting with the skill and the will to knock them back again. The exorcists. Probably we'd always been there, too—a latent tendency in the human gene pool, as I'd said to Louise, waiting for its time to shine. Whatever it is that we do, it's got sod all to do with sanctity or holy writ. It's just an innate ability expressing itself through the other abilities that we pick up as we go through life. If you're good with words, then you'll bind the dead with some kind of incantation; if you're an artist, you'll use sketches and sigils. I met a gambler a while back—nice guy named Dennis Peace—who did it with card tricks.

And with me, it's music.

I always had a good ear as a kid, but I never had the

patience or the concentration to survive formal lessons. This was in Walton, Liverpool, you understand—and although the image of the godforsaken North that persists down here in the smoke is a bit of a caricature, the mean streets I walked down would have been a damn sight meaner if I'd been walking down them with, say, a cello.

In the end, I took up the tin whistle because I found I could knock out a tune without really having to know what I was doing. Most of my little musical knowledge I picked up casually, either by jamming with better musicians or by not being ashamed to ask stupid questions whenever I was with someone who might be able to answer them. I learned to read music by watching a TV program aimed at six-year-olds, painstakingly practicing exercises set for me by a smiling, animated treble clef.

Along the way, after discovering to my bitter chagrin that you couldn't play tin whistle in a rock band, I stumbled across one application for music that I'd never dreamed of.

My first exorcism, though, didn't involve any instrument except my own voice. I was six years old—just. And when my dead sister, Katie, came back from the grave and visited me after midnight in the bedroom we shared back when she was alive, I sent her packing by singing the stupid taunts that kids use to make each other cry in the playground. I did it because it worked, found out much later why it worked—or rather, how—and, like many people I've met since, turned a strange knack into an even stranger career.

The more I did it, the easier it got. I found that I had a sort of additional sense, more like hearing than anything else. When I was close to a ghost long enough, I got a feeling for it—a feeling that translated readily into sound and usually into a tune, into music. When I played the tune on my whistle, the ghost would get tangled up in the sound, and when I stopped playing, the ghost would fade away on the last note like breath on a mirror. None of them ever came back after that. Bizarre and inexplicable as it was, what I did to them was permanent.

But what seems stranger now, as I look back on that time in my life, is that I did it all without ever once asking where the ghosts went when I played to them. Where did I send them to? Where did I send Katie to? Eternal reward, the world soul, or just oblivion? Answers on a postcard; except that the undiscovered country has no postal service.

It took a lot to shake me out of that complacent tree. I was an exorcist for well over ten years, and in that time I must have played a thousand tunes. The world changed around me as the dead started to return in greater and greater numbers. They made the first tentative steps toward creating their own infrastructure—zombies in particular have some very specialized needs—and predictably, the living responded by dividing into antagonistic camps, the Breath of Life movement calling for a recognition of dead rights, while groups like the Catholic Anathemata preached the imminent apocalypse and started stockpiling weapons for it. Meanwhile, people in the ghostbusting trade started to talk about encountering other kinds of creatures that had never been either human or, strictly speaking, alive: creatures that seemed to fit the mug shots of the demons described in medieval grimoires. I even met a few myself—encounters that I still relive in dreams and probably always will.

Two things eventually had to happen before I started to realize that tooting my whistle first and asking questions later was a flawed strategy. The first was me fucking up someone else's life beyond all possible unfucking, and the second was having my own life saved and handed back to me by a dead woman I was trying to exorcise. These days I don't do straight ghostbusting anymore—if you look at the sign over my office door, you'll see that it says I provide SPIRITUAL SERVICES. No, I don't know what that means, either, and it doesn't do a hell of a lot to bring in the passing trade. But that suits me okay in a lot of ways: The closest thing I've got to a philosophy is that I'll do anything for a quiet life except work for it.

―――――――

So what kind of a spiritual service was my old acquaintance John Gittings in need of? As I sidestepped out of the way of a broken-off chair leg that left a dent in the wall at the height of my crotch, I ran through some of the options, from the humane to the extreme. None of them looked good right then except slamming the door shut behind me and making a run for it.

Geist! It was like finding out that your best friend is a cannibal after he's just offered you a chicken sandwich.

Well, maybe not quite like that. John had never been a friend, exactly. Including one memorable skirmish with a werewolf at Whipsnade Zoo, in which John had modified our sketchy battle plan on the fly and almost gotten me eaten alive, I'd seen him maybe five times in the last three years.

It was still a shock, though, and I was having a hard time getting my head around it. Like I said, most ghosts are passive and harmless: It's only the most disturbed souls who go geist after death, their tortured personalities subliming through some terrible metamorphosis into an unliving storm of anger and frustration.

But John Gittings? In the words of Denis Healey, it was like being savaged by a dead sheep.

I turned to Carla, realizing what she'd been going through, why she'd asked me to come home with her, and what she'd tried and failed to say as we were driving back here.

I put a hand on her arm and gave her a firm push toward the door, seeing in her eyes that she was about to start crying again, and afraid that this time she might not be able to stop. "Wait in the car," I said.

She stared up at me, frightened and hopeful in about equal amounts, and some of what she was scared of was the same as what she was hoping for. "What are you going to do?" she demanded.

"What you asked me to do. Give him some peace."

"You won't—"

"Exorcise him? Send him away forever? No, Carla. I won't. I promise. Wait in the car. It shouldn't take longer than twenty minutes."

She took one last look past me into the room, where an invisible entity was trailing some extension of itself through the broken glass on the carpet, making it bristle and shift. Then she nodded and backed out the door, staring all the time, as if turning her back would have felt like a betrayal. I closed the door gently behind her, then knelt down and unshipped my whistle.

I keep it in a pocket I sewed into my coat myself, high up on the left-hand side. A paletot is handy like that—it's so voluminous you can carry around a drawerful of cutlery, a samovar, and a submachine gun with you and it won't even spoil the line. I generally keep just the whistle, a silver dagger, an antique goblet I've never had occasion to use, and a bottle of whatever booze I'm currently flirting with.

I blew a random sequence of notes to tune the whistle in, except that even then, even on this first approach, it wasn't quite random. There was an element of echolocation in it: of throwing out sounds to see how they'd come back to me, to see which the ghost absorbed and which bounced off and rolled away into the ether. These are just metaphors, you understand; but everything I do is a kind of metaphor. You choose the tools that work, or maybe they choose you.

Sometimes it comes hard and slow, sometimes quick and easy. This ghost was so big, so angry, that the sense of it filled the room. Notes ran from my gut up into my chest and lungs, through the bore of the whistle past my flickering fingers, and out into the air without me even needing to think about it. They built like a wave and broke like a wave, and the thing that had been John Gittings met them in full flood.

For a handful of moments the force of that meeting threw me off. I faltered in the middle of a phrase, pieced it out awkward and staccato, then found the flow again and began the laborious crescendo a second time.

This was the binding: the systolic beat, usually and inexorably followed by the diastole, which is the banishing. But not this time. By this point in my life, I'd had plenty of experience with a different kind of tune, with a different, more insidious purpose. I let a new phrase sneak in now, on a minor key—something I'd designed for my best friend, Rafi, after I lost the plot and let one of the most powerful demons in hell weld itself to his spirit. What I was playing now was something few exorcists ever bothered with, because for most of them, it didn't really pay its way in the standard repertoire.

This was a lullaby.

Gradually, I let the second phrase ride in over the first, run through it, and colonize it. Then I played the tune out until there was nothing left of it except three descending notes, each held as long as my breath lasted.

The silence afterward was like a roomful of applause. Nothing moved in the pillaged room. The ghost was still there, but its oppressive weight had lifted and faded. The sense I was left with was a dull, distant echo, not the roaring dissonance I'd walked in on.

I went out and down the stairs, back to the road. Carla was leaning against the car, smoking a cigarette. The dog end of another lay stubbed out between her feet. She stared at me—a wordless question.

"He's fine," I said, for want of any halfway adequate way of putting it. "I sent him to sleep, the same way I do Asmodeus when he's getting too frisky. Carla, how long has this been happening?"

She shook her head, looked away. "Since the day John died, Fix. Six days ago. It was almost immediate. It started maybe two or three minutes after I heard the shot."

I exhaled heavily. "Jesus!"

"It was how I knew he was dead. He'd locked himself in the bathroom, and I couldn't get in. I was hammering on the door, shouting his name. And then something—I can't describe it. Something went down the stairs behind me. I could hear each footstep. The boards creaking all the way down, as though—whatever it was—it was a massive weight. And I knew. I thought, That's John. That's my husband, going away from me. He's dead. Only he didn't go away. He stayed. He stayed and—"

Seeing the trembling start in her shoulders, I looked at the ground. "You should have called—" I began. Called whom? Me? That was a hypocritical bridge too far when I was standing there longing to be out of this. "One of us."

"I didn't know what to say." Her voice was thick and choked. "Fix, what am I going to do? I can't live like this."

"You don't have to. Have you got somewhere else to stay?"

She took a step back from me as though I'd pushed her, and her eyes registered shock and hurt. "Leave him alone? How can I do that to him?"

I threw out my arms, groping for words. "Carla, you said that John wasn't himself before he died. That you were scared he was losing his mind. I think that's why this is happening. It's best if you think of John as the man you used to know, and that thing in there as—"

"No. No, Fix." She raised her arms defensively, as if I'd just made an indecent proposal. "It's still him. Even if he doesn't know that himself, it's all that's left of him. I'm not going to just lock the doors and run and hide. I'm staying here with him, whatever happens."

I stared into her eyes. She meant it, in spades and with no room for argument.

"Okay," I said at last, cursing myself for not having the balls to shake her hand and walk away. You've got to have the courage of your lack of commitment; otherwise you keep getting dragged into the shit other people leave in their wake. But the ghost of a one-night stand that had never happened was clouding my judgment. "Coffee-maker still work?"

———————

It took a while to get the room to rights. I did the heavy lifting, and Carla went around behind me, putting the few intact ornaments back where they belonged, sweeping up the broken glass, throwing out what couldn't be mended or lived with. After we'd finished, the room still looked like a hurricane had been through but at least now you got the impression that it had stayed for tea and genteel conversation. You could tell that an effort had been made, anyway; it was the best we could do with the raw materials.

The kitchen was completely unscathed, which was a huge relief. I eyed the knife rack and wondered what it would have been like to meet the contents of that as I walked through the door. Memorable: like something out of a Tom and Jerry cartoon but without the perky sound track.

"Does he mainly stay in the living room?" I asked Carla as she heaped coffee into the Cona machine. She was scraping the bottom of the packet. When she'd finished, I took the empty packet from her and dumped it in the bin. Along the way, I accidentally kicked over a red plastic bowl on the floor. Dry pet food spilled out onto the tiles.

"Living room. Stairwell. Bathroom," she said tightly. It was obvious that there was a whole catalog of horrors behind that terse list. "I'm safe in the bedroom, and the hall outside the bedroom, and here." She switched the machine on, turned to face me, her face strained and earnest. "I said that wrong. Safe. He's never hurt me. He throws things around the room, but nothing's ever hit me. He's still my John, Fix. He's scared, and because he's scared, he's angry, but he'd never dream of harming me."

I mulled that over and found nothing to say to it. The stuff I'd dodged on the doormat had come a bit too close for comfort. But then John knew what I was and what I could do to him: He had good reason to want me to keep my distance. And if Carla had been living with this for six days and not taken so much as a scratch, it was hard to argue with her conclusions. Geists had been known to topple wardrobes on people's heads and push them out of windows. What was left of John Gittings was pulling its punches, at least as far as his widow was concerned.

I scooped the pet food back into the bowl and used it to change the subject. "I thought you hated animals," I said.

"Stray cat," Carla muttered, distracted. She tapped the Cona machine with a fingernail as it started to make slup-slup-slup noises. "It came in through the window one day, and John fed it some tuna. Then it wouldn't stop coming. I asked him not to encourage it, but he wouldn't listen. Haven't seen it in a few days, though. Maybe it's true that they know when someone doesn't like them."

Over coffee, she came back to the question of options. "I'm going to have to let them do it, aren't I?" she asked me glumly, staring at the cream swirling on the surface of her drink. "Dig him up again and burn him?"

I thought about that. "If the will's as specific as you say it is . . . Your only chance would be to prove that John wasn't in his right mind when he wrote it." I hesitated at that point, thinking about where I would be the following morning and what a tangled thicket the whole question of sanity was. In your right mind? Sure. But sometimes it all depended on who was in there with you.

"How do you prove something like that?" Carla asked, echoing my thoughts.

I took a swig of my coffee. I'd topped up both of the mugs heavily with what was left of the brandy, and it had a very pleasant afterburn. But the bitterness was there, too, and I let it seep through me. "I don't know," I admitted. "Usually, it comes down to expert opinions. In my experience, you can find an expert who's willing to say more or less anything, but it costs money. And since John wasn't getting any kind of medical help before his death, it'll be harder to make something like that stick." I paused for a few moments, then raised the next point very tentatively. "How important is it to you that he stays where he is?"

Carla sighed, made a vague, helpless gesture. "I thought it was what he wanted," she said, her voice a throaty murmur. "Underneath it all, I thought, This thing and this thing and this thing, that's all the disease. And these other things, they're still him. They're what's real. I couldn't believe he didn't still want to lie next to Hailey, because he'd told me so many times—" She faltered, glanced off in the direction of the pillaged living room. "But now that there's all this, I don't know. Maybe I got it wrong, Fix. And maybe that's why he's so angry with me."

I'd been thinking the same thing, but I was relieved that she'd gotten that far by herself. "Yeah," I allowed. "That's a possibility. When did he change his mind, exactly— about being buried, I mean?"

"I told you. End of last year. Before Christmas sometime. I don't remember, exactly."

"Did he ever talk it over with you? Give you any reasons?"

She shook her head. "Fix—" she said, and then there was a long pause. I saw the outline of what was coming, which helped: I kept my face deadpan and waited. "I don't think I can bring myself to talk to that man. Todd. I don't think I can do it without screaming at him."

"Well, with lawyers, you always want to be sure your shots are up to date."

Another pause. I guess she was hoping I'd take the hint without being asked: It can't be easy to beg favors from your dead husband's friends. But I was feeling like my humanitarian impulses had led me far enough astray today already. I drank off what was left of my coffee, put down the mug, and stood.

"Well," I said, "try to tell yourself that he's only doing his job. It's the truth, more or less. Thanks for the coffee, Carla. If you change your mind, call Pen. She's got a room free, and she'd love the company."

Carla nodded with only the very faintest sign of hurt in her eyes. "I've got something for you," she said, sabotaging my got-to-be-moving-along routine when it was just getting into second gear. Since I didn't have any other choice, I stopped and waited while she got up from the table and started to rummage through the drawers of the big Welsh dresser behind her. At last she found what she was looking for and brought it back to the table.

What she had in her hands was an antique half-hunter watch, Savonnette-style, with a silver case and a silver chain, tarnished but still very beautiful. There was delicate filigree work on the case, and the silver bar that was meant to attach the watch to a waistcoat was not a bar at all but a tiny figure of the crucified Christ, his outstretched arms providing the necessary perpendicular line. It was an amazing piece of work—pair-cased, too, I discovered, as I automatically opened the front and discovered the actual watch nestling inside its bivalved shell. It had to be two hundred years old, and it had to be worth a small fortune.

I looked at Carla. "I can't take this," I said.

"It belonged to his dad, and he wanted you to have it," she answered in a tone that brooked no argument. "It was one of the last things he said to me before—when he was still thinking straight. 'If anything happens to me, give this to Fix.' So it's not up to me or you. It's yours."

I put it in one of the inside pockets of the paletot, bowing to the inevitable. "Thanks," I said lamely. "I'll—Well, I'll think of John every time I look at it." Unpalatable though that prospect was right now.

"Thanks for driving me home," Carla said.

"It was my pleasure."

And then the twist of the knife. "Fix, I hate to do this. You've been so kind already. But if John's going to be dug up and then cremated, I've got to know where and when. And I hate that man so much. If it's not too much to ask—"

And there it was. No good deed goes unpunished. Come to think of it, probably most of the people you see lying rolled and robbed on the side of the road are Good Samaritans who stopped like idiots because they saw someone wringing his or her hands and looking helpless.

"Well," I said. "Yeah. Sure. I can check the details with him. Let you know." It was the minimum commitment that the situation seemed to call for. I tried not to sound too grudging as I gave it.

"Oh, Fix. I'd be so grateful. You're a sweet man. Thank you."

She kissed me on the cheek and we hugged again, even more awkwardly than before.

As she walked me back through the living room, I paused briefly, unfocused my eyes, and strained my senses for the ghost. It was still there, a faint, unmoving presence like a stain on the air. Dormant. Dreaming.

"The music should keep John quiet for a couple of days, at least," I told Carla. "After that, see how you go. If he's unhappy because you ignored his last request, then maybe after Todd's done what he needs to do—"

"Why does Pen have a room free?" Carla demanded, derailing my thoughts.

"Uh—because we had a bit of a falling-out," I admitted.

"You two? What could make you two row with each other?"

"Rafi," I said, and she let the subject drop. Everybody always does. Conversationally, that one word is the ace of trumps.

~ Three

IF YOU COME OUT of High Barnet Tube and head
uphill along the Great North Road, you pass the Magistrates' Court on the left, in between a bathroom supply
shop and a real estate agent's. Or you could stop right
there and save yourself a little effort, because it's not like
Barnet has anything more exciting saved up to show you.

It was the day after the night before, and the night
before had involved all the many units of alcohol I'd
failed to take in before the funeral. I felt fuzzy-headed and
sticky-eyed as I walked in off the street, finding myself
in a red-carpeted foyer where tasseled ropes barred off
some directions and steered you in others. It was like a
cinema, except there didn't seem to be anyone selling
popcorn.

Nobody challenged me. There was a single usher on
duty, but he was talking with strained patience to a belligerent young guy in a hooded jacket outside the door leading to court number one, and he didn't even look around

as I passed. I followed the arrows to courtroom three, where a sign said that the honorable Mr. Montague Runcie was presiding, and slid in quietly at the back. It looked like I'd missed only the warm-up. The magistrate, a man in his late fifties with a pinched, acerbic face and three concentric rings of wrinkles across his cheeks as though his eyes were wells that someone had dropped a pebble into, was still examining papers and holding a muttered conversation with the court clerk. Pen was sitting right at the front with her back to me, as tense as all hell if the set of her shoulders was anything to go by, but she hadn't started shouting yet, so that was good.

I sat down in an empty seat at the back of the room. There were a lot of empty seats; this was the sort of case that could easily make the local papers, but it didn't look like any of them had caught on to it yet. In the digital age, cub reporters don't bird-dog the courts and the cop shops anymore: They print out the press releases that come in over the wire, clock off early, and spend more time abusing substances.

Eventually, the magistrate looked up. He cast his eyes around the room as if someone at the back had just spoken and he was trying to work out who so he could hand out some lines.

"Miss Bruckner?" he said in a querulous tone. Pen got to her feet, holding up her hand unnecessarily. Her fall of red-gold hair made her hard to miss even sitting down. As always, she looked much taller than her five feet and half a spare inch. That effect is even more pronounced when you're facing her, staring head-on at her scarily vivid green eyes, but it's noticeable even from the back. Pen may be a small package, but what's in there was tamped down with a lot of force, and the lid barely stays on most of the time.

"And Professor Mulbridge?"

On the other side of the court, another woman who'd been scribbling notes in a ring-bound notebook looked up, flicked the book closed, and stood. She was older than Pen and made a strong contrast to her in a lot of ways. Matte-gray hair—the same gray as Whistler's mother or a German helmet—in a well-sculpted bob; gray eyes flecked with the smallest hint of blue; an austere, thin-lipped face, but with a healthy blush to her cheeks that suggested a warm smile lurking under the superficial solemnity. She was dressed in a formal, understated two-piece in shades of dark blue, looking like a probation officer or a Tory MP, whereas Pen was wearing flamboyant African silk. The professor's cool self-possession was clearly visible under the self-effacing smile and polite nod. Clearly visible to me, anyway; but then I go back a long way with Jenna-Jane Mulbridge, and I know where most of the bodies are buried. Hell, in a few cases, I even dug the graves. People who don't know her so well are apt to take away from their first meeting a vague sense of heavy-handed maternal benevolence; and to be fair, if I were going to describe Jenna-Jane to someone who didn't know her, "mother" might well be the first couple of syllables I'd reach for.

"Here, Your Honor," Jenna-Jane said mildly. Her voice said, "Trust me, I'm a doctor," and she is, as far as that goes. Then again, so were Crippen and Mengele, and they both sold patent medicines in their time.

The magistrate tapped the stack of papers in front of him. "And I presume Dr. Smart and Mr. Prentice are also in attendance?"

"Yes, Your Honor" and "Here, Your Honor" came from somewhere off to my far right.

The magistrate acknowledged them with a curt nod. "Thank you," he said dryly. "You can all be seated again. Now, from what I understand, this is a question of the disposition of an involuntarily held mental patient. A section forty-one case, Mr. . . . Rafael Ditko."

Someone who looked like an extra on *Judge John Deed,* impossibly young and suave and dark-suited, stood as if on cue on Jenna-Jane's side of the courtroom. The magistrate flicked him a glance but went on without giving him a chance to open his mouth. "Has there been a tribunal hearing?" he demanded, lingering on the word "tribunal" as though it were particularly tasty.

"Your Honor," the barrister said, holding up his own wodge of papers as if to prove that he was earning his salary here, too. "Michael Trevelyan, representing Haringey Health Authority. Yes, the review tribunal met three weeks ago. If you look in the court papers, you'll see the minutes of that meeting. It took place at the Charles Stanger Care Home in Muswell Hill. In attendance were Dr. Smart, Mr. Prentice, and your colleague Mr. Justice Lyle."

"And the recommendation?" The magistrate rummaged in the depths of the paperwork again, looking a little put out.

"The issue, Your Honor, is the transferral of Mr. Ditko from the Stanger Home to a separate, secure facility under the management of Professor Mulbridge—the Metamorphic Ontology Unit at Saint Mary's in Paddington."

"I'm aware of the issue, Mr. Fenster. I asked about the recommendation."

"Of course, Your Honor. But as you'll also note from

that document, the tribunal did not in fact manage to complete its deliberations. Miss Bruckner, who represents herself here today"—he glanced across at Pen—"was also in attendance and claimed—somewhat forcefully—that the tribunal was not properly convened."

The honorable Mr. Runcie had found his place now. He scanned the pages in front of him, tight-lipped. "Yes," he said. And then, a little later, "Oh yes." After reading on for a good half-minute longer while the rest of us examined our fingernails and the paint on the walls, he put down the paper and stared at Pen. "You disrupted the hearing, Miss Bruckner," he said with a slightly pained emphasis. "You're facing criminal charges as a result."

Pen stood up again. "I had to, Your Honor," she said levelly. "They were going to break the law. I needed to stop them."

I listened carefully to her words, or rather, to the tone of them, trying to assess how tightly wound she was. I estimated about three to four hundred pounds of torque: not terrible, for this stage of the proceedings. If anything, she managed to get an apologetic note into her voice, and she bowed her head slightly as she spoke in an understated pantomime of guilt. She knew she'd blown it at the Stanger hearing, and she was trying to undo that damage.

"You needed to stop them," Mr. Runcie repeated. "Indeed. Well, I've no doubt you feel very strongly about this. But still—the transcript suggests that you shouted and scattered documents, and you've been accused of actually threatening Dr. Webb, the director of the Stanger Home."

"I'm really sorry about that," Pen said meekly. "The threat, I mean. I did say all those things. But I didn't mean half of them."

For a moment I could see the proceedings being derailed by an itemized discussion of which threats Pen did mean: the one about breaking Webb's arms and legs, or the more elaborate ones involving objects and orifices? But the barrister interposed smoothly to keep things moving along.

"That case is pending, Your Honor, and it will be decided elsewhere. The crux of the matter here is that Miss Bruckner was asserting a power of attorney over Mr. Rafael Ditko's affairs and estate, and therefore a fortiori over the legal disposition of his person."

"On what grounds?" the magistrate asked, still looking at Pen. He was obviously trying to square the butter-wouldn't-melt picture of penitence in front of him with the written account of her exciting adventures at the Stanger. It didn't compute.

Pen answered for herself, again with really impressive restraint and civility. "On the grounds that I'm the one who signed the forms committing Rafi to the Stanger in the first place, Your Honor," she said. "And I pay his bills there, along with a Mr. Felix Castor. Dr. Webb has dragged me in every other week for two years, whenever he needed a signature on something. The only reason he doesn't want me to have a power of attorney anymore is because it's not convenient. Because now he wants to sign Rafi over to that woman, and he doesn't want anyone to be able to say no."

On "that woman," she flicked a glance across the court at Jenna-Jane Mulbridge, the demure mask slipping for a moment as her eyes narrowed into a glare. Jenna-Jane inclined her head in acknowledgment, the ironic glint in her eye barely perceptible.

"I see," said the magistrate. He turned to the barrister. "Well, if this *is* a section forty-one case, the safety of the public is the overriding consideration. Consent isn't necessarily going to come into the equation. Is that the only substantive issue, Mr. Fenster?"

"Your Honor, no," the barrister said, waving his wodge again. "Miss Bruckner further alleges improper collusion between Dr. Webb, Professor Mulbridge, and Dr. Smart, who, as the medical member of the tribunal, would have been making the initial recommendation as to its decision. That is where I come in, since the authority—which convened the panel—feels compelled to rebut these charges."

"Charges of collusion?"

"Just so, Your Honor."

The magistrate looked back at Pen with a frown. "Miss Bruckner," he said with very careful emphasis, "may I ask on what basis you are questioning the credentials and integrity of"—he scanned the paper that was still in his hand—"of a judge, a doctor, and a trained psychologist?"

It was time for me to take some of the pressure off Pen before she could get any closer to blowing. I stood up and gave the bench a friendly wave. "Can I answer that one, Your Honor?" I asked.

He gave me a slightly nonplussed look. Jenna-Jane looked around, too, and I took an unworthy pleasure in the way her thin lips thinned a little more at the sight of me. "And you are—?" the magistrate asked.

"Felix Castor. Like Miss Bruckner said, I'm the other side of the coin when it comes to paying for Rafi's fees at the Stanger and signing off on his monthly reviews."

"I see. And what is it that you do, Mr. Castor?"

Anything honest, I thought. Which rules out most of what you do. "I'm an exorcist, Your Honor."

"An..."

"Exorcist. Ghostbreaker. Provider of"—I ran my tongue around the white-bread phrase with a slight reluctance—"spiritual services."

The magistrate gave me an owl-eyed stare, the ripples seeming to spread away almost as far as his neckline. "I see. And you agree with Miss Bruckner's assertion that the tribunal's members are not fully impartial?"

I nodded. "Yeah," I said. "I do. Dr. Smart worked at the MOU under Jenna-Jane—Professor Mulbridge—for five years. He still does all his consultancy work at Praed Street. And that guy Prentice who's on the panel as the lay member—well, he's 'lay' in the sense of laying low. He's in my profession, and Professor Mulbridge is more or less his regular employer. She can't have exorcists on staff, so she hires them as security and puts their paychecks through a different budget. Prentice is as much of a fixture at Saint Mary's as the scum behind the toilet." Prentice, who'd been giving me a hostile glare ever since I mentioned his name, surged to his feet and opened his mouth to speak. "If you'll pardon the expression," I added punctiliously. "I wasn't comparing him to toilet scum in any personal or moral sense."

"Your Honor—" Prentice spluttered.

Runcie cut over him, giving me a severe frown. "Mr. Castor, if I hear any repetition of that pugnacious tone, I'll take it as a contempt of court. Are you seeing proof of association as proof of collusion?"

"No," I admitted. "Not automatically. But Professor Mulbridge is desperate to get her hands on Rafi because"—better pick my words with care here—"his condition is so rare and it chimes so well with her own interests. And you'd have to admit, Your Honor, it smells a little off if the institution that's trying to swipe Rafael Ditko, to take possession of him against his own wishes and the wishes of those close to him, is able to pad out the tribunal panel with its own staff. It looks like ballot-stuffing."

Jenna-Jane put her hand up, and the magistrate turned his eyes on her. "Your Honor," she said, sounding a little reproachful, "could I make an observation? Not to rebut Miss Bruckner's and Mr. Castor's allegations but to indicate the problem that the tribunal was faced with?"

Mr. Runcie indicated with a gesture that she could. Jenna-Jane nodded her thanks. "The facility I run at Saint Mary's," she said, sounding like a grandmother reminiscing about the queen's coronation, "is for the study, treatment, and understanding of a very specific range of conditions. Many of my patients believe themselves to be possessed by the dead, or to be themselves dead souls inhabiting animal bodies. As you know, the body of scientific evidence on such matters is small. In trying to enlarge it, I've had to call on the skills of a great many people whose knowledge is of an empirical rather than an academic nature."

Knowing the Jenna-Jane juggernaut and how it rolled along, I was listening to all this with a detached interest. I had to give her a 5.9 for artistic effect, but only 5.6 for technical merit. She'd gotten the respectful tone right, but she'd overdone the beating around the bush. "Your point, Professor Mulbridge," the magistrate chided her.

"My apologies, Your Honor. My point is that Rafael

Ditko claims to be demonically possessed. Dr. Webb's initial diagnosis was paranoid schizophrenia, but he admits that there's some anomalous evidence that brings the diagnosis into question. He wants Ditko transferred both because he represents a danger to the staff at the Stanger Home and because they don't have the proper facilities there to treat him.

"So a decision on Mr. Ditko's case requires an awareness of the paranormal as well as of the psychiatric factors presenting in his case. And it would be hard to find anywhere in the United Kingdom any practitioner in those areas—specifically, any exorcist—who hasn't worked with me or for me at some point in the last ten years. Why, Mr. Castor himself"—she turned to indicate me with a tolerant smile, our eyes locking for the second time—"was a very valued colleague of mine at the Metamorphic Ontology Unit until comparatively recently."

The magistrate looked at me with a certain mild surprise. "Is this true, Mr. Castor?"

Damn. Sometimes when you're not knife-fighting with Jenna-Jane on a day-to-day basis, you forget how strong her instinct for the jugular really is.

There was no point dodging the bullet. "As far as it goes, yeah," I admitted. "And it's also true that a lot of exorcists are going to have had associations with the MOU in the past. That's different from being still on staff there, though. And you could easily find a psychiatrist who isn't in Jenna-Jane's pocket."

"A psychiatrist with a background in the behavioral and psychological matrices of bodily resurrection?" Jenna-Jane inquired, tapping her thumbnail against her notebook.

"You don't have a monopoly on—" Pen broke in.

"Please," said Mr. Runcie with more of an edge to his voice. "I must insist that you address all comments to me and restrict yourself to answering my direct questions. Sit down. All of you, please sit down. I haven't asked anybody to stand."

We all complied, but the magistrate's feathers were thoroughly ruffled, and he didn't look any happier. "Thank you. It appears that there are two separate issues here— the one concerning Miss Bruckner's assertion of power of attorney, and the other relating to the legal constitution of the tribunal's panel. Mr. Fenster, are there any other heads under this case of which you've failed to apprise me?"

"None, Your Honor," the barrister said, taking the implied criticism on the chin. "Those are the two substantive issues."

The magistrate glanced at Pen. "And do you agree with that summary, Miss Bruckner? I mean, insofar as it states the matter at issue—the substance of your case?"

Pen hesitated, then nodded. "Yes, Your Honor."

There was a silence. The Honorable Mr. Runcie looked far from happy. "And the tribunal has no brief to review the terms of Rafael Ditko's detention—only his transferral from one facility to another?"

"Your Honor," said the barrister, looking profoundly sorrowful, "Mr. Ditko has been involved in incidents of damage or assault at the Stanger Home on five separate occasions within the last year. There are currently no plans—outside of the usual periodic authorization process—to review his sectioning and detention. Nobody is claiming that he can safely be released back into society."

Runcie gave Jenna-Jane a look that was fairly long and fairly hard. "Professor Mulbridge, I take it you were not yourself involved in the selection of the tribunal's members?"

Jenna-Jane spread her arms expansively. "Your Honor, these things are the province of the local authority—in this case, Haringey. As far as their internal workings go, I don't ask, and I'm not told."

The magistrate nodded agreement. "Yes. Just so. Still, I have the option of asking and presumably *will* be told. On the face of it, it does seem possible that there could be a conflict of interests. I'm keeping an open mind, but I'm going to order a three-day suspension of these proceedings while I look into the selection arrangements and make sure that all proper regulations were followed." He pondered. "On the question of power of attorney, that's an issue that goes far beyond these current events. I can't rule on the a priori assumption. Even if Dr. Webb has been dealing with Miss Bruckner and Mr. Castor as though they had such a power, that does not necessarily make it so in the eyes of the law. I believe you should take legal advice, Miss Bruckner, and perhaps give further thought to whether representing yourself is the wisest course of action here." He stroked the bridge of his nose self-consciously. "Given that Mr. Ditko can't legally give you his informed consent while he's sectioned on mental health grounds," he mused, "you'll almost certainly have to make an application through a higher court..."

Pen looked distressed. "But, Your Honor—" she interjected.

The magistrate raised a hand to forestall her. "I'm sympathetic to your position, Miss Bruckner. You clearly believe that you have Rafael Ditko's best interests at heart. But power of attorney would give you very wide-ranging rights over his estate and over any future decisions about his treatment. The safeguards have to be there, and they have to be observed. I'm sorry. But for what it's worth, I think you have a strong case. You should get yourself proper representation and do whatever it takes to prepare a full legal argument. My judgment, in the meantime, will focus on the makeup of the review panel."

He stood up, taking the clerk by surprise so that his "All rise" sounded a little panicked.

The magistrate gathered up his papers. "These proceedings are adjourned for three days," he said, "and will resume on Thursday, in the afternoon session. Make a note, Mr. Farrier, if you please."

He swept out of the room without a backward glance.

Jenna-Jane put on her jacket while Pen stood there looking like she'd lost a pound and found a plague sore. I knew what was going through her mind: With the power-of-attorney ploy kicked into the long grass, we had to shoot down Jenna-Jane's stooges on the review panel or the whole thing would go through on the nod. On the other hand, the Honorable Mr. Runcie—pompous and self-satisfied though he definitely was—struck me as being nobody's fool. I still felt like we were in with a chance.

There were exits on both sides of the courtroom, so it had to be deliberate that Jenna-Jane took the longer route and paused in front of Pen on her way out. "I'm so sorry, Pamela," she said, looking limpidly sincere. "I want you to know that if Rafi is given into my care, all of the resources of the unit will be brought to bear on him. If it's possible to make him well again, we'll do it."

Pen stared at her in stunned silence for a moment. Then she drew back her arm in a staccato movement, fist clenched. But I was already moving, and I stepped in before she could bring it forward again, sliding between the two of them with my back to Pen. Felix Castor, human shield.

"Jenna-Jane," I said, "you're a sight for sore eyes. Actually, let me rephrase that. My eyes are scabbing over just from looking at you. I'm carrying a voice recorder, so why don't you stop prejudicing your case and go play with your ECT machines?"

"Felix." Jenna-Jane shook her head with mock exasperation. "You're determined to hate me, but I have only respect and admiration for you. I'm hoping to welcome you back on board someday. There's going to be a war, and I want you on my side. I'm determined on it. Perhaps your friend Rafi might actually be the bridge that brings us together."

"You mean you're going to lay him down on the ground and trample on him?" I said. "Tell it to the court."

She raised her hands in surrender and walked on. I turned to Pen, who was trembling like a tuning fork. "Well, that went as well as could be expected," I said.

"Fuck off, Fix," Pen answered, her eyes welling up with tears and instantly overflowing. "Fuck off and don't talk to me."

She turned her back and stalked away along the seats, tripping at one point over somebody's briefcase and then kicking it out of her way as she righted herself. It wasn't a dramatic exit, but it did the job.

What's that old Groucho Marx line? No, never mind: "I've got plenty of enemies. But if they ever start to thin out, most of my friends are right there in the wings ready to audition."

There's going to be a war. Jenna-Jane Mulbridge actually believes that shit, and she isn't the only one.

The dead rose again only because they were running ahead of the demons, the theory went, and now the demons had started to appear. There was a gaping hole in the walls of Creation: Hell was throwing its legions into the breach, and so far our side not only didn't have an army, it didn't even have a poster with a pointing finger on it.

The first and greatest of the exorcists, Peckham Steiner, had believed, too, and toward the end of his life, he'd devoted his personal fortune to the building of defenses that would give the living a fighting chance in that war when it was finally declared: the Thames Collective, a barracks for ghostbreakers on running water, where the dead and the damned couldn't walk; the safe houses, protected by ramparts of water, earth, and air, which I'd assumed were an urban legend until I'd actually seen one and figured out how it worked; a dozen wacky schemes full of customized craziness in every flavor you can think of. It was classic paranoid stuff, but at this point in my life, I was finding it a lot harder to laugh it off.

If there was a war coming, then Rafi Ditko was conquered territory. Playing around with black magic, he'd opened up a door to hell inside his own soul, and something—a big, bad bastard of a something that called itself Asmodeus—had stepped through. Now Rafi was locked up in a ten-by-ten cell in a mental hospital, because the law hadn't caught up with the facts yet, and the only diagnosis that fitted his symptoms was schizophrenia. And the cell was lined with silver because—law or no law—you had to do what worked. Silver weakened Asmodeus and kept him from asserting full control over Rafi most of the time. The tunes I played to him had the same effect, pushing the demon down further into Rafi's hindbrain and giving his conscious mind a bit more wriggle room.

Unfortunately, it was also partly my fault that Asmodeus was stuck in there in the first place. After answering a panicked phone call from his girlfriend, Ginny, I found him burning to death from the inside out. I did what I could to stop it, but this was the first time I'd ever encountered a demon. To put it bluntly, I screwed up. In fact, I screwed up so badly that Rafi and Asmodeus had ended up welded together in some way that nobody had even managed to understand, still less undo.

And then a few months ago, when I'd had the chance to sever the connection permanently, I'd backed off because the price—letting Asmodeus loose on earth—had seemed too high. I still think I was right, but I'd never been able to explain it so that Pen understood. Actually, I'd never managed to get more than two words out before she either decked me or walked away.

Pen—Pamela Elisa Bruckner—is Rafi's ex-lover and my ex-landlady. Ex-friend. Ex- a whole lot of other things, one way and another. And what made relations between us even more strained was that this whole business at the Stanger kept throwing us together. The Stanger's director, Webb, had been trying to divest himself of Rafi ever since an incident about six months before in which the demon inside him had cut loose and almost killed two nurses.

Now he'd formed an unholy alliance with Jenna-Jane to get rid of him, effectively gifting him to the MOU at Paddington. And the MOU was a concentration camp for the undead, where Jenna-Jane talked about clinical care and pastoral responsibility while she performed experiments on her helpless charges that were increasingly sadistic and extreme. She was desperate to get her hands on Rafi because her menagerie—replete with ghosts and zombies and werewolves and one poor bastard who thought he was a vampire—didn't include a demon yet. So Pen and I had to work together to clog Jenna-Jane's works with spanners, whether we liked it or not.

Meanwhile, the war—if it was a war—was still in the "cold" phase. Maybe that's only to be expected when the enemy is the dead.

I'd had more than enough of the legal profession to last me for one day, but a promise is a promise, even if your arm is halfway up your back while you're giving it. I could have called, but I needed to pick up some silver amalgam from a dental supplier in Manor House, so Stoke Newington was almost on my way.

The offices of Ruthven, Todd and Clay turned out to be in a converted Victorian court built in chocolate-colored brick, on the corner of a slightly drab row of terraces from a later era. There were window boxes on either side of the door, painted bright blue, but they contained nothing except bare soil. No flowers at this time of year.

The front door was pretty bare, too—no wards, no sigils, no come-nots or stay-nots. Maybe the evil dead avoided lawyers out of professional courtesy, like sharks are supposed to do. I walked in off the street and found myself in a small reception area that, judging from its modest dimensions, must originally have been the front hall of a house. A wide, elbowed staircase took up a good half of the available space, and what was left was dominated by a large, venerable-looking photocopier. The inspection covers had been removed from the machine and were stacked up against the wall. An enormously fat, enormously pale bald man was on his knees in front of it, one hand thrust into its innards up to the elbow, looking like a vet trying to assist with a difficult birth. He glanced up at me as I entered, and then he kept on staring as if trying to place the face. He had a sheen of sweat on his forehead, and his half-open mouth hung down at the corners like a melting clock in a painting by Salvador Dalí. A young brunette sitting at the reception desk under the stairs watched him work with more attention than a busted photocopier seemed to merit. Maybe it was a slow day.

"I'm here to speak to Mr. Todd," I said to the brunette as she pulled her attention away from the exhibition of mechanical midwifery. "I called earlier. Felix Castor."

She ran her finger down the very full columns of a double-width appointment book. "Felix Castor," she confirmed. "Yes. Please take a seat."

There were several, so I took the one farthest away from Mr. Fix-it, picked up yesterday's *Times*, and started to flick through it as the receptionist called upstairs. I glanced across at the fat man once, out of the corner of my eye. He was still on his knees and still looking at me, although when I caught him at it, he dropped his gaze to the ground with a slight grimace and went back to the job.

"Any luck, Leonard?" the receptionist asked.

The man shook his head glumly. "There's no jam," he said in a higher voice than I would have expected, a voice that had a slight fluting quality to it, as though the big man had swallowed that weird little device that gives Mr. Punch his voice. "I think it's one of the rollers come off its bracket." He leaned forward and reached into the machine—with both arms this time. It shifted on its base and creaked ominously.

"Mr. Castor." I looked up. Todd was coming down the stairs, hand outstretched. He had on a different suit—mid-blue instead of gray, with a subtle dogtooth. Maybe he had one for every day of the week. I stood, and we shook.

Shaking hands is always a little jump into the unknown for me. The same morbid sensitivity that makes me good at sensing the presence of the dead sometimes allows me to pick up superficial psychic impressions through skin-to-skin contact. Nothing this time, though, or at least nothing revealing. Maynard Todd exuded only a cool aura of self-possession as immaculate as his tailoring.

"Thanks for coming," he said. Then he looked past me, and his expression shifted into a slightly perplexed frown. "Uh—Leonard, are you sure you know what you're doing there?"

"Yes," Leonard grunted tersely.

I could see Todd thinking about taking the discussion a stage further, and then I could see him giving up on the idea. He turned to the receptionist instead. "Carol," he said, "call the service number."

"Yes, Mr. Todd."

"I can fix it," said Leonard, not looking around.

"Come on upstairs," Todd said to me, ignoring Leonard's answer. "You want some tea or coffee?"

"I'm fine," I said, and followed him back up the wide staircase. When we turned around the elbow of the stairs, Leonard was still on his knees, intent on his veterinary duties.

"John Gittings," Todd said, glancing back down at me as we walked. "That's what you called about, right?"

"Right," I agreed.

"And I saw you at the funeral."

"Right again."

He nodded. "Yeah, I thought so. You were the one who stepped in when the natives were getting restless. Thanks for that."

I didn't answer. It would have sounded a bit graceless to say that I was more worried about Reggie and Greg picking up an assault charge than I was about his well-being.

The stairwell went up and up, and I lost count of how many turns we took before we got to Todd's office. It was surprisingly small, but then the courts had been the lower end of Victorian working-class housing: They meted out space as though it were gold. Todd indicated a chair as he walked around to the far side of the desk and pulled open the blinds, which looked onto the court's central light well and so didn't make much difference to the gray luminescence filtering into the room. It looked like the kind of place where you'd need the desk lamp on at noon on midsummer's day.

As he sat down, Todd flicked open a green hanging file that was already on his desk. It contained a thick wodge of papers. I took the chair opposite him.

"John Gittings," he said again, flicking through the documents on top of the file with quick, practiced hands. "I've been thinking about this one."

"Have you?" I asked, for form's sake.

Todd nodded. "About Mrs. Gittings's feelings on the matter, I mean," he clarified. "I'm going to go ahead and get the exhumation order, like I said. Have John disinterred and taken to Mount Grace for cremation. I don't have any choice about that."

"I'm sure."

He must have caught the sardonic edge in my tone, because he gave me a slightly injured stare.

"Seriously," he said. "You think I enjoyed turning up at the funeral looking like the bad guy in a silent movie, terrorizing widows, breaking up the show? I didn't. I didn't enjoy it one bit. But my client's wishes were absolutely specific."

I didn't answer right away; I was only here to check the dates. But since he'd given me the opening, it seemed churlish not to at least poke a stick into it. "Carla thinks that John was suffering from some kind of dementia."

Todd looked pained. "Mrs. Gittings has that luxury. I don't. Not unless she can prove it in court. I have to assume that John meant what he said, and I have to act on it."

"There's something else you should know about," I said. "Mrs. Gittings is being haunted by her husband's ghost."

I left it out there, looked at his face. Like I said, the law takes a while to catch up with how the world turns, and a lot of people with a rational mind-set somehow manage never to see anything that might challenge their basic assumptions. For all I knew, Todd was one of them: a vestal, to use Pen's word. Someone who'd never seen a ghost, or any of the other manifestations of the risen dead, and couldn't quite bring himself to make the conceptual leap in advance of the evidence.

But he surprised me. "I'm sorry to hear that," he said, and he looked as though he meant it.

"It gets worse. Whether or not John was in his right mind when he died, he's pretty much out of it now. The ghost is restless. Violent. It's become—"

"Geist," Todd finished, and I nodded, impressed that he knew the technical term. He blew out his cheek. "Damn," he said simply, and then for a long time he stared at the floor, his thumb running absently along the edge of his desk. "Well, that—yes, that's distressing. She must be very distraught. To see someone you loved—*still* love, I suppose—"

There was a long silence at the end of which Todd looked at me and nodded as though I'd been pressing an argument. "I want this to give her as little stress as possible," he said. "Especially after what you've said. So what I'm proposing is a wake."

I thought I must have misheard him. "A wake?" I echoed him. "You mean a party?"

Todd shook his head brusquely. "No, not a party. Just a night when the coffin goes back to the house—when Mrs. Gittings can sit with it, and John's spirit can become a little bit more reconciled to…his violent end. Do you think that would be a good idea?"

I mulled it over, and I had to admit—to myself, at least—that it did. It might or might not provide closure for Carla, but it ought to do John's ghost a power of good to see that his last request was being carried out to the letter. In theory, it ought to stop the haunting. You didn't need an exorcism if you gave the dead what they wanted.

What I said, though, was "It doesn't really matter what I think. I'll talk it over with Carla. See what she says."

Todd pushed the papers back into the file, closed it, and stood up very abruptly. "You do that," he said. "If there's a way of doing this that spares her feelings, then that's the way we'll do it. Thanks for coming in, Mr. Castor. I'm glad you told me all this."

"The cremation," I reminded him. "When is it going to be?"

"Wednesday, most likely. But it depends how soon I can get the disinterment done. It might have to be Thursday. Talk to Mrs. Gittings and let me know what she says. Oh, and please leave a number with Carol. I think under the circumstances Mrs. Gittings won't appreciate a call from me, so if you don't mind continuing to act as a go-between—"

"Happy to," I said stolidly. "Thanks for listening."

I went downstairs again and left my address and phone numbers with the bored brunette. The photocopier was in a state of even more advanced disassembly, and Leonard was nowhere to be seen.

I stepped back out onto the street. It was about five o'clock, and although there was still some light from the low, loitering sun, a roiling rope of heavy gray cloud was in the process of swallowing it whole like a python gulping down a guinea pig.

A scarecrow-thin old man crusted with the filth of years on the streets, dressed in a long, trailing outercoat so dirty and tattered you couldn't guess what color or even what kind of garment it might once have been, came shambling along the pavement toward me. I stepped aside automatically, but he zigged at the same time and walked right into me. His mad mud-brown eyes stared into mine.

"At the water hole," he said, his voice a dry, throat-tearing rasp. "With the others there behind you. Pushing. Pushing. Nowhere to go." He laughed out loud, delighted by some sudden revelation, and the stench of his breath hit me across the face like a solid slap.

I winced and leaned away from the searing smell, but he was already walking on—singing now in the same harsh, agonized tone. "'Oh, the devil stole the beat from the Lord, and it's time we put things straight...'" I didn't recognize the tune, but that ragged voice was shredding it pretty effectively.

An involuntary shudder went through me, and with it came a nagging prickle somewhere at the edge of consciousness—the slight sensation of pressure that comes when I'm being looked at by one of the risen dead. I looked around. Nobody in sight except the decayed tramp, who was heading away from me and had his back turned, and a woman on the other side of the street, wheeling a baby in a stroller. Maybe recent events had put me on something of a hair trigger: I slipped my hand inside my coat to make sure that my whistle was there and forgot about it. Probably nothing, but if it was something, I was all tooled up.

I headed north, aiming to grab a train at Finsbury Park. That gave me two choices—the immense dogleg of Stamford Hill and Seven Sisters Road, or the back cracks. I took the latter, turning off the main drag into a maze of terraced streets and narrow alleys. The sense of being watched—watched and followed—ebbed and flowed as I walked: It wasn't something that had ever happened to me before, and it made me wonder if I was experiencing some kind of aftereffect from my contact with John

Gittings's ghost. All ghosts impinge on my death sense, but geists have an intense, indelible presence that you can't just shake off afterward. Maybe it had been lurking in the background of my perceptual field ever since.

I took another street, another back alley, tacking alternately north and west so that ultimately, I'd break out onto the Seven Sisters Road somewhere past the reservoir. Meanwhile, the darkness leaked down out of the sky to cover the earth, and the prickle at the back of my mind became an itch, then an itch with a sick heat in back of it like the raw tenderness of sunburn.

I turned again, onto an alley that ran between the backyards of a row of terraces and a high blind wall that presumably had the reservoir on the other side of it. I took ten steps forward, then pivoted on my heel and waited, looking back the way I'd come. Now that I wasn't moving anymore, I ought to have been able to hear the footsteps of anyone approaching the corner, but the silence was absolute.

Before me was thick shadow, thick enough that if something dead or undead rounded the bend, I might lose the initiative because I couldn't get a clear enough look to know what it was. Impatient, I took a few steps back toward the corner I'd just turned, and my foot came down on something that moved. A black shape streaked past me with a whuff of air that I felt even as I yelled and jumped aside. The squawl of protest reached me a moment later.

Tomcat, big and fat, out on the pull.

With a muttered curse, I ran to the corner, then around it and back out onto the street. Nothing and nobody in sight. I'd have been surprised if there had been, after the early warning I'd just given out. As ambushes went, it was a sod of a long way from the Little Big Horn. And as if to confirm the futility of the endeavor, the extrasensory prickle faded out again into nothingness.

Which, for something so liminal and barely there to start with, wasn't a long haul at all.

I was about to say that I went home, but when I use that word, I still think of Pen's creepy old place on Turnpike Lane, with its Noah's ark freighting of rats and ravens and its Mobius strip architecture (it's built into the side of a hill, so the ground floor at the back becomes a basement at the front).

Now, though—just for a few weeks or maybe a month—I was living in a flat in a high-rise block along the Wood Green High Road: high enough up in the stack so I could look out of my window and see the Centrepoint Tower giving me the finger across the length of London.

It belonged to a friend of a friend, a guy named Ronald "Ropey" Doyle, who'd gone back to the Republic of Ireland to deal with some family crisis and didn't want to lose his place on the council housing list while he was away. He needed a sitting tenant who could pretend to be him if the need arose, and I needed a place to dump my stuff until I came up with a better idea. It seemed like a sweet deal.

It became less sweet when the lights went out and I discovered all the utilities were on a meter, and it soured altogether the first time the lift broke down. The flat itself smelled of root vegetables, and when it rained, the walls wept discolored tears that left brown-edged tracks down the paintwork. The decor ran to black leather and three-inch-deep orange shag pile. But to give it its due, it had four walls and a ceiling. Beggars can't be choosers.

Tonight, though, walking down Lordship Lane from Wood Green tube, I felt a definite desire to be somewhere else. If anything, that feeling only increased when I turned onto Vincent Street and saw what was parked in front of the block: a high-sided blue van with BOWYER'S CLEAN-ING SERVICES written in reverse over the windscreen.

Son of a bitch! I'd been solid-gold certain I'd ditched the Breathers on the M25. Now it seemed that they'd not only stayed with me all the way to Southgate, they'd planted a walking tail on me when I left Carla's and came home by tube. They knew where I lived. Taken in conjunction with Louise Beddows's tales of ambushes and punishment beatings, it wasn't a happy thought. More than anything, it made me ashamed. How could I have let myself be rolled up by a shower of amateurs? Normally, my instincts were better than that.

There was a guy sitting in the driver's seat of the van. The fractured sodium glare of a streetlamp was splattered over the curve of the windscreen, so that all I could see of him was an outline, immobile and sinister. I couldn't even tell if he was looking at me. I fought the urge to wrench the door open and have it out with him there and then. The back of the van was probably stuffed three deep with his mates.

An even nicer surprise was waiting for me when I got up to the flat. Someone had painted across the door in thick, still-dripping black paint the words EXORCIST EQUALS DISEASED EQUALS DECEASED. I stared at it in dead silence for about half a minute, considering my options. It wasn't my front door, of course, it was Ropey's, but still, I was living behind it, and it was my arse he'd want to kick when he saw this. But was it worth getting my head used as a baseball? On balance, probably not. I'd wait until the odds were more in my favor, and then I'd put these little fuckups through some changes.

The first thing I did when I got inside was to call Carla and tell her Todd's idea about the wake. She was iffy at first, but she talked herself into it. I said I'd call him and tell him it was a goer.

A pregnant pause at the other end of the line, punctuated in the middle by a muffled sob. "Fix?"

"Yeah?"

"Could you—could you come over and be here with me? When they bring John's body back?"

I thought about that one for all of two seconds. "I'd love to, Carla," I lied, "but I can't. I've got too much work on. I'll have my mobile with me, though. If the geist—I mean, if John gets overexcited, call me and I'll come over and play him to sleep again."

I hung up before she could find another angle to come at me from. A second call to Todd's office got me the answerphone, and I left a message there. That ought to have left me feeling off the twin hooks of guilt and duty and feeling a little better.

It didn't, though. I prowled around the flat, irritable and unsettled, wanting to pick a fight that I could win but not able to think of one right then. The wind was still high, and the noise it made as it broke on the northeast corner of the block was like a howl of pain sampled and played back through some aeolian synthesizer. It made me think about the late John Gittings, prowling invisibly around his own living room like a trapped animal. Worse still, the couple next door were in the throes of noisy passion, which meant they'd be swearing and throwing things at each other sometime within the next hour.

I felt the call of the wild, so I put my coat back on and went down to the Lord Nelson. Let the Breathers follow me in if they wanted to. If they did, they were going out through the fucking window.

Okay, "the call of the wild" is relative, because this is Wood Green we're talking about; but you've got to love a pub that's painted like a fire engine, even if the beer is shit. And the alternative was Yates's Wine Lodge, which for someone born in Liverpool arouses deep atavistic impulses of fear and suspicion.

It wasn't a football night, so the place was quiet. Quiet felt like what my nerves needed right then. A bunch of students were playing pool for pints over in the corner, and Mike Skinner was talking about his love life on the jukebox. I waited at the bar while Paul put a new barrel on, then, when he came over, I nodded toward the IPA pump. "Usual," I said.

"Someone wants to meet you, Fix," he said as he pulled the pint.

"What sort of someone?"

"Woman."

"Young? Old? Nun? Policewoman?"

"See for yourself."

As he handed me the pint, he nodded, barely perceptibly, off to my right. I handed him a fiver, took a sip on the beer, and casually took a glance in that direction.

There was a woman sitting by herself at a table off to one side of the door, dressed in a smart cutaway jacket over shirt and slacks, the whole outfit built around a motif of rust red and black. Something about her look reminded me of Carla: the intangible suggestion of widows' weeds, which was odd and unsettling because this woman couldn't have been over thirty. Dark brown hair in a tightly curled perm, bronzed eyelids, and metallic highlights on her lips. She was staring at the wall, but I was pretty sure she wasn't seeing it. The gin and tonic in front of her hadn't been touched.

I could have played coy, but I was curious about how she'd tracked me down here and what she wanted; and maybe I jumped at the chance of a distraction from the thoughts that were weighing on my own mind right then. I crossed to the table and gave her a nod as she turned to stare at me. "Paul said you were asking after me," I said.

She sat bolt upright, roused from whatever reverie she'd been in. "Felix Castor?"

"That's me."

"I'm Janine. Jan. Jan Hunter." She put out a hand and I shook it. "I got your name from Cheryl Telemaque. She said you're good. I'd like to hire you."

"Okay if I sit down?" I asked, and she took her handbag off the table to make room for me to put my drink down. I carefully neglected to ask what Cheryl had said I was good at. Given the way my relationship with her had gone, that seemed like it might be kind of a loaded question.

I took a seat opposite Jan, and she swiveled to face me. "So what's the problem?" I asked. The standard opening phrase for doctors, mechanics, and ghostbreakers.

"My husband," she said, then seemed to hesitate. "He's—" The pause went on. Whatever the next word was, she couldn't get over it. I tried to help.

"Passed on?" I suggested.

She looked surprised. "No! He's on remand at Holloway." Another leaden pause. "For rape and murder."

"Okay," I said, waiting for the other shoe to drop.

"And he didn't do it, Mr. Castor. Doug looks really tough, but he wouldn't hurt a fly. So it's—I've got to find the real killer. I want her to tell everybody what she did. So they'll let Doug go."

I noted the female pronoun in passing. This was getting stranger by the second. It was also veering gracefully away from what I think of as my core competencies.

"I'm an exorcist, Mrs. Hunter," I reminded her as gently as I could manage. "I could only find this killer for you if she happened to be—"

Before I could get the word out, Jan cut across me with the inevitable rejoinder. "She is, Mr. Castor. She's dead. She's been dead for forty years."

~ **Four**

I STARED AT HER for a moment, letting the idea grow on me.

"Okay," I said at last. "Provisionally, I mean. Okay with provisos. You'd better tell me the whole story. Then I'll tell you if there's anything I can do for you."

By way of answer, Jan Hunter rummaged in her handbag and came up with a photo that she handed to me. It showed a man the same age as Jan or maybe a couple of years older, with a suedehead haircut and slightly overlarge ears, looking to the camera with a goofy grin while holding up two fish on a hook. The background was a riverbank; the props, a canvas chair and a keep-net. He was wearing a lumberjack shirt, a wedding ring, and that was all I could tell you about him from memory. It wasn't a face that left a deep impression.

"Doug," I said.

"Look at that face," Jan said with a slight tremor in her

voice. "Can you imagine him hurting anyone? Let alone killing—"

"He did those two fish," I said, trying to inject a little reality back into the proceedings. She gave me a wounded look, and I shrugged an apology. "Why don't you just tell me what happened?"

She looked down at the photo, drawing in a long, ragged breath. It was mind over matter. I saw her shoveling the emotions back inside and locking them down. When she looked at me again, she was almost clinically calm.

"Just the facts, ma'am," she said, presumably being Dan Aykroyd rather than Jack Webb.

"To start with."

So she told them to me. And they were as nasty a set as I'd ever come across.

———————

The twenty-sixth of January. Sometime after four p.m. A man named Alastair Barnard, age forty-nine, checked in to a hotel room in King's Cross along with another, younger man—this other man described as having close-cropped mid-brown hair and brown eyes and wearing a black donkey jacket with a green paint stain on the left sleeve. The hotel in question was the Paragon; it rents by the hour because the clientele it caters to are the prostitutes who work the backstreets off Goodsway and Battle Bridge Road.

The desk clerk, one Christopher Merrill, gave them a key—room 17, which offered a fine view of the freight yard. He assumed that the younger man was a rent boy bringing his work in off the streets, but he didn't ask any questions or make any small talk, because you don't mess with your core business.

Normally, the clerk would have expected to see the two men emerge again half an hour later and walk away in different directions. In this case, it didn't happen, but the clerk didn't see anything unusual in that because he'd forgotten all about them. It was a Friday afternoon, and there were a lot of comings and goings—nothing compared to the traffic that would be coming through later in the evening, but plenty to keep the clerk busy.

But when nine o'clock rolled around and the pressure on the rooms started building up, he noticed that that key was still out. Five hours? Even with a double dose of Viagra and a pint of amyl nitrate, nobody can keep it up that long. And now they owed him money, because they'd only paid for an hour. With the sour suspicion that the men had fucked and run, he summoned the cleaner, Joseph Onugeta, who was the only other guy on the Paragon's daytime staff. Together they took the master key up to the second floor and unlocked the door.

"Barnard was on the floor," Jan said, frowning slightly as though quoting from memory. "He'd fallen off the bed, and he'd brought the sheets and the coverlet with him. He was all tangled up in them so you could only see him from the waist up. His head had been smashed into pulp."

The desk clerk started screaming, which brought people running from the other rooms. Most of them took one look at the devastation and fled. None had come forward since. It was the cleaner who called the police, explaining in heavily accented English that there'd been an accident of some kind and a man was dead.

The cops dismissed the accident hypothesis as soon as they walked in the door. Barnard had been hit more than two dozen times with something hard and heavy, wielded with frenzied energy. Other things—crueler and sicker things—had been done to him, too, presumably before the hammer came down. He'd died on his stomach, crawling across the floor away from the bed, trying to make it to the door.

As far as the damage to his skull went, there were two different kinds of wounds. Some of them had been made with something blunt and round-ended; some were narrower and had penetrated right through the bone instead of impacting on it. Preempting the forensics team who arrived later, one of the uniformed constables—the only one with the stomach to get close enough to see—immediately and confidently predicted that when the implement used on Mr. Barnard was found, it would turn out to have been a claw hammer.

"Was he right?" I asked.

Jan halted in her recitation, which had assumed a deadpan, running-on-automatic quality. "They haven't found it yet," she said. "Why?"

"If the weapon was a hammer," I said, picking my words carefully, "I guess you're talking about a certain degree of premeditation. It couldn't have been a—crime of passion, spur-of-the-moment kind of thing. The killer brought the thing in with him."

I was aware that I'd used the male pronoun, not the female. But unless I'd miscounted somewhere, there wasn't a woman in the case yet. In fact, if memory served—"You mentioned rape," I said. "Rape and murder."

Jan nodded. "This man—Barnard—he'd had what they call 'receptive anal sex.' And it had been rough."

"Rough enough to have been nonconsensual?"

"Rough enough to raise a doubt. There was—damage."

It was time for the make-or-break question. "Where does Doug fit in to all this?"

Jan dropped her gaze to the table, where the photo of her husband was still lying. "He hadn't even gone a hundred yards," she said almost matter-of-factly. "He had blood all over him, so people were staring at him, getting out of his way. Someone called the police, and they just routed the call to one of the cars that had been sent out to the Paragon. When the squad car got to Cheney Road, they didn't even have to ask—people saw them coming along the road, pointed the way, and they found Doug sitting on the edge of the pavement a block up from the station. Just sitting there, staring at his hands like he couldn't believe what he was seeing. They brought him in right there. Then they got a DNA match and charged him."

"A DNA match?" I echoed. "Then—"

She didn't flinch. Under the circumstances, that was mightily impressive. "Yes. It was my husband's semen they found inside Alastair Barnard."

I turned the expression "open-and-shut case" over in my mind, checking to make sure it had no sordid double meanings that would make it inadvisable to use. Before I could say it, though, Jan was carrying on at a rush.

"There's no denying that part of it," she said. "Doug had sex with this man. I suppose he went there, to that hotel, specifically to do that. But I don't believe he killed anyone, Mr. Castor. I don't believe he's even capable of doing that.

"We've been married three years now, and he's—despite the way he looks, despite the way he was brought up—he's the gentlest man I ever met. Really. He's six feet three, he works as a brickie, and he used to box, but really, he is. If he gets angry, he turns it on himself. He never even shouts. Doug could no more kill someone than you or I could."

I let that straight line sail right on by. It's true that I never pointed a gun at someone and pulled the trigger, or tenderized anyone with a claw hammer, for that matter. But I'd done things that had led to people dying, and I'd done them with my eyes open. It was enough to give me a twinge of unease as I listened to Jan Hunter protesting her husband's innocence on the basis that he was always nice to her.

"Did you know that he was bi?" I asked.

Jan shook her head violently. "No. No, I didn't. But in the last few months, I knew I wasn't satisfying him. We were scarcely ever together. He didn't want to touch me, although he was still—He still seemed to love me. There was just something he couldn't tell me. I'd wake up in the night sometimes, and I'd hear him crying in the dark. Sometimes I'd doze off and wake up again, and it would be hours later. But I'd still hear the same sounds. He was just crying and crying, all through the night. Something was eating away at him. Something he couldn't share.

"I'd started to think he had to be seeing someone else. It was the only explanation that made any sense. He was working on a big site over in East London—they're building one of those new super-casinos—and he was coming home later and later. Overtime, he said, but there's never that much overtime to go around in the winter. You can't mix cement in the dark.

"And then before the murder, he didn't even come home for a week. I hadn't seen him. He hadn't called, or..." Her voice trailed off. She stared at me, her expression bleak. "I was waiting for bad news. Just not this kind."

Face-to-face with her grief and her pain, I opened my mouth to tell her that I didn't think I could help her. That I couldn't think of anything that would get her husband off a rap as solid as this.

She saw my expression and forestalled me. "I've got evidence," she said quickly. "You have to hear this, Mr. Castor. Don't say no until you've heard me out."

"What evidence?" I asked with huge reluctance.

Jan picked up her gin and downed it straight before answering. She grimaced as the pungent liquor went down. "All right," she said, her tone hardening into something belligerent and stubborn. The students at the pool table looked around: It must have sounded as though we were having a marital tiff. "Something happened to me. About two weeks after Doug was arrested. I was sitting at home. To be honest, I was more or less drunk, even though it was only the middle of the afternoon. I was"— she made a sudden sharp gesture—"falling apart. I really was, just—bits and pieces. I couldn't keep a thought in my head. There was so much that had to be done. Not just talking to the lawyers. Bills. Letters. Doug had done all that, and now he wasn't there. I wasn't coping. I wasn't even trying to. I was just sitting there feeling sorry for myself."

That sounded reasonable enough to me, but Jan's face twisted in self-disgust. "Sitting there and waiting for something to happen. As though, you know, a light was going to shine down out of the sky and a voice was going to tell me what to do. Pathetic.

"And then the phone rang. It was an American voice. He told me his name, and I didn't hear it. I thought he was a friend of Doug's or someone from the site. His foreman or something. But then he said he wanted to talk to me about Doug's case.

"'Your husband didn't do it,' he said. 'He's innocent. You may even be able to prove it.'

"Well, I was sitting up straight now, but I still thought he might be, you know, some sort of crank. Like that nutcase who made the Ripper phone calls. One of these people who gets off on being close to a juicy murder, even if it's at second- or thirdhand. I asked him who he was, and he told me his name again. It was Paul Sumner. Paul Sumner Jr."

I vaguely recognized the name, but I didn't place it until Jan went on.

"He writes books. True crime. He wrote that history of the Mob that they made into a TV series. And a biography of John Wayne Gacy. Stuff like that. I'd never read any of it, but I sort of knew who he was. And he said he'd read about Doug's case on the Net. He's got all these news feeds on his desktop that link to weird crime stories from all around the world. Because that's how he makes his living. And he read about Doug's case, and it made his radar go off. He said he was waiting for something like this to happen, so he knew what it was as soon as he heard. Do you remember Myriam Seaforth Kale? She was a lady gangster back in the sixties. Sort of like Bonnie Parker was in the thirties."

I gave an eyebrow shrug. Of course I'd heard of her: She was one of these bad girls like Beulah Baird who go into folklore because of their connection with violent men, or because they do some of the things that violent men do routinely. I was nearly certain she'd turned up in a crappy movie that Roger Corman or someone had directed. *Daughters of Blood*? *Children of Blood*? *The Blood Family Robinson*? "Chicago Mob scene," I said. "She was Jackie Cerone's girlfriend or something, and then he used her on a job."

Jan was nodding vigorously. "That's right," she said. "That's absolutely right. She came from somewhere a long way down in the South. Brokenshire, Alabama. But she was already a killer before she ever got to Chicago. The first man she killed had stopped and picked her up on the road after she left home. The story is that he tried to rape her, and she killed him with a wheel wrench.

"Then later on, when she worked for the Mob, she only killed men. That was one of her rules. And she seemed to like humiliating them as well as killing them. She had a sort of ritual."

Some of the story was coming back to me in all its lurid colors. Myriam Kale: the homespun farmgirl who hitch-hiked up the interstate to Illinois and got lost in the big city, only to surface again as one of the few women ever to become a Mafia contract killer; the real-life femme fatale who inspired a hundred sanitized movie imitations, mur-dering nine men before the FBI cornered her in Chicago's Salisbury Hotel and brought her in alive so that they could try her, condemn her, and give her the electric chair. Or maybe it was lethal injection, I'm hazy on the details.

I had the barest beginning of an inkling of where this was going now. "Kale died in the sixties," I said. "Over forty years ago. On the other side of the world." It wasn't an absolute objection, I knew; just a place marker—some-thing we'd have to come back to.

But that was in another country, and besides, the wench is dead.

"I told you that Barnard had been tortured before he died," Jan said, using the unmentionable word this time rather than talking around it.

"Go on."

"When the pathology report came back, it turned out that one of his injuries was later than all the rest. Postmortem. It was a cigarette burn. On his face, just underneath his eye. That was her trademark, Mr. Castor. She did that to all the men she murdered. The first man, the one who picked her up, she burned with the cigarette lighter out of his car. All the rest she burned with a cigarette. It was the last thing she did, always after they were already dead. Like . . . signing off on the kill."

I tried not to meet Jan's overintense stare. "Anything like that," I said guardedly, "any detail that becomes associated with a particular murderer's style—copycat killers are going to pick up on it and use it as a matter of course."

Jan nodded again. She'd seen that objection coming, and it didn't faze her. "This is the third time Kale has killed since her death," she said. "And all three times have been here, in England, not in the States. Paul Sumner has been tracking her—that's why he knew what this was as soon as he read about Doug's case. The first time was in 1980, up in Edinburgh. The second was in 1993, in Newcastle. And now this. All three of them middle-aged men picked up on the street and taken back somewhere for sex. All three of them tortured, murdered, *then* burned. Do copycat killers rest up for over a decade between outings, Mr. Castor?"

"I've never known any," I admitted. "Maybe they're cyclical, like locusts."

"And there's something' else," Jan said with the look of someone who was turning over a hole card to reveal a big fat ace. "The cleaner at the Paragon Hotel—Joseph Onugeta—said in his statement that he walked past room seventeen sometime around five o'clock. That's about an hour after Doug and Barnard went in there. And he heard voices—people arguing. Two men and a woman, he said. Definitely three voices, because one of the men had a really cut-glass BBC voice—that would have been Barnard—and the other had a thick accent that he couldn't understand properly."

"Doug was—?" I interjected.

"He was from Birmingham, and he never lost it. I couldn't understand him myself when we started going out together. It used to really embarrass me. And then the third voice, the woman's voice, she had an accent, too. The cleaner said 'like on the TV or in a cinema.' I think that means an American accent. It was Myriam Kale, Mr. Castor. It was Myriam Seaforth Kale, and whatever else he may have done, my husband isn't going to prison for a murder that was done by some bloody ghost."

I assumed that when she said "whatever else," Jan was talking about the cottaging and the sodomy. So she'd somehow rolled with the blow of finding out that her husband was trawling the streets of London for anonymous sex with other men. I was torn between being impressed by her faithfulness and wondering what inconceivable, spectacular shit storm Doug would have to put her through before she decided that their ship was on the rocks.

I didn't say any of that. I just asked whether she'd mentioned her theory to the police. She snorted contemptuously. "Oh yes. Of course I did. The detective in charge—Coldwood—didn't even listen to me. He'd made up his mind already, and it didn't matter what I said, he wasn't going to—"

"Coldwood?" I interrupted, making sure I hadn't misheard.

"Yes. Coldwood. He's a sergeant." She read it in my face. "Do you know him or something?"

"I worked with him a few times. I used to do consulting work for the Met when business was thin."

That seemed to knock Jan back a little. "The police use exorcists?"

I nodded. "Sometimes exorcists can get a fix on how or where someone died. Sometimes we can confirm that someone who's missing isn't dead at all. It's standard practice now, although we can't give evidence in court. Most judges hate us like poison, just on general principle. Most cops, too, come to that. But I always got on okay with Gary Coldwood."

That was a slight exaggeration. Our relationship had actually gotten fairly strained when I was accused of murdering a thirteen-year-old girl whom in fact I got to meet only after she was already dead. My association with the Met was a dead letter now, and I hadn't seen Coldwood in four months or more; but we'd parted on good terms, more or less, and he'd stuck his neck out for me at least once when it would have been easier to leave me swinging in the wind. As cops went, I'd found he had a more open mind than most.

All of this was pushing me toward a decision. If Coldwood was involved, I could at least talk it over with him, get the bigger picture, if there was one.

"If I agree to take this on," I told Jan, "I'll be asking for a grand in all and at least three hundred up front. Is that going to be a problem?"

"No," she said, reaching for her handbag again. "I was expecting that you'd want some kind of down payment. I only brought two hundred and fifty, but—"

"Two hundred and fifty is fine," I said. "And it's refundable if I change my mind."

She froze, hand inside the bag in the process of drawing out her purse. "If you—?"

"If I look into it and it turns out there's nothing I can do. I'll give you the money back."

She looked at me hard. "And what about if you talk to your old friends in Scotland Yard and decide not to rock the boat?" she demanded.

"Victoria Street," I said.

She was false-footed. "What?"

"The Met moved to Victoria Street. Around about the same time that Myriam Kale was shooting G-men at the Salisbury. People just use the old name out of nostalgia." I lifted my glass for one last swig of beer, and changed my mind when I felt how close it now was to room temperature. "I said I knew Coldwood. That doesn't mean we're picking out curtains."

She gave a grudging nod, no doubt remembering Cheryl Telemaque's personal recommendation. Probably better if she didn't know how Cheryl and I had behaved back when our paths crossed. It hadn't been exactly my high point as far as professional ethics were concerned.

We exchanged contact details and Jan counted out the money into my hand, most of it in ten-pound notes. As I tucked it away in yet another pocket of my always accommodating greatcoat, she gave me a searching look. "You were going to say no," she said. "I could see it in your face. Why did you change your mind?"

I had to think about that one. "Two reasons," I said at last. "Coldwood's one. On a job like this, it helps if I can at least get some of the facts straight, and I know he'll level with me as far as he can. And then..." I paused, wondering how best to phrase this.

"And then?"

"Well, then there's the hammer. I'm presuming from what you said that Doug didn't have it on him when he was arrested?" I asked. She shook her head, eyes a little wide. "No. And I'm willing to bet that the boys in blue have been over every square inch of Battle Bridge Road—in fact, the whole of King's Cross—with a fine-toothed comb. If it was there, they'd have found it." I stood up to leave. "So it wasn't with Doug, and it wasn't out on the street. Which means that somebody else took it, presumably out of the hotel room."

"You believe me," Jan said with a slight tremor in her voice.

I gave a slight grimace. I really didn't want to lead her on when I knew so little about what I was getting into. "I'm prepared to believe—for the sake of argument—that there was someone else in that room." I finished the pint anyway, to fortify me against the night chill. "And if the someone else turns out to have been the ghost of an American serial killer, then we're in business."

———

Walking home, I got a repeat of the prickling premonitions—the sense of being watched that had dogged me all the way back from Stoke Newington. But this time

I was out in the open on a busy street. I looked around. Plenty of people walking by, plenty of traffic passing on the road. The feeling was oddly directionless, and there was no way to narrow it down. Reluctantly, I gave it up. I'd have to pick a better time and a better place.

The Breathers' van was still parked in the same place: two men sitting in it now, both older than the kid who'd been minding the shop earlier but not by much. No prickle or itch or tingling spider sense: Whatever I was feeling, whatever was watching me, it had nothing to do with these tosspots. I shot them a wave as I walked past, which they stoically ignored. I was almost sorry they didn't get out and try for a rumble. I would have welcomed the release of tension.

Back at the flat, I dumped my coat over the back of a chair, poured myself a whiskey, and then left it to stand while I picked out some bluesy chords on my whistle.

The couple next door were no longer coupling, which was good news. But though I'd missed the climax, I hadn't missed the epilogue, which as usual was taking the form of a stand-up fight. Sex and violence, always in the same order: They seemed to have a stripped-down, back-to-basics sort of lifestyle.

I gave up on the music practice after ten minutes or so because the bellowed profanities and the crash of break-ables breaking were throwing me off tempo. I put on one of Ropey's death-metal CDs instead, not because I like Internal Bleeding—with or without the capital letters—but out of sheer self-defense.

But the noises of destruction put me in mind of John Gittings's ghost, and my mood wobbled again. Thinking about John brought the pocket watch to mind. I went across to my coat and fished it out to check that it was okay. It was a beautiful thing, all right; you could see even through the black oxidation stains that the filigree work on the silver—a motif of fleurs-de-lys—was very fine. By a natural extension, I decided to wind it and see if it still worked. That meant taking it out of the outer case, since with a Savonnette watch, you can't always get enough of a purchase on the winding stem with the watch nestled inside its two separate shells.

As I took the watch out of the case, a small piece of paper fell to the floor. I picked it up and turned it over in my hand. It was the kind of very light, thin blue paper people used for airmail before there was e-mail. It had handwriting on it in a flowing, cursive script, and it had been folded over on itself several times.

I opened it out, three folds, four, five. When I had it fully open, I found that it was a complete page from a letter—from the middle of a letter, because there was no superscription and it started in midsentence. I read it with growing and slightly uneasy fascination.

could get along a bit faster, but its not a good idea to take risks. If they know youve got an idea about whats really happening, theyll take you out one way or another.

Youll just get the one pass, and its got to be on INSCRIPTION night, so you can get them all together. Take backup; take lots of backup, and warn them that as soon as there names in the frame there a target. It ends with you dead or them dead, that's the only way.

Dont make the mistake of reconasance: the wall isnt a wall, if you take my point. Not really. They can get out further than that, so they could attack you even when

*youre a long way out and you think theres nobody any-
were near you.*

*If you go in through the building, you better expect
there'll be heavy security. That may seem like the least of
your problems but dont underestimate it. Remember you
can still threaten them. Physically, I mean. If you pull
your foot back to kick, a man is going to cover his balls. I
know that sounds crude, but its the only*

And that was it—or almost. In the margin, opposite
the phrase "Take backup," someone had scribbled two
more words in red biro.

Felix Castor.

I was still staring blankly at those two words when
the phone rang. Actually, I became aware that it was
ringing—the sound had been going on for some time
underneath Internal Bleeding's relentless bass beat and
the equally unremitting noises of my neighbors disman-
tling their flat. Not my mobile; Ropey's phone. I picked up
and said hello by reflex, even though I couldn't remember
ever giving the number to anyone.

"Mr. Castor?" A man's voice, slightly breathless and
thin—not a voice I recognized.

"Yes."

"Interurban Couriers. Can you come down and sign for
a package?"

"A package?" I echoed, slightly false-footed. "Who
from?"

A short pause. "Well, the address is E14, but there's no
name."

The only guy I knew out that way was Nicky Heath, a
data rat who sometimes ran searches for me; but he wasn't
working on anything for me right then, and he wouldn't

be likely to use a regular courier service. Being both paranoid and dead, he had his own specialized ways of working.

"Mr. Castor?"

"Yeah, okay. I'll be right down."

I got up and went to the front door of the flat, unlocked it, and stepped into the corridor. A few steps brought me to the lifts. I pressed the buttons until I found the one that was currently working—the council tenant's equivalent of the "find the lady" game. The lift was on the fifth floor, only three floors below me, but instead of going up, it went down. Someone else must have pressed the button at the same time.

As I waited for it to make its stately way back up the stack, I listened—since there wasn't any other choice—to the shouting and swearing echoing from farther up the corridor. It amazed me that the other residents on this floor weren't poking their heads out to add their own shouts of protest to the overall row. Judging by their prurient interest in my comings and goings, it couldn't be out of an exaggerated regard for other people's privacy.

Something snapped in me at long last, and I walked back up the corridor to give my psychopathic neighbors' door a dyspeptic kick. "Turn it in, for Christ's sake," I shouted. "If you want to kill each other, use poison or something."

A door opened at my back, and I turned to find the woman in number 83 glaring at me.

"Noise was getting to me," I said by way of explanation. She just went on glaring. "Sorry," I added. She slammed her door shut in my face. While I was still staring at the NO CIRCULARS sign, I heard a ping from back the way I'd come, followed by a muffled thump: the lift warning bell and the sound of the doors opening.

I jogged down the corridor, determined to catch the lift before it changed its mind. I stepped inside, found it empty, and pressed G. Just as the doors started to close, I saw through the narrowing gap the front door of Ropey's flat standing open. In the five minutes that I was downstairs, the neighbors could have the TV, the stereo, and the three-piece suite. Irritably, I hit DOOR OPEN with my free hand, and the doors froze, jerked, froze, with about a foot of clearance to spare.

But before the doors could make up their mind whether to close again or slide all the way open, the entire lift lurched, the floor tilting violently. Taken by surprise, I staggered and almost lost my footing. From above me came a sound of rending metal.

I had half a second to react. As the lift shuddered and lurched again, grinding against the wall of the shaft with a sickening squeal, I fought the yawing motion, barely keeping my feet under me, and flung myself through the half-open doors back into the hallway. An explosive outrush of air followed me. I snapped my head around to look behind me and saw the lift drop like several hundredweight of bricks into the shaft. Some buried survival instinct made me snatch my right foot back across the threshold just as the roof of the car whipped past like the blade of a guillotine. The sole of my shoe was sheared off clean, and my ankle was wrenched so agonizingly that I thought for a moment my foot had gone, too. I didn't scream, exactly, but my bellow of pain was on a rising pitch—I think we're probably just talking semantics.

This time all the doors along the corridor opened,

and everyone on the whole floor came out to see what the noise was about. Well, all except one. My neighbors stayed behind their own closed front door and went right on calling each other obscene names at the tops of their voices. They probably had a quota to fill.

As I sat there staring into the darkness of the lift shaft, the asinine, obvious thought echoed in my head: Well, *fuck,* that was close. But it was followed by another thought in a different register.

All right, you bastards, you called it.

Let's dance.

~~ Five

I TOOK THE STAIRS three at a time, limping only slightly, until the last flight, which I cleared in a couple of frenzied bunny hops.

In the block's front lobby, to the right of the door, was a full-size red fire extinguisher. The damn thing weighed a good forty pounds. I hefted it in both hands, kicked the door open, and walked out onto the street.

The blue van was still there. I trudged around to the front of it, peered in. The light from a streetlamp shone full on the glass, so all I could see was a couple of dim, more or less human shapes inside. But one of them, the one in the driver's seat, gave a visible start of surprise as he saw me hefting the fire extinguisher. Maybe in the dark he mistook it for a bright red field mortar.

That was what it became a second later when I flung it at the van's windscreen.

It didn't go through—not quite—but it made a noise like a roc's egg hitting a concrete floor, and the entire windscreen became instantly opaque as the shatterproof glass gave up the ghost and sagged inward, transformed into a lattice of a million fingertip-size fragments.

The driver's and passenger's doors flew open simultaneously, and the two men leaped out onto the street, howling with rage. They were young and they were fast. When it came to handling themselves in a fight, though, their education had been sadly neglected. The first guy to reach me, the one coming from the passenger side, threw a punch that he might as well have put in the post with a second-class stamp. I sidestepped it and kicked him in the crotch. He folded in on his pain, his universe shrinking to a few cubic inches of intimate agony.

By that time, the gent from the driver's side had come to join us. He got my elbow in his face while he was still bringing his guard up. Then I barged him and tripped him, landing heavily on top of him with my knee on his chest in case he had any more fight left in him.

He didn't. He made a noise like the last gasp from an untied party balloon, then opened and closed his mouth a few times without managing to get out another sound.

I had my fist raised to deliver a knockout—which, with the assistance of the pavement, was virtually assured— but I hesitated. These guys had folded so quickly, it was frankly embarrassing. In my mind's eye, I'd had an image of Lou Beddows's bat-wielding thugs, which was why I'd gone in so hard and so fast. Belatedly, I began to wonder if this time I'd gotten the wrong end of the baseball bat.

I reached into the guy's corduroy jacket and searched the inside pockets, coming up with his wallet on the first pass. Flicking it open, I found an NUS card in the name of Stephen Bass of University College, London. Wolves in sheep's clothing? How hard could it be to fake an NUS card?

A glance over my shoulder showed me that the first guy—the one whose sex life was likely to be theoretical for the next few weeks—was still down. The one I was kneeling on was trying to speak again, but only the first syllable—"My—my—my—"—was making it out as he gulped for air.

I removed my knee, backing off and standing up. He rolled over onto his side and drew a few shuddering, raucous breaths.

"My—brother's—van!" he gasped. "You've—eurghhhh! Bastard! Bastard! My—brother's—"

"You think I give a stuff about the van?" I growled. "You tried to kill me, you psychopathic fuckwits! You're lucky I didn't torch the fucking van with the pair of you in it!"

He tried to sit up, failed, tried again, and still couldn't make his bruised chest muscles bend sufficiently to reach the vertical. He was staring at me in horror, and now he shook his head in tight, trembling arcs. "No!" he moaned. "Didn't—didn't—"

Righteous wrath was still propelling me, but with less and less momentum by the second. "What about the graffiti?" I demanded. "'Exorcist equals deceased'! You left me your fucking calling card. You wanted me to *know* you were setting this up."

The guy finally managed to get semi-upright. He looked across at his comrade, who was still curled up in a tight spiral like a dead wood louse. "I told you, Martin!" he wailed. "I told you we'd get into trouble!"

Those words put the whole thing beyond doubt. Stone-cold killers simply don't talk like that.

Anticlimax washed over me in a nauseating wave. Whoever had sabotaged the lift would be miles away by now, and I'd just torn into a couple of feckless students who were probably guilty of nothing worse than a preemptive paint job. My knees trembling slightly, I went across to check the damage on the other guy. He was beginning to be aware of the outside world again, and I helped him to his feet. By the time I'd done that, the driver—Stephen Bass, Esquire, if his NUS card was to be believed—had turned his attention back to the van and was trying to pull the fire extinguisher free without making the punctured windscreen collapse in on itself. He gave up quickly, because every attempt to move it precipitated a small shower of broken glass.

"He's gonna kill me!" he kept moaning. "He's gonna kill me!" Then he turned and pointed at me, tears in his eyes. "I'm calling the police, you bastard. You won't get away with this."

I shrugged. "Sorry, friend. Threatening to murder people can give them the wrong impression. I don't think the police are going to be too sympathetic under the circumstances."

He sat down on the van's step-up board, overcome with misery. "My brother needs the van for work," he said, his voice choked. "He only lets me borrow it when my car's off the road. He doesn't even have any insurance."

Any slight temptation I felt toward sympathy was quelled by the extravagance of his self-pity. Arseholes who play stalker when they should be writing term papers can't really complain when their world turns upside down. All I wanted to do was to make absolutely sure these idiots weren't the ones who'd just tried to kill me. Then I'd be only too happy to leave them to mourn their various losses in privacy.

I tossed Bass's wallet down on the road to get his attention. "Why were you staking me out in the first place?" I demanded.

"Oh yeah, like you don't know," Bass sneered, raising his head to glare at me accusingly. "We know all about you and what you've got planned."

"What I've got planned?" I echoed, interested in spite of myself. "What's that, exactly?"

"Mass exorcisms across London," the other guy said from behind me in a strained, trembly voice. "Spiritual cleansing—getting rid of all the dead in one go. You're the big wheel, aren't you? Felix Castor."

"Is this a joke?" I was starting to feel like I'd stepped into a parallel universe—one where Frank Spencer was God and lifts only went down. "I'm Castor, yes, but I'm nobody's wheel—big, small, or indifferent. Who's been feeding you this garbage?"

"The lieutenant—" the other guy started, but Bass cut him off with a brusque gesture.

"We had a meeting," he said. "You don't know it, but the Breath of Life have been keeping tabs on you for ages. We had an operative at that funeral watching you from undercover. She's from our underground task force. Afterward she made contact with us and told us to keep you under surveillance. And that's what we've done. Wherever you go, we'll be with you. Whoever you see, we'll see them, too, and we'll take down all their details and circulate them to everyone in the movement. You're ours, Castor, whenever we want to take you."

A secret operative? A Breather working undercover

among the London ghostbreakers? I tried that on for size, then I turned it upside down and discovered that it fitted a lot better that way. Dana McClennan. Dana McClennan stopping to talk to the pickets as she walked away from John Gittings's funeral. *You see that man over here? Well, he's not a man at all. He's the big bad wolf.*

"You fucking berk," I said sternly. "This secret operative—this sweet, blond, sexy, plausible secret operative who let you in on the big secret and made you feel so important—her name is Dana McClennan, and she's not even in your sodding organization. She was just using you to bust my balls."

Bass gave me a pitying look. "You can't trick me into giving away the names of our people. Your sort are finished, Castor. You just don't know it yet."

I walked toward him, and he flinched. But I wasn't interested in fighting anymore. I carried on past him, grabbed the handle of the fire extinguisher, and jerked it free from the remains of the windscreen, which fell like rice paper at a wedding onto the van's front seats. Bass gave an anguished wail. I hefted the extinguisher onto my shoulder and turned to face him and his blue-balled friend.

"Stephen Bass," I said. "UCL, wasn't it? I don't know which faculty, but it shouldn't be too hard to find out. If I so much as see your sodding face again, I'll come round to your hall of residence with some friends of mine, and we'll whistle your soul right out of your body. You'll be like a zombie, only with less personality."

Bass almost swallowed his tongue. "You wouldn't dare," he scoffed with less conviction than Bart Simpson saying "It was like that when I got here."

"Try me," I suggested. "Listen, you've been sitting out here watching the building all this time. Did you see someone go in?"

Bass hesitated, torn between wanting to play it cool in the face of my threats and not wanting to piss off a man who now knew more or less where he lived. "There was a big fat man," he said.

"And did you see him come out again?"

"What?" Evidently, Bass had worn himself out on the starter for ten.

"Did he come out again?" I repeated more slowly. "Did you see him come back out onto the street?"

"No."

Interesting. Very.

"Okay, thanks for your time," I said, dropping the fire extinguisher at Bass's feet and making him jump. "If you do feel a burning desire to talk to the police, I'm about to call them. All you have to do is wait right there. They'll be along presently."

I heard the doors of the van slam behind me as I went back into the block, and the engine started before I reached the stairs.

I went back up to the flat and dialed 999. The police rolled around about an hour or so later—a rapid-response unit, obviously. Performing for an appreciative audience of my neighbors, they checked the lift mechanism and took my statement. As I'd more or less expected they ended up putting the whole thing down to accident. The cables had snapped off clean, the nice constable said, which ruled out any foul play with bolt cutters or hacksaws. Probably down to metal fatigue.

Two things made me less than 100 percent convinced

by this diagnosis. The first was that the two other lifts had turned out, despite the OUT OF SERVICE notices pasted across them, to be working as well as ever. The second was that I'd checked out the name of that courier firm—Interurban—while waiting for the boys in blue to show, and it didn't exist. I hadn't really expected anything different. To quote Iago the parrot, I'd almost had a heart attack from not surprise. The whole setup had been too pat, the timing too convenient.

After the police had left, I waited a half hour or so for the last of the onlookers to go back to their interrupted evenings, and then I went down to the basement to look at the remains of the lift car. It had hit the bottom of the shaft with enough force to demolish the motor housing, and the splayed remains of it kept the lift doors open. Ignoring the incident tape and the warning sign, I climbed inside and inspected what I could see of the roof of the car, which was easy enough, since the inspection hatch had popped right out of its housing as the metal buckled under the force of impact.

Snapped off clean, like the man said. But the few feet of cable that were still attached to the roof of the lift were shiny and uncorroded. Metal fatigue doesn't show to the untrained eye, of course. But footprints do. In the sooty grease at one corner of the car roof, there was a nice one, size eleven or so, perfectly captured. If the Met boys had seen it at all, they probably would've put it down to the maintenance engineer, but this was a council block, and the lifts got inspected only on alternate blue moons.

The coincidence of this happening immediately after I'd read that letter hidden in the pocket watch had shaken me more than slightly. *Warn them that as soon as there names in the frame there a target.* And then my name scribbled in the margin. So had someone else read those words besides me? Was that why I'd nearly been bludgeoned to death by the force of gravity?

Probably not. Carla had said that John's mind was starting to go long before he died, and one sign of it was this business of hiding notes to himself all over the place. It was more than possible that he'd written the letter to himself. I didn't know his handwriting well enough to tell.

Either way, someone wanted me dead. And they didn't even have the decency to stick a knife in my back, like regular folks—presumably because they wanted my tragic demise to look like an argument for urban renewal rather than a murder.

And either way, I was feeling more curious about the job that John had been working on when he died. Maybe I would turn up for the wake after all. I'd probably kill the mood, but what can you do?

∼ Six

DETECTIVE SERGEANT Gary Coldwood had blood
on his hands, and it wasn't his. Not just blood, in fact:
Gobbets of red-black tissue hung from his fingers and
from the business end of the wickedly thin filleting knife
he held in his right hand. In his left hand was a heart that
would never beat again.

"Meter's running," he said. He liked to say things like
that because they fit in with his image of himself as a
tough, ruthless cop doing his balls-out thing in the can-
yons and arroyos of the urban wasteland. He had the
face for it, too—all squared-off chin and overluxuriant
eyebrows—and he used it to scowl at me now. "I don't
owe you any favors, Castor, and I'm not telling you anything that wasn't already reported in the papers, so don't
ask."

"Because a punch in the face often offends," I finished
for him.

"Exactly."

"Then why are we meeting here instead of down at the cop shop?"

"Here" was the kitchen of his maisonette in East Sheen. It was the afternoon of the next day, and given the Victor Frankenstein vibe that Coldwood was currently putting out, I was grateful for the touches of normality provided by the sinkful of dirty dishes, the Dress-up Homer Simpson fridge magnets, and the FHM calendar on the wall.

Instead of answering, Coldwood dropped the heart—a sheep's, judging by the size of it—back into the dish and wiped his free hand on an apron that was already foul. Then he picked up a pencil and stared at the sad, half-dismantled piece of offal with a hard frown of concentration.

"We're meeting here because I can't trust you to shut up when shutting up is the only sane option," he growled. He touched the business end of the pencil to a page in an open A4 pad and began to draw the heart with great care but no particular skill. A couple of pink smears extended across the paper like a wake behind his wrist. "You'll ask questions you shouldn't ask, make stupid guesses to see if you can gauge anything from my reactions, and generally show me up in front of people whose opinions matter to me."

There seemed no point in denying it, so I didn't bother. Might as well try the sympathy card, though, because you never knew. "Basquiat still got your balls?"

Coldwood laughed mirthlessly. "When the Paragon Hotel case broke, Detective Sergeant Basquiat was up in the Midlands talking to a roomful of local plod about the use of behavioral modeling in detective work. I think it's fair to say that if anyone is holding anyone's balls here . . ."

He tailed off, aware that the metaphor had unexpectedly run aground. Ruth Basquiat is as hard as tungsten-tipped nails, but her balls—unless she throws the kind that Cinderella likes to go to—are purely notional.

To show my good faith, I left that thought unspoken. "I'm not asking for any trade secrets anyway," I told Coldwood, comfortable with the outrageous lie because the next sentence exposed it straightaway. "All I need is an idea of how strong the case against Doug Hunter is."

"All you need for what, Castor?"

"Sorry, Gary. Client privilege."

He shook his head. "You're full of shit in an amazing variety of different shades and textures."

"Seriously," I persisted. "All I need are the basics, nothing that would compromise your professional integrity by even a half an inch." I pointed at one of the tubercles sticking out of the heart. "You missed that one," I added helpfully.

"I didn't miss it," Coldwood muttered. "I just didn't get to it yet. You want me to give you a walk-through of the whole case? Seriously? And you don't think that would *compromise* me?" The emphasis he put on the word was unnecessarily sarcastic. I could see that I was rubbing him the wrong way.

"Okay, Gary," I said. "Just meet me halfway, then. You know you want to. Deep down you're still feeling guilty because you let me get arrested for murder that time and then stood there and watched while Basquiat beat the crap out of me."

"No," he said, drawing in the little additional piece of cardiac plumbing. "I'm not feeling guilty, because that whole Abbie Torrington business was your own damn fault. And if I remember rightly, you got yourself *out* of arrest again in very short order. By driving an ambulance through the front wall of the Whittington Hospital, wasn't it?"

"I wasn't driving."

"Point stands."

He straightened up and looked at his drawing with a critical eye. Apparently, it passed muster, because he put the pencil down. I thought I could see a couple of other oozy bits of anatomy that he hadn't captured in his lightning sketch, but maybe they didn't matter from a policing point of view.

Coldwood's evening class in forensic science is his latest attempt to get ahead of the baying pack down at Albany Street and make inspector while he is still young enough to enjoy it. He goes up to Keighley College two nights a week, gets day release once a fortnight, and in theory, comes out in a couple of years with a BTEC Higher that he'll happily wave in the face of the aforementioned Detective Sergeant Basquiat—a willowy blonde with a pixieish disregard for interrogation protocol. In the meantime, he spends his free time slicing up internal organs that don't—anatomically speaking—belong to him.

"You don't have a murder weapon," I said, deciding to go for a direct approach. Sometimes there's such a thing as being too subtle.

"We'll find it. We still think Hunter ditched it in between leaving the Paragon and being picked up."

"Ditched it where? Out on the street?"

"Maybe, yeah. Or maybe in the boot of a car. Or in a skip behind a shop. It's a bloody claw hammer, Fix, with a two-and-a-half-inch cross section on the blunt end. We'll know it when we see it."

"What if you don't find it? Are you prepared to admit the possibility that there was someone else in that hotel room?"

Coldwood rolled his eyes and shook his head in something like disgust. He picked up the dish and overturned it, letting the heart slide out and fall into his pedal bin. "About a thousand someone elses," he scoffed. "You know the kind of place we're talking about. Revolving doors, hot and cold running whores. They're in and out of there like Tom and effing Jerry. We picked up three dozen sets of prints on the bedposts alone."

"I'm talking about someone who might not have left any prints," I said quietly.

That got his full attention. He wagged a finger at me, nodding to indicate that he understood now. "Oh, right. This is Janine Hunter's vengeful-ghost theory, is it?" he said derisively. "Myriam Kale back from the dead. How did she get to England? Through the phone lines?"

"You will admit, though," I pressed on regardless, "that without a weapon, most of your evidence is circumstantial—"

"Circumstantial?" Coldwood was incredulous. "DNA evidence from an anal rape?"

"Rape's a question of interpretation, especially if you walk into a bedroom in a knocking shop and lock the door behind you. But in any case, we're talking about the murder, not the sex."

"Look at the autopsy report and tell me it's all interpretation," Coldwood suggested. "Barnard had been beaten, burned, buggered, and bent backward. Then he'd been tenderized with a fucking hammer. Whether he went into that room for sex or not, I think it's pretty fair to assume that very little of what was done to him was as per tariff."

I was fighting a rearguard action here, but I wasn't ready to give up just yet. "Burned?" I repeated. "You mean on his face? According to Jan Hunter, that happened *after* he was killed, not—"

Coldwood waved the objection away. "Don't trip me up with semantics, Fix. This isn't a courtroom. Look, we can place Hunter in the area. We can place him in the room. We can place him—excuse my language—up Barnard's arse. What more do you want?" He turned his back on me, pulling a generous length of kitchen towel from a rack on the wall and wiping his gory hands on it. "We've done our homework," he went on. "Among other things, we talked to the rent boys around the back of Saint Pancras, and they say Hunter's been a regular down there for the past three months. They hate his kind—skindivers, they call them. Gay men who come down to head off a punter but don't charge for it. Hunter got into a fight with one of the street boys, and he threw some kind of a wobbly— very nasty. Went for the guy's face and marked him so he couldn't work. They left him alone after that. Just swore at him and gave him the finger from a distance."

He'd finished wiping his hands and gone on to wash them under the tap and dry them on a tea towel. He opened the fridge and took out two cans of Asda lager, one of which he offered to me. I took it for the sake of solidarity.

"Besides," he added, sounding very slightly, almost imperceptibly defensive, "we got someone to read the scene for us."

"Someone?" Taken slightly off guard, I snapped off

the end of the ring pull without actually opening the can. "What sort of someone? You mean an exorcist?"

"Yeah." He nodded. "Exactly. Your sort of someone."

"Son of a bitch!" I tossed the can back to him, suddenly not so keen on enjoying his hospitality. "You said you'd get me back on the roster as soon as the heat died down."

"It's not that easy, Castor. You resisted arrest."

"Wrongful arrest," I countered. "You dropped the charges."

"Yeah, we did. You still did eighty thousand quid worth of damage to the Whittington and left two injured officers behind when you walked out."

"When I was carried—"

"Fix, what can I tell you? The heat didn't die down yet. Your name is still John Q. Shit as far as the department is concerned. Frankly, they'd rather have Osama bin Laden on the payroll than you. At least he helps toward the ethnic recruitment quotas. Anyway, this is someone you know, an old friend. So you can ask her yourself, and she can tell you a fuck of a lot more than I can."

She? Someone I knew? Suspicion formed inside me, filling a small void left when my stomach dropped into my shoes. "Is this—?"

"I met her last year when I was interviewing Sue Book, the verger at Saint Michael's Church—you know, after it got set alight by those American satanists. Beautiful woman. I mean, you know—incredible. I was choked when I found out that she and Book were—"

"You mean Juliet Salazar," I said bleakly, cutting him off before he could go on to tell me what a waste it is that Juliet is a lesbian—or worse, start speculating on what it might take to turn her around.

"Salazar," he repeated distantly, looking past me in a way that made it quite clear he was still seeing her in the private theater of the visual cortex. "Yeah. Got it in one."

I waited patiently until he pulled himself out of the happy reverie. It cost him an effort. "So anyway," he said, "you said there were two things you wanted to see me about. What's the other one?"

"Someone's trying to kill me."

"Oh yeah?"

"Oh yeah." I told him about the falling lift and the man-size footprint in the oil and the shit on the roof of the car. He was interested, but he didn't want to show it.

"I hate it when you play junior detective, Castor," he said ruefully. "Some other poor bastard always ends up getting the sticky end of the lollipop."

"Yeah, well, everyone's entitled to a second opinion, Gary. Metal fatigue? Give me a fucking break!"

"If the cable's been tampered with, it'll be easy to tell," Coldwood allowed. "I'll send a team down to get an impression of that footprint, anyway. Probably get some virtuals off the cable, too, if the gent wasn't wearing gloves. You got any idea who he might have been? Whose cage have you been rattling?"

I didn't want to mention John's letter. It sounded too much like one of Nicky Heath's paranoid fantasies. I just shrugged.

"Your Breathers mentioned a huge fat man. Have you pissed off any huge fat men lately?" he asked.

"Not that I can think of."

"Have you even met any?"

"Well, yeah, there was one," I said reluctantly.

"Go on."

"Guy named Leonard. I don't know his last name. He works at a law office over in Stoke Newington. Ruthven, Todd and Clay. I saw him for, like, five minutes as I was waiting to see one of the partners. But he did seem to be staring at me a lot."

"He's a lawyer?"

"No, I don't think so. Some kind of clerk, maybe. He was fixing the photocopier."

"Okay." Coldwood looked thoughtful. "Ruthven, Todd and Clay. I'll look into it. Tell you if I find anything."

"Officially or unofficially?"

"The latter. I do homicide, Fix, remember? Not metal fatigue."

~ Seven

THERE'S SOMETHING you should know about Juliet, just so—unlike, say, Detective Sergeant Coldwood—you get the right picture in your head to start with. Oh, don't misunderstand me; she's every bit as drop-dead gorgeous as he said. It's just that in Juliet's case, the "drop-dead" part of that phrase is more than a simple intensifier.

Juliet is a succubus—a sex demon. Her real name is Ajulutsikael, so you can see why she doesn't use it much anymore. She feeds by stoking up your lust to the point where you're about to drown in your own drool and then consuming you, body and soul. She's tried to explain to me why the lust is a necessary component in all of this: It provides a conduit, a psychic drinking straw that she can use to suck up your spirit like a blood-warm milk shake.

There was a time, back when she was just starting out in the business, when we used to share a lot of our cases. You could say that I showed her the ropes, or at least taught her some knots that she didn't already know; but if I'm honest, what I was mainly doing was trying to domesticate a big, scary jungle predator into behaving like a house cat. It was a bumpy process with a number of very memorable upsets along the way.

Going back before that, Juliet tried to make a meal of me once but stopped halfway. In some ways, halfway is where I've been ever since—unable even to decide whether I'm relieved or frustrated that she didn't go through with it. Either way, I find it curiously hard to bear that she's shacking up with someone else—someone who (because she's female and Juliet's triggers are all male hormones) can get physical with her without arousing her other appetites.

All of which is by way of an explanation for why I didn't take up Gary Coldwood's suggestion and go and talk to Juliet as soon as I left his flat. There's only so much suffering a body can stand, and in any case, there was somewhere else I needed to be. I took the coward's way out and told myself that my duty to John Gittings's restless spirit came first: that and my curiosity as to what the letter hidden in the pocket watch was all about. If it had anything to do with me almost taking the express elevator all the way to Ropey Doyle's basement, I felt like I probably ought to know about it.

I was walking up the steps toward Carla's flat just as Todd was coming down. Four men in identical suits of funereal black, with identically impassive faces, walked behind him. Todd himself was jauntily dressed in a pale gray pinstripe.

"I take it you've just made a delivery," I said.

Todd glanced in mild surprise from my face to the

rolled-up sleeping bag I was carrying over my shoulder. "Yes," he said. "The coffin is in the living room. Are you staying the night, Mr. Castor?"

"That I am, Mr. Todd."

The lawyer nodded. "That's good. Mrs. Gittings probably shouldn't be alone tonight." He made to walk on past me.

"One quick question," I said. "When John came in to see you about changing his will, how did he look?"

Todd turned to look back at me with a stare that was suddenly all cold professionalism. "In what sense?"

I'd hoped to avoid specifics while I fished for random gobbets of information, but evidently, lawyers have built-in radar for that kind of thing.

I gestured vaguely. "In the sense of—did he appear lucid to you? Rational? Or was he looking a little frayed at the edges?"

Todd answered without even a microsecond's pause. "He was in his right mind. Entirely lucid, to use your expression. If he hadn't been, I wouldn't have been able to take legal instructions from him. He looked tired. Stressed, perhaps. A man with a lot weighing on his mind. But if his suicide was the result of any kind of—mental decay, then it hadn't started when I spoke with him. Or at least it hadn't begun to show in the way he talked and acted. I'd have said he was as sane as you or me."

"Then he wasn't talking about breaking and entering? Or kicking people in the balls?"

"Obviously not. Why? Is there some reason why you would have expected him to?"

I didn't have to answer that question, but I felt in some indefinable way as though I owed Todd a favor. Frankness was probably the only payment I'd ever be able to give him.

"They all came up in his correspondence," I said. "I think maybe they're related to whatever it was that was on his mind when he came to see you. He was working on something, and it had started to obsess him. I'd really like to know what that something was."

"Why?" Todd demanded again. He was looking at me with the lively mistrust that you show the nutter on the bus.

I shrugged. "He told Carla it was important. Maybe a professional commitment of some kind that his estate needs to take care of." It felt like a weaselly answer, but it was the best I could do without telling Todd about the lift incident and getting into deeper waters than I wanted to right then. Fortunately, he seemed already to have decided that this was something he didn't want or need to know any more about. He detached himself from me with almost indecent haste and led his four-man cortege away toward a massive hearse parked opposite. I went on up the stairs.

Carla had locked the door and bolted it at the top and bottom, so it took her a while to let me in. Her face lit up when she saw me. I guess she must have thought it was Todd coming back because he'd forgotten something.

"Fix!" she exclaimed. "You changed your mind!" She threw her arms around me, making me feel like a cynical, self-serving bastard because the reason I was here had so little to do with her and so much to do with my own near-death experience.

The coffin stood on two trestles in the center of the living room, cleaned and polished so that it was as good as new. It looked as though it ought to have a ROAD CLOSED sign hung from the middle of it. The place was as silent as the grave—maybe more, if my experience was anything to go by. The charm I'd laid on John the day before was still holding, although at the edges of my internal radar, I was aware of something stirring every so often, like the worm inside a jumping bean that makes the bean twitch as though it's alive.

I offered to put on some coffee, but it transpired that there wasn't any left; the packet that we'd emptied back on the previous Sunday had been the last in the house. It had been a while since Carla had remembered to do any shopping.

"Do you want to go out and grab a bite to eat, then?" I suggested.

"Sorry, Fix." She shook her head, her eyes flicking across to the coffin and then immediately shying away toward the neutral ground of my face. "I can't leave him here all by himself."

"No, I see that," I admitted. "Jesus, Carla, there's no need to apologize. This is the man you spent twenty years of your life with. Still, I think it would probably be a good idea if you took on some ballast. Could you handle a takeaway?"

She smiled weakly. "Not hygienic to handle it. I'll eat one, though."

I took things in hand, slipping out to the Romna Gate on Southgate Circus for some carry-out, and picking up a bag of other essentials from a minimart on the way back.

Carla perked up over gosht kata masala and a keema naan washed down by a glass of high-proof Belgian blonde. We were eating in the kitchen, where it was possible to forget the looming presence of the coffin for whole minutes at a time. Theoretically possible, anyway, but somehow the talk never seemed to stray very far from John.

I told Carla about the letter inside the watch case but not about the lift. She nodded, looking resigned. "That's what I was talking about," she said. "He'd hide things, and then lose them, and then find them and hide them all over again. I had it for months, Fix. I thought I'd gotten to know most of his hiding places by the end, but that's a new one."

I hesitated. All I knew about John's death was what Bourbon Bryant had told me, and that was the bare fact that he'd stood up one Sunday night while Carla was watching the omnibus edition of *EastEnders,* locked himself in the bathroom, and decorated the walls with the inside of his head. I found that after reading the letter, I wanted to know more. What I didn't want to do was to drag Carla over territory she'd rather not revisit.

"Did any of those other notes survive?" I asked. "The messages he wrote to himself?"

She thought about that. "No," she said after a few moments. "I'm pretty sure they didn't. Like I said, he was always changing his mind. Spending most of a day scribbling on bits of paper and envelopes, burning it all or tearing it up, and then the next day starting all over again."

"Those hiding places you mentioned—have you checked them at all since he died?"

Carla looked at me a little blankly. "Why would I want to do that?"

"I don't know. Because there might be something there that would tell us what he was up to. 'One for the history books,' remember? Maybe it was as big as he thought it was. Maybe there's a reason why it turned out to be too much for him to take."

Carla put down her fork, pushed her plate away. She blinked a few times quickly, as if there were tears in her eyes that she wanted to keep inside.

"I'm sorry," I said, lifting my hands in a gesture of surrender. "Forget I asked, Carla. You've got enough on your plate without this."

"No," she said. "It's all right, Fix. It just brought it all back, that's all."

"Exactly. I'll shut up."

"You don't have to." She stood up. "It's not like there's any getting away from it, is there? There are a few places we can look, if you want to."

She walked into the living room, then down a short hallway that led to the bedroom. I followed a little uneasily, sending up a silent apology to John's slumbering shade.

The bed had red satin sheets and a coverlet with the *Playboy* Bunny logo on it: matching his-and-hers pillows, with a halo for her and horns for him. You think you know people, but you never really do. Carla hauled a shoe box out from under the bed on the "his" side, rummaged inside it, and turned up nothing more interesting than a venerable set of check stubs.

Her next target was a safe on the wall behind a picture of a unicorn with a naked woman riding on it. The safe had a digital lock, which Carla opened by pressing the 1 key six times. "Factory default," she explained, glancing at me and rolling her eyes. "He never bothered to change it." Drawing another blank, she crossed to a rolltop desk next to the window. It had a single drawer, which was empty, but Carla didn't even bother to look inside it; she just pulled it out and put it on the bed, then knelt and put her arm into the space where it had been.

Faint bumps and thunks told me that she was feeling to the right and left in the hollow at the back of the desk. Then she stopped, and her eyebrows rose. "Bingo," she murmured.

With some difficulty, she pulled out a Sainsbury's bag wrapped around and around with brown duct tape. She held it out to me, and I took it. I hefted it in my hand, felt the weight. It didn't feel like there could be a whole hell of a lot in there.

I started to undo the tape, and Carla put her hand on mine to stop me. As if conscious of where we were, and how loaded even a momentary touch like that had to be at the foot of a double bed with Hugh Hefner's bow-tie-sporting were-rabbit giving us its one-eyed stare, she took her hand away again hastily.

"Open it somewhere else," she said. "Or—tomorrow. Not now. It would be too much for me right now."

I nodded and lowered the small package to my side. We were still standing too close to each other. We seemed to need another gesture to defuse the tension.

"You want another beer?" I asked her. "It's about eight percent proof—like Tennent's Extra but with taste. Guarantees a good night's sleep."

"I don't think I'll sleep much tonight, whatever I do," Carla said, turning away and taking a step toward the bed. She hauled the sheets and covers off in a single practiced movement. "Fix, I'm going to sleep in the living room, next to—I mean, with John. So you can have the bed.

There are more sheets and pillowcases in the top of the wardrobe, and a spare duvet in the divan drawer on that side." She pointed.

"I brought a sleeping bag," I said. "I'll just spread that on top of the mattress. Unless you want me to bring the mattress in for you."

She shook her head, looking at me with an expression that was only a couple of hard knocks away from beaten flat. "I'm fine with the duvet," she said. "I'll fold it like a sandwich and sleep in the middle." Seeming to reach a decision, she let the sheets fall to the floor and came back over to me. "Thanks for staying with me tonight," she said. "And for arranging everything. I don't know what I'd have done without you."

She kissed me on the cheek, and there was no tension or awkwardness in it. Not on Carla's side, anyway. I have to admit, her thanks sat heavily in my stomach right then, given my real reason for being here.

"It's part of the basic service," I assured her, deadpan. "The deluxe includes lawn care."

"I haven't got a lawn."

"Then the basic should suit you just fine."

I helped her take the bedding through, then went back down the steps to get a few other bits and pieces I'd brought with me. It was already dark, but the slate-gray mountains of cumulonimbus had made it dark for most of the day. The wind had blown most of that mass away to the west now, though, and a sliver of moon as thin as a sickle blade was cutting what was left of the clouds into grubby-looking tatters. Tomorrow was going to be fine, and as cold as charity.

I lingered out there because there was something about

the east wind, heavy with unborn frost, that felt clean and even refreshing. I called Juliet, got Susan Book. I asked if she could pass on a message: I just needed to talk to Juliet about some work she'd done for the Met. She said she'd tell Juliet as soon as she came in.

"We never seem to see you anymore, Fix," she chided me. "Where are you working these days? In some terrible wilderness on the edge of civilization?"

"Southgate," I said. "I think the nearest civilization is Wood Green Shopping City."

"Good grief, you're only twenty minutes' drive from here! You've got to come over for dinner. Jules would love to see you."

"Well, I will."

"Tomorrow."

Cornered. "Okay, tomorrow," I said.

"Actually, could you make it Thursday? I've got the prayer circle tomorrow night."

"Thursday it is, then. Thanks, Sue. See you then."

I hung up, pondering the mysteries of the human spirit. It was inexplicable, on the face of it, how someone who lived in sin with a succubus—a consenting adult demon of the same sex—could still be so active in the church and see no inherent contradictions in her lifestyle. Susan Book was one of a kind. I was getting to like her, even if she had stolen my woman.

I took my time stowing the phone away, collecting my things, and climbing the stairs again.

When I got back inside, I felt the difference even before I saw Carla frozen on the floor in a defensive crouch. Staining the carpet between her and the coffin was an elongated teardrop of spilled beer, with the starburst remains of the broken bottle at its narrower end. Clearly, during the few minutes I'd been outside, John had woken up in a pretty sour mood.

Carla was crying. I went over to her, knelt, and put an arm around her shoulders. She melted in to me, powerful sobs making her shudder and shake. "I just"—she managed to get out—"said good night—to him!"

I'm not good in this kind of situation. I'm familiar with the noises that have to be made, but people who know me, and know what I do for a living, find it as hard to take consolation from me as they would from a professional hangman. I tried anyway. "Carla," I said, "the reason he's so scared and so angry is because fear and anger are pretty much all he is. His body's gone—it's in the casket there. He's jumped the rails. Right now he's just a collection of emotions so strong there isn't even much room left for memories. That's why so many ghosts seem to spend their time replaying their own death: They're caught in a loop, going through the same events again and again because there's so much fear and pain tied up in there.

"John's not trying to hurt you. You said yourself that none of the things he's thrown has ever touched you. He's lashing out because he doesn't understand what's happened to him, and he doesn't know how to get free of it. But if he threw that bottle when you touched the side of the coffin"—with her head buried in my chest, she tried to nod, and I felt rather than saw the movement—"then that's a good sign. It means he recognizes the body as his own and wants to protect it. It means he remembers enough of his past to make that identification. On some level, he knows who he was. Who he still *is*. So you did the right thing, agreeing to this. I think you've helped him."

She still had to cry it out, but the point seemed to sink in, and she slowly started to calm. After a minute or so, I let go of her and took my tin whistle out of my pocket. "I'm going to play him some more music," I said.

That alarmed her all over again. She surfaced from the now slightly soggy depths of my lapels with a look of horror. "Fix, if you send him away now—"

"I didn't send him away the first time," I said. "I just made him drowsy. These are tunes I use on Rafi, so I've had plenty of time to get them down right. This time I won't even send John to sleep. I just want to calm him a bit so you don't have to go to bed in full-body armor."

I waited for her to respond. Finally, she gave me the merest hint of a nod, as though she didn't trust herself to speak.

I played a tune that was vaguely based on Neko Case's "Lady Pilot," I think purely because of the line in the song about not being afraid to die. Often in these cases, it doesn't seem to matter all that much what the song is when it starts out. Once I let it out into the open air, it grows and changes, as though the vibrations of the music are some sort of insubstantial extension of my own nervous system. It becomes something that I use to touch the world—the invisible world that seems to be idling next to our own right now at some interdimensional red light—and to operate on the things I see and feel there.

Opening my mind a little more this time, I met head-on the spirit that was waiting in the dark, and I was struck by the sheer intensity of its rage. It was like scalding water filling the room, unseen and unfelt until now. The strength of it—the strength of the will behind it—took me by surprise. None of the interactions I'd ever had with John had made me suspect that he could be capable of that kind of ferocity. Matching it high for high, low for low, I let the music fall into the anger like a calving iceberg and slowly, gradually, take away its power to hurt.

I lose track of time when I'm doing this stuff. Or maybe it's fairer to say that time becomes one of the dimensions of the music, and I can perceive it only as something that's moving in my chest and under my fingers, flowing out into the pattern I'm making. In any case, when I finally surfaced, I found that Carla was asleep next to me.

The geist wasn't asleep, but it was quiescent. It wouldn't be throwing any more beer bottles around for a while. I felt queasy all over again as I thought about the contrast between the vaguely well-meaning, more or less ineffectual man I'd known for the past fifteen years and this baleful ball of hate and wrath. Death changes you—in some cases, brings out the worst in you—but that didn't make this any easier to take. Particularly since I found myself wondering whether John Gittings might still be alive if I'd taken his calls.

My internal logic checker kicked in on my side at that point. You can't save someone from suicide if he's serious about making the effort. John had wanted and intended to die; that much had to be true. Even in New York City, where they're reputed to have those giant alligators in the sewers, people don't casually take loaded shotguns into the toilet with them.

And if it was murder dressed up as suicide? But that really sounded like Mr. Paranoia dropping in for tea.

On paper, in theory, in the cold light of day, I had nothing to reproach myself with. But this was the dark night of John Gittings's soul, and I couldn't let myself off the hook that easily.

I picked up my stuff and went into the bedroom, where I unrolled the sleeping bag on the stripped bed. There's something cold and unlovely about a bare mattress. I tried not to look at it as I unpacked the rest of my gear from a ragged-arsed overnight bag that used to belong to Rafi.

Then I slipped off my shoes, sat back on the bed with my feet up, and finally peeled the layers of duct tape away from the Sainsbury's bag that John had squirreled away so carefully. The bag started to tear, and a few small items fell out before I'd finished unwrapping it: a small key on a knotted shoelace and the torn back of a matchbook from someplace called the Reflections Café Bar. That left one bulky, rectangular object.

From what Carla had already told me, I wasn't expecting very much, but the biggest item in the bag was an object of such spectacular banality that I felt a sense of bathos and letdown even as I pulled it clear of the plastic and stared at the cover. It was an *A to Z of London*; one of the larger ones, spiral-bound.

I flexed it with my thumb and riffled through it. It had been marked up in black felt tip on almost every page— lines and circles sketched in, in some cases scribbled out afterward, so that you mostly couldn't see the features they were originally meant to be indicating. At least one of them was a church.

And that was it. Not much to go on at first glance; not much to indicate what John had meant when he'd said this was one for the books. Unless geographical gazetteers were the books he had in mind.

Further examination, though, showed that he'd used the *A to Z* as a notebook, too. The inside front and back covers and the blank spaces on the title and copyright pages were filled with dense writing. It seemed to be lists of names, and the ones at the front of the book included a lot of people I actually knew—my own name was there, along with Juliet's, Carla's, Bourbon Bryant's, Reggie Tang's. Some of them had been ticked off, others not; some had been ticked, the ticks crossed through, and then ticked again.

Other names, set off in a different column, were new to me or stirred faint echoes in my mind that I couldn't turn into meanings right then. Silver. Cornell. Moulson. Lathwell. Richardson. Lambrianou. Hart.

The list inside the back cover seemed to be of places rather than people: Abney Park, Eastcote Lane, St. Andrew's Old, St. Andrew's Gardens, Strayfield. They ran across five columns, written in a tiny, crabbed script; some of the names marked with symbols, some circled in different-colored inks, some crossed out and then written in again over the top. I remembered Carla's description of John writing messages to himself and then tearing them up. It seemed as though he'd been doing more or less the same thing here.

I flicked back and forth between the various lists, my eye drawn automatically to the parts that were easiest to read, avoiding other stretches where the density of the crossing out and rewriting made individual words hard to decipher. Eventually, my sight started to swim, and I gave it up.

I turned my attention to the key on its makeshift bootlace key ring. I looked at it with a certain degree of professional interest, because breaking and entering has been a hobby of mine at various points in my life. It was small, hollow-barreled, with the number 167 etched into the diamond-shaped bow end. It was a Lycett, the very distinctive product of that Midlands locksmithing firm, though it didn't bear the maker's name. That was interesting: Lycett did a great many job lots in the eighties and nineties, mostly for factories and offices, but very few of them were in London. A man with a lot of time on his hands and a prurient curiosity could probably find the lock that this key fitted. But what would be the point if it turned out to yield only a few more scribbled, near-illegible palimpsests like the one I'd just looked at?

I put the three items back in the eviscerated bag one by one, thinking that there must be some easier way of solving the John Gittings conundrum. The matchbook cover, I noticed, had a string of figures written on the back in red ink. A credit card number? No, only eleven digits, where a credit card would have sixteen. The first three digits were 832, so it didn't look like a phone number—but for the hell of it, even though it was well after midnight, I added a zero to the beginning and dialed it. The shrill, sustained note that means "no connection" was all I got in response.

I stared at the number for a while longer, wondering if I was missing something obvious, but I was finding it hard to focus through the fuzzy haze inside my head: long day, strong beer. This number would keep until the morning.

I put in one more phone call, this one to Nicky Heath. His name was in John's *A to Z,* too, but that wasn't why I called. Nicky's a ferret, skilled in the digital extraction of information. If anyone could make sense of John Gittings's annotations, it was him. Also, being a dead man himself—of the zombie persuasion—he might empathize with John's current situation.

That done, I stripped to my boxers, pulled on a T-shirt by way of a pajama top, and crawled into the sleeping bag.

I was expecting to fall asleep right away, but the atmosphere of the place made it hard for me to let go of the day's tensions. My playing had created a zone of silence in the room, where usually, I'm surrounded by a low-level psychic buzz of unformed energies. It was like the disconcerting hush you get when you're sitting in the kitchen and the fridge stops humming, filling your senses with an absence that's somehow louder than the sound it replaced.

I thought about Alastair Barnard's miserable death and Jan Hunter's absolute conviction that her husband hadn't been responsible for it. Where was the hammer? Why had it been worth taking away from the scene of the crime, since the evidence against Doug Hunter was already so strong? Maybe because it didn't fit with the rest of the evidence; maybe because it had the wrong fingerprints on it. In that case, it was either the real killer who'd waltzed off with it, or another someone had stepped in and swiped it after the body was found and before the police got there. A pretty narrow window.

In either case, Coldwood was clearly way off the beam when he said that Hunter had taken it himself. Walking through the streets of London with blood on his clothes, he'd attracted enough attention that people had stopped to watch him pass and then pointed out to the police where he'd gone. It was inconceivable that he'd been carrying a claw hammer all that time and nobody had noticed when and where he'd dropped it.

I dozed off at last, into the kind of fitful sleep where

you're sort of aware that time is passing and it's passing slowly. I had muddy, tedious dreams in which I was walking down long streets that I didn't know, looking for a train station because I had to go somewhere and time was running out. Night was coming on. If I missed the train, I'd be stuck here, and in the dream, that seemed like a very bad option. I turned corners at random, sure that I'd see the station in the distance, but each turning was either a blind alley or an avenue that stretched into the distance with no station in sight.

Then I passed a man sitting on the side of the road—in the same attitude, I guess, as Doug Hunter when the cops found him and took him in. But this wasn't Doug Hunter, a man I'd yet to meet. It was John Gittings.

I sat down next to him. It would have felt rude to just walk on by.

He gave me a look—more in sorrow than in anger, which came as something of a relief, considering his propensity for violence on the spirit level. He was dressed in the shabby brown jacket and tan chinos he'd worn on the day of the Whipsnade Zoo debacle the year before, when he'd taken his eye off the game during a tag-team exorcism and I'd come within an eighth of an inch of having my head bitten off. It was the last time I'd seen him alive.

He showed me his hands, which were bloody. My subconscious mind was definitely raiding Doug Hunter's story for narrative guidelines here.

"Not much left of me now, Fix," John said lugubriously. Psychologists tell us that you can't really hear voices in dreams, but this sounded like the John I remembered: as much vaguely comical self-pity as Morrissey, but John had played the drums when he was ghostbusting, and no group he was in ever stayed together for very long, so in most respects, you'd have to say he was more like Johnny Marr.

"No, mate," I agreed. "You've seen better days, that's for sure."

Since it was my dream, I checked my pockets for booze. Nothing there but a sprig of silver birch. Okay, that was stuck up on John's door to keep the restless dead out. I felt almost ashamed. As dreams went, this was turning into something of a busman's holiday.

I offered John the silver birch ward. It was looking a little ragged now, the white thread that bound it starting to unravel, but he didn't seem to notice it. He shook his head, staring somberly at the gutter where a trickle of black water was running along past us, detouring around the toes of his shoes. "Nobody wants to know, do they, Fix?"

"Wants to know what, John?" I asked.

"How the bastards killed me."

I put the birch twig back in my pocket. "Umm—you killed yourself, John," I said as tactfully as I could. "You didn't take any chances about it, either. You stuck a shotgun in your mouth and pulled the trigger. It took Carla two days to get your brains off the walls."

John looked up at me, his expression slightly reproachful. "I might not have had to," he said, "if you ever picked up your phone."

I'd been expecting that one. You didn't need to be Freud to know why I was dreaming about John Gittings while I was sleeping in his bed with his dead body in the room next door. "Yeah, I'm sorry," I said. "Really, really sorry. On the other hand, you could have left a message that made some kind of sense. You never told me what was at stake, John. You never tried to meet me halfway."

He was rummaging in his pockets, patting his jacket, a distracted frown on his face. "I thought I could handle it," he admitted. "By the time I decided to bring someone else in on it, I was already in way over my head. I always was an arrogant sod, Fix. Almost as bad as you. I think I was supposed to give you something."

"The letter? I got it."

"No, not the letter. The score. The final score, after the whistle blew."

"The whistle?"

"Or the drums. I forget. It's like a skeleton, Fix. The skeleton of a song."

"Yeah, well, thanks for the thought, John. I guess I'll live without it. What's inscription night, by the way? It sounds like something you'd get at the local bridge club."

John sighed and stood up, very slowly, with great reluctance. There was a faint splash as he disturbed the water in the gutter, the rippling aftereffects lasting longer than I would have expected. I looked up into his pleading hangdog face.

"I've got to go," he said. "It'll have to wait for another time. You won't let them get me, will you, Fix? I can rely on you for that much? Blow me away, if you have to. Play me a song and blow me out like a candle. I don't mind. Just don't let them get me."

I stood up, too, because the street was filling with water. The trickle in the gutter had grown into a flood while I wasn't looking, and it was already up to our knees. It was cold and completely opaque, like a rising tide of ink.

"Who, John?" I asked. "Who wants to get you?"

"The same ones as before," he said with a helpless shrug. He stared into my eyes, his jaw tightening with fear. "Always the same ones, again and again and again. That's the point. Kill me if you have to, Fix. Better you than them, God knows."

He took a few steps away from me out into the road. He stopped and looked off to the right and then to the left, as if unsure which way to go, or maybe as if checking for traffic—you've got to keep your wits about you when you cross the road in London. As if to underscore that point, he tripped and fell, vanishing into the water almost up to his shoulders. There was a hole of some kind in the middle of the street. Roadwork, maybe. But it wasn't roadwork, and I knew.

I stepped out into the still-rising flood, feeling the vicious undertow trying to pull my legs out from under me. I picked my way forward one step at a time, feeling with my toes for the edges of the unseen pits. The road was a cemetery, the open graves hidden by the water so that you couldn't see them until you fell.

Who'd dig graves in the middle of a road? Maybe it was like housing: Location was all-important, and a dead man with somewhere important to be would want to be buried in a place that was handy for the shops and the tube.

I rounded one of the graves and almost stepped sideways into another. The water was up to John's neck now, and he was staring in all directions, his eyes wide with dread.

Before I could get to him, something pulled him under. He gave a wail of terror, cut off very abruptly when his head went below the surface. When I got to the spot, there was nothing to show where he'd been except a ragged stream of bubbles, drifting away on the midnight-black flow of the urban river.

Something brushed against my leg under the surface—something big enough to push me aside as it glided past, unseen. I jumped away, watching the roiling water it left in its wake. It turned in a vast, lazy arc and headed back toward me. I took one step back, and then another, and on the third step, there was nothing to put my foot down on. I slipped on the rim of the submerged grave pit and went under, my mouth clamped shut.

I woke up gasping for air as though I really had half-drowned. Like someone in a movie, I came bolt upright, my body sheathed in already cooling sweat. I groped for a bedside light, found one, and after a few seconds of floundering, succeeded in turning it on. A big calico cat that had been sitting at the foot of the bed yowled in protest, jumped down to the floor, and padded to the door, shooting me a glance of cool disapproval as it left. The stray that Carla had told me about, obviously.

Shit! That had been the worst nightmare I'd had in years. With slightly shaky hands, I unzipped the sleeping bag and swung my legs out. There was no way I was getting any more sleep until my pulse rate had come back down to normal.

I went to the door, then trekked along the short passage and looked out into the living room. Turning the light on had robbed me of my night sight, so I couldn't make out many details in the scene before me. I could hear Carla's rhythmical breathing, though, and I could see the shadowy bump that was her sleeping form.

The coffin still stood on its trestles, undisturbed. The cat walked under it, rubbed its cheek against the legs of the nearer trestle, then strolled on with regal indifference.

A couple of cautious steps into the dark brought me to the foot of the coffin. I put a hand on its lid, the smooth wood chilly under my fingertips.

All right, mate, I said to myself. Nothing formal. No promises, because when all's said and done, I don't owe you a damn thing.

But I'll do what I can.

~ Eight

TODD HAD MADE all the arrangements for the cremation, too. He'd told Carla that the hearse would call at ten in the morning, but he was there himself at nine-thirty to supervise. Carla was in the shower, so I opened the door for him, feeling like I'd been rolled up wet and put away dry.

I must have looked fairly rough, too, because as he came inside, Todd gave me a look that was almost supercilious. "Sleep well?" he asked blandly.

I picked up my mug of coffee, which I'd rested on the coffin lid while I was opening the door, and took a deep swig of Carla's bitter espresso before I answered. "Like the dead." Todd actually winced. They say that if you can make a lawyer blush, you get a free pass to heaven. I wondered if this would be good for a day trip to purgatory.

He outlined the route to me, although this time we'd be traveling in one of the official cars, so there was nothing to memorize. "Mount Grace Crematorium is on Bow

Common," he said. "Behind Saint Clement's Hospital. We'll drive down to Primrose Hill, around the Outer Circle, and then east all the way from there. Is Mrs. Gittings ready?"

He could hear the sound of the shower as well as I could, so I gave him the only answer the question seemed to deserve: "Almost." He wasn't listening, in any case; he was prowling around the room looking at the damage that the ghost had done, which of course he was seeing for the first time. He assessed it with a thoughtful, even professional eye, as if considering what it might be worth as part of a lawsuit. I finished my coffee and watched him in silence. He seemed nervous and eager to be on his way, which he probably was. I didn't know how much he charged for estate work, but it didn't seem likely that John had paid him enough to cover two visits to Waltham Abbey and a slap-up funeral in the East End. Or maybe I was underestimating John's determination to have his last wishes respected. Maybe he'd given Todd a big enough retainer to cover all eventualities.

The lawyer's circuit of the room brought him back to the door at last. It was still open; he hadn't closed it on his way in. He looked at John's old wards with the same clinical eye, then glanced at me. "These ought to go," he said. "Before we take the body out."

It was slightly embarrassing that I hadn't thought of that myself. Of course that could be what had caused John's ghost to be separated from his body and stranded here in the first place. It was hard for the dead to cross magical wards if they'd been put together right—and although they were used mostly to keep ghosts and zombies out of places where they weren't wanted, they'd work just as effectively to imprison them. Jenna-Jane's cheerfully sadistic experiments at the MOU in Paddington had proved that a hundred times over.

I took down the birch sprig myself; it brought back my dream more vividly than I liked. "Not much left of me now..." Todd wiped over the chalked *ekpiptein* with the palm of his hand, and I levered off the mezuzah. Between the two of us, we cleared the doorway inside of a minute. Tactfully, Todd didn't point out that as the resident exorcist, I ought to have done it myself before he arrived.

Carla still hadn't put in an appearance, and the cars weren't here yet, either, so I went back into the kitchen and brewed some more coffee—I'd bought a packet the night before, on my expedition for the curries and beer. Todd accepted some—black, no sugar—and then left it to cool as he paced around the room some more.

"Did John ever mention why he was so dead set on being cremated at Mount Grace?" I asked. "Is there something special about that one place?"

Todd turned to glance in my direction, looking a little surprised. "Well, perhaps I played a part in that," he said. "I thought I mentioned this already, but maybe I was talking to someone else. Mount Grace is something of an oddity. The owners—the Palance family—are clients of ours. They bought the crematorium from the borough in the twenties, although they founded a blind trust to take care of the actual running of the place—its running as a historical site, I mean. It's hardly ever used for its real purpose anymore, except in very rare cases—family and friends, mainly. I had the file on my desk one time when John came into the office. He was talking about cremation, and I told him about Mount Grace. The idea of a crematorium that's something of a select club seemed to appeal to him."

So whatever it was, John's concern hadn't been narrowly geographical. He'd been concerned about what exactly was done to his body, rather than where it was done or where the remains were put afterward. Burning rather than burial. Why? To close the door on his return? But it hadn't. Although a lot of ghosts tend to stay close to their mortal remains, far more linger in the place of their death, just as John had done. Being cremated only ruled out coming back as a zombie, not coming back per se.

"Any reason why you suggested Mount Grace, then?" I asked for form's sake. "Did John ask for something specific in the way his body was disposed of?"

Todd shook his head firmly, looking bored and perhaps even a little resentful at being questioned. "It was nothing like that. It was just that he wanted the whole thing settled quickly, almost on the spot. Because of my firm's connection to the Palances, I was able to make arrangements at Mount Grace with a single phone call. And it seemed to meet John's requirements in other respects, too. The cost is nominal, because as I said, the trust sees the place mostly as a site of historical interest, and there's a bequest that covers its maintenance.

"There's a garden of remembrance where Mr. Gittings's ashes will be laid, and it's in a rather beautiful spot. At least it *was* beautiful, and I'm sure it will be again when the building works on the site next door are finished. The crematorium has its own formal gardens. I think they were designed by Inigo Jones. In fact, that's why the Palances acquired the site in the first place: The buildings and the grounds are very fine, and there'd been some talk of bulldozing them and building houses there. Michael Palance, who's dead now, tried to get the building adopted by the National Trust, which was fairly new in those days, and when that failed, he bought it himself."

Carla walked in at this point, looking more than a little stunning in her widow's weeds. She clearly wasn't all that happy to see Maynard Todd in her living room, but almost at the same moment, there was a knock at the door—the four pallbearers reporting in for duty. They hefted the coffin, and we got under way immediately, avoiding any need for an unpleasant scene. A few of the neighbors watched from their front gardens or from behind lightly twitching curtains as John went off to the next installment of his eternal reward. Carla walked regally down the steps and into the car, not sparing any of them so much as a glance.

Since all three of us rode together in the hearse, conversation was sparse and strained. That left me plenty of time to mull over the change in John's will, and to chase my thoughts around in decreasing circles until I was sick of them. Cremation. Why had it mattered to John so much that he had drawn up a new will and gone to a new law firm to make sure that his instructions were followed, no matter how much distress it might cause Carla?

Nicky Heath, who, as a zombie, took a lively [*sic*] interest in stuff like this, told me once that in early civilizations, cremation was kind of a patriarchal thing. "You could think of the smoke as a ghost phallus if you want to," he said. "The 'dead man's last stand' kind of thing. Or if that strikes you as a little off-color, you could go for the official symbolism. You're seeing the soul ascend to heaven to sit at God's right hand. Matriarchies didn't go for that whole heaven argument so much—they favored burial because it was going back to the womb of Mother Earth. Closing the big circle. You can't get born again until you put yourself back." Needless to say, Nicky sided with the mothers on this one. Anyone who came near him with a can of kerosene was likely to return to Mother Earth in a lot of separate pieces.

But John was a ghostbreaker through and through: There are very few of us who have any time for religion. When you spend your life dealing with the crude mechanics of life and death, you tend to find the elegant theories less than compelling. So maybe Carla was right—maybe his mind had started to go, and maybe that explained both his aberrant behavior in the last few weeks of his life and his scary transformation after death.

Or maybe there was something else going on, although it was hard to imagine what sort of something that could be if it required him to burn his body after he died, as though it contained a secret message of some kind. For just a moment, an idea stirred in the fuzzy depths of my mind, but it submerged again before I could reach for it.

Todd brought me out of my thoughts by leaning forward to tell the driver to hang a left. The unexpected sound made Carla tense, showing how strained the silence in the car had become even as it broke. As though the ice had been broken, too, Todd turned to Carla and offered her an affable smile.

"I haven't made any specifications about the service, Mrs. Gittings," he said, "but I believe there will be a clergyman on hand. If you want any kind of a prayer spoken over the casket, or a hymn—" He left the sentence unfinished, no doubt realizing as he said it how pathetic the three of us would sound striking up a chorus of "Guide Me, O Thou Great Redeemer."

"I just want it to be over," Carla said in a low, curt tone that left no room for further conversational pleasantries.

Our route took us through a part of London that's one of my favorites. Mile End is steeped in tragic and tragicomic history in the same way that, say, a pickled pig's trotter is steeped in vinegar. This was where the first of Hitler's flying bombs rained down; where the spectacularly cocked-up launch of H.M.S. *Albion* killed dozens of local kids who'd taken the day off school to see it glide off the slipway; where the resurrection men plied their trade; and where Bishop and Williams murdered the Italian Boy. The rising of the dead is a fairly recent thing, but in Mile End, the ghosts have soaked into the stone.

We drove on through Stepney to Bow Common, and just after Mile End Station, we turned off the main drag, skirted the shapely backside of Saint Clement's, and drove in through the gates of the Mount Grace Crematorium. We had no choice, because the bottom of Ropery Street was blocked off. The building site that Todd had mentioned extended on both sides of the road, and oversize earthmovers prowled behind the plywood hoardings like wind-up dinosaurs in some mechanical equivalent of Jurassic Park.

Mount Grace had a small frontage on the street, but the grounds were deceptively spacious. They opened in front of us as we rounded the oxbow drive, lined on both sides with tall yews, and we got a glimpse of the formal gardens off to our left. They were a pretty but slightly somber prospect dominated by funereal cypress trees and heavy, po-faced stone balustrades. Two massive stone urns flanking an arched gateway with passionflowers trained up it on both sides marked the entrance to the garden of remembrance. Kind of an odd choice, was my first thought; then I remembered someone telling me that the passion referred to was the passion of Christ, so I guess it was all as per the party line. Death and resurrection: Pay now and live later.

The crematorium itself was pretty damn impressive, though. It was built in cream-colored stone, its main mass coming forward to meet the drive while two wings extended toward the rear of the grounds on either side. It was crenellated, with scalloped curves rather than straight ups and downs. The overall effect made it look as though the building had been assembled out of jigsaw pieces.

I enjoyed it while I could. As I got closer, the presence of the dead announced itself first as a pressure, then as something like a continuous bass throbbing at the limits of my perception. As I think I mentioned before, I hate cemeteries. Crematoria are no better and no worse: They're places where my death sense wakes up like a jumpy nerve in a tooth.

The cortege rolled onto the gravel drive, the hearse itself taking pole position in front of the crematorium's massive oak door. From this close up, I got an even better view of the architecture. There were ornate carved crowns over the windows, and the remains of some very weathered bas-relief sculptures on the corners of the building—faceless caryatids supporting the actual cornices on their bent backs, scarred and blackened by generations of rainwater to the point where you couldn't even guess what figures they'd been meant to represent. The four winds? The four elements? The Four Tops?

Our bearers had been traveling in the car behind. They·
got out first, opened the back of the hearse, and slid out the
runners, ready to move on Todd's command. At the same
time, a man who had been standing on the front steps of
the crematorium came down to greet us. From his appearance, I guessed that he wasn't the clergyman Todd had
mentioned. He was in his late twenties or early thirties,
with white-blond hair and a craggy, stolidly handsome
face. He was built like a rugby forward, but he wore a solemn, measured expression that made me wonder whether
my first impressions had been wrong. Maybe he *had* taken
holy orders, out in Beverly Hills. His slate-gray linen suit
was as good as Todd's, maybe better. The one I was wearing came from Burton's. I generally pick them up in the
sales, when they'll throw you in an extra pair of pants for
free, so you'll appreciate that there are gaps in my sartorial
education. Once you get past the thousand-quid mark, my
eye's not good enough to make the fine distinctions.

We got out of the hearse. Todd and the newcomer
locked eyes in a way that was definitely hostile: viscerally, bitterly hostile and bleeding out of the pores despite
the constraints of the situation.

"Maynard." The blond man held out his hand, and
Todd stared at it for a moment, nonplussed. Then, looking cornered and unhappy, he took it, shook it in a single,
staccato up-down movement, and let it go again.

"Mr. Covington," Todd said. "I didn't expect to see you
here. It's very good of you to come." There was a slight
thickening in his voice. It had cost him an effort to get
those words out.

The blond man shrugged easily. "I was in the neighborhood," he said. "It seemed silly to pass the keys on to

Fenwick or Digby when I could just come and open up myself."

There was a perceptible pause. "Yes," said Todd. "I see. This is Mrs. Gittings, and this is Felix Castor. And—umm"—turning to us—"this is Peter Covington."

Covington gave me the briefest of nods and turned his attention to Carla. I could see she was impressed: There was a sudden warmth that I could feel from where I was standing—a wave of easy benevolence that made the air around us ripple with a virtual heat haze. "I was sorry to hear about your loss," he said, and I think she believed him. Certainly, she let him take her hand and squeeze it. He looked soulfully into her eyes, and for a long moment, she looked back. Like I said, Carla generally went for older men, but when she finally took possession of her hand again, I thought I could detect a little reluctance on her side, at least.

I was half hoping that Blondie would offer the same hand to me, for curiosity's sake—he had a lot of poise for a guy ten years my junior, and I would have been interested in reading him, but he just stepped back and indicated the doors with a gesture that was almost a bow.

"I presume everything is ready inside," he said. "I haven't been able to check—I've got a lot to do elsewhere, and I'm running late already. And I wouldn't presume to join you for the actual ceremony. But my very best wishes to you all—and especially to you, Mrs. Gittings. If there's anything I can do to help, please don't hesitate to call." He took a card from his pocket and gave it to her with a decorous flourish.

Carla took it without even looking at it. "Thank you," she murmured throatily.

The personable young man swept us all with a frank, blue-eyed gaze, then with a final murmur of farewell to Todd, he headed off toward a small, sleek black sports car parked at the other end of the drive. Todd watched him go, his attention taken up to the exclusion of everything else around him.

"The owner?" I said as the bearers slid John's coffin noisily onto the runners and drew the lawyer out of his reverie.

Todd looked surprised, then laughed with a slightly odd inflection. "No, Mr. Castor. The owner is a man named Lionel Palance. He lives a long way from here, in Chingford Hatch, and he hardly ever leaves his house at all now. No, that was Peter Covington, a man Mr. Palance employs as a sort of... personal assistant." He rattled off these facts with a lawyer's precision, as though it mattered that I should get the details straight in my head. Then he seemed to recollect himself, and his tone became more formal and solemn. "Mrs. Gittings, shall we go in?"

We crossed the drive, following behind the bearers. Carla was still holding Covington's card because she'd left her handbag inside the car. "Fix," she said. "Would you...?" I took the card and secreted it away in the well-worn leather wallet where I keep my mostly useless credit cards.

The front doors of the crematorium opened onto a narrow entrance hall, almost long enough to count as a corridor, whose dark woods and vaulted ceiling confirmed the impression of age I'd gotten outside. Four huge inlaid panels dominated the space, two to either side of the door: a lion and an eagle to the left, an ox and a robed angel to the right. The symbols of the four evangelists. The carpet was royal blue, scuffed pale in places by the passage of many feet.

Ahead of us was another door. Black-suited men, presumably also hired by Todd, stood on either side of it and nodded respectfully to us as we passed. They looked like bouncers at a nightclub.

We walked into a large, high-ceilinged room that looked like any church hall anywhere, except for the dumbwaiter-like doors at the far end and the slightly sinister platform placed in front of them—a platform whose surface was a plain of slick, frictionless plastic rollers. I abreact to furnaces, probably because of having to take my dad his lunch a couple of times when he worked behind the ovens in a bread factory. Places like this one always put me in mind of Satan's locker room.

The bearers placed the coffin on the platform and stepped back, and at the same time a very short man in a black ecclesiastical robe came out through a curtained doorway off to one side. Todd went forward and had a brief, murmured conversation with him, presumably along the lines of "This is the action replay, but let's dispense with the slow motion and get it over with." The man nodded briskly. He had a slender face with a very long, sharp nose that made me think of a fox or a wolf. I'd seen a Japanese ivory once—a tiny figure, barely bigger than the top joint of my thumb—of a fox dressed as a priest, with a long robe and a staff and a pious expression. Maybe it was unfair, because the nose must have been enough of a burden in itself, but this young cleric brought the statuette vividly into my mind.

Todd had presumably mentioned that Carla didn't want any prayers said, but the cleric clearly wasn't happy to let the occasion go by without ruminating on mortality just a little. Force of habit, I figured, although technically, he was wearing a surplice.

"In the midst of life," he said, "we are in death." Two cheers and a thump on the tub for Ecclesiastes. Sitting in the front row, with Carla to my left and Todd to my right, I let my attention wander. Unfortunately, it wandered to the furnace doors, where it found no comfort and shied away again pretty fast.

I was still feeling tired and rough, worse than I had when I woke up, if anything. The chill in the room was creeping into me, and the half-floral, half-chemical smell was turning my stomach. It didn't help that beyond the walls, the dead souls were massed thickly, sounding to my overdeveloped senses like a swarm of desert locusts.

There was another soul here, too: stronger, or at any rate, closer. It hovered around our heads like an invisible cloud, making the lights in the room seem a fraction dimmer. But a cloud suggests something dispersed and diffuse, and this presence was localized. As my gaze panned across the room, it reached the coffin and stopped as if the coffin were a black hole pulling light and matter and everything else in toward it.

The priest's voice had taken on a hollow echo. There was an arrhythmical vibration rising behind it like a pulse, and the vibration danced against the surface of my skin, wave after wave, as though looking for a way in.

Neither Carla nor Todd seemed to be aware of any of this. They were both watching the priest, whose lips were still moving, although I was damned if I could hear a word he was saying. For a moment I wondered if I was just imagining the whole thing—if the nightmare and the lack of sleep were just taking their toll—but then the feeling of general overall pressure narrowed in on the front of my head and intensified into one of actual pain.

Todd slipped something into my hand, and I found myself staring down dully into a hip flask a little like my own, except this one was slimmer and cased in black leather. Reflexively, I raised it to my lips and took a hit. The liquor was very potent and very bitter, and it took a real effort not to gag. I passed the flask back to Todd, and he slid it away into some recess of his suit where it didn't spoil the hang.

The priest pressed a switch on the catafalque, and the coffin moved forward on its rollers. The waves of pressure in my skull built to a new crescendo as John Gittings's body trundled toward the double doors like a very short wagon train rolling over black plastic prairie. The doors slid open on either side to receive him into the furnace beyond.

The pain was so intense that I actually gasped. It was as if John had thrown out an invisible grapnel, trying to keep a purchase in this world, and one of the flukes had embedded itself in my skull.

Carla looked around at me in surprise. She put a hand on my arm, but I waved it away. I had to get out. As casually as I could, I lurched to my feet and stepped out into the aisle. I was heading for the door, but suddenly, I wasn't even sure which way the door was. Instinctively, I walked away from the force that was pulling on me so hard— away from the coffin, half convinced that I was dragging it along behind me like a sheet anchor. The sensation of weight, of resistance, was so palpable.

The doors loomed into my field of vision, and I took another step toward them. Carla was on her feet at my side, and Todd, too. Hot air that must have been entirely imaginary billowed across my back. The hook bit deeper, and I couldn't move, couldn't move at all now; couldn't make myself walk forward, because a force as unanswerable as gravity was pulling me back toward that hot mouth behind me, pulling me back and down into the dark.

Someone shouted a name, a single syllable. My name? Possibly. I wouldn't have wanted to be categorical on that subject right then, because I didn't seem to have a name of my own, only a vague sense of a space that was me and a space that was everything else. And the oven's searing heat was making the space that was me shrink away like the film of breath you leave on a windowpane.

Then the doors ahead of me were thrown open, and something miraculously beautiful filled my sight. It was Juliet. Vivid, ineffable, irreducible Juliet, a bookmark in the stodgy, samey script of the world that always let you find your place. I fell into her arms like a drowning man, aware even through the sweltering ruck inside my head of her strength, the incredible ease with which she took my weight. The last thing I saw as the red of the furnace rose before my eyes was her face staring down into mine, a little surprised.

She said something too long and complicated for me to catch, but I was pretty sure that my name was in there somewhere.

Castor. Yeah, of course. I knew that.

―――――――――

Voices came toward me across a fractal landscape of synesthetically throbbing shadow. They were raised in argument.

Todd telling Juliet that this was a private ceremony and she couldn't just walk in off the street and interrupt it.

Juliet telling Todd in a calm and neutral tone that if he didn't step way back out of her face, he was likely to lose some internal organ that he couldn't do without. No more from Todd after that.

The foxy priest asking if everyone would please, please sit down again so the cremation could continue. Juliet telling him that he could go ahead and burn whomever he liked, she hadn't come along to watch.

Carla asking Juliet who in the hell she was, and Juliet saying it was funny she should ask.

I must have been out for all of ten seconds. Ten seconds was more than enough, though, if Juliet was in a sour mood. It was lucky for all of us—and probably for Todd most of all—that she'd gotten out of the right side of Susan Book's bed this morning.

I was lying on the ground, though, and that was a bad sign. If she'd put me down to free up her hands, things could be about to escalate. I started to sit up, my stomach lurching slightly as gravity sloshed around me like cooling soup.

"Fix, are you all right?" Carla knelt beside me and supported me as I tried to get my upper body vertical.

"I'm fine, Carla," I said, and it was true that the blood-red haze was fading out to the corners of my eyes. I could think again without feeling as though my brain were about to explode out of my ears like Silly String. It was obvious I could think, because I was doing it: I was thinking about Juliet's legs, which were on a level with my face. Juliet's legs are long and shapely, and they deserve a lot of very serious thought—especially when, as now, they were encased in tight black leather pants and stiletto-heeled boots. But it wouldn't help restore dignity to the proceedings if I started howling like a wolf.

I stood up, taking in the rest of her outfit only in peripheral vision. More blacks—her favorite color, and she goes for every possible shade of it. Her arms and shoulders were bare because her shirt was really only a vest, made out of something almost diaphanous that allowed you to guess at the shape of the body underneath it. Sometimes, with Juliet, even peripheral vision was too much.

Todd was taking her in stride, which was an impressive feat. Her threat to eviscerate him had made him stop talking, but he was staring at her with a cold composure that I still haven't managed to master. Maybe lawyers are wired differently from the rest of us.

"Mr. Castor," he said, "is this a friend of yours?"

"Yeah," I said. "Juliet, this is Carla Gittings, John's widow. And Maynard Todd. John's solicitor. Both of you, Juliet Salazar, my—associate."

She gave each of them a glance that you could only call minimal. "You left a message with Sue," she said to me. "Something you wanted to ask me about."

"Yeah, but—" I was about to ask how she'd found me here, but I realized before I got the question out that it was like asking a dog how it had found a bone it had once buried. Juliet was a predator, and she had my scent—she could find me anytime, anywhere, without the benefit of my number, my address, or my permission. "I meant... afterward," I finished lamely, conscious of the little priest looking at me with bristling resentment. "Could you wait for me outside? I'll just be another ten minutes or so."

Juliet considered, then nodded. "Ten minutes," she

agreed, and she turned and walked out without another word. Again, Juliet walking out stayed in your mind for a long time after you'd seen it, but I wouldn't want to give you the impression that I'm obsessive in any way: It's a side effect of what she is, that's all. I tore my eyes away, apologized to Carla, and discovered with wry amusement that she was still staring at Juliet's departing back.

The bride forgets it is her marriage morn;
The bridegroom too forgets as I go by.

But this wasn't a wedding, it was a funeral, and I'd disrupted it more than enough. We went back to our seats. I looked across at the coffin, and listened, too—listened on the frequencies that the living don't use all that much. Nothing. The dead still kept up their cricket-chirping from the garden of remembrance, but from John, there wasn't so much as a tinker's fart. I had my answer now, at any rate: John's vengeful ghost had anchored itself in his flesh again and come along with us for the ride. But if I'd been hoping that falling in with his plans for the afterlife would sweeten his disposition, it looked as though I'd been mistaken.

On the credit side, that last attack, if it was an attack, had spent him. As the priest pressed the switch, John Gittings rolled in his sustainable hardwood casket through the furnace doors into eternity without valediction. What happened next would be a combination of the banal and the unknowable. His body would burn; the rest of him would start out on a different journey, and there were no maps or roadside services. I was obscurely sorry that my last goodbye to him had taken the form of a psychic wrestling match. Even sorrier, maybe, that he'd had me on the ropes.

When it was all over, I asked Carla if she'd be okay going back without me. She was easy on that score, because she'd already decided to cut loose and take a cab. She found a little of Todd's company went a long way, and it didn't help at all to know that he was going out of his way to be friendly. From her point of view, he'd still played a major part in the nightmare of the last few days, and he stuck in her craw no matter what.

I gave her a hug, promised to be back in touch the next day to see how she was, and headed for the door. Todd ran an intercept, and I stopped because otherwise I'd have had to trample him. He gave me a firm handshake and a hard, speculative glance.

"Thanks for all your help, Mr. Castor," he said.

"My pleasure."

"You feeling okay now?"

"I'm fine."

"Nervous condition?"

"Something like that." I pushed on past him. I liked the man well enough, but I wasn't interested in talking about it right then.

Juliet was leaning against the wall in between the Lion of Saint Mark and the Eagle of Saint John, looking like the odd one out in a police lineup. She checked her watch meaningfully as I appeared. It was kind of cute. It wasn't like she gives a damn about time in the days, hours, and minutes sense, but it was exactly the sort of human mannerism that fascinated her—and watching her reproducing it was like hearing someone talk in a sexy foreign accent.

"Pushed for time?" I asked.

"I've got other places to be, yes," she confirmed, kicking off from the wall and falling in beside me. "I came all the way over here because Sue said you sounded worried. She thought it might be something urgent. If it's not, just tell me. I'll go back to where I belong, and you can send me a letter."

"Where you belong?" I raised an eyebrow. That's something of a loaded proposition when you're an earthbound demon.

"You know what I mean."

We walked down the steps and out into bright, clear winter sunlight. The clouds had rolled away while we were inside, and the day had taken on an entirely different cast. I welcomed it with something like relief.

"It's about a crime scene you read for Gary Coldwood," I said as we walked down the curved drive back toward the street. Silence from the gardens. The dead were in communion, maybe welcoming a newbie into their hallowed ranks.

"Alastair Barnard," Juliet said.

"Lucky guess."

"Gary called me. He said you were taking an interest in the case, and he reminded me that I'd signed a confidentiality agreement with the Met when I took their retainer."

"Good money?"

"You did it for three years, Castor. I assume that's a rhetorical question."

"So he told you not to talk to me?"

"Not in so many words. But he's concerned about doing things by the book. He has a past association with you, and you've taken on a commission from somebody—the accused man's wife?—who has a real interest in sabotaging his case. He doesn't want to make life difficult for you, but he doesn't trust you overmuch."

I laughed at that. "He's right not to," I admitted. "But I like the delicate nuances there. He's saying that he *could* make life hard for me if he wanted to."

Juliet shrugged. "He's a policeman."

"Say 'cop,'" I suggested.

"Why?"

"Just say it. For me."

"All right. He's a cop."

"Better. It's like looking at your watch when you want to say you're in a hurry. It sounds more authentic."

She shot me a sardonic glance. "Thank you, Castor."

"It's my pleasure."

We came out through the gates onto the street, the noise from the building site making further talk impossible for a few moments. As we turned right and back up toward the main drag, a very tall and very lean man in a full-length tan Driza-Bone coat walked right in between us. Juliet kept on going, but I swerved to avoid a collision and was struck by the guy's pungent smell, which sat oddly with the way he looked and walked.

I went on a few more steps, then stopped dead. Something about both the smell and the circumstances triggered a small avalanche in my memory: the tramp who'd accosted me on the street outside Todd's office. He'd looked very different, but he had the same rancid sweat-and-sickness stink about him. There couldn't be two smells that bad in the world: They'd have to meet and fight it out to the death.

I turned and looked back, but the guy was already out

of sight, which was interesting, because the only place he could have gone was in through the crematorium gates. As Juliet stared at me, bewildered, I sprinted back the way we'd come, rounded the nearer gatepost, and stared up the long, clear drive. There was no one in sight.

"Did you leave something behind?" Juliet asked.

I shook my head as I went back to join her. "Nothing I need right now," I said. "It'll keep. Okay, you already did pretending that you're worried about the time. You want to go pretend you need to eat?"

She nodded. "Certainly." She put her hand in her pocket and drew it out with something small and dark glinting between her fingers. She pressed it with her thumb, and the car that was standing beside her on the pavement—a very jaunty-looking little number that was wasp yellow and sleek and elongated at the front end in a way that suggested a great amount of discreetly stabled horsepower—made a self-satisfied warbling sound. Juliet opened the door. "Get in," she said.

I stared incredulously at this transport of delight. I'm not a car fetishist by any means, but I know something way out of my price range when I see it. The badge on the hood bore the distinctive trident logo of Maserati—a sweet little touch for a demon's wheels. It had a very low center of gravity, the sculpted cowling underneath the front bumper almost touching the road. It had the look of a car that might have Gransport in its name, and maybe Spyder, too.

"Is there something wrong, Castor?" Juliet asked with an edge of impatience.

"No," I assured her. "No, I'm fine. It's just—you can *drive* now?"

"Obviously. I've been living among human beings for over a year. I'm not intimidated by your technologies."

"And—you drive *this*?"

"It was a gift," Juliet said simply, sliding in behind the wheel with the sinuous grace of a cat curling up to sleep.

I didn't ask. But don't think I didn't want to know.

~ Nine

Iᴛ's PROBABLY NOT a great idea to kid Juliet about her diet, considering I once came close to being an item on it. And what I said about pretending that she needs to eat wasn't even strictly accurate, because she can take a certain amount of nourishment and even pleasure from things that you and I would call food. It's just that when you strip away all the niceties and get down to basics, the fuel that drives her best—the stuff she's made to run on—is the flesh and blood and souls of sexually aroused men. Her jaw-droppingly good looks are an adaptive mechanism along the lines of the sweet liquid in the calyx of a pitcher plant that tempts bees and wasps with its scent and then digests them when they fall into it.

Of course, knowing that doesn't make me want her any less. Most of the time, it's hard not to feel that being devoured in the middle of coitus would be a price worth paying for Juliet's undivided attention. But it's no damn good. Men make her hungry in all the wrong ways. Now she's discovered a way to keep her sex life and her nutritional needs apart, and she says she's sticking to it.

"How's Susan?" I asked her, probing the wound— mine, obviously, not hers—as she cut her twelve-ounce steak into two pieces and filled her mouth with one of them. The trip here had been rough going—Juliet drove with a focused aggression that made most road-rage incidents seem like brief, contemplative interludes, and she punished the sleek, overpowered sports car as though it had done her some terrible harm—but it didn't seem to have dented her appetite at all. We'd driven more or less at random, it seemed to me, but always bearing west until we finally fetched up in the ragged borders of King's Cross, where we stopped at a bistro called something like Fontaine's or Fontanelle's or something equally Euro-gastric. I'd gone for pasta; Juliet, as usual, was interested only in large slabs of animal flesh.

She swallowed once without chewing, then dabbed her mouth fastidiously with her napkin. "Overworked," she said. "They've put her in charge of children's events at the library, and they haven't even given her a budget. She's on the phone all day, trying to find authors who'll come in and read for free, and she spends every evening inventing competitions with prizes that she buys out of her own salary. I keep telling her to get out of it. I can make enough for both of us."

"Nobody wants to be a kept woman," I pointed out tactfully. "It causes all sorts of stresses in a relationship."

"So does being too tired for sex," Juliet growled.

"So anyway," I went on, my cheerfulness sounding a little brittle. "Alastair Barnard. Claw hammers. Want to talk, or are you sticking to Gary Coldwood's big red book of Metropolitan etiquette?"

She shrugged, spearing the other half of the steak. "I'm not interested in politics. Coldwood is a friend, but so are you. Don't put me in a position where I have to choose, and we should be just fine."

"More than fair," I said. "Should I order you another one of those?" It was a reckless offer. I still had the remains of Jan Hunter's cash burning a hole in my jacket pocket, but given that Jan was currently my only client it would be a good idea to eke it out.

Juliet shook her head. "I'm meant to be cutting down," she said. "Susan's fully vegetarian now. She doesn't like the smell of it on my breath."

I boggled slightly. "So you'll… what? Eat green salads?"

"And oily fish. It doesn't matter much to me, Castor. The kind of meat I really want to eat, I'm abstaining from right now. I took the pledge eleven months and nine days ago, and I'm managing very well, all things considered."

"Still keeping count, though."

She favored the space where the steak had been with a very long, very serious stare. "Yes," she said simply. "Still keeping count."

"What do you think happened to the hammer?"

She didn't bat an eyelid at the change of subject, but then, from my limited experience, a demon's brain is probably a bit like a hurricane in a box. The illusion of calm can be maintained only as long as you keep the lid nailed firmly down.

"Hunter hid it somewhere, presumably." She ate a piece of the broccoli that had come with the steak, but the gesture lacked conviction, in my opinion.

"Somewhere in the hotel or somewhere out on the street?"

"Why?"

"I just want to know what you think."

She looked at me thoughtfully. "It's not likely he could have taken it onto the street," she admitted. "Someone would have seen what he did with it, and it would have been recovered by now."

I nodded. "And if it was anywhere in the hotel, the police would have turned it up inside of ten minutes."

She put her fork down, giving up on the broccoli. "That's an interesting point, Castor," she acknowledged. "However, it's a point that holds equally well no matter who killed Barnard. So it doesn't particularly point toward Douglas Hunter being innocent."

"I know that," I said. "I'm not saying that Hunter is innocent—just that there may be more to the story than Coldwood is seeing. I was hoping you might be able to fill me in on what you read in the hotel room. It might give me a better idea of whether or not I'm wasting my time."

Juliet tapped an incisor with the tip of one immaculate fingernail. "I think you are," she said. "Wasting your time, I mean. But yes, I can do that."

"Thanks. So when would be good for you?"

"Now." She pushed the plateful of vegetables away with a decisive movement and stood. "Now would be good for me. That's why I drove us here. The Paragon is just around the corner."

The Paragon Hotel lived up—or maybe down—to all my expectations.

Like a lot of early-twentieth-century London architecture, it's the type of building that was thrown up to take advantage of negative space. In other words, it fit into a gap between older buildings that somebody decided to exploit even though it had no rational shape. You can tell what you're getting as soon as you round the bend of Battle Bridge Road and see the frontage ahead of you: a narrow slice of soot-blackened mulberry brick inelegantly slotted in between a stolid warehouse and a bigger hotel that was trying to look respectable—not an easy trick with the Paragon clinging to your leg like an amorous dog.

The interior managed to be both constricted and sprawling at the same time. The lobby went back a long way, but it was ludicrously narrow, and it had a dogleg, the front desk thrusting out into a high-ceilinged space no wider than a corridor, which seemed to flinch away from it in a nervy zigzag. Naive anthropomorphizing, I know, but when you deal with the risen dead on a day-to-day basis, you tend to see the life in almost everything. The death, too, which is maybe the down side.

The clerk looked up from a computer monitor as we came in, his gaze flicking from Juliet to me and then back to her, and he hurriedly hit a button on his keyboard. He could have been hiding a solitaire game, but something about his studiously blank expression as we walked up to the desk made me suspect that whatever window he'd closed had been a little more incriminating. Then again, this was a whore hotel, and the last time he'd seen Juliet, she'd presumably been part of Detective Sergeant Coldwood's traveling circus. He had good enough reason to be circumspect.

He ran a hand through his thinning sand-brown hair,

which I was seeing in a glorious 360-degree perspective because of the huge mirror behind him. He seemed to have some kind of thyroid condition, or at any rate, he had the bulging-eyed stare that sometimes goes with hyperthyroidism. His beaky nose and hair-trigger blink reminded me irresistibly of the dead comedian Marty Feldman. There was a long loose thread on the shoulder of his herringbone jacket that stuck out to the side as though he were on a fuse.

"Can I help you?" he asked us in a slightly nasal voice.

"I'm with the police," Juliet said, which I guess was a white lie. "Investigating the Barnard case. You remember, I came in about a week ago to read the room."

The clerk nodded. Of course he remembered. You didn't see Juliet and then just forget about it.

"We need to go over it again," Juliet said. "I presume it's still locked off."

"Oh yes," the clerk said, already reaching for the key. They were ranged behind him in pigeonholes, each one with a thick wooden fob five or six inches long.

"If you meet any of our other guests," the clerk said, handing the key over to Juliet with some diffidence, "I hope you'll be discreet. It's been very hard for us over the past few days, and we've cooperated in every way we could. We'd really like to start putting the whole thing behind us now."

"I'm sure," said Juliet. His hand smoothing down his hair again, the clerk watched us unhappily as we walked around the dogleg to the stairs.

There was no lift, but then the Paragon was only three stories high, and the whole point of the place was to give people healthful aerobic exercise. We went up one flight and came out onto a corridor somewhat broader than the entrance hall. Thick pile carpet in shades of dark red created the right carnal ambience, but bare hospital green plasterboard let the side down a little. The place was silent, and there was nobody in sight.

Juliet already knew where room 17 was, so she led the way. "Was that Merrill?" I asked as I followed, dredging up the name from Jan Hunter's account. "The guy who called the police on the day of the murder?"

"That was Merrill," Juliet confirmed. "But it wasn't he who placed the call—it was the cleaner Joseph Onugeta."

"Sorry, you're right. I wouldn't mind talking to him. I'll have to ask if he's here."

Juliet stopped in front of a door that badly needed a paint job—or maybe a surgical scrubbing. Its dark brown surface had a smeared, rucked look to it as though the paint had been plastered on too thickly and run as it dried. "I think they're both here every day," she said. "They seem to run the place between them. The owner lives in Belgium somewhere and only turns up on the quarter days to check the books."

She turned the key in the lock and pushed. A sour, musty smell came out to meet us as the door opened, and I hesitated for just a moment to step inside, not sure how much of the physical evidence would have been left in situ.

Juliet went on in, and as she swung the door wide, I could see that the room was almost bare. There was a bed frame standing against one wall, taking up most of the available space. No mattress or covers and no pillows, just two dark rectangular spaces in the divan that had once held drawers and now looked like the empty eye sockets of a skull. On the pale beige carpet were dark and very extensive stains. Square windows had been cut into some of these, the bare boards showing through where small, regular sections of carpet had been taken away by the police forensics team. There were similar stains, rich rust brown in color, down the near side and the bottom of the divan. Alastair Barnard might be gone, but "gone" was a relative term. The air reverberated soundlessly with his suffering and his fear—an emotional effluvium like the ghost of a bad headache.

"So this is where it happened?" I said unnecessarily— as much to disturb those silent echoes as anything else.

Juliet nodded in the direction of the fouled divan. "X marks the spot," she said coolly.

"When you read the room for Coldwood," I asked, looking around the chilly, claustrophobic space, "was it like this? Or was the body still here?"

"It was still here," Juliet said in the same disinterested tone. "Nothing had been touched. Coldwood wanted me to read it while it was still fresh."

"So tell me what you saw."

She looked at me for confirmation. "With which eyes, Castor?"

I waved an expansive hand. "All of them. What was physically there, in front of you, and anything else you saw."

She stared at the ground, thought for a few moments, then pointed to a spot almost at my feet—a point midway between the bed and the door. "Barnard was lying there when I came in," she said. "What was left of him. His body had been hurt—damaged—very extensively. I knew he was a man mainly by the smell. There was too little left of his head to tell what he'd looked like when he was alive. But then when I looked backward, into the past, I saw him clearly enough."

The quality of her voice changed, making me look up from the carpet's intricate organic geography and check her face. I'd caught an emphasis that seemed a tiny bit off. "Was there something else that you couldn't see?" I demanded.

She didn't seem to hear. She was staring right through me at the door, and I could tell that what she was seeing was not me but the events of January 26. She was squinting into the middle distance, along a dimension that wasn't there for members of my particular species.

"They walk in together," she said slowly. "Barnard is the older man, obviously—the one in the suit, his face all red from climbing the stairs. Hunter is the big, well-built one who moves like a fighter."

"He used to box when he was younger," I said.

"Yes. He's aware of where his weight is. He stands solid, foursquare, as though someone is going to come at him and try to knock him down. He crosses to the bed, puts down a bag that he's carrying—a long green canvas holdall that looks as though it's used to carry tools—and then he turns to say something to Barnard. He grins as he speaks. One of the words is 'now.' Barnard is nervous, but it's the nervousness of arousal. He closes the door, fumbles with the lock for quite some time. He doesn't want to be disturbed, obviously.

"Hunter is already taking off his clothes. Barnard crosses to the bed and starts to undress, too, but Hunter stops him. He pushes Barnard down onto his knees—"

"I think we can take the next part as read," I said.

Juliet nodded. "They copulate," she confirmed. "For a long time. Hunter takes the dominant role; takes it very aggressively, and the violence is part of the sex. Barnard doesn't mind. Not yet. He's excited. Enjoying it very much. Then..." Her voice trailed off. She was staring at the bed, her eyes narrowed.

"Then?"

"Then it starts to hurt."

She walked around the bed, her gaze still fixed on it, triangulating on the past with her exquisite dark-adapted eyes. "What Hunter is doing now will leave marks. Barnard doesn't want that. It makes him afraid, and it makes him indignant. He says something, tries to sit up. Hunter—hits him, hard, on the side of the head, and Barnard falls down again. He's dazed. His mouth is bleeding, not where the blow landed but where he bit his lip because of the force of the impact.

"He tries again. Hunter straddles him, forces him down with his own weight. He's hitting Barnard with his closed fists, and at the same time, he enters him again. He beats him and rapes him at the same time."

I opened my mouth to speak, to ask her to skip forward again, maybe, and spare me some of the gory details. But the details were what I needed to hear. There was no point being in this room if I didn't take a good, long look at what had happened. At the same time, Juliet's words had sharpened my own responses to the place. I couldn't see its history the way she could, but I could feel the emotional afterwash of the events with a terrible clarity, and everything she said fell into place with a dull, heavy inevitability, anchoring the emotions and giving them form.

"He twists Barnard's right arm behind his back—up and back, as far as it will go. He's leaning on it with his full weight. He's still riding him at this point. And then..."

There was a long silence. I didn't realize I'd been holding my breath until I let it out. "...And then he gets the hammer out of the bag and smashes Barnard's skull in," I finished. But there was something in Juliet's expression that I couldn't read. I waited, resisting the urge to throw another question at her.

She was still staring into the past with minute, almost furious attention. "I don't see that," she said at last.

"You don't see—"

"The end of the torture. The hammer coming down. The moment of death. Something moves across the room. Something very big. It's been there all the time, but it's been standing very still. I only see it when it moves."

"What sort of something?" The words sounded banal, but I needed to ask because I had no referent for what she was describing. An elephant that had been disguised as a standard lamp? A battleship making an awkward right turn out of the bathroom?

"I don't know," Juliet admitted reluctantly. "Not something solid—not something that's physically there. A darkness. A darkness without a body of its own. I don't know whether they brought it in with them or it was waiting for them. But it doesn't seem to do anything to interrupt what's happening. It hovers for a few minutes, almost filling the room. I can see through it, but it's a little like seeing through thick fog. The two men are still there. They're still on the bed, moving together, with Hunter on top. Then they separate, come together again.

"It gets even darker. Even harder to see. When the

shadow passes, Hunter is gone. Barnard is lying there"—
she pointed—"on the floor, not on the bed. There's nothing left of his head but a bloody smear."

"And the hammer?"

"There." She pointed again to a place just under the
window. A smaller cluster of old bloodstains marked the
spot she was indicating, although it was some distance
away from the bed, in the opposite direction to the one in
which Barnard had crawled in his last pathetic attempt to
escape from this brutal, arbitrary death.

Silence fell between us. Juliet glanced from bed to
window to door, measuring distances and angles with the
abstract curiosity of a professional.

"What happens to the hammer after that?" I pursued.
"Can you carry on watching it?"

"No." She shook her head. "It's the intensity of the
emotions here that lets me see into the past. With Barnard
dead and Hunter gone, that intensity fades very quickly.
Fades to black, you could say."

I thought over what she'd said. "So it's possible," I
summed up, "that someone else was present in the room
when all this was happening? It's possible that someone
else came in at the kill, as it were, took the hammer, and
used it while Doug was . . . doing his thing."

Juliet looked at me a long time before shaking her
head. "No. I don't think so."

"But this shadow—"

"I told you, it's not like a physical thing. It's more like
an accident of the terrain."

"I don't get your drift, Juliet."

She frowned impatiently. "I'm trying to describe invisible things, Castor. Most of this is metaphor."

"Are you absolutely sure there was no one else here?" I persisted doggedly. "You said yourself that something blocked your...perceptions. Something got in your way, whether it was solid or not, and if we stick with the metaphor, you were seeing through a glass, darkly. Anything could have happened behind that fog."

"If there was someone else there, I'd sense them on some level," said Juliet coldly.

"And you don't?" This was coming to the crunch. I stood facing her, held her blacker-than-black gaze without flinching. It wasn't easy: It was like standing up in a stiff wind that sucks you in instead of blowing you backward. "You don't sense anything else at all? Anything that makes you doubt for a fraction of a second that Coldwood's got his hand on the right collar? Barnard and Hunter were meant to be in here alone, but that cleaner, Onugeta, heard a woman's voice when he walked past the door. Three voices, he said: two men and a woman. Was he wrong, or was there a woman here? Is there any emotional trace in the room that you can't explain by two men coming in here to fuck each other's brains out?"

Thinking about Alastair Barnard's shattered skull, I wanted to drag those words back and scrub them clean with Dettol as soon as I'd said them, but Juliet didn't bother delivering the hideous punch line. She didn't say no, either.

"There've been many women in this room," she said slowly. "Many and many, and most of them were sad. Most of them resented what was done to them here, or hated the men who were doing it to them. Perhaps that's all the shadow was—the stain left by their unhappiness."

My gaze broke first: I'm only human, after all. But it

was Juliet who was being evasive here, and I didn't have to say anything else. I just waited for her to fill in the blanks, staring out of the window at the King's Cross marshaling yards while my pulse came down again.

"There is something else," she admitted at last. "A residue that's very strong and very noticeable. Perhaps it *is* a woman. The physical scents are of the two men, but perhaps yes. A woman's feelings. Angry, negative feelings. Disgust, and fear, and defiance—all feeding into anger."

"Was it here already?" I asked. "Or did it come in with Hunter and Barnard? Was it following them? Does it leave with them? Was one of them being haunted by this...residue?"

I glanced at Juliet as I delivered the last word. She shrugged eloquently, her breasts shifting under the tantalizingly translucent fabric of her shirt. "I don't know," she said with visible reluctance.

I couldn't resist pressing my advantage. "I want to go and visit Doug Hunter in jail," I said, "and get his take on what happened. Will you come with me?"

Juliet looked blank. "Why?"

"Well, have you ever met him?"

"No."

"Wouldn't you like to meet him if your testimony is going to send him down for twenty or thirty years?"

"No."

I was amazed and a little exasperated. "What, you're not the slightest bit curious?"

"Not the slightest bit," Juliet confirmed equably. "However, I will admit one thing. The possibility that I might have made a mistake in this does trouble me. I take my reputation very seriously."

"So is that a yes? You'll come with me?"

After a fractional pause, Juliet nodded. "Yes. Very well. Not today, though. Today I have other things to do."

"I'll need to arrange it with Jan Hunter, in any case," I said. "I'll call you."

"Fine. If I'm not home, leave a message with Sue."

She turned and walked out of the room without another word. In a human woman, it would have seemed spectacularly abrupt, but with fiends from the pit, you have to make allowances. After all, Juliet had been living on earth only a little over a year, and you have to assume that in hell, a lot of the normal conversational rules don't operate in quite the same way. For example, tearing someone's head off and spitting down his or her neck probably has an entirely different meaning down there.

I lingered in the room for a few minutes more, searching it myself with my eyes tight shut. But the susurrus of fright and cruelty was everywhere; it was like trying to echolocate in the midst of a ticker-tape parade. I gave up, let myself out, and closed the door again. The lock had an automatic catch, and Juliet had taken the key with her when she left, so that was it as far as examining the crime scene went. There was no way I could get back in.

The desk clerk, Merrill, had his back to me as I approached the desk again. He was putting some keys back in the pigeonholes—including number 17, I noticed. I waited until he realized I was there and turned to face me.

"Can I talk to Joseph Onugeta?" I asked. "I wanted to check a couple of details in the statement he gave."

"He's not in today," Merrill said.

"I thought he was in every day."

"He called in sick."

"Well, is it okay if I come by and talk to him tomorrow?"

"It's okay with me, yes. His shift starts at six."

I chanced my arm. "Did a woman check in here on her own on the day of the murder?" I asked.

He looked surprised. For a moment I thought I'd insulted his professional standards. "We cater to couples," he said shortly.

"Yeah," I agreed, "I know that. I was just wondering if—"

"There wasn't any woman in that room. I don't care what Joseph says he heard."

I felt the weight of words not yet spoken. "But—" I prompted.

Merrill stared at me in silence. "A *man* came in by himself," he said at last. "I was in the back room there, and I saw him walk straight past the desk. I thought maybe he was a cabdriver and he'd come to pick someone up. But then he walked out about ten minutes later and was still by himself, so if he was a driver, he came to the wrong place."

"When was this?" I asked. "Before Barnard and Hunter arrived, or after?"

"I think after," he said. "But it must have been before we went up and opened the room, because after that, we had the police here, and they closed the place down for the whole of the rest of the day."

"What did this guy look like?"

Merrill thought. "Pretty old," he said. "That's all I remember. I didn't get to see him up close."

I threw a few more questions at him, but he wasn't

throwing very much back. He wasn't kidding about his mind going blank. I probably could have gotten more circumstantial details out of a six-year-old. Then again, everyone's got his own way of dealing with stress, and Merrill looked like the kind of man who stressed easy.

I left my number and asked him to call if anything else occurred to him. To make that slightly less unlikely, I slipped him a couple of tenners. Doing that made it very clear, if he needed the confirmation, that whatever connection I had with Juliet, I sure as hell wasn't a cop. I guessed that was probably a plus rather than a minus for a man who worked in the hinterlands of the sex industry. And I doubted there were any lands from London to silken Samarkand that were much more hinter than the Paragon Hotel.

On the way back to Wood Green, I stopped off at Charing Cross Road and kicked around a few of the bookshops there until I found Paul Sumner's biography of Myriam Seaforth Kale. It was out of print, so Borders and Foyles couldn't help me at all. I turned up a copy at last in one of the secondhand bookshops farther down the street, past Cambridge Circus. It was an American paperback, and the badly glued interior signatures had come loose from the cover, so I got it for the knockdown price of seven pounds fifty.

No blue van staking out the entrance to Ropey's block. On the downside, the two lifts that hadn't been used recently for murder attempts both seemed to have broken down in the course of the day. I slogged my way up to the fourth floor, closed the door on the world, and put some soothing music on the stereo—I think it was Rudra's *Primordial* this time, described in the sleeve notes as "seminal Vedic thrash metal." Then I lay back on the bed, cracked the book open, and immersed myself in the last death throes of the American mobs.

Sumner wrote in a spare, almost bald style, using adjectives only when they were already clichés and therefore guaranteed not to convey any actual information. The Alabama farm where Kale—then just plain Myriam Seaforth—had been born and spent the early years of her life was "humble," and her family's poverty was "grinding." She herself was "fresh-faced" and "comely." Okay, she had a chickenpox scar over her left eye that some people thought was disfiguring, but she was still a statuesque redhead, very tall and very full-figured. Most accounts seemed to agree that she was 100 percent bombshell. She "left the family nest" at age fifteen, given in marriage (legal from fourteen in Alabama) to Tucker Kale, a well-to-do feed store owner from neighboring Ryland.

The next seven years of her life were very sparsely documented, and Sumner got through them in a couple of pages. Tucker Kale died in a car crash when Myriam was twenty-two, and she headed north to try out a different kind of life in the big city, pausing only to say a last, fond farewell to her family.

The big city in question was Chicago, which was almost seven hundred miles away—a long way to go even with money in your pocket and a place to stay at the other end. Myriam Kale didn't have either of those things. She just packed a suitcase one day and jumped into the wild blue yonder, hitching all the way up Interstate 65 with no idea where she was going or what she'd do when she got there.

Along the way, it was pretty well documented now, she met up with a man named Luke Poulson, whom Sumner described as a traveling salesman, and one of two things happened. Either, as Kale herself would later tell some of her Mob friends, Poulson tried to rape her and earned himself a short, eventful, and terminal encounter with a tire iron, or else Kale lured him to his death with an offer of sex, intending all along to kill and rob him as soon as they were out on the open road.

Either way, she beat Poulson to death with thoroughness and enthusiasm, and she stole his car. But before she left, she heated up the cigarette lighter and used it to burn the dead man on his cheek as though she were a rancher branding a steer. Every man she killed would be burned in a similar way, usually—once she took up smoking—with the lit end of a Padre Gigli cheroot. In the last year or so before her death, she would come to be known in the Chicago underworld as the Hot Tomato. This was partly a tribute to her physical charms, but it was also a wry reference to the fact that if you picked her up, you were likely to get burned.

Arriving in Chicago, she ditched Poulson's car and hit the streets—literally. She worked as a hooker for a couple of years on the meat markets of South State Street, working briefly for a pimp named Lauder Capp before going solo (Capp was supposed to have sworn to cut her throat for her disloyalty). She met Jackie Cerone at the Red Feather Club and took him up to a room in a hotel probably not much different from the Paragon for a night of passion that turned into a new job opportunity.

She knew who Cerone was. She'd seen his picture in the papers, and she made the connection. This man who was hiring her for the whole night was a big player in the Outfit, currently riding high after Sam Giancana had made his run for the border, leaving Battaglia (with Cerone as kingmaker) to pick up the pieces of the Chicago rackets.

Kale's relationship with Cerone was the turning point in her life, according to Sumner. She impressed him with her get-up-and-go and her entrepreneurial spirit, and after two more paying dates, he employed her in a different capacity—as the bait for a surviving Giancana lieutenant who was high up on his shit list.

There was a photo of her from around this time, and I had the vague feeling I'd seen it before. A smeary black-and-white image taken in a crowded nightclub, it showed Kale dangling on Jackie Cerone's arm, both of them mugging for the camera with bottles of champagne in their mitts. Kale's mouth was open on a laugh that looked like it must have been loud and indelicate, but her eyes weren't closed or crinkled with laugh lines; they were wide and staring. They looked to me like the eyes of a wild animal peering out at the world from behind the thickets of her own face, where she was either hiding or looking for prey. The only other figure in the picture, a blond man whose bodybuilder's physique was encased in a double-breasted jacket that screamed "gangster," was staring at her with a sort of covetous wonder.

Before long, Sumner assured his readers, this real-life femme fatale was undertaking hits on her own. Jackie provided the gun and the training in how to use it. Over the next five years, Kale became something of a celebrity in Mob circles without ever coming to the attention of the police. She made at least nine hits (Sumner argued passionately for the higher and more headline-grabbing score of thirteen) and was paid sums of up to eighty thousand dollars a time. At one point, Phil Alderisio reputedly kept her on retainer.

Meanwhile, the cigarette-burn motif had become a tabloid legend, and incorruptible police chief Art Bilek made a public commitment to bring in "the Mob killer who signs his work in this odious manner." In 1968 he caught up with her in yet another hotel room, on the top floor of the Salisbury. The trappings this time were opulent rather than sleazy, and Kale was a guest of Tony Accardo, but neither the exclusive surroundings nor the distinguished patronage saved her when Bilek's men surrounded the building and moved in to arrest her.

She added another man to her score as the cops broke down the doors of the suite and burst in on her. She was stark naked, according to the papers—fresh out of the bath, manicured and smelling of Madame Rochas, she shot the first man to walk through the door, twenty-two-year-old constable Dermot Callister. Hit in the face, he died instantly. She herself was shot seven times within the next few seconds (the bullets were later removed, counted, inventoried, stolen, and sold for souvenirs), but she managed to wound three more officers before being taken alive. Her will to live must have been truly extraordinary, Sumner pointed out, because one of those bullets hit her liver, and another collapsed her left lung. It was a miracle she survived long enough to go to court; long enough to spend three years on death row; long enough to die, at last, at a time and place of the state's choosing.

That was the rough outline of the story, but Sumner embellished it with some fairly elaborate reconstructions of Kale's sexual encounters with the made men of the Chicago Mob scene. I wondered what his sources were for some of the more circumstantial accounts. Maybe Kale kept a journal or something. "Dear Diary, you'll never guess with which widely feared psychotic gang lord I had a knee-trembler in the lift at Nordstrom's today—or what he likes to be tickled with."

I was only skimming, but even so, my attention was starting to wander long before I got to the end. It's not that I'm prudish, or even morally fibrous, but pornography that's written as a list of sexual positions and uses the word "turgid" as though it were punctuation gets old fairly quickly.

I skipped to the end, which turned out to be an account of Myriam Kale's last two hits—the ones she was supposed to have carried out from beyond the grave. In 1980 a guy who lived on George Street in Edinburgh was murdered in his own bathroom. Forensic evidence suggested that he'd been murdered immediately after sex, and his cheek and temple were scarred by postmortem cigarette burns.

Ditto in 1993. Some middle-aged sales rep in Newcastle left work on a Friday night, announcing his intention to "get laid, get wrecked, and get to bed early." He was found the next day in the laundry room of a hotel on Callerton Lane, stuffed into one of the baskets. Again, his face had been burned, and again, there was evidence that he'd been engaging in coitus before meeting his violent death.

Cause of death in both cases was blunt-instrument trauma, and the weapons were never recovered. Sumner offered no explanation as to why Kale should have chosen the British Isles as the site of her postmortem adventures. He just presented the facts, humbly and pruriently, for our consideration.

For a change of pace, I dug out the bag of bits and pieces that Carla had retrieved from behind John's desk drawer. I flipped through the pages of the *A to Z* again, this time with my own oversize hardcover London street guide beside me on the bed, and got slightly more out of it this time. The list of place-names—Abney Park, Eastcote Lane, St. Andrew's Old, St. Andrew's Gardens, Strayfield, and the rest—turned out to be a list of London cemeteries. A pretty exhaustive list, I was guessing, because it ran to more than a hundred sites. Most had either been struck through with a single line or had a large cross next to them. Whatever John had been looking for, he had exacting standards.

At the bottom of the page, set off from the list by a couple of inches of glaringly empty space, was a single word: SMASHNA. It wasn't crossed out, but John had circled it again and again in red ink. He'd then added three question marks in green. It was a powerful graphic statement; it just didn't mean a damn thing to me.

The other lists—the ones that consisted of people's names—were even more opaque. I checked through initial letters, last letters, and a bunch of other assorted things to see whether some kind of acrostic message was hiding in there, but they were still only names. Some friends, some the opposite of friends, most strangers.

That left the key and the matchbook. I picked up the matchbook and looked at that number again, and this time, maybe because I was coming to it in a code-breaking frame of mind, the truth hit me at once. The final digits were 76970. That could be a phone number after all, if the phone were a mobile and the number had been written backward.

I keyed the number into my mobile and it rang. I had a brief sense of something like vertigo: a peek down the sheer vertical colonnades of a mind under terrible stress. Whom had John been keeping secrets from? What had made him so obsessively careful? Nicky Heath, who ought to know, once told me that paranoia was a survival trait as well as a clinical condition. It hadn't been that for John, but it looked as though he'd done all he could to keep what he was working on from falling into the wrong hands. Or any hands at all.

The ring tone sounded three times, then someone picked up.

"Hello?" A man's voice, brisk and cheerful. "What's the score?"

"Hi," I said. "I'm a friend of John Gittings—"

There was a muttered "Fuck!" and the line went dead with a very abrupt click. Interesting. I tried again, and this time the phone rang six, seven, eight times before it was picked up. No voice at all this time, only an expectant silence.

"I really am a friend of John's," I said, trying to sound calm and reassuring and radiantly trustworthy. "My name is Felix Castor. I worked with John on a couple of jobs a little while back. His widow, Carla, gave me some of his things, and your number was in there. I called because I'm trying to find out what he was working on before he died."

That was enough to be going on, I thought. I waited for the line to go dead again. Instead, the same male voice said, "Why?" Not so cheerful now—tense, with an underlying tone of challenge.

Actually, I had to admit it was a pretty good question. "Because he seemed to think it was something really important," I said slowly, because I was picking my words with care in case any of them turned out to be loaded. "But he didn't tell anybody what it was all about. I'm thinking that maybe finishing the job for him might make him rest easier. Because right now he's not resting easy at all."

There was a long, strained silence.

"Not tonight," the man said at last. "Tomorrow. Twelve o'clock. The usual place."

He hung up before I could ask the obvious question, and this time when I dialed, the phone rang until I got voice mail. I tried twice more with the same results. For some reason—maybe creeping paranoia—I didn't want to leave a message. But I thought I knew where the usual place had to be. There was presumably a reason why John had written this number down on the matchbook from the Reflections Café Bar, and fortunately, he'd left the postcode showing when he tore off the cover. That plus the Yellow Pages ought to be enough to get me there. The timing was going to be tight, though. I needed to be back at the courthouse in Barnet at two p.m. for the start of the afternoon session, when Rafi's hearing would resume.

I'd have to make sure the meeting was a short one.

~ Ten

A HUNDRED AND FIFTY YEARS AGO, **HM** Prison
Pentonville was considered a model of the perfect nick.
Politicians made millenarian speeches about it; penal
experts came from all over Europe to see it and coo over
it; and no doubt many an old lag committed imaginative
new crimes so he could get banged up in it.

It was the first prison in England built to an American
blueprint known as the separate system. It was sort of a
refinement of the Victorian panopticons, where sneaky
little architectural tweaks and twiddles allowed the prisoners to be watched every second of every day, no matter
where they went.

In the separate system, though, the cruelty was a bit
more refined than that. The designers still made a big deal
out of having clear lines of sight and high-mounted guard
platforms, but the main inspiration was to knock the fight
out of the prisoners by denying them any human contact.
Not only was the prison split up into a sprawl of different

wings that had no contact with one another, but the same separation was enforced at meals, in chapel, even in the exercise yard. Inside, cubicle walls divided every shared space into a honeycomb of miniature rooms, so you were always alone even when there were a thousand people sitting or standing right next to you. Outside, you wore a specially designed cap with a downward-extended peak to hide your face, and nobody ever used your real name. As with Jean Valjean or Patrick McGoohan, your number became your official identity. If you failed to answer to your number, you got a week in a punishment cell. If you gave your name to another prisoner, you got another year nailed onto your sentence.

It was a roaring success in terms of making the prisoners docile. After a few months of this treatment, most of them were as meek as lobotomized lambs. Okay, a few of them—maybe more than a few—would slip a little further along the bell-shaped curve from passivity into apathy, then into psychotic withdrawal or catatonia, but some people are never going to be happy no matter how much you do for them.

After a high-profile lawsuit brought by the family of a guy named William Ball, who went into Pentonville sane and came out a frothing berserker, they started to liberalize the regime, and the whole idea of control by dehumanization went into a bit of a decline in the UK until they opened Belmarsh in 1991. Pentonville's not that bad today, if you compare it to somewhere like Brixton or the Scrubs. It's even got its own poolroom and a big bare hall where you can show movies, and its blindingly whitewashed frontage is so meticulously maintained that it causes regular pileups when drivers coming along the

Caledonian Road incautiously glance across at it as the sun breaks out of cloud cover.

All the same, as Juliet and I checked in at the clanging gates and banging doors the next morning, it didn't seem like the jolliest place on earth. The acoustics in a prison are unique: Every echo sounds like a taunt or an insinuation, and there are always a lot of echoes. It didn't help that the sky outside was blue-gray like a bruise, with the first drops of rain starting to fall, or that the security procedures, even for remand prisoners, are so much like decontamination protocols—as though you're bringing the outside world in with you, and they don't want any atom of it touching the prisoners.

We were randomly chosen to be searched, but given the effect that Juliet has on people of all sexes and persuasions, I wasn't sure how much randomness was involved. The women officers who searched her certainly took their time, and I had to loiter outside the guard station long after their male counterparts had impounded my hip flask and ceremonial dagger and given me a receipt. When the doors opened and Juliet strode out with her hands nonchalantly in her pockets, the women warders who followed her looked a little dazed and haunted. It was a standard nonintimate search—a "rubdown"—but if you gaze into the abyss, the abyss also gazes into you.

Reunited, we were ushered through another set of doors—more bangs and clangs, more echoes, like the opening credits of *Porridge*—to the interview hall.

Remand prisoners have their own visiting room, and although there's a guard present, the regime is a bit more relaxed than it is for other inmates. Instead of the glass shields and wall phones you see in the movies, there's a room like the common room in a school—bare walls enlivened by a few yellowing posters advertising long-defunct public information campaigns, semicomfortable chairs set up around low tables, and a coin-op coffee machine.

The room was empty, and I threw a questioning look at the guard, who wrenched his eyes away from Juliet with an effort. "He's on his way down, sir," he said. "Won't keep you more than a minute or two."

Juliet crossed to one of the clusters of chairs and sat down to wait. I got a coffee from the machine before I joined her. She watched me approach with detached interest. "You're walking a little stiffly," she observed as I sat down. "I noticed that yesterday, but I forgot to ask."

"Someone tried to drop me down a lift shaft a few nights ago. It's okay. I dodged."

Stuff like that doesn't faze Juliet in the slightest. She noted my unwillingness to talk and didn't ask any more. The truth was, that whole incident with the faulty lift had been preying on my mind more than somewhat. If someone tries to kill a private detective, it's almost a mark of respect. It means you're getting close to something, and the opposition is taking you seriously. If someone tries to kill a jobbing exorcist, and if said exorcist is as badly in the dark as I felt right then, it's probably a sign of a basic character flaw.

Or maybe I was close to something and I was too dense to see it when it was right under my nose. That was a sobering thought, and I was still soberly thinking about it when a man walked into the room. It obviously wasn't Doug Hunter: too old, for one thing, and for another, he didn't fit the description Jan had given me in any respect

at all. He was slightly built, almost bald, and very pale.
He wore a nondescript light gray suit that looked as faded
as his skin, but his eyes were a darker, colder gray, magnified by strong prescription lenses, and his thin face wore
an expression of brusque impatience.

"Mr. Castor?" he inquired. I was expecting him to do
the usual comic double take when he saw Juliet, but from
where he was standing, she must have been out of sight
behind me.

"That's me," I said.

"My name's Maxwell. *Dr.* Maxwell. I'm one of the
medical staff here at the prison. Douglas Hunter is a
patient of mine, and I need to speak with you before you
see him. If you've a moment?"

I nodded, but he was taking my assent for granted and
already carrying on. "Douglas's condition is still deterio-
rating," he said. "Even in the last few days, there's been a
marked change, and it's all for the worse."

My confusion must have shown on my face. "He's not
well?" I said. "I didn't realize—"

Maxwell made a palms-out "don't put words in my
mouth" gesture. "The medical situation is complicated by
the legal one," he said. "Not unusual in here. I've made a
diagnosis, but you'll forgive me if I don't share it with you.
The point is that Douglas has had to be quite heavily medi-
cated. With aripiprazole, if that means anything to you."

"It doesn't," I admitted.

Maxwell raised his eyebrows expressively. "It will
mean something to the defense, mark my words," he
said. "The point is, since this is your first visit, you're apt
to find him a little odd to talk to. He'll be drowsy and
unresponsive, but at the same time, he's likely to show a

certain restlessness and discomfort. These are side effects of the drug, not of his condition."

"And his condition is?" I probed.

Maxwell made the same gesture. "I can't discuss that with you right now," he said, "although I've discussed it at length with Mrs. Hunter. The other reason for me coming in to talk to you like this is that I'm advising you very strongly not to excite or upset Douglas in any way. If you do, it could have an adverse effect on his condition, and it could be unpleasant—physically unpleasant, I mean—for you. The governor is keen that you should express understanding of these conditions. He would have liked you to sign a waiver, but he's aware that everything I'm saying here has nuances that could be significant in a court of law."

I shook my head in complete mystification. I had the unusual and uncomfortable sense of meanings flying over my head, unapprehended. "You mean that he's mentally ill?" I asked, groping blindly in the dark.

"The governor? No, he's very well balanced, taking into account a constitutional tendency toward depression."

"Doug Hunter."

"That would fall under doctor-patient privilege," Maxwell said with a rigidly impassive face.

Juliet appeared at my side, and he blanched. It took some doing with a face that was already so pale.

"What *is* aripiprazole, Doctor?" she murmured in her throat. "I've always wondered."

Maxwell looked like a distressed fish, if a fish could be simultaneously caught on a hook and out of its depth. "Well, that information is in the public domain," he floundered. "You could look it up very easily."

"And if we did?" Juliet pressed without mercy. "What would we find?"

"It's a partial—a partial agonist to the D2 receptor. A dopaminergic modulator, if you will, in the mesolimbic—"

"In English?"

"An antipsychotic!" Maxwell blurted. "I really have to—this comes under—"

"Doctor-patient privilege," Juliet finished. "Of course. Thank you, Doctor."

She moved her head a fraction, and Maxwell seemed to wake from a trance. He excused himself with as meaningless a combination of syllables as I've ever heard and fled back through the door.

"You could have cut him some slack," I chided Juliet. "He was just trying to do his job."

"I was only asking for clarification, Castor."

"Sure you were."

"And I respected his holding to those professional standards. I admire men whose passions are intellectual and moral. In fact, I find that really arousing."

I gave her a hard look to see if she was taking the piss, but she bowed her head demurely and sat down, so I didn't get a good look at her face. At that moment the door opened again, and Doug Hunter came in between two burly guards.

He made quite a strong impression, even in his prison grays. As Jan had already told me, he was big and well muscled; handsome, too, I was prepared to assume, in that his face was symmetrical and featured a square jaw and vividly blue eyes, two perennial favorites. Or three, if you count each eye as a separate feature. His striated mid-brown hair looked as though it might originally have been a darker brown but had been bleached by years of working in the open air until it looked like flax and straw bundled together. He stood slightly stiffly, legs together, almost standing to attention.

But his eyes were vague, vacant, the motor behind them rumbling along on idle. He reached up and scratched his temple above his eye. His nails left livid marks on his pale skin: three parallel lines, like the feverish crossings out in John Gittings's *A to Z*.

"Mr. Hunter." I stood up and held out my hand for him to shake as he crossed the room toward us. The guard who'd come in with him moved off to one side but stayed close, keeping him in view, and the other guard who'd been waiting with us took up a position off to the other side, about the same distance away. Remand or not, they knew what Doug was up for—probably knew what Doc Maxwell's diagnosis was, too—and they weren't taking any chances.

Doug ignored my hand. His gaze flicked from me to Juliet, where it lingered for a long time. That wasn't unusual, but maybe it was worth noting in this case. Whatever flavor of sexuality Doug generally favored, he seemed to be capable of responding on some level to Juliet's charms. I filed that fact away for future reference.

"You know why we're here?" I asked him.

He nodded slowly, turning to look at me again with a slight widening of the eyes, as though he'd forgotten in the interim that I was there. "You're here," he said simply.

His voice was different than I'd expected. Hadn't Jan said he had a Birmingham accent? This voice had no discernible accent, and it was so strangely uninflected, it was almost like a robot's voice. Except that most robots these days use sampled sound from human voices, so they sound more animated and a whole lot warmer than Doug Hunter did.

Coldwood's sexual-psychopath hypothesis made sense to me at that moment. Doug sounded like a man whose brain was currently operating only a minimal service during extensive refurbishments. Then again, how much of that was the man and how much was the drug?

"Right. Exactly. We're here to talk to you. Would you like to sit down? I'll tell you what I've found out so far, which isn't very much, and where we can go from here."

He didn't take the invitation, so that left the two of us standing face-to-face, me slightly awkward, Hunter foggily indifferent. Juliet hadn't gotten up from her seat or spoken yet. She was watching Hunter intently, unblinkingly.

"From here," Hunter echoed. For a second I thought he was so zoned out on the antipsychotics that all I would get out of him was echolalia, but then he shook his head very slightly, left and then right and then left again. "Never getting out of here," he commented, not in the tone of a lament but looking slightly mystified that I'd raised the issue at all. "Not now. Not after all that—everything. Everything else. Going to miss the inscription. Only three days left now. Till the dark of the moon. They told me never to get lost. Never to miss it. They won't be happy."

The inscription? The mention of that word sent a slight frisson down the back of my spine. "Well," I responded, making an effort not to let any reaction show on my face, "you know what Jan has hired me for. She doesn't believe you killed Barnard, and she thinks your best bet at trial might be to try to establish that someone else was in that room along with the two of you. A dead someone else, which is why she came to me. But obviously, I'd like to hear your version of what happened."

"My version." He looked down at his hands momentarily, palms up, as though checking to see if they were clean. "Nothing," he muttered, as if to himself. "Nothing."

This was getting us nowhere fast. I sat down next to Juliet, hoping Hunter might follow my lead, but he wasn't even looking at me. He was looking up at the ceiling.

"My version's older than that," he murmured, so low I almost didn't catch the words.

"Was there someone else, Doug?" I asked, trying again. "Did someone else come into the hotel room with you? Or afterward? How did Barnard die?"

He lowered his head slowly and made eye contact with me almost accidentally at the bottom of that long, gradual arc. "The hammer," he said. "Isn't that what she used? I'm not sure anymore, but that's what I remember. His head—was very—I can ask her. If you like."

"Then there *was* someone else?" I demanded. The eerie dissociation of his mood was in the air like something you could breathe in and catch. I had to fight the urge to push my chair away from him, and to force myself to take normal breaths instead of sipping the tainted atmosphere as shallowly as I could.

Hunter shook his head. "Just me," he muttered. "Just me and her. Nobody else. Maybe a dead man. Maybe some people who were dead. Nobody else." A ponderous frown passed across his face like a ripple across muddy water. "I think he sucked me. My cock. But I can't remember why now. That's really disgusting."

He sighed long and deep and sat down at last, opposite

me. "I sprained my ankle," he said, sounding slightly wistful. "And they took me next door. To the church. If they'd had a first-aid kit—but it was all cash in hand, no tax, no pack drill. Nobody to keep the site up to code. Thought they might have some painkillers or a surgical bandage. Stupid."

There was a long silence that I didn't try to fill. I had a feeling that if I let him free-associate, he might lead me to something important. But after a minute or two, I realized that he'd retreated back into his own head and wasn't coming out again without coaxing.

"When was this, Doug?" I asked. "When you were working at the site?"

He blinked once, twice, three times. "They gave me—glass of water," he said. "Called an ambulance. Told me to wait. Too late by then. That was when she came, you see? That was what it was for. Something in the water. I think so. Something in the water."

His eyes seemed to clear abruptly, and he stared at me with intense, unreadable emotion. His eyes were opened so wide it looked like it had to hurt. I kept waiting for him to blink, but he didn't.

"You don't know," he said with aching bitterness.

"No," I agreed, feeling more and more uneasy about how this was going. "I don't. But I'm trying to find out. I'm an exorcist. Your wife hired me to try to find out whether there's any possibility that Myriam Kale—the ghost of Myriam Kale—was involved in Alastair Barnard's death. She believes if we can find evidence that Kale's ghost was in the room at the time of the murder, we might be able to raise a reasonable doubt about your guilt. Is that something you have an opinion on?"

I was assuming that most of this would wash over him, but to my surprise, he responded with something coherent. His blue eyes were still locked on my face, but they narrowed now, which I'll admit was something of a relief.

"I think that'd be a good one," he said, "if anyone could do it. Not in the room, though. Not when he was lying there. If you'd seen what it was like when she was working on him, you wouldn't ask. You wouldn't want to know. She's not a ghost. She's never been a ghost."

"What is she, then?" I asked, fighting the urge to push my chair back and get some distance from that tortured, unblinking gaze.

To my surprise, Hunter laughed. It wasn't a pretty sound. "She says she's the one thing they never wanted to happen. Because it's not a game for her. It's not a job. She can't stop. They want to make her stop, but they don't know how. And she doesn't know, either. So she works and works and works at it, one man at a time, and—she used a hammer. I'm pretty sure it was one of mine. But there aren't enough hammers in the whole damn world for—"

He frowned, and it was like a light going off behind his face. "An exorcist?" he demanded, and I understood that he was echoing what I'd said a minute or so before.

"Yeah," I confirmed. "I'm an exorcist."

Hunter shook his head in pained wonder. "Won't work," he said, sounding angry and impatient. "If it was that easy, they'd all have gone years ago. But they won't like it all the same. If I were you, and believe me, I'd sooner be the shit on your shoe, I'd be running now. I'd be taking a train to somewhere a long way away and changing my name to—to fucking *Smith* or something. You idiot. What do you think you can do? You can't do anything."

"I'm still going to try," I said, for the sake of saying something.

"Jan sent you, didn't she?" Hunter demanded, his voice modulating weirdly so that the wrong words were emphasized and the sounds fought against the sense. "She can't help me now. You—just leave. Just get out of here. And you tell her—tell her to forget about him. He didn't ask any of you to get involved in"—he hesitated, blinking rapidly—"in my life, or in what's happening to me. In fact, I'm telling you not to. You don't have the right." The guards stepped closer, alert to the change in Hunter's tone, but he didn't make any move toward me. He seemed to be in pain as well as angry.

"I'm sorry about Jan," Hunter said, and the catch as he spoke her name made me pretty sure he meant it. "Really, really sorry. I know—how much she's got to be missing me. But he's not coming back. Not after what I did. I can't help that now. She should find somebody else. She needs to."

He stood up, kicked the chair away with his heel. "He's not coming back," he repeated. "I'm going to sort this out for myself, and I'm going to go my own way. Don't try to save me. She killed a man. She doesn't deserve to be saved, and she doesn't want to be."

I opened my mouth to speak, but Juliet stood up abruptly, stepped around the table, and came up very close to Hunter, her face only an inch or so from his, her eyes and his locked in a point-blank staring contest. He froze, then a shiver went through him. I had a worm's-eye view from directly underneath, so I saw his fist clench.

The guards saw it, too, and they all moved at the same time, but I was closer, so I got there first. I caught the fist two-handed as it came up and back, using Hunter's own momentum to pull him off balance so that he lurched and had to shift his weight to keep from falling. He tried to yank his hand away from me but succeeded only in pulling me to my feet. I kept my two-handed grip as long as I could, until finally, the guards got hold of Hunter by the shoulders and forearms and hauled him backward out of my reach. Even then I followed for a couple of steps, letting go at the last moment as the guards half marched, half carried him back through the doors and out of the room.

"Leave me alone!" he shouted at me. "Don't come near me! I'm not doing this anymore! I've had enough! Just let me go! Just let me—"

The doors slammed with a terminal click, drowning out the rest of his words.

I sat down again, feeling a little like a puppet with its strings cut. Juliet stared down at me with measured curiosity. "You felt it," she said. It wasn't a question.

I nodded, but when she opened her mouth to speak, I raised my hand in a stop sign. "Outside," I parried. "Not here." The truth was that I didn't want to put it into words. I didn't want to look at it yet, although I knew as I sat there and finished my cold coffee that it was impossible to look away from. Juliet waited in silence, making no attempt to hide her impatience.

A guard—one of the two who'd come in with Hunter—came in through the prisoners' door and let us out through the visitors' one.

"Is he all right?" I asked.

"Not really, sir, no," the guard said. "He's quieter,

though. And Dr. Maxwell will come along in a little while and give him another shot."

Yeah, I thought. I just bet he will.

We threaded our way out through the door and gates and screens, reclaimed our effects at the front desk, and escaped back out into the big wide world, where the chains are mostly metaphorical and easier to cope with.

"What are you going to do now?" Juliet asked as we walked toward the tube station in a chill, soul-sapping drizzle.

"I don't know," I hedged. "If Hunter is losing his mind, a lot of this becomes academic. Even if he ducks a murder rap, he's going into a secure mental unit, and he's not coming out for a long time."

"*Is* he losing his mind?" Juliet countered.

"I'm just talking about how he'll come across to a jury," I said. "Nobody hearing him talk is going to believe his picnic is fully catered."

Juliet stopped, so I had to stop, too. We stared at each other. I didn't enjoy that as much as I usually do.

"All right," I admitted, feeling eerily detached from myself so that I heard my own words as I spoke them. "Kale is in there with him. He's possessed."

Juliet nodded brusquely. "Of course he is."

"Although we both know that's not possible," I added, feeling the need to wave a feeble flag on behalf of common sense.

"It's possible for my kind. It's *easy* for my kind."

"Yeah, but not for human ghosts," I pointed out. "You know what the loup-garous are, Juliet, and *why* they are. And the zombies, come to that. If human ghosts could possess living human bodies, they wouldn't cling to their own dead flesh or take up residence in fully furnished vermin. A demon versus a human soul, that's one thing. But soul against soul is different: The home team always wins. There isn't a single example on record of—this. Of a dead soul driving out a living one."

Juliet ladled a lot of sardonic emphasis into her next words. "I'm sorry, Castor. You're the expert. But you said yourself that the situation is more complicated than that. She hasn't driven him out; she's merely cohabiting. As you said, they're sharing that body. Sometimes he spoke as Hunter, sometimes as Kale. It probably wouldn't take you very much effort to cut her loose."

The casual, brutal observation took me by surprise. "Exorcise her? Yeah, I could do that. But I'd have to get in close to Hunter and stay there for a good long while, until I got a strong enough sense of Kale to be able to play her out. He's not going to let me do that, is he?"

"Or *she* isn't."

I grimaced and carried on walking again. Juliet's footsteps don't make any sound unless she wants them to, so I had to look out of the corner of my eye to make sure she was still with me. We walked along in silence for a while, and then I threw her own question back at her.

"What are *you* planning to do? I suppose you're good now, right? You fingered Hunter for Gary Coldwood, and now we know that Hunter did it. Or at least Hunter's body did it. And if Kale is still in residence, then you got the right man. Woman. Whatever." Something that had occurred to me briefly while Hunter was talking came back to niggle at me again. What about the missing hammer? My hypothesis that someone had taken it to shield the real killer looked pretty sick, if the real killer was the one whom all the rest of the evidence already pointed at. You might as well steal a pillow off the bed or a towel out of the bathroom. Unless—

"I think we need to know more," Juliet said bluntly, sending the fugitive thought skittering.

"About Hunter?" I demanded. "Or about Kale?"

"About both, probably. Coldwood hired me to tell him what happened in room seventeen of the Paragon. I thought I'd done that, but now I'll have to go back and tell him I was wrong. That he's brought in a dead murderer as well as a living one. When I do that, I want to be able to answer any questions that he might have."

"And is that all?"

She shook her head emphatically. "No, it isn't. You don't catch ghosts like you catch a cold, Castor. If Kale is inside Hunter, there's an explanation for how she got there, and we ought to know what that is. We *need* to know. Because it changes the nature of the game for all of us. All the ghostbreakers. Everyone who binds the dead and the undead for a living."

I was relieved that she was still along for the ride, because giving up wasn't an option for me. Apart from anything else, it meant I'd have to look over my shoulder every time I got into a goddamn lift. And Hunter—or the thing speaking through Hunter's mouth—had used that word. *Inscription*. The same word that had cropped up in the fragment of notepaper inside John Gittings's pocket watch. And, probably less significantly, in my dream.

"We can backtrack Hunter's movements," I suggested. "See if we can figure out where and when he picked up his passenger."

"By talking to his wife?"

"To start with, yeah. And there's something else we can do, something a little bit more radical, but it'll take some time to set up."

"Go on."

"We can raise the ghost of Myriam Kale."

Juliet looked at me and laughed—a liquid, musical sound. "Raise? You don't think she might already have ideas above her station?"

"I mean pull as opposed to push," I snapped, her cold amusement stinging me probably more than it was meant to. "It's another way of getting to the same place. If we can find something that belonged to her when she was alive—something she's got a strong enough link to—then we don't need to get close to Hunter. We can call her from a distance. Bring her out from inside him and make her come and talk to us. Two birds with one stone: We set Hunter free, and we have a chance to get the story out of Kale's own mouth."

"Well, that's going to the source," Juliet observed dryly. "I like it. But to bring up the obvious objection, do you think you can obtain something that was hers?"

You can use clichés on Juliet with a certain amount of impunity, because most of them aren't clichés in the ninth circle of hell. "No," I admitted, deadpan. "But I know a man who can."

———————

I'd agreed to meet Nicky Heath in St. James's Park—his idea, and coming from him, it was a pretty weird one.

Nicky has as little to do with daylight as he can. He isn't afraid of it, exactly, but he's morbidly aware of his core temperature, and he keeps it as low as he can. That means staying in the dark whenever it's an option, using eco-friendly lightbulbs because they produce less waste heat than the regular variety, spending a part of every day sitting in a big chest freezer with the lid down, and not getting too close to anyone who's warm and breathing.

For Nicky, being dead was a lifestyle.

When I first met him, he'd been a hot-shot data analyst, selling the secret history of the future to greedy CEOs who were in awe of his ability to predict share prices based purely on the flow of information across digital exchanges. He was an arrogant son of a bitch, too: He pissed people off outrageously for the hell of it, showing them up with pointless displays of expertise whenever he could. After a friend introduced us at a party, I used Nicky a couple of times to chase down information I had no legal right to access. I couldn't pay him a tenth of what he was worth, but he got me the stuff anyway because it made an interesting change from what he did the rest of the time.

He died young, of a heart attack, which didn't surprise anybody.

Then he came back, which kind of did.

There were already a lot of zombies around, so it wasn't the plain fact that Nicky clawed his way out of the grave that was unusual; it was how skillfully he rolled with the situation afterward.

The dead still don't have any legal rights, despite endless parliamentary debates and a few orphaned white papers. In theory, Nicky's living brother and sister could have waltzed off with all his worldly goods and left him cooling in the gutter. But they didn't, because he hid his money so successfully that—apart from a couple of grand in a current account—no lawyer was ever able to find a penny that was his. And while they were hunting, he was setting up a maze of blind trusts and offshore-shelf companies that would give him full control over how the money was used without it ever legally, incontestably, belonging to him.

Then he brought his data-rat brain to bear on the question of survival. Zombies enjoy a whole lot of advantages over ghosts. Having bodies, they can interact with the world in most of the same ways that the living can—touch and taste and smell and all the rest of it. But the downside is that the body they're anchored to is basically a slab of rotting meat. They've set sail in a sinking ship, and for most of them, it's a short voyage. Even though it's probably raw will rather than nerve impulses that makes their limbs move, decay and decomposition gradually reduce the body to a state where it can't hold itself together anymore. The inhabiting spirit may still carry on clinging to the increasingly rancid carcass, or it may give up the unequal struggle and strike off on its own, but either way, the ship is aground at that point. You can't make disarticulated legs move, or see through eyes that have closed up like dead flowers.

Nicky was very keen not to reach that stage, and he realized that the key to long-term survival was to learn as much as he could about his own internal workings. He picked up a stack of biology textbooks and read through the parts on human anatomy, supplementing what he learned by posting queries on medical message boards and talking to real doctors—mostly dead ones—at remorseless length.

He became an expert on butyric decay, dry decay, and

decomposition. And then he went to war against them, with a single-mindedness he'd never applied to anything when he was alive. He stopped eating and drinking, something a lot of zombies like to keep doing for reasons of nostalgia and emotional reassurance. When you're dead, your alimentary system can't process food, so it rots in your stomach and creates another vector for infection. By contrast, Nicky began to take a whole pharmacopeia of virulent poisons, mostly by injection. He pickled his flesh, not in formaldehyde but in embalming compounds that he brewed up from recipes he found online, and he steeped his body's cells in a cocktail of inorganic compounds so potent that at one point he started to sweat contact poisons.

There was more to it than that, I knew. He hooked up with Imelda Probert, more generally known as the Ice-Maker—a faith healer who offers a bespoke deal to the living dead—and now he visits her a couple of times a month for a mystical/religious tune-up. He learned meditation techniques and claims to be able to visit different parts of his body on a cellular level, repairing damage with the cement of self-belief. And, like I said earlier, he stays out of the sun in case he spoils.

But today he was sitting out in the open on a bench on the Pall Mall side of the park, his arms spread across the back of the bench and his crossed legs sticking out in front of him, looking relaxed and expansive. Okay, there was a heavy overcast and a chill wind, but even so, it was shocking to see Nicky out in full daylight.

I sat down next to him on the edge of the bench, because he didn't bother to move up and make room for me. His gaze flicked sideways to acknowledge me, then he went back to staring up through the leafless branches at the swag-bellied gray clouds. He was wearing black jeans and a bright red T-shirt. It made his unnatural pallor look all the more unsettling by contrast, which I guess was the point. Given the time of the year and the unkindness of the weather, it also flaunted the fact that he didn't have a circulatory system.

I tilted my head up, following his gaze. There was nothing to see up there except the black lattice of the branches against the sky—the rib cage of a monster waiting to be reborn. "Isn't Mother Nature wonderful?" I remarked.

Nicky snorted dryly. He does everything dryly, of course: no body fluids. "Castor," he murmured, "the only mother around here is you. Don't try to small talk me, and don't piss me off, because I'm not in the mood."

"Fine. I won't. I'd hate to spoil your mood, Nicky."

"So you want something or not? I didn't come all this way to hear your usual bullshit."

"I offered to come to you," I reminded him. "You saw me, raised, and I folded: And I've got to say, this is a whole new you."

He looked at me again, for a second or two longer this time, and shrugged as he looked away again. "I'm having some work done on my place," he said simply.

That was intended to shut me up, and it worked. Ever since he died, Nicky has been keeping house in a derelict cinema in Walthamstow, and it had been trashed not so long ago by a pack of crazed American satanists who knew about Nicky in the first place only because of his association with me. He'd been able to claim a heap of money back on the insurance, and he'd told me he had some big ideas about what to do with it, but he'd refused to be pinned down on the specifics.

The whole experience seemed to have changed him subtly—or maybe not so subtly. He'd been turning into one of those life-forms whose house is part of their bodies, like a snail or a tortoise. Now, apparently, he'd entered a different phase of his afterlife cycle.

By way of changing the subject—and coming to the point—I handed him the key and the *A to Z,* which I'd been carrying around with me all day. He pocketed the key without a word, knowing that I wanted it matched to a batch number and a location. Then he switched his attention to the book. He turned it over in his hand as though checking it for bugs, then flipped it open at the first page and started to scan the list on the inside front cover.

"It belonged to John Gittings," I said. "And you're in the middle column. Any idea why?"

Nicky looked bored as he scanned the names. "John the Git was one of my regulars," he said.

"You did data raids for him?"

"Occasionally."

"Recently?"

"No."

"But you did *see* him recently?"

"What are you, Castor, my father confessor? Yeah, I saw him."

"In the line of work?"

"Yes. And before you ask, no, I won't tell you what the work was. It was his business, now it's mine. You'd be choked if you heard I was advertising your wheelings and dealings to everyone else who waved a fifty under my nose."

I nodded. He had me there. "Okay," I said. "I respect your professional integrity. But could you look through the rest of the shit in there and see if it makes any sense to you? John spent the last few weeks before he died writing out those names again and again, so they must have meant something to him. Or maybe there's a code that I'm not picking up. Either way, I'd be grateful for a second opinion."

Nicky flicked to the back of the book and looked over the list there. The final word, SMASHNA, glared up at us from the nest of ink swirls.

"Smashna," I mused aloud. It didn't sound like a real word. Maybe it was an acronym of some kind.

"It's Russian," said Nicky. "Russian slang. It means great, cool, wonderful." He closed the book and leaned slightly toward me so that he could slide it into his jeans pocket. I caught a strong whiff of aftershave, riding over a harsher but fainter chemical smell that I couldn't have pinned a name on even if I'd wanted to. "What did you have in mind by way of remuneration?"

"Let's leave that open for now," I parried. "There's something else I need, and it's big."

"Yeah?" Nicky's offhand tone suggested there weren't many jobs in the whole wide world that counted as big for him. "So what's that?"

"I was wondering if you could pick up something for me," I said. "The kind of something that doesn't change hands too often."

"Go on."

"Memorabilia."

"Relating to?"

"A dead gangster. A killer from way back."

Nicky's head swiveled around fast, and he stared at

me for a few moments in perplexed silence. It seemed like something of an extreme reaction. Okay, maybe this sounded pretty sleazy, but I knew him well enough to be sure he didn't have any moral objections. Still, something was bothering him enough that he hadn't been able to hide it.

"I thought we had a no-bullshit rule in place, Castor," he said, his tone unreadable.

"You think this is bullshit, Nicky?"

"Isn't it? You give me Gittings's book, you pump me about what I was doing for him, and now—" He hesitated, shrugged, as though I ought to be able to join the dots for myself.

"It's not about John. It's a different case." I put out a hand, palm out in a gesture of reassurance, but didn't actually touch him. He hates to be touched by the living because their skin is a germ factory where the assembly lines are always running. And since he hates to hang out with other zombies for aesthetic reasons, it's been a while since anyone got inside his personal space. "Pull it back, Nicky. I swear, I'm not trying to get you to compromise your one last professional ethic, even though I didn't know you had one until now."

He didn't answer, but he was still giving me the fish-eye, so I rolled straight on. "It may not be something you can help me with, in any case. There was a gangster back in the sixties named Myriam Seaforth Kale. I don't know if you ever heard of her. She killed a dozen people, all of them men, then the FBI shot up a hotel to get ahold of her and sent her to the chair."

"An *American* gangster," Nicky said with careful emphasis.

"Yeah. Sorry, I thought I said that already. Anyway, you know the way these things work, probably better than I do. There's always a market for celebrity souvenirs. And it's kind of like an iceberg—some of it's above the water, most of it isn't."

"Sure," Nicky said. He seemed mollified. Whatever I'd said to upset him, he'd either bounced back from it or filed it away for later. I still couldn't figure out what had gotten under his skin, but right then didn't seem like the best time to ask.

"So," I summed up, shielding my eyes as the sun unexpectedly broke through the clouds, "you think you could lay your hands on something?"

He nodded a few times, not in answer to the question but acknowledging that it was an interesting commission. "Funnily enough," he said, shooting me another narrow-eyed stare as if warning me off making any smart one-liners, "I've got some contacts in that line of business."

"No kidding?"

"No kidding." He slid along the bench, out of the patch of sunlight. He might have reclaimed the day, but he was clearly going to be selective about which parts of it he kept. "I'm not making any promises. Stuff like that doesn't come up for sale too often, and when it does, it tends to go for crazy prices. Supply and demand. There's a whole lot of sickos out there, and only so many dead serial killers. You might not want to pay the asking price."

"Yeah," I agreed. "That's why I said we should keep the payment issue open for the time being. We'd only be looking to have this thing in our hands for, like, a day. Maybe we could rent it."

"Buy it, sell it on again," Nicky mused. It was obvious

that he saw the potential there: two transactions in quick succession, with a commission to be made twice over. "Yeah, maybe. Who's this 'we,' by the way, and what do you want the little keepsake for?"

I got up. "Call me if you get a bite," I said. "Or if you click on what the fuck is going on in that notebook. Sooner the better, Nicky. I'm kind of under the gun on both of these."

"Yeah, well, that's life," Nicky observed.

When a dead man says that, he means it's somebody else's problem.

~ Eleven

SOMETIMES SYNCHRONICITY is your friend. Everything flows together, and the thing you're looking for turns out to be in the first place where your groping fingers come down. Much as I complain about my luck, even I get days like that. But this wasn't feeling like one.

I had an appointment at noon at the Reflections Café Bar, which, going by the postcode, was somewhere around Victoria. Didn't know whom I was going to meet there, or what light he might be able to shed on John Gittings's weird little list, but I didn't want to miss it. In the meantime, I called Jan Hunter from the middle of Trafalgar Square to tell her how my meeting with Doug had gone. I didn't try to explain about Juliet; I just said that I'd taken along a colleague for a second opinion. I didn't mention Kale, either, not at first. I was afraid of offering Jan any shred of hope, because I was nearly certain that whatever I turned up would still leave Doug in the frame for murder. So instead of telling her that her husband was carrying a passenger, I asked why she hadn't mentioned the prison doctor's theory that Doug was suffering from a psychosis. The line went very quiet for a moment.

"*Incipient* psychosis," she corrected me at last. "Not full-blown." She sounded defensive but not apologetic. "I just thought that if I told you Doug was losing his mind, you might not agree to help me. And really, it's not relevant—not to the case. It's only come on since he was arrested. It's that place. And the stress of everything that's happened. He was fine before."

"I think you said he was increasingly distant and hard to read before," I reminded her. "And then he went AWOL for a week and didn't even call you."

"But he was still himself." Her voice was thick with tears. "Some of the time, anyway. And when he wasn't himself, it wasn't like he was mad. Just...like he wanted to be somewhere else. I don't believe a week would be enough to turn him into a murderer. I don't believe a lifetime would be enough!"

"Maybe not," I allowed. "Anyway, for what it's worth, I think Dr. Maxwell got the wrong end of the stick. Whatever's wrong with Doug, I don't think he's going crazy."

"You don't?" Through the tears, hope and relief showed like the shiny edge of a fifty-pence piece in the muddy ruck of a sewage trench. Fuck it. I really needed to watch my mouth. "Then what is it? What's happening to him?" she asked.

"I'm not sure," I hedged. "And Jan, I hate to say this, but it may not make any difference. Not in terms of the verdict. But there's a lot more to it than the police have their little pointy heads around. And whether it helps or not, I'm going to get you some answers. We've got a window—probably a few weeks, at the very least. Going on what Gary—Detective Sergeant Coldwood—had to say, the trial date hasn't come down yet. The police are still looking for the murder weapon and not having much luck, so nobody's pressing for an early hearing. If I can turn up something solid—" That word felt a little odd, given how tenuous and formless all of my speculations were. "Well, whatever I turn up," I finished lamely, "I'll hand it over to you, and you can decide for yourself what to do with it."

"So you believe that Doug is innocent, Mr. Castor?"

I grimaced. I would have preferred not to be pinned down on that score right then, because the truth was that I didn't have a bastard clue. "I believe Myriam Kale was in that hotel room," I said. "But I'd dearly love to nail down the how and the why of it, or at least get some idea of—"

"'Why' isn't an issue," Jan broke in, her voice strained and angry. "She killed dozens of men when she was alive. They don't know how many. And she's still doing it. And we don't need to know how she got there, either. If she's a ghost, she can go where she likes. She doesn't have to knock on doors or take trains and planes and taxis. She can walk through walls, and she can be gone when the police get there. She wouldn't even show up on cameras."

"And she'd have a hell of a time swinging a hammer."

Sudden silence from the other end of the line. I waited for Jan to ask the obvious question, to which I'd have to give the obvious answer: *Your husband's soul has run off with another woman*...Meanwhile, my gaze wandered around the square almost as if I were subconsciously looking for a way out of the conversation. A Japanese tourist a few feet away was unfolding a map of London that ended up being so big it spilled all the way down to the ground. A big feral cat, black with dirty white splashes across its back, was watching the pigeons fly from one equestrian statue to the next; the cat's tail twitching in tight arcs like a severed cable with a thousand volts pouring through it. An art student, or maybe a hobbyist, was sketching Charles I in pastels, a bottle of Red Stripe resting at her side as she sat cross-legged on the stones.

It was almost as though Jan could see the chasm yawning up ahead of her and knew instinctively to veer away from it. "I don't understand any of this," she said. "Whatever you can find, Mr. Castor—whatever you can tell me—"

I could have taken the invitation right there, but like a coward, I veered, too. I grabbed a question from my mind's cluttered desktop and waved it like Chamberlain waving his famous autograph from Adolf Hitler.

"Doug mentioned spraining his ankle," I said. "Was that something that really happened?"

"Yes." Jan sounded surprised. "A few months ago. He was coming down a ladder, and his foot slipped. He was in agony. The stupid bastards running that site didn't even have a first-aid kit. And that meant they wouldn't even let anyone call an ambulance, because they didn't want anyone to twig that they weren't up to code. Doug had to limp around the corner—two of his mates carried him part of the way—so he could make the call from somewhere else and not get them into trouble. Sodding cowboys. He's always worked for sodding cowboys!"

I looked at my watch. It was half past eleven, and I really needed to be hitting the tube. I told Jan very quickly what Juliet and I were going to try to do, and I told her I'd let her know how it came out. Then I hung up and went underground.

———————

The Reflections Café Bar turned out to be on Wilton Road, directly opposite the front entrance to Victoria Station and offering a top-notch view of the bus shelter.

The name promised something eclectic and cosmopolitan. The reality was a narrow glass booth jutting out onto the pavement, containing a coffee machine, a fridge full of Carling Black Label, a countertop, and six chairs. A teenage girl in a maid's uniform that looked as though it had been ordered from a fetish shop took my order for a double espresso with a nod and a smile, and I sat down. She was the only person in the place apart from a stocky, balding man in a drab-looking mid-brown suit. He had a film of sweat on his face as he worked through the *Times* sudoku, as though sudoku were an illicit thrill of some kind.

I sat down well within his field of vision, but he didn't react and didn't seem to see me at all. It was five past twelve by this time, so there was a chance that my man had already been and gone. That seemed more likely when my coffee came and he still hadn't shown. Taking a sip of the tepid liquid, I stared out the window at the bus shelter across the street and idly scanned the faces of the people waiting for the number 73. None of them so much as glanced at the window of the café; none of them looked as though they were trying to pluck up the courage to step inside.

The waitress was lost in the intricacies of cleaning out the coffee machine's drip tray. The bald guy was working

on his puzzle. Nobody seemed to want to make contact
with me. Probably time to chalk this one up to experience and walk away. Might as well finish my coffee first,
though.

And while I did that, I scanned the faces at the bus
stop again. Most of them were new, but one of them had
been there while half a dozen buses came and went. He
was a skinny guy in his late twenties or thereabouts, in an
LL Cool J T-shirt, black jacket, and jeans. His nose was
the size and shape of a rudder and made the rest of his
face look like it had been arranged around it in a space
that wasn't quite wide enough. He had a sallow, unhealthy
complexion and the trailing wires of a pair of headphones
dangling from his ears. His crisply ringleted head nodded
gently, double-four time, as he soaked up the vibrations of
whatever was playing on his iPod. He still hadn't looked
at me, or if he had, I hadn't caught him at it.

The usual place. Maybe I'd jumped to conclusions.
Maybe the late Mr. Gittings had outparanoided me yet
again. Leave the matchbook, yeah, and the phone number, but don't quite join the dots, because then everyone
else will see the shape of what you're making. Maybe the
usual place was somewhere you could *watch* from the
Reflections Café Bar.

I finished my coffee, paid up at the counter, and walked
out onto the street. The guy at the bus stop moved off
at the same time, still—as far as I could tell—without
glancing in my direction. I followed him at a medium-fast
stroll, crossing the street as he tacked away to the south
toward Bridge Place.

We were in the maze of bus lanes and bollards in front
of Victoria, and I thought he might veer off to the right

and go into the station. He didn't, though, and he didn't look behind him. He kept ambling along, his head still bobbing slightly in time to his personal sound track. I kept pace with him, ten feet behind. I slid my hand inside my coat, found my mobile, and took it out. Almost out of charge, I noticed—already showing empty, in fact—but there ought to be enough juice for this, I thought. Pressing the recent calls button, I found the number I'd dialed the night before—the one John had written down on the matchbook cover—selected it, and called it up.

A second. Two. Then I heard the tinny, boppy, tooth-jangling strains of the Crazy Frog sound from right ahead of me.

The skinny guy's head jerked in a belated double take. His hand snaked into his jeans pocket to turn off his phone, and he turned to look back at me, locking eyes with me for the first time. He must have had the phone set to vibrate, too—either that or there was no music on his headphones in the first place.

Abruptly, without warning, he bolted.

I sprinted after him, instinctively bearing right to cut him off if he headed for the station concourse. If he got inside there with even a few seconds' lead on me, I'd never see him again.

But he wasn't trying for the station. He sprinted straight out across Bridge Place, almost getting sideswiped by a bus, which cost me a second or two as I slowed to let it pass. He plunged into a side street.

I was almost thirty feet behind him, and by the time I got to the corner of the street, he was already out of sight. I kept running anyway, scanning the street on both sides to see if there were any clues as to where he might have gone. Only one turnoff on the left. I took that and was in time to see him vanish around another corner away up ahead of me.

Maybe I don't exercise as much as I should; I know health experts recommend half an hour a day. I did half an hour back in 1999 and then sort of fell behind, what with all that excitement about the new millennium and all. I was already feeling winded when I reached the next corner, while the guy I was chasing seemed to be accelerating, if anything.

I got a lucky break, though, when a door opened ahead of him and a woman came out into the street leading two children by the hand. They turned toward us, forming a pavement-wide barrier and giving him the choice between trampling them underfoot or making a wide detour. He skidded to a halt, almost slamming into the startled woman, then swerved across the street, past a skip full of someone's defunct living room furniture, and into an alley.

I took the hypotenuse and won back enough time to snatch the base unit of a standard lamp from the skip as I passed it. Aerodynamically, it was piss-poor, but this was no time to be picky. Putting on a last, desperate spurt of speed, I held it out beside me like a vaulter's pole, but then I flung it like a javelin.

It didn't have the balance of a javelin, and the heavy end dipped at once toward the ground as it flew. Another couple of feet, and it would have hit the pavement and spun away end over end. But I was riding my luck, and it stayed with me. The shaft went squarely between the guy's pounding feet, and he tripped, smacking down heavily on the stone slabs.

He was winded, but he managed to scramble up and limp forward another couple of steps. By that time, I was on him. I knocked him down again with a shoulder charge; then I jumped on top of him, planting one knee in the small of his back to pin him to the ground. He squirmed and tried to get up, but I had the advantage of weight and position.

"What the fuck!" he spluttered. "Let go of me! Are you frigging insane?"

"We haven't met," I panted, my pulse pounding and my breath coming in ragged hiccups. "Well, except on the phone. But I'm hoping we can be friends. I'm Castor. Who are you?"

"I'm gonna scream," the guy snarled, still struggling. He snaked his head around to glare at me, his nose looking like a raptor's beak. "You think you can do this in broad daylight? Out on the street?"

"I think," I said, still breathless, "that you wanted to take—a look at me without—committing yourself. And for some reason, you got cold feet. I told you, I don't want to hurt you. I'm just a friend of John's."

"Then let me up!"

I did. He looked to be in even worse shape to run again than I was, but I could see that the alley was a dead end. There was nowhere for him to run. I stood up and stepped back, letting him climb slowly to his feet.

"What's your name?" I asked him again. "And tell me the goddamn truth. I was in a bad mood when I got here, and it's not getting any better."

He rubbed his knee, favoring me with a sneering grin. "Yeah, I'm not surprised. Sitting there in the café like you're waiting for a blind date. Should've worn a white carnation in your—Chesney," he added hastily as I took a step toward him. "Vincent. Vincent Chesney." He threw up his hands to protect himself.

I grabbed his right hand, much to his surprise, and shook it hard. It probably looked absurdly formal, given the fact that I'd just chased him down like a dog chases a hare, but I didn't give a damn. I was here to collect information, and one way was as good as another.

Sometimes the impressions I pick up from skin contact are fleeting and ambiguous; other times they're so sharp and immediate, it's like a movie with five-point surround sound. Vincent Chesney didn't have any psychic barriers to speak of, and his emotions arrived in my head unmediated, with almost painful clarity.

The grin was bravado; underneath it, he was afraid. Afraid of me, mostly, but not just on a physical level. There was something else in the back of his mind—something else at stake.

I released his hand, and he snatched it back, suspicious and faintly indignant.

"Okay," he said. "Yeah. I did want to get a look at you first. What's wrong with that, man? Calling me in the night. You could have been frigging anybody, seen? I've got to watch my back. I'm in a delicate position here."

"Are you?" I asked politely. "Why is that, then, Vincent?"

"Vince."

"Question stands."

"Okay," he said again, hesitant, unhappy. "You've come for the items, right?" He put the same sort of heavy, loaded stress on the word that the till assistant in a chemist's would put on "something for the weekend."

"The items that John left with you?" I hazarded. Chesney nodded, looking even glummer. "They're one of the things I've come for," I lied.

"Well, okay. Yeah. That's what I thought. It's just around the corner."

The switch from plural to singular threw me. "What is?" I demanded.

"The place where I work. I can get you the stuff, right? It's just around the corner. But you'll have to wait here while I—" He broke off because he could see from the look on my face that I wasn't going to buy it. "If you come up with me," he snapped sullenly, "you follow my lead, yeah? I mean, back me up, whatever I say about you. This is gonna look bad enough anyway. I don't want to lose my frigging job, seen?"

"I'll follow your lead," I promised. I stepped aside and let him walk past me back onto the street. Then I followed him—not back toward Bridge Place but farther south. I was getting my breath back, and Chesney was getting back some of the cocky cool I'd heard in his voice when he picked up the phone the first time.

"So what are you?" he asked as we walked. "You said you worked with Gittings. Does that make you another ghosthunter? 'Get thee behind me, Dennis Wheatley' kind of thing? Nothing wrong with it, mind you. Bit macho, bit paternalistic, not my cup of cocoa, but someone's got to do it. Is someone you?"

"Yeah," I confirmed when I'd figured out what the hell he was talking about. "Someone is me."

"Well, fine. And you scare up a bit of business by looking at the tea leaves. I get it. Sounded wacko at first. But then you start looking at the evidence, and you think,

Whoa, fuck, that's scary. The same patterns unto the third and fourth generation and all that. And then he died, and I had to wonder."

"Wonder what?" I asked, hoping against hope for a coherent sentence.

"If maybe he got too close to the flame," he elaborated, pantomiming the flight of a moth with vague gestures. "You know, if he was chasing after this stuff and he went to the source, someone might have taken it personally. That's what I was scared of. That's why I put the phone down when you called. I mean, you could have been anybody, as far as I was concerned. You could be one of the really cold geezers with the most to lose, yeah? And someone comes along, wants to buy something with your fingerprints, what are you gonna think? Maybe you just take out a gun and bang. Maybe you even watch the message boards, listen to the wires. Like, who's this guy going around picking up my leavings? What does he want? Bring his body down here. Most likely not, but hey. You get me?"

I nodded, but only for the sake of form. Either this guy was assuming I knew a hell of a lot more than I did, or else he always talked like this—in which case I'd have to beat him to death with his own iPod.

We stopped in front of an anonymous Georgian edifice that had once been someone's house and was now three sets of offices. I say three because there were three small plaques on the wall next to the door: VITASTAR FILMS; NEXUS VETERINARY PATHOLOGISTS; DEACON LLOYD EDUCATIONAL PUBLISHING.

The door was unlocked, but it opened into a tiny vestibule. The inner door was operated by a swipe-card lock, and Chesney had the card hanging on a chain at his belt. He swiped us through, putting two fingers up at the security camera mounted on the door frame.

"Nobody there," he said dismissively, and it was true that the security desk in the hall was deserted. "There's a guard comes on at nights, but he never checks the camera footage. It's just *pour encourager les cretins*. Most of this shit is. If I wanted to fake the swipe reader, I could do it with an old bus pass."

We ascended the stairs with Chesney in the lead. The first landing was Vitastar Films, but we kept on going. "Porn," said Chesney, who seemed to have taken on the role of tour guide. "You get one girl and ten guys standing outside here every Monday morning. I think they put out a lot of *bukkake* titles." He pronounced the word "buck cake," which had the side effect of making it seem a lot more wholesome than it was. I thought of the Waltons. Then tried hard not to.

The second landing was Nexus Veterinary Pathologists. The door was open, and Chesney walked inside. There was no receptionist's desk, as such. The room was big and open-plan, and it had a vaguely unpleasant chemical smell. A cluster of chairs in the near corner was a token gesture toward a waiting room; the rest of the space was taken up with glass-fronted storage cupboards, steel lockers, and uniform olive-green filing cabinets. Against the wall off on my left were three different-sized desks, like the bowls of porridge in "Goldilocks." The biggest had a brass nameplate that read JOHN J. MORETON, MSC, DAP.

A young Asian woman in a white medical coat was squatting on her haunches on the far side of the room, stacking bottles on the lower shelves of one of the cupboards. It was too far to read the labels on the bottles, but the HAZCHEM sign on the box she was taking them out of was clear enough. Right next to her was a closed door plated with dull gray metal and marked NO ADMITTANCE TO GENERAL PUBLIC.

She looked around as we came in, and she gave Chesney a severe frown. "Thanks, Vince," she said, in a flat Brummie accent. "That's half my bloody lunch hour out the window. Why've you got mud on your knees?"

"Sorry, Smeet," said Chesney. "I got held up."

The girl looked from him to me as if she expected either an introduction or an explanation. "Mr. Farnsworth," Chesney said after too long a pause. "He brought a poodle in last year, yeah? Before my time. And now there's another one from the same litter who's got the same kind of tumor, or it might be a different one, so he needs another copy of the report for his insurance claim because there's a clause about genetic predisposition. I said I'd dig one out for him."

Smeet nodded. She'd already lost interest, I think maybe at "Farnsworth." Chesney had done a good job of making me sound too boring to live. She pointed at the box, which was still half full of bottles. "You can finish those off," she said bluntly. "I'm not even supposed to handle them until I get my B2 through."

"Yeah, no worries," said Chesney, throwing his jacket down on top of one of the filing cabinets. "You go ahead. Take a full hour if you want. Morpork won't be back until four, will he? Not if he's at one of those RSPCA thrashes."

He went to one of the filing cabinets, opened the top

drawer, and started to rummage around without much conviction. His acting stank, and Smeet was taking her time getting ready—taking off the white coat and hanging it on a rack behind one of the desks, then putting various items from the desktop into her handbag.

"Busy?" I asked her, just to draw her attention away from Chesney.

"Busy?" she echoed. "Yes, we are. We're working until ten o'clock most nights. Bird flu is our main money spinner at this point in time. Rabies has been a niche market since the pet passport came along, but bird flu was a very timely replacement. It's even outselling canine thrombocythemia. I'd say, on average, Vince gets to do the parrot sketch from *Monty Python* once every other day."

She was done loading her handbag, and she hit the high road without looking back, deftly snatching up a brown suede jacket from the same rack and putting it on as she headed for the door. One hand raised for silence, Chesney listened to her footsteps as they receded down the stairs.

"Bitch," he said with feeling when the front door two floors below us slammed to. He shut the file drawer with unnecessary force, opened the bottom one, and took a box from it with a certain amount of care. It was about the size of a shoe box but made of wood with a hinged lid. It was painted in green and gold to resemble an oversize Golden Virginia tobacco tin. "She'd report me in a minute, you know? I have to do everything on the sly. Come into my parlor and I'll give you the stuff. Happy to get rid of it, to be honest."

He opened the door that the general public couldn't pass through and went inside. Following him, I found myself in a room that fitted my preconceptions of a pathology lab pretty much to the letter. There was a massive operating table in the center, with a swiveling light array above it on a double-articulated metal arm. White tiles on the walls and floor and gleaming white porcelain sinks inset into white work surfaces with kidney-shaped steel dishes stacked ready to hand. I'd always wondered why those dishes were so popular in medical circles, given that the only internal organ that's kidney-shaped is the kidney. The chemical smell was a lot stronger here, bordering on the eye-watering, but Chesney didn't seem to notice it. He closed the door behind us and then drew a bolt across. That struck me as overkill, given that we were alone in the place.

"Okay," he said again. It seemed to be his favorite word, unless the repetitions were just a sign of frayed nerves.

He set the wooden box down on the operating table, swinging the swivel-mounted light array out of the way with his left hand. He flashed me a significant glance but undercut it by opening his mouth again. "We are controlling transmission," he said in a heavy cod-American accent. "Do not adjust your set. *The Twilight Zone*, yeah? That's where this stuff belongs."

Chesney was quoting the opening credits of *The Outer Limits,* but this didn't seem like the time to split hairs. He opened the box and started to unpack its contents. On top of the pile was a CD marked CD+RW and scrawled over in black marker with the single word FINAL. Underneath were a dozen or more resealable plastic bags of the type that the police use for physical evidence. They held a slightly surreal variety of objects: a penknife; a Matchbox toy car; a big commemoration crown piece from some forgotten royal event; a playing card—ace of spades—that someone had signed illegibly; a fountain pen; a pair of pliers; a glass paperweight; a tie pin; and unsettlingly, in this innocuous company, a bullet.

"I'm not paranoid," Chesney assured me, as if anxious to dispel a specific rumor. "I just hid the stuff because I knew bloody well Smeet would blow the whistle on me if she found it. I'm not supposed to use the lab for private stuff, seen? It's a hanging offense, and my boss doesn't need much of an excuse right now."

I looked through the weird stuff in the bags, turning up a few more surprises—a toy soldier that looked really old, the paint flaking off it to reveal bare metal underneath; and a Woodbine cigarette packet that had been signed like the playing card. The name in this case was Jimmy Rick, or maybe Pick, and it didn't mean a thing to me.

"And these were all John's things?" I asked, making sure I had this right.

"Yeah." Chesney nodded. He was looking at me very closely, trying to read my reactions. "Worth a bob or two," he observed slightly wistfully.

Which told me all I needed to know about his weird behavior on the phone and his skittishness today. When he heard about John's death, he must have thought Christmas had come two months late.

"Yeah, probably," I agreed. "I imagine there's people out there who'd eat this stuff up."

Chesney nodded eagerly. "Yeah, and I could shift it for you. John more or less promised I could have the lot once he was done with it. He always said this was about the data, seen? Not about the items. He wasn't a ghoul or a pervert or anything. It was just something he was interested in—his own private Idaho kind of thing. I never thought anyone would come round asking after this stuff."

"And the stuff is valuable because of who it used to belong to?" I demanded, making sure I'd gotten the right end of this increasingly shitty stick.

Chesney looked blank. I don't think it had occurred to him until then that I was flying blind, but it was a little too late to decide to be coy. "Well, yeah," he said. "Obviously. They're—you know—" He hesitated, presumably looking for a polite turn of phrase.

"Death row souvenirs," I finished. It was the words "ghoul" and "pervert" in the same sentence that had clinched it for me. Well, those and the fact that I'd just asked Nicky to find me something exactly like this: some banal object made magical and precious by the fact that it had once been in the hands of a killer. Big thrill. I'd been in the hands of killers so many times it wasn't even funny, and nobody was looking to sell me on eBay. Maybe that was a blessing, though. It's probably best not to have too clear a picture of your market value.

Chesney looked a little sick, because he could see in my face that I'd never seen any of the stuff in his bran tub in my life. He was counting up the cost of lost opportunities. I would have sympathized, but time is money, and right then I was all about the bottom line.

"Yeah," he said lugubriously. "The ace of spades was from a deck that Ronnie Kray used to play poker in his cell in Parkhurst. Some minor villain named Alan Stalky got him to sign it and then took it instead of the winnings. That's worth a fortune. George Cornell used the paperweight in a fight—broke some bloke's head open with it—and the pen is the one that Tony Lambrianou signed his confession with. It's still got his blood on it, allegedly because the police beat the living shit out of him before they let him sign. The crown piece belonged to Aaron Silver…"

He carried on talking through the contents of the baggies one by one, but I was only half listening because the names he'd already mentioned had made something groan on the dangerously overstacked shelves of my memory. Cornell. Lambrianou. Lathwell. Silver. Every single one of those names had turned up in the lists in John Gittings's notebook. If Kray had been there, too, I'd have made the connection. It occurred to me to wonder where the hell John had been getting the money. If these things were as valuable as Chesney said they were, they ought to have been way out of the reach of someone living on an exorcist's earnings.

"So what?" I said, wrenching my attention back to the present. "John was picking this stuff up on the fan-boy circuit?"

"He had a dealer. A zombie guy."

Yeah, of course he did. Nicky, you cagey bugger, I thought, we are going to have some very harsh words. "Right. And he was passing it all on to you so that you could—?" My mouth had outrun my brain, but Chesney had mentioned data, and the fact that we were in a pathology lab—even if it was one where most of the corpses on the slab were named Fido—was a big clue. "You ran tests on them," I finished ungrammatically. "What kind of tests, Vince?"

"The whole works," Chesney said with a touch of professional pride. He tried to take the box back from me, but it was a try that expected to fail, and I made sure it did by putting my full weight down on my right hand, the one resting on the box lid. He straightened up and pretended not to notice. "Fingerprinting. A fuck lot of that. Hematocrit when he could get something with a bloodstain on it. And DNA. I can do DNA. Okay, I'm working with puppies right now, but that's just for the work experience. I trained in human pathology, and I'm gonna do real forensic work as soon as I'm out of this shithole. John's nineteenth-century time-warp 'criminals are gorillas' thing may have been piped shite, but from where I was standing, it was good practice."

"And good pocket money," I guessed.

Chesney bridled. "Hey, look, he came to me. I was doing him a—"

"—a favor. Absolutely. Why do you keep talking about criminal physiognomy, Vince? Is that what John said this was about? Recapitulation theory? I can't see that kite getting very far off the ground."

"Me, neither." Chesney was still stiffly on his dignity. I'd hurt him where his professional ethics pinched the tightest. "But the customer's always right, and John had this thing, you know?"

"What kind of thing?"

"A Cesare Lombroso reductionist taxonomic criminal-anthropology kind of thing."

"Go on."

He glanced toward the box with longing, bereaved eyes. "He was making up a big database," he said. "Criminals, yeah? Killers especially. He wanted to measure them every way they could be measured. I did the tests and passed all the stuff on to him, and that was that. I didn't have to clap hands and believe in fairies."

"Fairies in this case being—?"

"Oh, Christ, you know the song. The idea that there's a criminal type. That by pooling data from a thousand people who've already done bad things, you'll be able to predict the next rapist or serial killer before he or she cuts loose. It's not just bullshit, it's the bullshit that the century before last left out for the binmen."

I tapped the box. "Sounds pretty thin. The disk in here, that's all the data you put together for John before he died?"

Chesney nodded, but by now he wanted rid of me. A nod wasn't enough.

"All of it?" I pursued. "All the test results for all the 'items'?"

"It's all there." He was indignant, seeing his nest egg about to waltz out through the door and knowing there wasn't a thing he could do about it.

I straightened up. "Thanks for your help, Vince," I said. "If there's anything on the disk that a layman can't get his head around, would you rather I called you here or someplace else?"

"Don't call me at all," Chesney said, in something of a sulk. "I don't owe you anything, man. I didn't even need to give you the disk. That's my intellectual property."

"True," I conceded. "But let me put it another way. If there's a fine point of interpretation and I want a steer, should I come to you or to your boss?"

"Fuck!" Chesney waved his arms wildly. "I wish I'd never gotten involved with any of this crap. It's not like the money was any good."

I cut him a small amount of slack, because it's generally easier to lead a horse to water than to hold it under for the time it takes to drown it. "There could be some more money on the table at some point," I said. "I'll see what I can do."

"You can call me on my mobile," he said, very slightly mollified. "The number you got from John, yeah? I'll get back to you when no one's listening over my shoulder."

"Okay." I hefted the box. "Thanks for your help, Vince. John's smiling down on you from heaven, if that's any help."

I made my own way out, leaving him cursing me under his breath. Smeet was coming back up the stairs as I went down. She eyed the box curiously. "Dead dog," I said, and kept on going.

John's own private Idaho, Chesney had said. Yeah, maybe it was, but I could have wished he hadn't reminded me of that song. The B-52s warbling about the awful surprise in the bottomless pool tied in too neatly with the dream I'd had the night before.

I felt like I was following the trail that had led John to that final encounter with the business end of his own shotgun. And I wondered for the first time where the gun had come from.

Another souvenir, maybe.

～ Twelve

NICKY WAS KIND of surprised to see me again. I was surprised, too, walking into the formerly empty shell of the old Gaumont to find a team of six men resurfacing walls and putting the seating back in. Nicky was supervising loudly and officiously, ignoring the plaster dust in the air because he didn't have to breathe it. He turned and saw me and threw out his hands as I approached, as though I were going to frisk him.

"What?" he said. "Castor, it's only been four fucking hours. I didn't even look at your stuff yet. I'll call you if I've got any bones to toss to you, okay?"

By way of answer, I lifted the lid of the wooden box, which I had tucked underneath my arm like Henry the Eighth's head, and showed him its contents. He couldn't blanch: Zombies have a natural pallor that makes albinos look like dedicated sun-bed addicts. But he did look a little sick.

"How about we go gnaw on a few together?" I suggested.

Nicky nodded slowly and put out his hand to touch the box lid, pushing it down so that it covered the objects inside from view. He turned to look over his shoulder at his task force. "The rest of the stall seats are over there, guys," he said, pointing. "If they're not all in purple plush, do alternate purple and blue. Or make a star pattern or something. But tasteful—I don't want to end up with something that looks *ongepotchket*."

We went up to the projection booth, our footsteps echoing on bare concrete. This was Nicky's inner sanctum, cluttered with whatever he was obsessing on at any given time and the rich and varied detritus of previous obsessions. It was generally pretty hard to move in there, but today it looked worse than ever because he'd moved a lot of stuff up here from downstairs, out of the way of the builders. Once we were inside, Nicky closed a steel door like the door of a vault and turned to face me, looking stern and pissed off. I guessed he'd decided that attack was the best form of defense.

"I've got to maintain a professional relationship with those guys," he said, pointing at the floor. "They're working for me. And it's kind of hard to get past their touchingly naive assumption that zombies are shambling retards who can be ripped off with total fucking impunity. So another time, Castor, you want to have something out with me, you do it in private, okay? Entre fucking nous. Now what's this about? And for the record, before you start, you don't have any beef with me. I didn't lie to you. I just didn't talk to you about other people's business."

I might have made a snappy comeback—in fact, I normally would have felt obliged to—but I was looking over Nicky's shoulder and was momentarily distracted by the colossal seventy-millimeter projector sitting behind him, in a position previously occupied by his stinking hydroponics vats.

"You're reopening this place as a cinema?" I asked, amazed.

"Sure. Why not?"

"Is that a trick question, Nicky? How about because you hate people?"

Nicky shrugged. "Yeah, I do. The live ones are too warm, and the dead ones are mostly falling apart and bleeding self-pity out of the joins. Fuck them all, is my motto."

"So opening a cinema—that's facing your fears with a vengeance, wouldn't you say?"

Nicky looked peeved. "I didn't say I was afraid of them, Castor. Just that I hate their guts. I also didn't say that when this baby is up and running, anyone else is getting in to see the show. It's gonna be for an audience of one. Cinema Paradiso. Me and the dark and the black-and-white dream machine."

I still couldn't get my head around the idea, and I put the bollocking that I was about to give Nicky on the back burner while I tried. "What about making a small footprint?" I demanded. "You'll have to order prints of movies. Get on distribution databases. Deal with shipping companies." Staying inconspicuous had been Nicky's highest priority from way back before he died. The world is a web, he said, and every time you touch one of the strands of the web, you tell the spiders where you are.

When he accessed the Internet, he did it through a string of proxy servers as long as the Great Wall of China—and like China, he treated information as though it were both a weapon and a shield. You couldn't get a fix on Nicky; you couldn't find him in any search. Even his electricity was hand-pumped from deep artesian wells rather than coming straight out of the national grid. He was the closest thing I'd ever met to an invisible man, and his paranoia was a thing of beautiful, terrible purity.

So this had to be not the real Nicky but some kind of lifelike—or rather, deathlike—facsimile.

"The small footprint is still a good working goal," Nicky said almost off-handedly. "But think about it for a second, Castor. I kept a small footprint for years, and it didn't stop this place from being torn apart by Fanke and his fucking satanists. I'm working on a different strategy now."

"Which is?"

"Which is my business. When it turns out to be yours, I'll tell you about it."

"Okay." I gave it up. The most likely diagnosis, as far as I could see, was that being winkled out of his shell by a crazed mob had made Nicky's psychosis metastasize into a new form. And he was right. I'd find out about it somewhere down the line, so there was no point in worrying about it now.

I threw the box down on top of what looked like a baby's changing table and strolled past Nicky into the room. He backpedaled, keeping pace with me and staying in between me and his nice, shiny new projector. Evidently, it was a look-don't-touch kind of deal.

"So let's get down to business," I suggested. "I asked you what you were doing for John Gittings, and you came out with all that client-privilege palaver. Then I asked you to find me a curio that used to belong to a dead killer, and you almost jumped out of your dry-cured skin. I noticed it at the time, but I didn't know what it meant. Now I do. It was because John had been asking you to do the same thing on a bigger scale—death row souvenirs by the bucketload—and you thought I might be playing some kind of mind-fuck on you. Trying to make you give yourself away."

Nicky spread his hands in a "there you have it" gesture. "And I don't know what in our previous relationship could have caused me to have so little trust in you," he said sardonically.

"It's not about trust." I put my hand on the curve of the projector's lens turret, and Nicky swatted it away. "It's about not making me run around in circles when life's short enough already. Was there some reason to keep me in the dark about John's hobby? Was there anyone whose interests could have been harmed in any way at all by you leveling with me?"

"Not my call," Nicky deadpanned, wiping the turret with his shirt cuff where my hand had touched it. "His widow, maybe? His kids? Fuck do I know? First do no harm, is my motto."

"Since when, Nicky?"

"Since now."

"Right. Or maybe you had the same idea Chesney had. That if nobody got to find out about this shit, you could have a garage sale in due course and pocket the profit."

"Chesney?"

"Never mind."

I'd been looking at the projector. I didn't know enough

about these things to tell if it was high-end or low-end, state-of-the-art or shoddy; I was just looking, like a prospective buyer in a secondhand car dealership. Now I looked at Nicky instead. "Sit down," I said.

"I'm happy standing."

"No," I explained patiently. "This isn't 'Sit down and make yourself comfortable.' This is 'Sit down or I'll have to sit you down, and then you might break.'" There was an office chair on rollers within reach of my outstretched arm. I snagged it and rolled it across to him. It took him a moment or two to decide, but when I actually took a step toward him, he sat down hurriedly.

"This is bullshit, Castor," he said angrily. "And you wouldn't pull it on someone who was still alive."

I wheeled the chair back over to the changing table where I'd dumped John's box. I opened the lid again, took out Vince Chesney's disk, and thrust it into Nicky's hands. "You're going to look this over for me," I said.

"Yeah? Why am I going to do that?"

"Because I'm asking you. Nicely, so far."

Nicky turned the disk over in his hands, examining it with a remote, bored expression.

"You know Cesare Lombroso?" I asked him.

"Sure. I golf with him."

"Nineteenth-century anthropologist."

"Yeah." Nicky nodded. "That's the guy. Starting to smell pretty fierce now. And his elbow gives on the backswing."

"He came up with this idea about criminal physiognomy," I said. "He called it recapitulation, and it made him the poster boy for the early eugenics movement."

He dumped the disk back in the box. "Eugenics? That was Annie Lennox and Dave—"

Moving quickly, I slammed the box lid down on his hand, trapping it. He yelled, but not in pain: His nerves were closed for business, so pain wasn't a feature of the landscape for him anymore. But that had made him obsessively careful about organic damage, since he knew he didn't have the advantage of the early-warning system that the living take so much for granted. He also didn't have self-repair: no white corpuscles, no platelets, no cell division. So where anyone still warm would have tried to snatch his hand back out of the box, Nicky froze up stiller than a startled possum.

"Castor, enough with this stupid fucking schoolboy shit!" he shouted. Shouting meant inflating his lungs fully and emptying them again—again, not easy for a dead man—and that meant a few moments of total silence after he was done.

I went on as though I hadn't been interrupted. "Recapitulation," I said. "It's a bankrupt concept, but it seemed sexy enough until Darwin drove a stampede of finches and Galápagos turtles through it."

"What the fuck are you—"

"The idea, Nicky, is this." I leaned a little more weight on the box lid, and his free hand clenched as though he were considering punching me; but that's a good way to break a knuckle, so I knew he wouldn't. "Babies in the womb, so the story goes, run through all the previous stages of evolution before finally reaching full human form. It's like Mother Nature has to scroll down through every template in the book before she can get to the human one, because that's the one that's most fully evolved. It's bullshit, like I said, but are you with me so far?"

"Let go of my fucking hand, Castor!"

"But Lombroso thought there were glitches in the program. Sometimes babies get stuck on one of the more primitive forms, he said, and instead of being born fully human, they're born with apelike features that really belong much earlier on in the series.

"See, he'd taken a good look around, and he'd noticed how many hardened criminals have thick, heavy brow ridges like orangutans, or abnormally long fingers like gorillas, and he had this lightbulb moment. Criminals are the way they are because they're throwbacks to our nonhuman ancestry. And once you know that, you can spot them up front and run intercept. You don't even have to wait for them to commit a crime." I nodded at the box. "That's what John said he was doing with this stuff, if anyone asked. But that was just his cover story, and I'm hoping you might have some idea what it was covering. See, I know this isn't really about your Hippocratic Oath, Nicky. It's about protecting the bottom line. And part of that is not giving away for free any information that I might be persuaded to pay for later. So you want paying, fine, you come up with a starting price, and then we'll haggle. But time is fucking money, and right now I'm hypersensitive to people who waste any of mine because someone tried to kill me the other night by dropping me down a lift shaft. So this is personal, and it's at the top of my things-to-do list. Is that understood?"

"Yes!"

"Yes what?"

"Yes, it's fucking understood. Open the box, you frigging arsehole!"

I took my weight off the lid, and he retrieved his hand, checking it for damage in a frigid, resentful silence. There wasn't any. I'd been careful.

"He started collecting around the end of October," Nicky muttered sullenly. "And he was throwing money around like it had a use-by date on it. It wasn't just me—he had a whole team of us working on commission, buying everything we could pick up."

"Anything that had belonged to a killer?"

"Belonged to. Been used by. Been touched by. You see the bullet? One of my coolest finds. Les Lathwell loaded that into a gun that he carried to the Barclays bank massacre in sixty-nine. It was used in evidence when the case came to trial. That bumped the price up. It cost three grand, if I remember rightly."

"Cost you or cost John?" I asked, to keep things clear.

"The dealer asked for two five," Nicky conceded. "I took my cut. That was understood. Hey, I don't normally do this stuff. It was a personal favor because John wanted to work through proxies."

"You're a friend in need, Nicky."

"That's the Samaritans, Castor. I work on margin."

"Tony Lambrianou. Ronnie Kray. George Cornell. Les Lathwell. Aaron Silver." I counted off the names on my fingers. "They're all there in John's notebook. What else have they got in common, Nicky?"

He grimaced as if he found the question hard to swallow. "We didn't name a price yet," he said.

"Put it on the slate."

"Not what you said. You said I could name a—"

I opened the box lid wide, and the hinges gave a creak that was surprisingly eloquent and persuasive.

"They're all from the East End," he said, holding up his hands in surrender, or maybe just to keep them well away from the box. "That was the brief, right? Lambrianou and Lathwell were in the Kray gang. Cornell worked for Charlie Richardson and was murdered by the Krays. That leaves Aaron Silver as the odd one out."

"Why?"

"Because he's a couple of generations earlier. Prewar, even. He was a mad rat-bastard Jewish immigrant who came over from Poland and tried to get work as a tailor. But his needlework sucked, and he couldn't get a start-up. So he had a brainwave one day and started going around all the other tailors, taking voluntary contributions for the Brick Lane Fire Service. You pay up front, they don't burn your house down."

"It's not exactly the Krays."

"You're wrong. He was the ur-Krays. The Krays before the Krays, the great precursor. Protection was where he got his foot in the door. Pretty soon it was prostitution, gambling, the tail end of the opium business—you name it. Silver wasn't his real name, by the way. He was born Aaron Berg, but he went by Aaron Silver so his family wouldn't be ashamed. Nice boy. Loved his mother."

I nodded, turning over these dusty old facts in my mind. I'd been wondering ever since I met Chesney whether any of this might turn out to be connected in some way with Jan's theory of a vengeful Myriam Kale wandering around London forty years after her death, but it seemed not. An American contract killer would still sit oddly with a bunch of East End gangsters. "You did your homework," I said to Nicky.

He looked at me and pulled his lower eyelid down with

the tip of his middle finger—an unsettling gesture when a zombie does it, because the eye is desiccated, and it's not that firm in its socket to start with. "Only way to avoid getting ripped off is to know your stuff," Nicky told me. "John the Git was hungry for anything to do with those East End bad boys. Big premiums for stuff that hadn't changed hands too many times since, and for stuff that they'd owned as kids."

That explained the lead soldier and the toy car. But it still didn't give me even the beginning of a clue as to what John had been looking for. I only knew—with absolute certainty—that the Lombroso stuff was a smokescreen. John had dropped out of university without finishing his degree, just as I had, but while my discipline was English, his was biology. And what little I knew about Lombroso came from a late-night drunken conversation in which John had told me at length what an utter wanker Lombroso had been.

"So what was he looking for?" I asked Nicky.

"Why don't you tell me?" There was a sneer lurking behind the words. Nicky pushed the box away and stood up.

I said, "He had some animal pathologist running tests on these things. Checking them for fingerprints; for blood and DNA in the few cases where that was possible; probably for a lot of other things, too."

"Then I guess he was looking for correlations. For patterns in the data."

"Like?"

"Like I'll have to look over the disk myself and get back to you. It's way past time we named that price, Castor."

"So name it."

"Five hundred. Plus I get to keep what's in the box."

"Jesus!" I did my best to sound appalled. "You just told me one item in there is worth three grand, Nicky. Why the hell should I let you pocket the whole lot?"

He threw his arms in the air. "Because it's no skin off you," he said.

"The five hundred is. I'm not going to clear that myself. Carla isn't paying me, and the Myriam Kale thing is pretty much on spec."

"Okay, say two hundred," he conceded magnanimously. "And the stuff in the box."

"Two hundred is fine. You sell off the stuff in the box and split the proceeds fifty-fifty with Carla Gittings."

"Agreed."

"But everything stays here until I tell you it's okay to sell it. I still don't know where we're going with this. I'd hate to come back here looking for something in particular and find you've already hocked it on eBay."

"Fair enough," Nicky said. "Better than fair. I'm on the case, Castor, in spite of the shit you just pulled. And as a token of good faith, so you know I'm on the level, I'll tell you something for free."

"Yeah?" I asked. "What's that, Nicky?"

"You were stiffed. There should be at least thirty or forty other things in the box."

I blinked. "You're sure?"

"Am I sure? I can give you the fucking inventory if you want me to. It's a lot of the choicest stuff that's missing, too—lots of Kray memorabilia. Including a pair of leather bondage pants that I bought from a priest in Flitwick, Bedfordshire. Long, sordid story. And that's only the items I got for John. There's a lot more that he bought through other people or picked up himself."

Son of a bitch. So that was why Vince Chesney had caved so fast. He'd given me the bargain-basement stuff and kept the top drawer for himself.

"I'll get you the rest, too," I promised. "In the meantime, work through whatever the fuck is on that disk and give me a précis. Anything at all you think looks interesting. I'm completely in the dark on this, Nicky. A single candle might be all I need."

"Sure, sure." He herded me toward the door, anxious to be rid of me now that the deal was sealed. But when I was halfway down the stairs, he called out to me. I stopped, and he came down to meet me, fishing in the pocket of his jeans. "Here," he said. He handed me the key, which I'd forgotten I'd given to him. "I almost forgot. Left luggage lockers, Victoria Station."

A hundred yards from where John and Vince Chesney had had their meets. Yeah, it figured. "Thanks," I said.

"You're welcome. I await your lavish apology."

"It's coming," I said. "Sooner or later. This makes it sooner." I tucked the key away in one of the many hidden pockets of my coat. "What's your first screening going to be, Nicky?"

"That Friedkin movie." He snapped his fingers, pretending to consult his memory. "The one where the exorcist gets thrown through the window and bleeds out on the pavement. I'll do it as a double bill with *Day of the Dead*. You know me. I love a happy ending."

"Call me," I said.

He nodded. "A single candle. Sure. Just don't leave the gas on, Castor. Naked flames are dangerous things to have around. Hey, is your mobile turned off?"

"No," I said, knee-jerk, without checking. "Why?"

"Because I'm turning into your fucking answering service. That cop friend of yours called to say he might have something juicy for you in a day or so. And I do not appreciate you giving him my number."

"And?"

"And Pen Bruckner rang three times since I got back from seeing you this morning. Wants to know where you are. She said you were due in court or something."

From Walthamstow to Barnet isn't that far as the crow flies. As the taxi crawls along the North Circular Road, though, it's a fair way. Out of sheer desperation, I offered the driver an extra twenty if he could cut some corners, and he peeled off onto some backstreets where we seemed to go faster but covered less ground.

I was right about the phone; it was still turned on. But the battery, which was old and needed replacing, had run out of power, so the point was moot. Sometimes I could coax a minute or two longer out of it by ejecting it and then sliding it back into place, but not this time. It was definitively dead.

By the time I got to the courthouse, it must have been almost four o'clock. I was hoping that the case might have started late, but as soon as I saw Pen sitting on the courtroom steps, I knew it was beside the point to hurry now. I also knew from her face how the hearing had gone.

I sat down next to her. She didn't look around or seem to notice.

"What happened?" I demanded. She didn't answer, so I asked again. "Pen, what happened?"

"He said he'd looked at the composition of the panel,"
said Pen slowly, sounding almost as though she were reading the words from a badly printed sheet. "And it wasn't
right. They were supposed to make sure the panel was
completely independent—no conflicts of interest or anything—and they hadn't. So any decision the panel made
wasn't valid."

I blinked. That sounded like good news, as far as it
went. "Then we're—"

"But he also said he'd thought about the power-of-
attorney thing, and he'd changed his mind about it not
being in his jurisdiction." She looked at me, her face
strained and pale. "He said someone had to look out for
Rafi, and it had to be someone who could be trusted to
make decisions in his best interests. Someone who understood the medical background and knew what was at
stake and wasn't going to act out of emotion or prejudice.
Someone with an independent mind and an expert grasp
of the issues."

I saw what was coming, but common sense rebelled at
it. So did my stomach. "You're not fucking telling me—"
I protested.

Pen nodded. "He gave it to Jenna-Jane Mulbridge. She's
got power of attorney now, and she's already signed the
consent forms. She brought them *with* her, Fix. She knew
this was going down. Then Runcie let them convene the
hearing right there because all the panel members were
present, and it was one, two, three, you're done." She
blinked away tears. "I thought he was trying to do what
was right for Rafi, but he's just railroaded us. That cow is
going to take Rafi away to the MOU tomorrow, and then
she can do what she likes to him.

"Over my dead body," I promised.

But that was the kind of knee-jerk response you have to be wary of. It took only a few moments of sober reflection before I thought better of it.

"Better yet," I amended, "over hers."

∼ Thirteen

I WAS STARING DOWN the barrel of another long night, and I knew it. I had the ultimate ordeal of dinner with Juliet and the lovely Mrs. Juliet to look forward to. But first I was going to get some errands run.

I got to the Paragon at about six, which, according to the desk clerk, Merrill, was when Joseph Onugeta's shift began. Merrill was sitting at the desk reading the *Evening Standard* when I walked in. He gestured with his thumb backward over his shoulder. "He's in the cupboard," he said, and went back to his paper.

The cupboard turned out to be a room on the ground floor—the same size as the bedrooms, or at least the one I'd seen—lined with shelves and stacked with boxes of cleaning materials. Joseph Onugeta was changing into his work overalls when I knocked and entered. I'd been seeing Onugeta as an East African name, but his skin was the rich near-violet black of the Orissa Dalits. He had a frizz of ash-gray hair, so tightly curled that it almost looked sheer, that came down to a widow's peak above intense brown-black eyes with heavy lids. His mouth was set in the dour line of someone who's seen a lot of shit and expects to see a lot more. Then again, I have that effect on a lot of people.

I introduced myself and told him what I was there for—that I was interested in what he'd seen and heard on the day of the murder. He listened with gloomy indifference, his mouth tugging down at the corners as though it made him very sad to have to listen to me.

"I told the police already," he pointed out.

"I know that," I agreed. "I'm just checking the details. Especially this thing about you hearing a woman's voice from the room..."

At the word "woman," the man's whole demeanor changed. A tremor went through him. He seemed to still it with some difficulty, clenching his hands into tight fists.

"Can you tell me anything about her?" I asked. "You didn't see her go into the room?"

Silently, he shook his head.

"Can you remember anything she said?"

Another jerk of the head that I took to be a negative, but before I could throw another question at him Onugeta was speaking in a tense, urgent monotone. "'I hate you,'" he muttered. "'I fucking hate all of you. If I could kill every rat bastard of you, one after another after another, I'd do it.'" It took me a second to realize that he wasn't talking to me but quoting from memory. "'I want it to fucking hurt you so bad, so bad. I want to see in your eyes how much it hurts. And when you're dead, I wish I could bring you back and make it hurt some more.'"

He fell silent, turned his back on me, and took down

a pair of marigold gloves from one of the shelves. "Like that. On and on like that. And the one man, he was saying, 'You don't mean that, you don't mean that.' Scared. Really scared. And then the other man said, 'Make her stop.'"

I had to be careful with the next question—careful not to let it sound like an accusation. "You didn't think of going into the room?" I asked.

Joseph shot me a bitter look. "I hear worse than that every day," he said. "Much worse. I-love-you-I-hate-you-I'll-fuck-you. Everyone says that here. Or thinks it. I kept on walking. None of my business. All I do is empty the wastebins. There's nightmares enough for anyone right there.

"But then when we turned the key and looked into that room..." He was staring at nothing, and his face was set hard, the gloves dangling forgotten in his hand. "It wasn't any kind of love that did that," he muttered. "Love can turn into a lot of things, but—there wasn't a square inch of him that hadn't been—" He gave up on that sentence, shaking his head rapidly like a dog trying to get itself dry. "It takes a lot of hate to do that. To keep on hating someone after he's already dead."

He discovered the gloves in his hand, put them on, and wriggled his fingers into them one at a time with repetitive, robotic care. His eyes were hooded, his mouth twisted slightly as if he were in pain. I got a glimpse of the truth, then, about what had made him too sick to come into work. He was talking about a sickness of the soul.

"Joseph," I said, although I wanted to stop and get the hell out into the fresh air. "You didn't see her? You never got a glimpse of her, going into the room or coming out?"

It was a question I'd already asked, but given his state of mind, it was worth one more throw of the dice. Since he couldn't get away from these memories, maybe if I kept hovering around the edges of them, some kind of enlightenment, some kind of clue, would come to me.

"I'll know her if I see her," Joseph said, tapping his gloved finger against his right temple. "I dreamed about her that night. Dream about her most nights. My daddy had the sight, and I got it, too, whether I want it or not.

"She's not a woman, though. Not a real woman. It sounds stupid, but I don't care. I'll say it anyway. She's got a devil face. Long red hair. Tall as a man, strong as a man. And a circle here, over her eye, like a crater. Like a little bomb hit her and left a crater. Or like someone shot her and the bullet bounced off."

The hairs rose on the nape of my neck as he talked. He was describing Myriam Kale; he'd even gotten the chickenpox scar. But the look on his face told me that carrying on with this line of questioning was going to lead to some ugly eruption that I probably couldn't handle.

"Joseph," I said, switching tack, "your boss, Merrill, said something to me that didn't get a mention in the police evidence. He said another man came into the Paragon a little later than Barnard and Hunter. An old man. By himself. Does that ring any bells with you?"

"Yeah." Joseph nodded. "I bumped into him in the corridor. I was coming out of a room with an armload of sheets and stuff. Next thing I know, I'm going backward instead of forward. I hit him and bounced off." He picked up a plastic bucket and hung two J-cloths over the side of it. "He wasn't an old man, though. I don't know where Mr. Merrill got that idea from. I didn't get a good look at him, but he was solid. Very strong. And he walked like—you know—like a big strong guy walks. All swaggering. That wasn't any old man."

Something stirred in my mind as he said that, but I didn't try to drag the thought up into the light. Not yet. It would come in its own good time if I didn't reach for it. I thanked Joseph for his time and offered him a twenty from my dwindling stash. He took it without even looking at it. Where he was living right now, money couldn't bring much solace.

I had to get out to Kingsbury next, for my dinner engagement with Juliet and Sue Book, and the easiest way to do that was to hoof across to Baker Street and change onto the Jubilee. That was what I was going to do, swear to God, but I had that locker key of John's burning a hole in my pocket. How long would it take to open a locker and pick up the contents? Five minutes at the outside. I could still do it and get to Juliet's in plenty of time. So I found myself heading south instead, without any recollection of making a decision about it.

The left luggage lockers at Victoria were scattered randomly across the whole station, but the densest concentration was next to the Pret A Manger at the northern end of the concourse. I tried there first, but locker number 167 wasn't among them. I zigzagged back toward the escalators that lead down into the underground, going from one row of lockers to the next, and finally struck paydirt on the fourth or fifth. But paydirt was a relative term in this case, because when I opened 167, it was empty.

I felt the sudden prick and slow deflation of bathos,

but only for a moment. Then I thought about how John had played the earlier moves in this game. There was the plastic bag, for starters, taped to the space in back of the desk drawer; then the backward phone number, written on the matchbook of a café that turned out not to be his rendezvous point with Chesney but a place where the rendezvous point could be spied on. Always that extra, paranoid little wriggle, like the innovations of a mind determined to catch itself out as well as everyone else.

Going down on hands and knees, and mentally consigning the trousers I was wearing to the dustbin of history, I took a closer look inside the locker. Still nothing to be seen, but when I stuck my arm inside and felt over all the inside surfaces, there was something there—something fixed to the top of the locker space. It gave slightly under my hand and was the wrong texture for metal. I managed to get hold of a corner of the something and pull it free. It was a big, chunky envelope, fixed to the roof of the locker with duct tape.

I carried on looking, wanting to make absolutely sure that I wasn't missing anything, but I didn't unearth any further treasures. I left the key in the locker and took the package over to the station bar, where I ordered a whiskey and water and then opened the envelope while I was waiting for the drink to come.

After the *A to Z*, the matchbook, and the key, I was expecting something else with an aura of cheap dime-store mysteries about it, but the envelope was full of music. At least it was full of sheets of music paper. The notations that were on the paper, though, made no sense to me at all. The sequences of notes—if that was what they were—had been set down as mere vertical strokes of a felt-tip pen, with no indication of how long they should be sustained, and they ricocheted all over the scale without rhyme or reason. If they looked like anything, it was the way Woodstock speaks in the *Peanuts* cartoon. It sure as hell wasn't music. And in among the thickets of vertical lines were letters of the alphabet, asterisks, and horizontal dashes.

It was going to be another code, I realized wearily. Another stupid secret message from John to himself that, when decoded, would probably reveal the secret location of another secret message, and so on to the goddamn crack of doom.

My whiskey arrived, and I studied the sheets as I drank, trying to figure out if there was any way they could be laid on top of one another or read from an odd angle to yield actual words. It didn't work: The letters that were present were all D's, T's, and K's, and they were sprinkled around the page seemingly at random. As far as I could tell, there was nothing there, which just meant that I was still missing too many jigsaw pieces to guess what the picture was.

Missing pieces. Yeah, there were a lot of those. The other death row souvenirs, for starters—the ones Chesney had swiped for himself after he heard about John's death and before I scared the shit out of him by calling him up.

An idea dropped into my head out of nowhere. I was reaching for my phone when I realized that I hadn't managed to recharge the goddamn battery. I delved into my pocket instead, fished out my remaining small change, and sifted it for silver. Enough for a local phone call, surely, and this was very local.

I crossed to the pay phones. It was stupidly late, but

hadn't Chesney's colleague Smeet said that they worked until ten o'clock? There was a good chance that Chesney would still be at the lab. Good enough to be worth a try.

I dialed Chesney's mobile number, the one from John's matchbook. He picked up on the third ring. "This is Vince," he said brightly. "What's up?"

"Funny you should ask," I said.

"Castor!" Not so bright suddenly. I seemed to have this effect on him every time we talked.

"Hi, Vince. Working late at the office?"

"Yes." He sounded surly and defensive. "So?"

"So I was wondering when it would be convenient for me to come over and collect the rest of John's stuff."

"What rest? I gave you all there is."

"Please, Vince." I did my best to sound world-weary and bored. "Don't make me read you a fucking itemized list. For one thing, leather bondage pants would be on it, and I don't want casual passersby to think I'm some sort of pervert. I'm assuming you kept the stuff you thought was going to bring the highest prices. I'm also assuming—because I like you and I'd hate to see pieces of you twisted or broken off—that you've still got them. Now, if both of those assumptions are correct, the next word you say should be 'yes.'"

A long pause, during which I had to feed the phone the last slender remnants of my small change. "Yes," Vince said finally, with flat, tired resignation.

"Good. Thank you. Here's another question for you." I tried to keep my tone casual, but this was the big inspiration that had come to me as I sipped my whiskey, and the real reason why I was calling Chesney now rather than the next morning. I phrased it as a bluff, because my instinct was to give him as little room to maneuver as possible. "Did you get anything useful out of the Myriam Kale piece?"

Silence from the other end of the line, which stretched. I waited as long as I could bring myself to, but in the end, I had to prompt him. "Well?"

"I'm just checking," Chesney snapped back sullenly. "I gave you the disk, remember? All I've got here are the backup files, and I didn't index them all that—Oh. Okay. Yeah, here it is. Just a fingerprint. The stain wasn't blood, it was lipstick or something. Carnauba wax, lanolin, petrolatum...yeah, it was lipstick. The print's pretty good, but her print's on record anyway. Why?"

I didn't answer him. The implications blinded and deafened me for a moment or two. Paydirt. It wasn't just the fact that we now had the Kale artifact we needed to do a summoning. It was the link: the proof of what had been looking more and more likely ever since Doug Hunter let slip the word "inscription" when we dropped in on him at Pentonville. John's dead killers and the born-again Myriam Kale. Not two things but one. It was hard to imagine what unlikely chain of skulduggery or coincidence could tie a bunch of East End hard men from the sixties and before to a dead American gangster's moll surfacing for a last bite of the cherry in a King's Cross hotel room, but some massive subterranean chain of cause and effect was there, had to be there, just out of my line of sight. I felt like I'd been strolling along the banks of Loch Ness and I'd glimpsed one coil of an unseen monster breaking the water in front of my startled eyes.

"Castor? You still there?" Chesney's voice brought me out of my trance. "I said, why did you want to know?"

I checked my watch. Okay, it was going to be a tight squeeze. Tighter than tight: I'd turn up at Juliet's late, and Sue Book would look at me with reproachful tears in her eyes and a burned casserole in her oven-gloved hands. Then Juliet would rip out my intestines for making Susan cry.

"Because I need it right now," I said. "Have it ready for me, okay? I'm at Victoria, so I should be with you inside of ten minutes."

"No!" he protested. "I'm not on my own here. Smeet's in the lab doing a dissection. This is a lousy time."

"Chesney, I don't care. I'm coming over."

"Fuck! Okay, I'll be waiting on the stairs. Outside the porno studio, yeah? On the first floor?"

"Fine. See you there."

I hung up and headed for the exit. Belatedly, I realized that I should have called Juliet, too, and told her I was going to be late. But I could do that on the return arc, and at least then I could tell her, with my hand on my heart, that I was on my way. And maybe the trophy I'd be bringing back with me would take the edge off her demonic strop.

I left the station and crossed the road, looking behind me by force of habit. No tails, and no sense of a tail—no premonitory prickling at the back of my neck or the back of my mind. If something dead had been sticking close to me over the past few days, it was gone now.

I turned into the small cul-de-sac where Nexus Veterinary Pathologists had set up their shingle. I could see from the other end of the street that their door was standing open, presumably because Vince had already come downstairs and left it ajar for me.

But hadn't he said that there was a security guard on

at night? The bare foyer beyond the door was brightly lit, and it seemed to be deserted.

I was a little wary as I approached the door and stepped inside. I'm prolific with threats, but I didn't want to get Vince disciplined or sacked if there was nothing to be gained by it.

The security post was empty, but the monitor behind the counter was switched on, showing a stretch of empty stairwell. Perhaps the guard was on his rounds.

Or perhaps not. As I came past the security post, heading for the stairs, I caught a glimpse of something dark behind the counter, close to the ground. It was a slicked mass of hair, the top of a man's head. I stopped and leaned over the counter, looking out and down.

The guard was lying on the floor, his back propped against the rear wall of his narrow domain. It was hard to see his face because his head was bowed forward onto his chest, but the sheer amount of blood dribbling down onto his torso and spreading across the floor around him suggested there might not be that much face left to see.

Still dribbling. Still spreading.

This had only just happened.

The urge to run away from danger is one of the hallmarks of sanity, and I like to think I'm as sane as the next man, although in London that's probably not saying very much. There were two reasons why I sprinted up the stairs rather than back out into the street. One was the conviction—maybe unreasonable—that whoever had done this was the same whoever who'd tried to drop me down a lift shaft; the other was that I wanted answers, and sticking my head into the lion's mouth seemed to be the only way I was going to get them.

The thought that Vince and Smeet might still be alive up there occurred to me as I hit the first landing, so I can't say it was part of the initial impetus that launched me. Maybe it kept me moving as I took the next flight, running toward the door of the vet's office, which was not only open but off its hinges.

I slowed on the threshold as a wave of stink hit me—hot, sharp animal pheromones, so pungent they thickened the air. A loup-garou: It had to be. Nothing natural smells like that. I reached inside my coat for my tin whistle, turning slowly as I advanced into the room to minimize the chances of an attack from behind. But whatever it was, this thing would probably be quick and ruthless. The guard downstairs had died at his post and seemed to have fallen where he stood, with no sign of struggle or flight.

There were plenty of signs of struggle up here, though. The lab had been trashed with spectacular thoroughness and violence, desks and cabinets upended and thrown around the room, splintered shelves sagging and bleeding books and files onto the floor. Broken glass crunched under my feet as I circled.

I saw Vince first. Or to be more correct, I saw his head staring blindly down at me from the coatstand onto which it had been embedded. A trickle of blood traced a thin straight line from the corner of his mouth to his chin, and his expression was one of mild consternation and puzzlement. The rest of his body was a good few feet away, under a ruptured radiator against which it had been thrown with casual violence.

A second after that, I caught sight of Smeet. She was crouched underneath the only desk that was still upright, and both of her hands, balled into fists, were pressed to her mouth. Her impossibly wide eyes were staring at me in uncomprehending shock. It took me a moment to understand that she was still alive.

"It's okay," I said inanely, going against all the evidence. Before I could think of anything stupider to add, the lights went out, plunging the room into absolute blackness.

There was a sound in the darkness a few feet away from me. A hiss? Yeah, let's call it a hiss. That probably makes you think of snakes, but this wasn't like a snake. It was the kind of hiss that a big carnivore—say, a tiger—makes involuntarily when it opens its jaws as wide as they'll go.

It wasn't a very comforting sound to hear right then.

～ Fourteen

THE GOSPEL ACCORDING TO Castor, Chapter 1, Verse 1: When in doubt, duck.

I threw myself forward into the debris, and something went over my head fast enough that I felt the wind of its passing.

I landed heavily on splintered wood and broken glass, cutting my hands as I threw them out to break my fall. There was a rending crash as my attacker made his own involuntary touchdown away to my right. Then I rolled, coming up on one knee to bring my whistle to my lips and blow a shrieking discord.

It was a place marker, really, nothing more than that. I didn't know this were-thing well enough yet to play a tailor-made tune for him. But loup-garous are more vulnerable than ghosts and demons in one respect, precisely because they're composites: human souls holding animal flesh in an immaterial full nelson. All you need to do to weaken them is to slide a crowbar between the human and the animal and start working it loose.

That is, assuming they'll sit still and let you.

The unseen thing I was fighting roared, basso profundo, and the floor shook, or maybe that was just me. There was a swirl of motion and a scrabbling, as of claws on polished wood.

I was planning to duck again, but I didn't get that far. Something very solid made contact with my left shoulder, knocking me sprawling and sending the whistle flying out of my hands into the dark.

I would have used my momentum to roll, getting some distance from the thing, but some overturned piece of furniture was right behind me. I hit it hard, went arse over tip, and came down headfirst on the far side of it. What with the odd angle and the force of the impact, I couldn't stop my head from hitting the floor hard. Lights danced behind my eyes, and I fought against unconsciousness with fierce desperation, because if I blacked out for even a second, this was over.

I groped in the blackness for a weapon, knowing that I wasn't going to find one that would work, knowing that I'd need luck, light, and backup to make a dent in this thing, and that none of them were likely to come my way.

But something came to hand: something rounded, with the texture of wood. The leg of a chair or a desk, maybe. Whatever it was, it was all I had, and it's a poor workman who picks a fight with his tools. I heard that scrabbling sound again, from right in front of me, as my unseen assailant scaled whatever it was I'd fallen over. I made myself wait for an agonizing second and then brought my makeshift club up with all the strength I had left, two-handed, with a silent prayer that the thing would be jumping down on me as the club came up. Its own speed and weight would give the blow a lot more heft than I could.

The shock jarred my arms right up to the shoulder. Something went crunch, and then the thing bellowed in agony even as its weight came down on me. I felt claws pierce my shoulder, and I yelled, too, kicking and rolling to try to get out from under it before it recovered from the pain and the shock.

No dice. I managed to lever my upper body a few inches up off the ground, but then the claws tightened, sending bolts of agony into my captive flesh, and hot stinking breath played over my face like a flameless blowtorch. I threw my head back, heedless of concussion, and the jaws clashed above me close enough for me to hear the sound. Something warm and wet showered over my face, but at least it wasn't bits of me.

Out of options, running on pure instinct, I rammed my stick into the place where that mouth had to be and was rewarded with another shuddering impact. No bellow of rage this time. It's hard to make primal screams with a five-pound toothpick lodged in your gullet. I kicked and flailed and pulled myself out from under, pulling myself off those clutching claws and trying not to think how much of my own precious skin I was leaving there.

It wouldn't stay down; I knew damn well it wouldn't. I'd hurt it, and I'd given it something to think about besides me, but this wasn't a fight I could win—not without my whistle and a fair bit more lead time than the couple of seconds I probably had.

My eyes were starting to adjust to the dark, at least a little, and I could see the crazy diagonal of the unhinged door up ahead of me. I half ran, half staggered toward it. At the very least, if this bastard followed me, I'd be leading him away from Smeet and giving her a fighting chance.

I made it out onto the landing, but my head was still reeling from the whack it had taken earlier, and I almost fell down the stairwell before I could skid to a halt and orient myself. Down or up? No contest. If I went up, I'd be cornered as soon as I ran out of stairs. At the bottom, there was the street and a slim but measurable chance of getting out of this.

What happened next was kind of a mixed blessing. The loup-garou came cannoning out of the door right behind me and hit me squarely in the back with its full weight, sending me tumbling down the stairwell. I got to where I wanted to go a whole lot faster. Unfortunately, it also meant that I reached the bottom in a sprawling heap, one arm twisted painfully under me. All breath had been slammed out of my lungs on the second or third bounce, so all I could do was lie there, sucking in air in a shuddering, drawn-out gasp.

By a happy chance, I fetched up on my back, looking the way I'd come, so I got to see the thing that was about to kill me in the light from the street outside. Despite its impressive size, the loup-garou padded down the stairs with an incongruous daintiness, slow at first but accelerating because the stairs were steep and built for two legs rather than four. It was sleek and black—or maybe some dark shade that looked black in the inadequate light—and it had the basic shape of a panther: more mass in the shoulders and forelegs than in the back, claws as long as the blades of Swiss army knives, and with a tendency to carry its weight close to the ground. The head was more eclectic, though: The mouth was too wide, and studded with too many different kinds of teeth, to be convincingly catlike. And the forehead was high, like a human forehead, like the dim memory of a human face stirring behind the bestial shape.

For a second, in the near-dark, it reminded me of a face I'd seen before.

When it got halfway down the flight of stairs, it launched itself into the air in a graceful, almost lazy leap that would land it right on top of me. Unable to muster enough strength to move, I tensed, balling my fists uselessly for a fight that wasn't going to happen. If the impact didn't kill me, those claws would, and either way, I wouldn't get to express an opinion about it.

But the loup-garou's leap ended prematurely as something came streaking in out of the night, jumped, and met it in midair.

The new something was a whole lot smaller. The loup-garou massed around four hundred pounds, and it had gravity on its side. Logically, it should have kept on going, the interloper smacking uselessly into it and being brought down by its superior weight and momentum.

Instead, the two of them seemed to hang impossibly in space, all that downward energy canceled out by some arcane counterforce; then they both crashed together through the delicate balcony rails and came to the ground in a spitting, snarling heap five yards away from me.

The newcomer was a man: long-limbed, lean, cadaverous, and dressed in a full-length coat that had looked momentarily like wings as he made his jump. The loup-garou's claws raked him, shredding his clothes and laying bare white flesh, red meat, but he paid them no heed. His own blows fell sledgehammer-hard, sledgehammer-heavy, so that I could hear the impact, and the were-thing spat and snarled as it struggled under him.

Yeah, I said *under* him. He'd managed to come down on top somehow, and he was taking full advantage of the position. A scything claw opened up his throat, but he still laughed, a liquid, musical gurgle, as blood fountained from the wound. His fists kept rising and falling like pistons, threshing the flesh of the loup-garou, smacking and splintering, breaking and entering.

Under that relentless rain, something grotesque and unexpected happened. The loup-garou started to fracture and fall apart, its flesh sagging and separating, its human form melting away. Its head rolled free from its shoulders, sprouted legs, and fled away, miraculously transformed into a huge black tomcat. Cats clawed their way free from its huge shoulders, its splayed legs, its broken back, and they scattered in all directions. Once again, I felt the shiver of déjà vu.

The skeletal man caught some of the cats as they ran, twisted them in his hands with malicious glee until they broke and bled. He held them over his head so that the blood rained down into his mouth. He was still laughing, his head tilted back in manic joy. Most of the cats got away, but half a dozen or so ended their lives in pieces in those slender-fingered, impossibly strong hands.

Suddenly, it was over. The man tossed the last dead animal to the ground, staring down at it with something like regret, and bared long brown teeth in a skull-like grimace.

It was the tramp—or rather, it was the man I'd met as a tramp outside Maynard Todd's office and then in a somewhat more respectable guise at the Mount Grace crematorium. He didn't look like a tramp now. His coat was shiny black leather, and his thin face was austere and patrician, dominated by a rudder nose and a fleshy, pouting mouth that made him look like an out-of-work Shakespearean actor. His clothes and his flesh hung in tatters here and there where the loup-garou's blows had landed, but he didn't seem to care very much.

"Fuck!" I exclaimed weakly.

He glanced around at me as though only then remembering that I was there. "We'll talk," he said, his voice the same dry, agonizing rasp I'd heard when I first encountered him—when he sang his crazy song about heaven and hell. "But not yet. Not until you know what I'm talking about. I don't like wasting my time."

"Wh-who—?" I slurred inarticulately, trying to sit up and not getting very far. A lance of white-hot pain went through my back from shoulder to coccyx, stopping me in my tracks. Shit, my spine could even be broken.

"A friend," the thin man said with a leering snigger that robbed the word of any warm connotations it might have had otherwise. "Because fate makes our friends, doesn't it, Castor? And I'm certainly your enemy's enemy." He walked across to me, looking down at me with a cold and clinical interest. "You've got some of it," he murmured. "You must have, because you're not a fool. And only a fool would refuse to see the obvious because it happens to be impossible. But you have to go to the source. Otherwise

they'll kill you before you're in a position to kill them."
He paused, frowning. "Sequence. Cadence. Rhythm," he
said. "Let's get this right. My name is Moloch, and you
may pass on my best wishes—with an ironic inflection—to
Baphomet's sister."

"To—"

"Your ally. The lady. We have ... history."

He stepped over me and back out into the dark, and I
was in no position to stop him.

In fact, it was all I could do to crawl to my feet—back
not broken after all, just agonizingly bruised—and limp out
of there before the sirens started to sound in the distance.
I cast a longing look back up the stairs to where the rest of
Chesney's notes and trinkets might still be lying, no doubt
with his own blood added to the patina of ancient violence
that made them so collectible. No good to me now, no good
at all, because even if they were still there—even if they
weren't what the loup-garou had been sent here to fetch,
and I was nearly sure they were—I couldn't afford to hang
around long enough to find them. Even with Gary Coldwood's grudging patronage, this was one crime scene I wasn't
going to be reading for the Met if I could possibly help it.

———————

Susan Book's doorbell played the first four bars of
"Jerusalem." For some reason that made me laugh, even
though laughing hurt right then.

Juliet opened the door and stood there staring at me in
silence, taking in all the details—the bruising on my face,
the split lip, and the blood on my shirt. She nodded slowly
as if acknowledging that I probably had a valid excuse.
All the same ...

"You're an hour and a half late, Castor," she said sternly.

"I know," I answered. "And I'm sorry. I got held up."

"At gunpoint?"

"At clawpoint. Can I come in before I fall down?"

She considered for a moment longer. "Yes," she said. "All right. But we ate without you."

She held the door open for me, and I lurched in out of the night. Susan Book bustled out of the kitchen wearing a Portmeirion apron—PASSION FLOWER, it said and showed—and opened her mouth to speak, but then she changed her mind and shut it again. She stared at me instead, blinking a few times as if to clear her vision.

"I'm really sorry, Sue," I said. "I hope I didn't spoil your evening. I was on my way here when something came up."

"Would you like a drink?" asked Juliet, who knew me pretty well. I nodded. "Then come on through into the living room," she said. She pronounced the phrase with careful emphasis, as though it were still a little alien to her. Some concepts were harder for her to get her head around than others.

"I think," Susan said hastily, "that we should probably take Felix into the bathroom first."

Juliet stared at her, momentarily puzzled. Susan pointed at the crusted blood on my shoulder, where the loup-garou's claws had pierced the cloth of my greatcoat and dug deeply into the flesh beneath.

"Oh," said Juliet. Wounds are something else she has to be reminded about, mainly because her own flesh (if that's what it is) flows like water to heal itself on the rare occasions when she sustains any damage. "Yes. Of course. Do we have any disinfectant and bandages?"

It turned out they had both, and Susan did a good job of cleaning my wounds, although she drew in her breath slightly when she first saw them, her eyes widening. Examining myself with queasy fascination in the bathroom mirror, I could understand her reaction. I looked as though some huge bird of prey had scrabbled at my right shoulder, trying to pick me up, and then—judging from the bruising all over my torso—had given up the effort and dropped me from a great height onto some rocks.

"You met one of the *were*," Juliet said. An observation, not a question.

"Yeah," I confirmed. "You remember Scrub?"

She frowned, consulting her memory. "The rat-man that worked for Lucasz Damjohn," she said with no obvious emotion, although she had hated Damjohn enough to linger over his death and add a number of artistic flourishes to it. "You killed him at Chelsea Harbour."

"I *spiked* him at Chelsea Harbour," I corrected her. "Hit him with a hard enough chord sequence to push him out of the flesh he was hiding in. But you know how it is with the were-kin. They're old souls, mostly, and they're tough as hell. Most of them are used to migrating to a new host when the old one dies." I winced as Susan applied TCP too enthusiastically to a tender area of torn flesh.

"Are you saying this was Scrub?" Juliet demanded.

I shrugged, then gritted my teeth because shrugging seemed to draw the disinfectant deeper into the wounds. "I don't know. For a second it kind of looked like Scrub. Then it looked like someone else. But Scrub was the only loup-garou I ever met who was a colony. I mean, he made his body out of rats, not out of *a* rat. And this thing I met tonight was made out of cats in the same way."

I had to suppress a physical tremor at the memory, half disgust and half fear. All at once an identity parade of cats filed before my inner eye: the stray that was hanging out at the Gittingses' house; the tom I almost trod on as I was walking home from the law offices in Stoke Newington; the feral moggy in Trafalgar Square when I was talking to Jan Hunter on the phone. I would have bet the farm there was a cat lurking under the left luggage lockers at Victoria, too—that it had heard my conversation with Chesney and somehow contrived to get there first. I'd sentenced Chesney to death by calling him.

Juliet raised an eyebrow, unconvinced. "If one were can make that transition—from monad to gestalt—then presumably others can, too."

"Presumably. Most of them—ow!—*don't*, though. It would help to know, because if it *is* Scrub, I can probably remember the tune I used to smack him down."

"I'm sorry if I'm hurting you," Susan said, looking up from her work. "But they're nasty, ragged wounds. It would be really easy for them to get infected."

I nodded. I'd been there, and I wasn't likely to forget. But at least my tetanus shots were up to date this time. "Go for it, Sue," I muttered, trying hard to dismiss the specter of Larry Tallowhill from my thoughts.

As Susan moved from cleaning the wounds to dressing them, I told them both about what had happened at Nexus. Susan was pale by the time I'd finished, but Juliet seemed moved in a different way.

"Moloch," she said. She spat, very precisely, onto the floor. Without a word, Susan Book took a piece of toilet tissue and wiped up the mess.

"Yeah. He told me he knew you. Asked me to pass on

his best wishes—with a broad hint that he didn't really mean it."

"He doesn't," said Juliet, her teeth showing in a genteel snarl. She usually managed to rein herself in around Susan, who frightened easily, but clearly, the mention of Moloch's name had touched Juliet at a level below the pretensions of civilization. "I left my mark on him once, a long time ago. But it goes further than that. His kind and mine—we were old enemies even before the great project."

"Before the what?"

Juliet seemed to remember herself. "Nothing," she said, a little too quickly. "I was remembering things that happened before you were born. Let's just say that his kin arc cats and mine are dogs. Or vice versa. Where the succubi and incubi settle and build their houses, the *shedim* can't live. He'd love to hurt me if he thought he could. But what is he doing on Reth Adoma?"

"You know," I groused, "if you keep doing this, I'm going to ask for a simultaneous translation. What is he doing *where*?"

"On earth. Among the living. There's nothing he can eat here. He'll starve if he stays too long."

"He looked like he was halfway there already," I agreed. "At least that's how he looked when I first met him a few days ago. Today he looked a fair bit sleeker. And he was strong enough to make this loup-garou run for cover."

Juliet frowned, her eyes slightly unfocused as she followed a train of thought she didn't bother to voice. To be honest, I didn't want her to. It was hard to think of hell as a place, and even harder to think of her walking there. It had a whiff of bad Bible stories and undigested metaphors.

"This is bigger than we thought," she said, looking at me again. "Something—something important, perhaps—is at stake here. Something has brought him up through the gates and made him stay long enough to weave a body for himself. I think—"

The pause lengthened.

"What?" I prompted. "What do you think?"

She shrugged dismissively. "Nothing. So you think Kale might have been involved somehow in John Gittings's death?"

"I don't know," I admitted. "Not directly, obviously. He killed himself. But the big case he was working on—the one he kept saying was going to get him into the history books—had something to do with dead killers. And now we know that Kale was on his list."

Juliet thought about this. "And the problem with Kale is that she isn't dead enough," she finished, voicing my own thoughts. "Are there any urban legends about the great East End gangsters coming back from the grave?"

"None that I've heard. Maybe it's a foreign-exchange kind of thing. Kale does London and the Krays do Chicago."

Juliet nodded. "It's possible," she mused. "But it goes against everything we know about the dead. And it raises far more questions than it answers."

"I meant it as a joke," I said.

"Then you should have smiled."

"I've finished," Susan said, standing up and inspecting her handiwork with profound and obvious misgivings. "But you should probably go to a hospital as soon as you can, Felix, and let a doctor take a look at you."

"I will," I lied. "Thanks, Sue. You're an angel of mercy." Living with a sex demon, I added in my mind. Life throws you some funny curves.

"I saved you some ratatouille," Susan said, embarrassed. "You can eat it on a tray, if you like."

Downstairs in the living room, I ate and drank and began to feel less like a piece of windblown trash. The room had changed a lot since I'd been there last. Then it had still been full of Susan's late mother's ornaments and antimacassars and framed samplers like a mock-up of a room in a museum of Victoriana. Now it was kind of minimalist, with red Chinese calligraphy hung on white-painted walls. I knew enough about Juliet's tastes to recognize them here, and I wondered how Susan felt about the changed ambience. She seemed comfortable enough.

"So how's work?" I asked her. "Juliet said you're kind of snowed under." She'd been the verger at a church in West London when she'd met Juliet, but she'd bailed out when they started living together and gone back to her old career as a librarian. It was a principled decision based more on the fact that she was in a same-sex relationship than on her shacking up with a demon. The modern Anglican church regards hell as a state of mind and doesn't officially believe in demons (unlike the Catholics, who hunt them with papally blessed flamethrowers), but it still has problems with church officers who are openly gay. As an atheist with issues, I have to say I love that shit.

Susan smiled, genuinely pleased to be asked. "No, I'm fine, really," she said. "I'm enjoying it. It's a little hard sometimes, because I'm trying to do a lot of ambitious things on no money. But it's lovely to be working with children. They're so open-minded and spontaneous. And you'd be amazed how many children's authors will do readings for the fun of it. We had Antony Johnston in last week. He wrote the graphic-novel version of *Stormbreaker*. And he was wonderful. Very funny and very... whatever the opposite of precious is. Very matter-of-fact about what he does. We got the biggest audience we've ever had."

"*Stormbreaker* being?" I prompted, feeling a little lost.

"It's one of the best-selling children's books of the last decade, Felix," Susan chided me schoolmarmishly.

"Oh, *that Stormbreaker*," I bluffed.

"They made a movie of it."

"Not a patch on the book."

"You don't need to work," Juliet said to Susan, putting a broom handle through the spokes of my small talk.

There was an awkward pause.

"I like to work, Jules," Susan said.

Juliet met that statement with a cold deadpan. "Why?"

Susan didn't seem very happy with the question. Generally, anything that looked like an argument looming in the distance made her run for cover, but this time she stood her ground. "Because it's part of who I am. If I just made your meals and cleaned house for you and warmed your bed, then—well, I'd be a very boring person. And then you'd want to see other people, and then you'd leave me. And then I'd kill myself."

Juliet considered. "Yes," she said at last. "I can see the logic. I've never been romantically infatuated with anyone before, so it's difficult right now to see how my feelings for you could change. But there's plenty of evidence from human relationships, so you're probably right. Go on."

But Susan couldn't. She forgot what she'd been saying, tried to start again, floundered into silence. For the first time in many, many months, I felt sorry enough for her to forget how much I envied her. I changed the subject by main force, swiveling it back around in the direction of shoptalk, and ended up regaling both of them with some of my favorite ghost stories. Most had happened to other people, not me, but I stretched the truth to pretty good effect. The moment passed. The tears that I'd seen in Sue Book's eyes never actually fell.

"Moloch said I should go to the source," I told Juliet when I was a fair way into my fourth glass of Glen acetone.

"Did he?" Juliet's tone sounded hard and cold. But when Susan topped up her glass, she reached out to touch her hand for a moment: a very delicate touch, expressing both affection and something a little more proprietorial. After what had passed between them earlier, it was a healing touch—or something close. "And did he say what he meant by that?"

I shook my head. "No," I admitted. "He didn't. But I've got some ideas of my own. Have you got anything tomorrow afternoon?"

"No. Why?"

"There's something happening in the morning over in Muswell Hill—something I want to be around for. But I'm free after that, and I was wondering how you'd feel about leaning on some people while I ask them a whole bunch of leading questions."

"Which people?"

"I'll know when I see them," I said evasively.

Juliet rolled her eyes. "Where?" she demanded. "Where do they live?"

I swirled the brandy in my glass, studiously avoiding her eyes. "Alabama," I said.

~ Fifteen

IT MAY DENT my image of macho, gung ho capability to say this, but the next morning I felt rough. I'd stayed at Juliet's long enough to work out the logistics of where we were going to go and who we were going to see, and then I'd made some calls before she could change her mind: one to a travel agent to book a couple of cheap tickets to Birmingham, Alabama, and another to Nicky to tell him what was up and ask if he could work out an itinerary for us. He said he wanted to talk to me before I left, but that was all he'd say.

A third call, to Gary Coldwood, got me his answering machine. "What does something juicy mean?" I asked it, and hung up.

I had one last errand to run before I could limp off home, and I'd managed to get it done with the minimum of fuss even though it involved a certain amount of blackmail—both the emotional kind and the kind that's a felony.

When the alarm woke me at seven, I felt like my brain had been melted, decanted through a pipette, and left to stand in the petri dish of my skull until it congealed again. The only thing that could possibly have gotten me out of bed was the thought of what was going down at the Stanger this morning—and the knowledge that I had to be there to make sure it went down my way rather than Jenna-Jane's.

The Charles Stanger Care Home in Muswell Hill was never designed for its current usage. It was originally a set of Victorian workmen's cottages before it was converted to a residential and holding facility for the violently disturbed after the former owner—the eponymous Charles Stanger, an enthusiastic psychopath in his own right—bequeathed them to the crown. The interiors were gutted and replaced with ugly, functional cells, and a much larger annex was built on as demand grew. It seems that lunatics, like ghosts, are one of the growth industries of the early-twenty-first century.

But Rafael Ditko isn't a lunatic; he is just someone for whom the criminal justice and psychiatric care systems have no other label that fit. After all, he does hear a little voice inside his head, telling him what to do: the voice of the demon Asmodeus, who took up residence about four years ago and—thanks largely to me—has never gone home again.

It was almost eight when I got to the Stanger, which I hoped would still put me ahead of Jenna-Jane's agenda. I nodded to the nurse at the reception desk, relieved to see that it was Lily. She'd known both me and Webb long enough to have no illusions about the score, and she nodded me through without asking me to sign the visitors' book.

One of the male nurses, Paul, who knew I was coming (another late-night call) was waiting for me outside Rafi's cell. I gestured a question at him, thumb up and then down.

He shrugged massively. "He's quiet," he said. "Kind of. Had a rowdy night, and I guess he's resting now. Still wide awake, though." He was unlocking the door as he spoke, but he paused with his hand on the handle to look me full in the eye. "You're not gonna like what they've done to him," he warned me. "Try to keep your cool, okay?"

"Okay."

He swung the door open, and I stepped in, announcing my arrival with an echoing clang because the floor inside Rafi's cell is bare metal: steel, mostly, but with a lot of silver in the mix, too. I know because I paid for it to be installed—cost a small fortune, but worth it because for at least some of the time, it keeps Rafi's passenger from getting too frisky.

Friskiness didn't seem to be an issue right now. In preparation for transit, Webb had Rafi trussed up tighter than a Christmas turkey.

They'd built—or perhaps Jenna-Jane had supplied—a massive steel frame, about seven feet high by four feet wide, standing on three sets of wheels like a mobile dress rack. The resemblance didn't end there, either: Rafi was hanging inside this construction in an all-over-body straitjacket fitted with a dozen or more steel hoops to which lengths of elasticated cable had been attached. Like a spider trussed in his own web, he dangled at the center of the frame on a slight diagonal, his face the only part of him that was visible. I would have expected that face to be livid with demonic rage, but it was a near-perfect blank, the eyes—all pupil, no white—staring at me and through me.

"OPG?" I asked Paul.

"Yeah."

"Inhaled or injected?"

"Both."

"Bastards." I could smell the stuff in the air, although it was the propellants rather than the gas itself that I was smelling. OPG itself is too volatile to linger for longer than a couple of seconds after it's been used. It was produced as a weapon—a nerve toxin derived from the less potent Tabun—but was banned for military use decades ago. You could still use it on the mentally ill, though, because of a sweet little legal loophole. In tiny, almost homeopathic amounts, it had been proved to slow the onset of Alzheimer's and to have a sedative effect on manic patients. I was willing to bet that the amounts we were talking about were more in the bulk-haulage range.

"I'm gonna leave you to it," Paul said. "And if anyone asks, I'm gonna lie and say I never saw you. Sorry, Castor. Bastards they are, but for now I still work here. We're meant to be wheeling him out to the front in a few minutes, so you'd best keep it short." He stepped out and pulled the door almost shut behind him.

"Hey, Castor," said Rafi, his voice crystal-clear despite the zoned-out stare.

"Hey, Rafi," I answered, giving him the benefit of the doubt until I could be sure. I came in a little closer, but not too close. I wasn't sure how much give there was in those elastic straps. "Asmodeus in there, too?"

"Yeah, he's here. He's not happy with you."

"I bet. Can I have a word?"

There was a long silence. I waited it out, knowing from past experience that there was no way of rushing this. Asmodeus rose or fell under his own steam and at his own pace, and the massive OPG hit, whimsically cross-connecting the circuitry of Rafi's nervous system, wouldn't help much, either. But slow ripples began to pass across Rafi's face, each one leaving it subtly altered. The effect was slow enough that you could convince yourself it was an optical illusion, but it didn't much matter how you rationalized it. After half a minute or so, the fact was, you were looking at a different face.

The new face, wearing Rafi's features like a savagely ironic quote, stared at me with a sour grimace twisting one corner of its mouth.

"Can't hear the cavalry," Asmodeus said, sounding like he was crunching down on a mouthful of ground glass.

"They're coming," I answered with more confidence than I felt. "In the meantime, I was going to ask a favor."

"I love doing you favors, Castor. Come in a little closer. Kiss me on the lips."

"I want you to burrow down as deep as you can. Go all the way to sleep if you can. I'll play for you: Listen to the music instead of trying to avoid it. Let it work through you, and use it to get as much distance from Rafi as you can."

Asmodeus smiled politely. "And why should I do this thing?"

"Because someone who looks like one of my species but acts like one of yours is coming to get you. And she'll pick you to pieces with tweezers, and she'll mount you on slides, and she'll label all the pieces of you. You know this is true."

There was silence except for the punctured-tire hissing of Asmodeus's breath. "The bitch," he said at last, without heat. "The bitch with the fishing rod and the big ambitions. When she hits the wall, it will make a very sweet sound."

"Maybe," I allowed. "Maybe not. She's a crafty player, Asmodeus, and too fucking big for you right now."

"And for you, Castor."

"Goes without saying." Knowing what Asmodeus was, I felt seriously uncomfortable with all of this—almost, as if the phrase had any meaning at all, like a species traitor. I was discussing tactics with a demon, trying to keep him out of the hands of the closest thing the human race had to a predator of demons. This was what Jenna-Jane Mulbridge had brought me to, and at that moment I hated her for it.

"The people outside need to see Rafi," I said, taking my whistle—it was the first alternate, and I hadn't properly worn it in yet—out of my pocket. "They don't need to see you. If they see you, they'll think she's right. You understand?"

"Humans can't think, Castor. They can only think that they think."

"Point stands. Maybe I'll see you later, but I sure as fuck don't want to see you now. And I've said all I'm going to say."

I stopped talking and played. It started out as a recognizable tune but then became a crazy medley, fast at first but decelerando, working down through the scale with a certain doleful urgency. Asmodeus bobbed his head in time with the beat, ironically showing me that he was keeping up. He sang improvised words in a guttural language that the human voice box was never shaped for, and I hoped I'd never meet anyone who could provide me with a translation.

But his eyes were closing, and his voice was faltering. His head dropped out of sync with the music, then slowed and stopped. When the door finally swung open behind me, he was still.

"Got to move the patient," Paul said brusquely.

I turned around, tucking the whistle back in my coat. Paul wasn't alone; a Welsh guy named Kenneth and a third Stanger staffer whom I didn't recognize stood shoulder to shoulder with him on either side, while farther back I could see Dr. Webb, the Stanger's director, directing proceedings along with a bald, austere stick figure of a man in a dark gray suit. Paul's face was impassive; he barely even looked at me. Webb, on the other hand, was dismayed and outraged to see me there ahead of him.

"Castor!" he exclaimed, spitting out my name in much the same way a cat spits up a hairball. "Who let Castor in here? He's trespassing! Move him aside!"

"Sorry," I said, stepping determinedly into the path of the little party as they came forward. "Got to move the patient where, exactly? Who says? What are you talking about? I'm the patient's next of kin, so why don't I know about this?"

"You're not his next of kin!" Webb snarled. He snapped his fingers under Kenneth's nose and pointed at me imperiously. While the stick man was still talking at me, Kenneth put a hand on my chest and pushed me firmly to one side, allowing Paul and the other male nurse to walk past me and take either end of the metal frame.

They maneuvered it so that they could wheel it end-on through the door, but I wasn't done yet. I ducked under Kenneth's hand, crossed to the door, and slammed it shut. The mortise lock clicked home, which meant that Paul would have to leave off what he was doing, get his keys out, and open it again. And that meant he had to come through me.

Webb bought me another few seconds, obligingly. Turning three shades south of purple, he stalked toward me, then stood in front of me with his clenched fists hovering an inch from my face, paralyzed by an approach-avoidance conflict so painfully visible that I couldn't look away. He wanted to hit me; he knew there were witnesses. But he wanted to hit me—but then there were those darn witnesses...

"I'm sorry," I said to the room at large, "but I'm performing a citizen's arrest."

Kenneth looked pained as he advanced on me again, having to step around the good doctor. "You're performing a what, my lovely?" he demanded.

"A citizen's arrest. I'm arresting all five of you for the attempted abduction of a mentally ill person against his—" Kenneth clamped a massive hand on my lapel. I swatted his hand vigorously away. He came back with both hands, and although I parried again, he managed to get a better grip this time and keep his purchase.

He outweighed me by a good fifty pounds. I could have taken him, but only by playing dirty, and getting myself banged up for assault at this stage of the game wasn't a risk I could take. I let him pull me aside and pin me into a corner of the cell while Paul got the door open and he and his colleague manhandled the massive steel frame through it, hindered rather than helped by Webb's unnecessary instructions and ubiquitous presence. "To the right, Paul. No, to the left—"

"Mind your feet, Dr. Webb," Paul rumbled, and then there was an agonized yelp from Webb that did my heart good. But they were out in the corridor and picking up speed. My delaying tactics had foundered.

"Okay, boyo, you just stay put," Kenneth growled, wagging his finger sternly in my face. But as he turned to follow the others, I shouldered past him and got to the door first.

We trotted along the corridor in a strange and unwieldy procession. Paul and the other nurse pushing the frame along after Dr. Webb, the ugliest drum majorette in history, flanked on one side by Jenna-Jane's tame lawyer and on the other by me, with Kenneth bringing up the rear.

When we got to the reception area, they faltered to a stop, staring out through the double doors onto the small apron of the Stanger's front drive. In theory, I knew, there should have been a van waiting there, its back doors open and a ramp in place, with a happy crew of psychiatric interns and burly removal men all ready to take Rafi aboard and whisk him away to his new life in Paddington.

The van wasn't there, though. Presumably, it was still out on the road, or stranded at the Stanger's gates. Meanwhile, the drive had been colonized by three or four hundred young men and women who were singing "You can't kill the spirit" with as much wild energy as if they knew what they were talking about. They were mostly in casual dress, but black T-shirts dominated, and on a lot of them, I could pick out the slogan DEATH IS NOT THE END.

"Holy fuck," Paul muttered under his breath.

"What?" Webb demanded, words seeming to fail him for a moment. "Who are all these people?"

"Mostly the local chapter of the Breath of Life movement," I told him helpfully, relieved that they'd all made it on time. "I met some of them a couple of days ago. Really nice guys once we got past the small talk and the mutual fear and loathing. They were fascinated when I told them what you and J-J were up to." I didn't mention the frightener I'd had to put on Stephen Bass—threatening to tell his tutors and the police about his hobbies of vandalism, stalking, and criminal damage—before I could get him to agree to this. That seemed to fall under the heading of a trade secret. "Oh, and I think those guys over there," I went on, "are from a national TV network. You see the letters on the side of the camera? They stand for Beaten, Butt-fucked, and Clueless, and they're talking to you."

Webb shot me a look of horrified disbelief and opened his mouth to speak. But his words were lost to posterity, because at that moment the double doors of the Stanger swished open and Pen strode across the threshold, bang on cue.

"Where's my husband?" she demanded, projecting beautifully for the cameras and standing dead center between the doors so they slid impotently back and forth on their tracks, unable to close on her. "What have you done with my husband, you bastards? I want him back!"

Webb blinked, his jaw dropping. He turned to face Pen, at bay, and took a step toward her, but then he stopped as flashbulbs popped out on the drive—one, two, then a whole cluster all at once. The paparazzi were moving into position on either side of the doors so that they could enfilade anyone coming out from a variety of photogenic angles.

"Miss Bruckner!" Webb struggled with the polite

form of words, forcing them out through clenched teeth. "I don't know what you're talking about. You and Ditko aren't married. You don't even—"

"He's my common-law husband!" Pen shouted. "We're married in the sight of God! And I'm not letting you put him in a concentration camp!"

Webb was struggling to make any sound at all, his complexion getting darker and more alarming by the second. "The—the MOU in Padddington is not a—a—"

"Oh, look what they've done to him!" Pen wailed, pointing at the frame and Rafi's glum, limp form hanging in the center of it. "He's not a criminal! He's not a monster! Why are they torturing him?"

"Rights for the dead and the undead!" Stephen Bass bellowed from the front ranks of the Breathers. "Soul and flesh are friends! Soul and flesh will mend! Death is not the end!" The chant was taken up by his undisciplined but enthusiastic cohorts. It didn't mean a damn thing, as far as I was aware, but it sounded great.

"Your move," I murmured to Webb in a lull between the twenty-first and twenty-second repetitions. "My advice would be to—"

"I do not," Webb gurgled, swallowing hard several times, "want your advice, Castor. And this—this will not make a difference."

"Well, that's not strictly true," I demurred with a mild shrug. I caught Paul's eye, and he winked solemnly at me over Webb's shoulder. "I think it's going to make a difference of at least—let's say—four or five days. Maybe a week. Depends how cold it gets at night and how much staying power these kids have. They're young and idealistic, so I'd be surprised if they didn't make it at least up to the weekend. After that, I'll have to think of some other way to make your life a misery."

I walked away from him before he could answer. I passed Pen in the doorway. "You can take it from here?" I murmured. "Keep things percolating? Make sure they don't get Rafi out the door?"

"Trust me," Pen snarled back. There was a dangerous gleam in her eye as she stared at the restraint frame. She wasn't faking it. She was really angry.

"Play it cool, though," I cautioned her, a little worried. "You've already got one assault charge pending. Be the victim and let Webb be the monster."

"I'll be fine," Pen told me a little curtly. "Where are *you* going, anyway?"

"The United States. Alabama."

"Looking for a change of scene?"

"I'm looking for a dead woman."

"Get Jenna-Jane Mulbridge to come down here. I'll make you one."

I put a hand on her shoulder and squeezed, but only for a moment. I didn't want to lose it.

I was hoping the crowd might part for me, but I'm no man's Moses. I picked my way through the massed ranks of the Breathers, trying not to tread on any fingers or toes, trying not to meet anyone's eyes. They were in a volatile mood, bless their rabid little hearts.

———————

The flight I'd booked was going out of Heathrow at a few minutes past noon. I checked in with hand luggage at a little after ten and went to wait for Juliet in the grotesquely named Tap & Spile bar.

She was already there, waiting for me. So was Nicky, dressed in black from head to foot and wearing shades indoors like some vampire wannabe. He gave me a sardonic wave. He had a full glass of red wine in front of him, and Juliet had an empty one. She also had a UK passport in her hands. That was a relief. Nicky hadn't been sure he could cobble something together at such short notice and have it pass muster.

"Another?" I asked Juliet, pointing at her empty glass.

She shook her head. "It reminds me of blood," she said.

"Is that a bad thing?"

"I'm about to spend ten hours in a confined space with three hundred people, Castor. You tell me."

I let that one go and went to the bar, where I ordered a whiskey and water for myself. I took it over to the table and sat down between them.

Nicky nodded at a folded sheet of paper sitting on the table. "Names and addresses," he said. "Juliet's got one, too, in case you get separated."

I unfolded the sheet. "Fair enough. Who's on here?"

He waved vaguely. "Anyone I could find who might remember Myriam Kale or have anything interesting to say about her," he said. "I've given you the address of the Seaforth farm—where she lived until she got married—but there's no phone number I can find, so my guess is nobody's living there now. There's a maternal uncle—Billy Myers. You've got his last address. And I called through to the local paper, the *Brokenshire Picayune*."

"The what?" I winced at my first taste of the lousy blended Scotch.

"*Picayune*. Means trivial or everyday. Great name for a newspaper, huh? 'It doesn't matter a tinker's fuck, but you read it here first.' Anyway, the editor's a guy named Gale Mallisham. I told him you were digging for information about Kale and might have some to trade."

"And he said?"

"'Fuck. Another one? Why won't anyone let her lie in her fucking grave?'"

"Thanks for priming the pump there, Nicky."

"Don't mention it." He put his wineglass underneath his nose and inhaled deeply, eyes closed. Since he died, that's been Nicky's most sensual pleasure. I let him spin it out as long as he wanted to. Juliet was following all this with a detached, almost bored look, but I knew she was taking everything in. You don't get to be as old as she is by letting your attention wander.

When Nicky put the glass down, I shot him an expectant look. By way of answer he sat back in his chair and made himself comfortable.

"The stuff in the box," I prompted.

"Sure." He was still in no hurry. "I notice Johnny boy's gopher is dead."

"Meaning Vince Chesney?" I frowned. "Yeah, he is. How'd you know?"

Nicky looked smug. "Two and two, Castor," he said. "The baggies that Gittings's souvenirs were packed in had a name label printed on them—some animal pathology outfit called Nexus. And this morning Nexus was all over the news on account of having lost one of its employees last night in an inexplicable bloodbath at their premises in Victoria. Some security guard got to join the choir invisible, too. No witnesses, no leads, at least when I hacked the Police National Computer at four a.m. Juliet tells me you were there."

"Yeah. I was there." I glanced at Juliet, who shrugged. I hadn't told her it was a big secret, but I'd still have liked the right of veto on telling Nicky about it.

"It was a loup-garou, right?"

"Right. Nicky, have you got something for me or not? Because twenty questions was never my game."

He gave me a languid grin, stubbornly determined not to pick up the pace. "I know your game, Castor. It's blind man's buff." I opened my mouth to curse him out, and he raised a hand, forestalling me. "Okay, don't start on me. I'm just in an expansive mood, that's all. I like days when I throw out the questions and the answers bounce right back."

"So you're saying . . . ?"

"I went through the stuff on the disk and cross-checked it myself in a couple of places. It was mostly bullshit— your man measured everything he could touch a ruler to, whether it mattered or not—but if you want a smoking pistol, then I think you got one."

"Go on." I could tell by his lingering smile that he had a bombshell to drop, or he thought he did. He reached into his pocket and handed me one of the evidence bags. I remembered the object inside the bag pretty well, because it stood out from the mostly innocuous stuff in Chesney's treasure chest like a dildo in a nun's bootlocker.

"The bullet," I said, resigning myself to the role of straight man.

"Bullet *casing*, actually. It's from a ten-millimeter auto round, and according to your now deceased doggy pathologist, it was fired out of a Smith and Wesson 1076. Got a lovely clear print on it, too—Les Lathwell's. You know, the East End gangster? The one they called the Krays' heir apparent?"

"To be honest," I said, "I'm a little hazy on social history. I know the name, but—"

"Kind of an entrepreneur in the violence and intimidation line. He went to America to learn from the greats. Came home and built his own little mafia on the Mile End Road. You should read about this stuff; it's inspirational. Anyway, I went online and did some rooting around—that's why I hacked the PNC—and the print checks out A-one at Lloyd's. I'm no expert, but I think the ballistics do, too. And that's where things get interesting."

"Oh? Why's that?"

"Lathwell died in 1979. The ten-millimeter round didn't even get introduced until 1983, in a Swedish hand pistol that kicked like an unlimbered cannon and broke people's arms if they weren't expecting it. It didn't get popular—and I use that word in heavy quotes—until the FBI picked it up in eighty-eight. In other words, Lathwell couldn't have fired that round, or loaded it into a gun, because he died before the gun ever came off the assembly line. So there's your Rod Serling moment. Enjoy."

He indulged in another deep snort of the wine breath, drawing it out for maximum dramatic impact. He got the timing just about right, because I was struggling to fit that spiky fact into what I already knew—which was possible only because I knew jack shit. Looked at from one angle, though, it made a queasy kind of sense.

"You think Lathwell rose in the flesh, then?" Juliet asked, voicing my thoughts. "As a zombie?"

Nicky put down his glass, basking in our undivided attention. "Could be. Or maybe someone flayed his fingertips and wore them for a joke. There are a couple of other tidbits like that in the notes on the disk. Anachronisms, I mean. My favorite is a letter from Tony Lambrianou to his brother, Chris. You know the hearse that carried Lambrianou's body had a message from Chris, in the middle of a wreath the size of Canary Wharf? It said, 'See you on the other side.' Well, this letter is dated about six months later, and it's exactly three words long: 'I made it.' Sick joke or mystical revelation. You decide."

He leaned forward, more animated. "Okay, that's what's on the disk, so that's what your dead pal Chesney told your dead pal Johnny G. But I'll give you something else for free, and this is part of the Nicky Heath service. You get this because I'm obsessive and because I'm dead—in other words, because I'm a stubborn bastard who doesn't need to sleep ever, if he's got something on his mind. Look at this—and look at this."

I was expecting him to give me some more of the evidence bags, but instead, he held out two badly photocopied fingerprint charts—copies of copies of copies. I scanned them as carefully as I could, trying to compare them through the smudges and smears.

Juliet looked over my shoulder. Her pattern recognition skills were evidently a lot faster than mine. "They're the same," she said. "Or almost the same. The differences are very few and very small. Is that the point?"

"Yeah, that's the point. But here's the kicker. The one on the right is Les Lathwell again. The one on the left, which is different by about three ridges and one friction artifact, is Aaron Silver, who was the great-granddad of all East End psychopaths. There's about eighty years between them, and they're meant to be two different guys. Only they're not. They're the same guy twice."

I gave a long, low whistle. Nicky was right. This was

a smoking pistol in anyone's book. In fact, it was a whole roomful of smoking machine guns. Something that John had said when I met him in that bad dream came back into my mind.

Who wants to get you?

The same ones as before. Always the same ones, again and again and again.

"They're coming back," I summarized. "All the East End bad boys. All the biggest bastards."

"But how are they coming back?" Juliet demanded, dragging me back to the incontrovertible facts and rubbing my nose in them. "Ghosts can possess animals, but they pay the price. They lose their own humanity a little at a time—become more like the flesh they inhabit. In the long term, the human consciousness becomes completely submerged in the animal, diluted to the point where it's really not there anymore. As for the revenants—the zombies—their bodies seldom last longer than a year, two at most. And the loss of function is progressive. Inevitable. When they begin to fall apart, there's nothing that can keep them together."

The silence after she finished speaking was somewhat tense. She looked at Nicky, saw him staring at her with a grim deadpan. "I'm sorry if that was tactless," she added. "I'm talking in general terms."

"Sure," said Nicky tightly. "I appreciate that. Present company excepted, right?"

Juliet raised an exquisite eyebrow. "No, obviously you're subject to the same—"

"Shut the fuck up. Please." Nicky's voice was an intense snarl; he'd drawn in a large breath beforehand for exactly that purpose. "I'm giving you information here, not asking for a prognosis. You just—Don't talk, okay? Don't talk about things you know fuckall about."

The tough-guy tone rang hollow. The two subjects with which Juliet was intimately familiar were sex and death: their declensions, and conjugations, and the inflexible metaphysics that governed them. Tactfully, though, she made no reply.

I tried to pull the conversation back to less controversial topics. "They've still got their own fingerprints," I said, answering Juliet's question. "So somehow it's got to be their own flesh. If Les Lathwell was Aaron Silver, that means he was born well before the end of the nineteenth century. Died—"

"Nineteen oh eight," Nicky supplied sullenly.

"Nineteen oh eight. So if he was still leaving fingerprints in the sixties and seventies, his body would have been spectacularly well embalmed."

Juliet shook her head. "It doesn't work, in any case," she pointed out. "This other man—Les Lathwell—he had friends? Family?"

"Two brothers, both dead," said Nicky. "A sister who's still alive."

"And there's documentary evidence of his growing up?"

Nicky nodded slowly, seeing where she was going. "Sure. Lots of it. School photos. Home movies. All that kind of shit."

"Then how—and when—did Aaron Silver insinuate himself into Lathwell's place?"

It was a more than reasonable question. Something was niggling at me, something that felt as though it might be part of the answer, but I couldn't tease it out into the light.

"Not plastic surgery," Nicky said. "They could do it now, fingerprints and all, but in the sixties the technology wasn't that advanced. Except on *Mission Impossible*. You know, that guy with all the masks."

"Flesh is plastic enough, in any case," Juliet said, and I almost had it.

But then Nicky spoke again, and I lost whatever connection my subconscious was trying to make. "I haven't managed to find any Myriam Kale memorabilia," he said. "Turns out East End gangsters are easy compared to sexy American assassins for hire. A few things came up, but they all smelled like scams. I'm still looking. But since you're going to where she lived, maybe you'll pick something up along the way. In which case, throw it to me when you're through with it, and I'll find it a new home."

So Chesney's Kale piece had come from some other source. I decided not to mention that. Nicky was touchy enough already without being told that someone else had outscored him. "I'll do that, Nicky," I said, blandly. "In the meantime, could you check something else out for me?"

"I'm always at your disposal, since, obviously, I don't have a fucking life," Nicky observed dryly, flicking a cold glance at Juliet.

"Can you find out where all these guys are buried?"

"Yeah, sure. That's easy. Why, you want to put some flowers on their graves?"

"I want to find out if there's any connection here to John Gittings's list of London cemeteries. If there's a pattern—if they all ended up in the same place—"

"Yeah, I get it, Castor. The thing about the flowers? Joke. Is your mobile triband?"

"I don't have the faintest idea. But the battery's flat, in any case."

"Fine." Nicky gave it up, getting to his feet and shoving away the untouched wine with a disgruntled air. "So you get yourself a stack of dimes and call me. I know you don't travel much, so I probably ought to make it clear that dimes are what Americans use for currency. Have a nice flight, the both of you. I'll see you when I see you." He was about to walk away but then turned and held out his hand, palm up. I almost shook it, misinterpreting the gesture, but he clicked his tongue impatiently. "The bullet casing. You go through the metal detector with that in your pocket, there could be all kinds of humorous misunderstandings."

I gave it back to him. "Thanks for everything, Nicky."

"You're more than welcome." There was something in his tone, in his face, that I couldn't read. "You want to pay me back, then keep me in the loop. I want to see how this comes out. By the way, someone else knows you're coming." He threw that out with carefully measured casualness, playing for the double take.

"What? What do you mean, Nicky?"

"When I got your names off the airport data system, there was a nice little trip wire set up there. I saw it because I was coming in on a machine code level."

"A trip wire?"

"Yeah. Like, a relay. So if your name comes up on any flight, someone gets told."

"My name? Or Juliet's?"

"Just yours, Castor. Anyone wants to know a demon's whereabouts, they only have to stick their nose into the wind."

He walked away without waiting for an answer. "I hurt his feelings?" Juliet asked. She wasn't contrite; she was asking for the sake of information. Something to add to her database of human foibles.

"You shoved his face in his own mortality," I said. "Nobody likes that much."

"He's already dead."

"Doesn't make it any easier to live with."

A few moments later, the tannoy told us that our flight was ready to board at gate 17. I just about had time to finish my whiskey. When we left, Nicky's wine remained on the table behind us, untouched.

In the departure lounge, Juliet stood at the window and watched the planes taking off. She seemed fascinated, and it made her oblivious to the covetous stares she was collecting from the male passengers sitting around her. I hadn't thought about it much, but this was her first flight.

Joining her at the window, I told her about some of the side effects she could expect to encounter. She wasn't troubled about the changes in pressure and what they might do to her ears. "I'll adjust" was all she said. She seemed to be looking forward to the experience.

We boarded at the tail end of the line because Juliet preferred not to join the crush until the last moment. Our seats were forward of the toilets at the very back of the cabin, in what once would have been the smoking seats. Explaining the concept of smoking seats to Juliet took us all the way through the safety lecture. She was amused at the fences and barricades that humans had built around their pleasures, but then she was amused at the whole notion of deferred gratification. Demons, she said, tended to work more in terms of reaching out and grabbing.

Well, anytime you feel the urge, I gallantly didn't say.

She took an almost childlike interest in the takeoff, swapping seats with me so she could look out the window, and remaining thoroughly engrossed right up until we were in the air.

But after that her mood changed. She seemed to withdraw into herself somehow, her expression becoming cold and remote. I checked out the in-flight movies, none of which looked particularly exciting, and then looked around again. Juliet had her head bowed and her eyes closed, and her hands were clasped—very tightly, it looked to me—in her lap.

"You okay?" I murmured.

"I'll be fine," Juliet answered tersely.

I left her to it while the cabin staff came around with complimentary beverages. I opted for coffee, bearing in mind the risks of deep vein thrombosis, but hedged my bets to the extent of asking for a brandy to spike it with. Juliet shook her head when the stewardess asked if she wanted a drink; she didn't even look up. Was she nauseated? Could demons get travel sickness?

I waited awhile to see if she'd come out of it by herself. I didn't want to irritate her by seeming too solicitous. But when we'd been in the air for half an hour, her expression had become a rigid mask of suppressed suffering. Juliet wasn't capable of going pale, because she was already pale enough to make most albinos look ruddily healthy, but something had happened to her complexion, too. It was as though the radiant white of her skin was losing some of its intensity, some of its definition.

As tactfully and neutrally as I could, I showed her the sick bag and explained its function.

"I'm not sick," she said, her voice low and harsh.

"Okay," I allowed. "But you're not your cheeky, chirpy self. What's the matter?"

She shook her head, but only a half an inch in either direction, so the movement was barely visible. "I don't know."

I wasn't going to press it any further, bearing in mind how fiercely Juliet defended her privacy, but she spoke again after a pause of almost a minute. "I feel—stretched," she muttered. "Strained. As though—part of me is still down there. On the ground."

I could hear the tension in her voice and see it in the set of her shoulders. The whole of her body was clenched tight, like a fist. The nails of her latticed fingers were digging into the backs of her hands.

"Maybe it's a kind of travel sickness that only demons get," I suggested tentatively. "If it is, you'll probably get over it soon. It's just your body adjusting to the weird input—the cabin pressure and the motion of the plane."

"Yes," Juliet growled. "Most likely."

But she didn't get better. She got worse. Two hours out, I saw a sheen of sweat on her forehead, and I could hear her breathing. Both were alarming signs, because for all her scary sexiness, Juliet wears human flesh at a jaunty angle. She's not human, so a human body is only ever a disguise for her, or a craftily designed lure, like an anglerfish's light. She doesn't have to breathe or sweat if she doesn't want to. There are, of course, times when she wants to do both, but this seemed to be involuntary.

A little while later, when I looked at her again out of the corner of my eye, trying not to make a big deal out of it, she'd either fallen asleep or passed out. At any rate, she'd slumped sideways in her seat, her head sliding over until it almost rested against my shoulder. She didn't respond when I whispered her name.

And her sharp, sweet scent—the smell that, more than anything else, defined her in my mind—was gone. She smelled of nothing except a faint, inorganic sourness, an almost chemical odor.

What was going on here? I turned over some possibilities in my mind. Maybe it was because demons were chthonic powers, linked in some way to the earth itself—as though, in addition to the biosphere everyone knows about, there's another meta-biosphere that includes the fauna of hell. Maybe demons were like the children of Gaea in Greek mythology, who were invincible as long as they were standing on terra firma, but weak as kittens if you could manage to lever their feet off the ground.

Or maybe this was something completely different: an anti-demonic casting that we were flying into, like the wards and stay-nots that people put up over their doors to stop the dead from crossing the threshold. Maybe the whole of the U.S.A. had wards on it, and they were already operating even this far out and this far up.

Either way, there might be something I could do about it. I started to whistle under my breath, so faintly it was barely voiced and wouldn't carry beyond the row of seats we were in. The tune was Juliet, the sequence of notes and cadences that represented her in my mind. No summoning, no binding, and certainly no banishing, just the bare description. Perhaps it might work as a kind of anti-exorcism, to give her immune system a boost and help her fight against whatever was happening to her.

She slept through the whole flight. When the steward-ess came around with our meals, I ate one-handed so as not to disturb Juliet. It was an odd and unsettling experi-ence. Normally, any part of me touching any part of Juliet would have been so agonizingly arousing that I wouldn't have been able to think about anything else. After a few seconds, I'd have been physically shaking. Now, though, it was as if something inside her had switched itself off, as if she were only a lifelike model of Juliet, and if I tapped her skin, she'd ring hollow.

For the second half of the flight, I dozed, too—fitfully and intermittently, waking every so often to check the flight progress screen on the back of the seat in front of me and discovering that we'd inched forward another couple of hundred miles. Juliet didn't stir, but her chest rose and fell arrhythmically. I let her be, figuring she was better off asleep than awake. Even the changes in pressure as we started to descend didn't wake her.

But as soon as we hit the runway at Birmingham, her eyes snapped open.

Then she leaned forward in her seat and dry-heaved for a good long time.

~ Sixteen

THE BIRMINGHAM in Alabama took its name and inspiration from the one back in England, but as soon as we walked out of the terminal into the heavy, humid, soupy sledgehammer air, I knew that comparison would turn out to be fanciful.

Nicky had taken care of car hire with his usual near-mystical thoroughness, so all I had to do at the Hertz desk was wave my passport. We found our car, a trim little Chevrolet Cobalt in a fetching red livery, parked only a hundred yards or so from the airport entrance. For most of those hundred yards, though, Juliet was leaning her weight on my arm and walking like a frail octogenarian. I felt light-headed myself. It was midafternoon here, the air hot and heavy with the day's freight of sweat and tears.

Inside the car, Juliet slumped back in the passenger seat with her eyes closed.

"Is there anything I can do?" I asked.

"No," she said, her voice faint. "I started to feel better

as soon as I was back on the ground. But—it's taking me a while to get my strength back."

"You think it's something to do with flying, then?" I asked.

She nodded slowly. "It must be. It's not something I'd heard of before. But then—your species left the ground only very recently. Perhaps—I'm the first of the powers to try it out."

"What about demons with big, leathery bat wings?"

Juliet smiled one of the least convincing smiles I'd ever seen. "They fly low," she muttered.

"You want to find a motel and lie down for a while?"

That got a faint rise out of her, at least. "What a great idea. And you'd watch over me while I slept?"

"Like a mother hen."

"Just drive, Castor. I'll be fine."

Brokenshire is southwest of Birmingham, out toward Tuscaloosa. We found our way out of a maze of crisscrossing sliproads onto Interstate 59 and headed down through the heart of the city. The skyline of Birmingham's financial district floated off my left shoulder on a haze of dawn mist, the inaccessible towers of a distant Camelot. Nearer at hand, we drove past derelict factories with eyeless windows and weeds growing taller than man height across the endless, deserted aprons of their parking lots. Most cities have at least two faces. I was seeing both the Magic City and the ashes from which it periodically got to be reborn. I was aware that neither was the truth, but they were all the truth I was going to find this time out.

South of Birmingham was Bessemer, but I wasn't really aware where the one ended and the other began. After a couple of hours' driving, with Juliet awake but silent

and unmoving beside me, we turned off the interstate and
then off the state highway onto the back roads, rapidly
exchanging cityscape for something a lot more rural and
homespun. The houses we were passing were made of
wood, with big front porches. Some of them were pretty
grand, the porches extending to two stories with burnished
banister rails gleaming in the slanted morning sun; others
were cramped bungalows whose porches seemed to serve
the same function as garages in England, piled up with all
the detritus of living that never gets used or thrown away.
In one yard, a huge black dog tethered to a post barked at
us and ran around in crazy circles as we passed. A man
who looked like the male half of Grant Wood's *American
Gothic* couple stood with a pair of secateurs in his hands
and—although he had a lot more self-possession than the
dog—he, too, kept us in sight until he faded into the distance in the rearview mirror.

Tiny townships alternated with vast, open farmland
and the occasional patch of forest. There was a lot less
traffic on the roads here, so I was able to give the Cobalt
her head. I was also able to positively identify the car that
was following us. I'd been nearly certain it was there when
I was lane-hopping in Birmingham. Certainly someone
way behind us had been zigging when we zigged and
zagging when we zagged. But the press of traffic and the
need to keep my eyes on the road in an unfamiliar car had
meant that I never got a decent look at it. Now I could see
that it was a big dark gray van with an ugly matte-black
bull bar, the driver and any passengers invisible behind
tinted windows.

It kept pace with us as we drove south and east. It kept
a long way back, but then it could afford to. There was no

traffic besides the two of us, and the turnoffs were five miles apart.

———————————

Brokenshire is a town of twenty-eight thousand, situated in a valley close to a railhead serving a now defunct copper mine. Literally and figuratively, it's the end of the line. Where Birmingham mixed affluence and entropy in roughly equal measure, Brokenshire looked as though it had quietly sailed past its sell-by date without anyone caring enough to mark the occasion. On the map, a small creek runs through it, but I saw no sign of it as we drove toward the town square past postwar houses as small as egg boxes, many of them burnished with the variegated silver and red of half-rusted aluminum siding. I guessed at some point in the town's history, the creek got covered over. Probably just as well. If we'd had to drive across running water, there would have been logistical problems for Juliet. In fact, in her current weakened state, she probably couldn't have done it.

We parked up in the town square, in front of a prim granite courthouse like something out of *Gone with the Wind,* and got out to look around. The scratched, dust-streaked car got some looks, and so did we. Juliet's mojo was slowly starting to come back, which meant that the unsubtle aura of sexual promise hung over her again like an invisible bridal gown. We ignored the hungry stares and did a slow, ambling tour of the downtown area that took us all of half an hour.

Unsurprisingly, Myriam Kale had been turned into something of a local industry. The town's bookshop had given its whole window display over to books about great

American gangsters, with a—presumably secondhand—copy of Paul Sumner's out-of-print biography as its centerpiece. It was the same edition as mine; maybe there was only ever the one. Beside it was a reproduced photo: the photo of Kale and Jackie Cerone in the nightclub, which Sumner had included in his book. It brought home to me how small a pool of facts and images about Kale was being recycled.

A sign in the bookshop window advertised maps of the Kale Walk, taking in the street on which her first married home still stood, her grade school out in nearby Gantts Quarry, the old Seaforth farm where she'd grown up. There was also a museum of local history, which turned out to be 90 percent Kale to 10 percent prizewinning pigs. No insights there, either; just the familiar photos, the familiar truncated history.

"I think we're ready for something harder, don't you?" I said to Juliet.

"Do you mean hard information, Castor," she asked. mildly, scanning one of the photos with narrowed eyes, "or hard alcohol?"

"Neither." I headed for the door. "It was sexual banter. But the nice man at the desk says the offices of the *Picayune* are on the next block. And since we're expected..."

In fact, it was barely fifty yards to the modest two-story brownstone building that bore the *Picayune*'s masthead in German black letter type over the door. It looked like the kind of newspaper office that might have had a preteen Mark Twain as a copyboy. The bare lobby smelled of dust and very faintly of fish. That turned out to be because they had an office cat, lean and calico, and I flinched in spite of myself—recent memories sparking inside my head—as it uncurled itself from a mat beside the open door that led through into the newsroom. It rubbed itself against my leg, refusing to take offense, then looked up at Juliet and let out a long, yowling cry. Juliet mewed back, and the cat turned tail and fled.

"You talk to cats?" I asked her.

"Only when they talk to me," she answered shortly.

She let me lead the way into the newsroom. It was a tiny space with only two desks but lots and lots of shelves and filing cabinets. The shelves were full of box files, the desks were groaning with papers, and I was willing to bet the filing cabinets were stuffed to bursting, too. The good news about the paperless office hadn't penetrated as far as Brokenshire yet.

They had computers, though, and the only thing in the room that looked like a journalist was hammering away at one with a lot of superfluous violence. He was a heavy-set black guy in his shirtsleeves, with thinning salt-and-pepper hair. As he raised his head to look at us, his face was as rucked up as a bulldog's. "What can I do for you people?" he snapped, as if he didn't want to know but was working from a script he had to follow. He had much less of an accent than Hattie or the guy in the museum. I wondered whether that was because he'd come here from someplace else and hadn't quite blended in to the local idiolect, or if it was a relic of a college education in another state.

"My name's Castor," I said, "and this is Juliet Salazar. I think Nicky Heath wrote to you and asked if it would be okay for us to pay you a call."

He frowned, trying to place the name. "Nicky Heath?" Then it came to him, and his face sort of unfolded, some of the seams disappearing as his eyebrows went up and back. "Oh, wait. Dead man with a dot-co-dot-uk suffix?"

"Yeah, that'd be him."

He got to his feet and thrust out a hand. "Sorry about that," he said. "Gale Mallisham. Pleased to meet you. A lot of people walk in here in the mistaken belief that their lives qualify as news. I find it's a mistake to let such people get a head start."

I took the hand and shook it, and I got the usual instant telegraphic flash of information about his mood, which was calm and only mildly curious. I got my fingers crushed, too, because he had a fierce grip.

He gestured us to sit down, realized there was only one chair on our side of the desk, and went off to steal one from the other, empty desk. "The dead man said you were in a position to offer me a quid pro quo. He was deliberately vague about what you were offering, though."

"Well," I said cautiously, "he probably told you that we're chasing information about Myriam Kale. And yeah, we've got some to trade. *Recent* information, if you take my drift. Something that might make a story."

He wheeled the other chair back across to us, and Juliet took it with a smile and a nod. Gale Mallisham caught the smile full in the face and didn't stagger, so it was clear that Juliet wasn't back to anything like full proof yet, but his eyes stayed on her as he walked back around to his own side of the desk. Even without her lethally addictive pheromones, Juliet is beautiful enough to make people walk into furniture and not feel the pain.

"Something that might make a story," he repeated, swiveling his gaze back to me. "And would that be a Paul Sumner story, by any chance?"

"Meaning?"

"Meet me halfway, Mr. Castor. I won't be coy with you if you're direct and honest with me."

I sighed and nodded. "Yeah," I admitted, "it's that kind of story. Kale reaching out from beyond the grave to claim another victim."

Mallisham sat back, resting his hands on his stomach with the fingers intertwined and steepled. "We don't cover stories of that type," he said. "Not as a rule, anyway. You've got an uphill struggle now, but I'm still listening."

I told him in stripped-down form about the murder of Alastair Barnard, then about the events of the past few days, touching not only on the testimony of Joseph Onugeta but also on John Gittings's weird collection of gangster memorabilia and what Nicky had sieved out of it. Mallisham listened in complete silence, except when he wanted a detail repeated or clarified. About halfway through, he found a notebook and a pencil in the clutter on his desk. He looked at me for permission, waving the pencil in the air, and I nodded, not breaking stride. After that, he scribbled notes while I talked.

When I'd finished, he set down the pencil and massaged his wrist. "Shorthand hurts more and more as I get older," he grunted. He looked at what he'd written, reading it over silently with his lips moving slightly as though he were reciting the words to himself under his breath. "Quite a story," he said when he'd finished. His tone was dry.

"It's only half a story," I said. "I'm looking for the other half."

"To stop this man Hunter from going to jail."

I shifted in my seat, uncomfortable at having to define

my stake in this. "I think Doug Hunter's going to jail whatever we do," I said scrupulously. "Even if we turn up evidence that Myriam Kale was in that hotel room—in the spirit or in the flesh—there's a better than even chance that the judge will kick it out of court. And it's nearly certain that it was Hunter's hand on the hammer, whoever was in the driving seat at the time."

"Then why is this worth crossing the Atlantic for?"

"Because if there's a connection between Myriam Kale and the East End gangsters my dead friend John was researching, then she's the odd man out. And the odd man out is sometimes the best way to crack the puzzle."

Mallisham was staring at me thoughtfully. Perhaps he'd heard the slight hesitation in my voice when I described John Gittings as a friend. Perhaps he was wondering how much of this was made-to-measure bullshit to prize his lips and his files open. But when he spoke, it was only to summarize again.

"You've got a lot of dead men—dead *bad* men—turning up alive again," he said. "Or at least you got one or two, could be, and your friend was prodding a whole lot more with a stick to see if they moved. That right? But they're all from your side of the water. Myriam would be the only woman and the only American."

"Yes. Exactly."

"So it's about your friend, and his...unfinished business." He took off his glasses and stroked the red pinch marks on the bridge of his nose. "Would I be right in saying that finishing the business would make it more likely he'd lie down and stay down instead of distressing his nearest and dearest?"

"Yes," I said again. I thought about Carla and realized

that I hadn't called her before I left. I didn't even know whether John's violently unhappy spirit had resurfaced since the cremation. I had to admit to myself that there were other factors operating here besides altruism. One of them was that when someone tries to kill me to keep me from finishing a job, it touches a stubborn streak in me that goes fairly deep.

"Okay." Mallisham put his glasses on again, squinting and grimacing them into position. "I'm going to buy that. One out of two of you's got an honest face, and these days that counts as better than average."

"One out of two of us?" Juliet queried blandly.

Mallisham gave her a hard look. "You're a long way away from being what you look to be, missy," he said to her. "I'm not sure whether you're dead or just something that never got born in the first place, but that body that looks so good on you—it isn't really *you*, is it?"

There was a long silence. I didn't rush in to fill it. This was Juliet's question, and I figured she'd field it by herself.

"No," she murmured at last, looking down demurely into her lap. "It's not me. It's not even a body."

"Just something you ran up for the occasion, eh?" Mallisham's eyebrows flashed. "In a way, that makes me feel a little better. You're, what, *her kore aperigrapta*? Succubus, maybe?"

Juliet's gaze jerked back up to meet his. She blinked. "You want to guess my lineage?" she invited with an edge to her tone. I hadn't understood the ancient Greek, but it was clear that something Mallisham had said had hit home.

He laughed and shook his head. "No, no. I'm not of

a mind to play twenty questions with you. I used to do a little exorcism on the side in my early days, is all. That's how I knew what you were. I gave it up a long time ago, on account of how journalism was what I really wanted to do. My daddy said God had put a sword in my hand for the smiting of the ungodly, but there're lots of different ways of doing that." He shook his head again, a bit ruefully this time. "Well, well. Succubus. But not hunting."

"No. Not hunting."

"Passing for human."

Juliet shrugged.

"You're the second I've met who's taken that course." He stared at Juliet with intense, unashamed curiosity. "I wonder—I hope this doesn't give offense—I wonder if I'd have had a chance against you in a straight draw."

"You're not seeing me at my best," Juliet said with a cold smile.

Mallisham smiled disarmingly back. "That's hard to believe. Anyway, Myriam Kale. What was it you wanted to know, exactly?"

I took over again. "Any gaps in the official story," I said. "I mean, if you know of any link she had to England—any factor that might help to explain her turning up in London, alive or dead—then that would be gravy. But really we just want to get more of a handle on her as a person rather than a legend."

"That's a laudable goal," Mallisham mused. "Not all that easy, though, after forty years of disinformation. You've presumably read Sumner's... well, some call it a book."

"*Inside Myriam Kale*? Yes," I said, "I've read it."

"Then your best move would be to forget it,"

Mallisham rumbled, making a sour face. "I don't like to speak ill of the dead, but that man made a career out of telling the kind of lies that would have turned Pinocchio's nose into a goddamn national monument. To listen to him, you'd think Myriam Kale was two parts nymphomaniac to one part Mob assassin."

"And that's not an accurate summary?" I hazarded.

The bald man snorted in a mixture of amusement and indignation. "No, sir," he said curtly, "it is not. It takes no account of what made her the way she was, and it ignores the way she killed—the reason why she killed. Paul Sumner blithely assumes that most of the murders attributed to Myriam Kale were bought and paid for purely because the men concerned were known or thought to be Mobsters. But after she was picked up by Jackie Cerone, most of the men she *met* were Mobsters. It's a skewed sample."

"If not money," Juliet asked, "then what?"

Mallisham stroked the bridge of his nose again, this time leaving his glasses in situ. "Well," he said, studying the clutter on his desk, "I'm not claiming to be an expert. It's just that if you look at how the story starts, you come to different conclusions. Or maybe you hold off from conclusions. Are you going to take notes, Mr. Castor?"

"No," I said. "I'm not."

"Or a recording?"

"No."

"Good. I'd like it best if all of this stayed off the record. Use the information, by all means, but don't use my words. And if by any chance you've lied to me and you belong to my own and Mr. Sumner's journalistic profession, I'll deny any words you put in my mouth and collaterally sue your ass into a sling."

"Agreed."

"Okay." He settled down in his chair as if hunkering down for what he knew would be a long haul. "First off, you ought to know that Myriam Scaforth—as she was then—was almost certainly abused by her father and one or more of her brothers. I can't prove it, but it's the damn truth all the same. It happened to her sister, Ruth, and it happened to her. 'Course, all the Seaforth men are dead now, so there's nobody left to give me the lie, but people around here take reputation pretty seriously. None of this is ever going to make the front page of the *Picayune*. Or the Sunday supplement, for that matter."

"How can you be so sure she was abused?" Juliet threw in. There was a stillness about her, an intensity of attention that was almost intimidating. She had this thing about battered women, a kind of razor-edged sentimentality.

"How can I be sure?" Mallisham echoed her. "Well, let's say I know people at the county hospital over in Sprott, and I know people in the sherriff's office. Myriam was brought in for stitches once, in a place where she didn't ought to have got torn, and Ruth said something at school another time about something a twelve-year-old girl doesn't have any right to know. A lot of people got a piece of information and never tried to find out more. I'm a newsman, first and foremost. I collect those pieces, looking for stories. But some stories I know better than to tell."

"You mean," Juliet said with dangerous calm, "that you knew these girls were being hurt and you did nothing to stop it."

"No," Mallisham said, neither angry nor defensive. "I knew later on—after they were all grown up—that someone had hurt them back when they were small. Don't be so quick to judge, missy. I wouldn't have sat by if blowing the whistle would have done any good. But like I said, the Seaforth line's dead now. Lucas Seaforth died thirty years back, and the brothers all perished in various accidents and drunken brawls, so Myriam's generation is the last there ever was."

"Ruth never married?" I asked.

Mallisham pursed his lips. "Nope," he said. "She still lives out there on the farm. The only Seaforth left. And she's seventy years old, so she's left it a little late to think about starting a family. But when you look at the kind of marriage Myriam made, you can understand her feeling a mite chary about getting spliced herself.

"Tucker Kale was a drunk, and a nasty drunk. There's some people who say he bought Myriam off of Lucas Seaforth, cash down. I doubt it was that simple, but Lucas was a farmer, and Kale ran the feed store, so I'd guess there was more of commerce than of love about the whole thing. I knew the man pretty well—my house is only a half a mile from where the feed store used to be—and speaking personally, I wouldn't have given him a kitten if my cat dropped a litter of ten. It's certain that he beat Myriam, and he liked to show her up in front of people, too. He was the kind of polymorphous sadist who can take his recreation intellectually as well as physically.

"So he was another brick in the wall, so to speak. But Myriam was damaged when he got her. Her own family had already given her more hurt than anyone should ever have to take."

He spoke with a weary finality that made me ashamed my own interest in Myriam Kale was so tangential. "How

long were they married?" I asked, conscious of Juliet's
scary stillness on my left.

"Seven years, give or take."

"And then he was killed in a car crash."

Mallisham shrugged. "If you like."

"If I like?"

"Well, I told you good name was kind of an issue
around here." He got up, pushed his chair back, and went
across to one of the bookcases, where he started scanning
the box files with his face thrust right up close to them. He
held his glasses up out of the way of his eyes as he squinted
at the writing on their spines. "That's what they said at the
time. And sure enough, the man was found dead in his
car, which was kind of a wreck. But it was kind of a wreck
when he bought it, and when he drove around town in it.
At the time I didn't ask any questions because there didn't
seem any reason to doubt that things happened that way.
But a long time later, after Myriam became such a celebrity and all, I took a look at that autopsy report myself.
Got it here somewhere, I'm pretty sure."

He tapped one of the boxes, then another, as if touching them helped him to remember what was in them.
But it was a completely different box he hauled out from
the next shelf down. He brought it over to the desk and
opened it up. "Now, if old Tucker got drunk and drove
himself into a ditch, which is what the police said he did,
then some of those injuries he took to the head require a
little explaining. Looks to me like he must have backed
up and taken a good few runs at that ditch until he got
it right, because his head sure was dented in a lot of different places." He held up a very old foolscap sheet, on
the kind of glossy paper the earliest photocopiers used.

"Yeah, here it is. You can look at it if you want, but I'd rather you didn't take a copy. This one is traceable to me, and like I said, I'm not going on the record with any of this."

"Just summarize for us," Juliet suggested.

Mallisham nodded. "There were also the injuries to his rectum. They didn't even get a mention when the county coroner sat and gave his verdict, but they're all down here in black and white. Tucker Kale was anally raped after he died."

"Raped?" I echoed. Images of Alastair Barnard, whose dead body I'd fortunately never had to see, inconsiderately flashed before my eyes anyway, as if they had a right to be there.

"Artificially raped," Mallisham amended. "I wouldn't normally be talking about this in front of a lady, but you're... what you are, so I guess it's nothing new to you. I guess nothing that one body can do to another body is news to you.

"Something had been put inside him. With a lot of force. And it was something made of wood, because there was a wood splinter that they found. Handle of a hammer? Fence post? I don't know, but I'd lay odds that whatever Myriam used to kill him, she put to this other use afterward.

"But what clinches it for me is the burn mark on Tucker's forehead."

"Myriam's signature," I muttered, but Mallisham waved that away.

"I don't mean that," he said. "Yes, it's part of what became her modus operandi, but I think this was the first time she'd ever killed a man. And she didn't do it in cold blood. It wasn't planned or practiced, I'm willing to lay long odds. It wasn't something she had any kind of a choice about; it was something that came up from inside her and had to let itself out. 'It was the reasoned crisis of her soul,' as some poet on your side of the water put it.

"So I wasn't thinking of it as evidence that Myriam was the one who killed old Tucker Kale. I've known that ever since I covered this story back in the sixties—for this newspaper, where I'd started as a cub reporter seven weeks previously. But it took me a while of being out in the world and watching people at their worst to see what it was that Myriam was doing."

He shrugged massively. "Maybe this is fanciful," he said. "But I think she was making a point to herself. For her own satisfaction. She'd been sexually abused by a lot of men. I think she enjoyed being on the other side of that particular transaction. The anal rape is part of that. And the burning is part of it, too. She burned him with a cigarette. She smoked a cigarette and stubbed it out on his forehead. Does that suggest anything to you?"

I would have got it, but Juliet, to whom the rituals of sex were second nature, got it first. "The cigarette afterward," she said, and Mallisham nodded, holding out his hands as if surrendering the entirety of his argument into her hands.

"The cigarette afterward. Yes. It was all symbolic, in my opinion. And what it was symbolic of was sex. Bad sex. The kind where you don't respect the other person, you just use them for what you want and then get up and walk away."

There was a silence as we mulled this over. Mallisham eventually broke it.

"It seems pretty clear to me," he observed in a brisker tone, slotting the sheet of paper back into the box and closing up the lid again, "that Luke Poulson—the man Myriam met and murdered on the interstate—was her second victim, not her first. The pattern was already established when she killed her husband. And she followed it in every kill she made thereafter."

"Jesus," I said involuntarily, and then "Sorry, Juliet." She hates it when people use that kind of language.

"Jesus is not part of this equation, Mr. Castor."

"No, I suppose not. But you're saying that Myriam Kale was driven to kill because of her background and her childhood experiences. That after she went to Chicago, she became a serial killer—like Aileen Wuornos—rather than a Mob enforcer? Or is the whole Chicago thing just part of the legend, too?"

"No, that part is true," Mallisham confirmed. "She did go to Chicago, and she did work as a prostitute for a couple of years. I think she killed one or two of her customers, but they're not part of the official tally, and there's no way of knowing now. I'm just going on Chicago coroners' court records documenting corpses with postmortem burns.

"But I believe Aileen Wuornos is a valid comparison. Myriam Kale wasn't a Mobster. She was a psychotic who killed because she had to. Because her mind was so damaged from the hurt that had been heaped on her, hurting was all she knew. There isn't a shred of evidence that Cerone ever paid her to carry out a hit. In my humble opinion, she killed hoodlums because she mixed with hoodlums. And in one or two cases, she killed people Sumner *assumed* were hoodlums because Kale killed them. Kind of a circular argument, but there you go. The plain fact is, she killed most of the men she slept with. Only the women she took to bed got away clean."

"She was bisexual?" Juliet asked.

Mallisham looked almost comically shocked. "Good Lord, no. She was a lesbian. Even when she was married to Tucker Kale, I think, although she may not have done anything about it until after she killed him and went north. Men forced themselves on her sometimes, and she used men sometimes to get what she wanted. Sex with men was never a pleasure for her, unless she enjoyed raping them with household tools. When she chose her own partners, she chose women.

"Now, unless there's anything else you specifically want to ask me, I need to get back to work. I've got a couple of articles to type up and some ad space to sell. These days, as you may have gathered, I pretty much am the *Brokenshire Picayune*. What I don't buy off the wire, I write myself, and it's a long day."

I stood, and Juliet followed my lead. I held out my hand, and Mallisham took it again, gave it another of those wrist-crushing shakes. His mood was a lot less placid than before. Going over this old ground again seemed to have unsettled his mood.

I thanked him for making the time for us, but he waved the words away brusquely. Juliet offered him a hand, too. After a moment's hesitation, he shook his head.

"I'd rather not," he said. "No offense. Just natural caution."

I tensed momentarily, wondering how Juliet would take that, but she seemed, if anything, impressed with Mallisham's solid common sense. She nodded. "I understand," she purred. "If I were in your situation, I wouldn't want one of Baphomet's sisters to have my sweat on her hands, either."

Mallisham gave a double take, then nodded with a slightly rueful expression, acknowledging the insider information.

"That would have been my second guess," he said. "But of course, if I'd met you in the field, I wouldn't have lived long enough for a second guess. So—it's lucky for me I didn't, isn't it? Enjoy the rest of your day."

Juliet and I headed for the door, but as we were about to leave I remembered something he'd said that I wanted to follow up on. I turned on the threshold, Columbo-style, and looked back at him. He was already back at his keyboard, but he paused with his fingers poised and waited for me to speak.

"Mr. Mallisham," I said, "when you mentioned Paul Sumner just now, you talked about speaking ill of the dead. How long ago did he pass on?"

"Couple of years back," Mallisham said, "to the best of my recollection. Why? Were you hoping to look him up while you were here?"

"It was a possibility," I said. "Now it isn't."

Which was true as far as it went, but it was a different impossibility that I was thinking of. Jan Hunter had said Sumner called her up in January, under two months ago, and that conversation was what had started her off on asking questions about Myriam Kale—had made her approach me and enlist me in this bizarre search.

One more open grave to go with all the rest? Or something else?

As Juliet and I walked back out into the sunshine and

the heavy air, I imagined puppet strings dangling down out of the clouds, attached to my arms and legs. If I found out who was pulling on those strings, I was going to wrap them around his throat in a lover's knot and pull it tight.

～ Seventeen

THE SEAFORTH FARM was seventeen miles out of town, but they were country miles, and I was tired. Jouncing around on the dirt tracks, our progress punctuated by potholes and thick roots, I brooded on what Mallisham had told us. On the one hand, if Myriam Kale was a psychotic serial killer rather than a paid enforcer who carried out bespoke murders for a living, that might explain the terrible strength of purpose that would be needed to keep her from sailing on down the river of eternity—to bring her back out of the grave forty years after she died so that she could carry on her interrupted killing spree. But on the other hand, it seemed to weaken Kale's connection to the Chicago Mob, and therefore to make her even more of a pickle in John Gittings's fruit salad.

"I'm not figuring this," I confessed to Juliet, who hadn't said a word all this time. "There's something we're still missing, and it has to be something big."

"More deaths," she mused.

"Say what?"

"More deaths," she repeated. "Myriam Kale's father. Her brothers. Paul Sumner. Everyone who knew her first-hand and could have told us anything about her."

"Not everyone," I pointed out. "There's still Ruth."

Juliet nodded thoughtfully. "Yes," she allowed. "There's still Ruth. Perhaps we ought to be asking why—"

Whatever the next word was going to be, it was lost as something rammed us hard from behind. The Cobalt bucked and bounced like a startled horse, and metal ground loudly against metal.

"Shit!" I exploded, fighting the car back under control as the back end tried to slew off the road. My eyes flicked to the rearview mirror. The gray van filled it, which meant it was already accelerating toward us for a second pass. There was no room on this narrow track to swerve aside, and no way we'd hold together if we left the road and tried our luck among the trees—too many rope-thick roots, too many leaf-camouflaged pits and troughs.

I did the only thing I could do, flooring the accelerator and jumping away from the van as we put on speed. But they were already closing the distance again, and there wasn't a scratch on those black bull bars from where they'd rammed us the first time. Mass and momentum and position were all on their side; they could run us off the road and not feel it. The tinted windows didn't allow me to see who was driving, but whoever he was, I cursed his name and his Ray-Bans.

Juliet was looking over her shoulder, too. "We should stop and deal with them," she said with an amazing degree of calm.

"Great," I growled, weaving from side to side on the

road in the hope of presenting a slightly less easy target. "The only problem with that idea is that if we stop now, they'll ram us into the side of a tree, and we'll fold like a concertina."

Juliet gave me a slightly puzzled look. "Like a what?" she said.

"A concertina. Musical instrument. Makes sound by drawing air in through a bellows and then pumping it out through a—Shit, can I explain later?"

"Yes," said Juliet, just as the van caught up with us again. There was another shuddering impact, and our back end actually left the road for a couple of moments, then smacked down again hard enough to rattle my teeth inside my skull. I rode it out, slightly better this time because I'd seen it coming, but a stench of burning rubber reached my nostrils. I had no idea what that meant. My best guess was that we'd come down with enough force to make the suspension momentarily irrelevant, and the tires had scraped against the inside of the wheel arches at however many thousand revs per minute we were currently hitting. If I was right, another impact like that would probably blow at least one of them.

But Juliet was putting down her window with as little haste as if she wanted to spit out some gum. She'd already unbuckled her seat belt, and there was a barely audible sigh of cloth on metal as the belt reeled itself back into the holder. "Keep driving," she said laconically. Then she slid out through the window and up onto the roof of the car, out of my field of vision, for all the world as if we weren't driving along a narrow dirt track at 130 miles an hour.

I caught the jump in the side mirror. It was something to see: The van was ten yards behind us at this point, but Juliet cleared the distance in a heart-stopping, balletic giant stride that landed her on top of the bull bars, so perfectly poised that she didn't even hit the windscreen. Instead, she punched a hole right through it. Then she reached inside and hauled the driver out through the ragged circular hole in the shatterproof glass as though she were delivering an oversize baby.

She dumped him under the wheels of the van, and it jounced over him, making his arms flail and whip like a shirt on a washing line. He died without ever knowing what had hit him. The van started to veer left, losing speed now that there was no one to lean on the gas, but still with a terrific amount of momentum to burn off and nowhere to spend it.

There was a thunder-crack sound that was repeated two more times. Juliet pivoted on one arm as someone moved inside the van, gun raised to fire again. If Juliet had been hit, she didn't show any sign of being hurt. The van's side ground against the thick trunk of a mature tree and ricocheted away across the narrow track, slewing more violently and starting to lean over sideways at a steeper and steeper angle. Juliet swarmed up onto the roof, rode the movement with unconscious grace, and was already jumping off as the van's side smacked down into the dirt and it bounced end over end.

I hit my own brakes, aware that I should have been watching the road ahead of me instead of what was coming up behind. There were no other cars in sight, but I took a broad bend way too fast and skidded to a halt in the middle of the road with a hand-brake turn that would have been elegant and accomplished if I hadn't blown out both of the driver-side tires in the process.

It had all happened so fast that the echoes of the van's

crashing fall were still dying away as I leaped out of the
car. The trees hid it from my sight for a couple of seconds,
though, and by the time I rounded the bend, the action
had moved on a little.

Juliet was down in the road, and the surviving occu-
pants of the van were crawling out as best they could
through doors and windows. One of them—judging by
the gun in his hand, he must have been the guy who'd
been blazing away at Juliet from inside the van—raised
his arm to shoot her at point-blank range. She ducked
under the bullet and pirouetted so fast she was a blur.
The roundhouse kick that caught him high up in the chest
must have staved in half his ribs. He folded up, fell, and
didn't move again after that.

That left three: two men and the woman, whom I saw
now for the first time. She was a petite, washed-out little
thing dressed in shades of beige, streaked with vivid red
here and there because she'd just struggled through a
shattered window and hauled herself to her feet in time
to watch Juliet dispatching her colleague only a few feet
away. Incongruously, she was barefoot. Maybe that should
have tipped me off, but it didn't.

The two guys were dressed in finest mafioso chic, but
the black suits and wraparound shades looked less menac-
ing given how the situation had spun out of their control.
One of them was down on his hands and knees, crawling
away from the van toward the undergrowth in desperate,
indefatigable slo-mo. The other stood facing Juliet irres-
olutely, fists clenched but not knowing what to do. She
took a step toward him, opening her arms as if to embrace
him. He staggered back, groping belatedly at his waist for
some weapon he carried there.

That was when the woman struck. She was only waiting for Juliet to be broadside to her. Now she moved in a staccato blur, slamming the heel of one hand into Juliet's left temple and then, as Juliet turned to acknowledge her, following up with a raking slash from the other hand. Juliet's head snapped to the side, and blood sprayed up into the still, sun-speckled air.

The woman was already changing, had already changed, more like a stiletto blade snicking out of its sheath than like the slow, camera-friendly metamorphoses of horror movies. She seemed to stand up taller as her torso narrowed and elongated. At the same time, her elbows and her knees bent and locked into a new configuration that a human being wouldn't have been able to achieve without ripping a dozen bones out of their sockets. Hairs as thick as porcupine spines bristled on her flesh, like a cat's hairs standing up when it's making a squalling, spitting last stand.

Juliet struck out at the loup-garou, but she was blinded by her own blood, and the sleek, monstrous thing leaped over the wildly hazarded punch to land on Juliet's shoulders. Its hands, long and slender now and ending in two bristling thickets of unfeasibly long claws, flashed in and out, raking at Juliet's face. Another jump and it was away before her opponent could get a proper grip on it. Juliet staggered like a drunk as the loup-garou landed foursquare in the dust and turned for another pass.

By now I was racing hell for leather toward them. There was no time to think it through. I stuck out my hand, grabbed a handful of something from the bushes to my left, and tore it free as I ran. *"Benedic, domine meus,"* I panted under my breath, *"hunc florem, et noli oblivisci—*" Coming from me, it was bullshit, but it would have to do.

The loup-garou went low this time, diving under Juliet's flailing guard and laying open her stomach with a scything kick from one backward-slashing foot. I was almost there, and all I had to do was to lay my loaded foliage on the loup-garou before it turned and saw me coming.

The surviving guy, whose existence I'd completely forgotten, tackled me from the side and sent me sprawling, coming down on top of me. The force of the impact knocked a lot of the wind out of me, and before I could get it back, I felt his fingers closing on my windpipe. His flushed, sweating face glared down into mine, his lips drawn back from clenched teeth. I couldn't get my right hand up to prize his fingers loose; the injury to my shoulder had left the entire arm too weak and stiff to give me any purchase. But my left hand—the one that was full of greenery—was in full working order, and since he'd obligingly come in so close, I threw it around his neck, hugged him closer still, and butted him in the face with nose-flattening force. He sagged, and I rolled again so he was under me. I kneed him in the balls en passant to make sure he didn't get up anytime soon. I scrambled free and managed to get upright again, leaving him wrapped around his pain.

Juliet was down on one knee, her face a mask of blood but her guard still up despite the terrible damage she'd already sustained. The loup-garou was dancing around her, looking for an opening. It danced right into my open arms, and I nailed it with the flowering branch right in the kisser.

"Hoc fugere," I snarled.

The beast jackknifed like a sideswiped truck, its head snapping back, its eyes wide but unseeing. A ripple of pain passed through it, and its feet found no purchase for a second or two as its shorted-out nerve endings popped and fizzed with agonizing static. I used those precious seconds to shift my balance and slam both of my fists into its throat.

For all its wiry strength, it didn't weigh all that much, and the effect was gratifying. It hit the ground hard at an oblique angle, tumbling and rolling in a cloud of dust across the full width of the dirt track.

My sense of triumph was short-lived, though, because it touched down on all four feet like a cat and was suddenly heading my way again as though I'd never landed a finger on it. I'd known the punch wouldn't do much damage, but I'd had better hopes for my makeshift ward. I guessed its lack of efficacy had something to do with my lack of faith. A Christian blessing spoken by an atheist isn't likely to hit as hard as one spoken by the archbishop of wherever the fuck.

Claws raised to rend and tear, the loup-garou launched itself into the air with a miawling scream that rooted me to the spot. If it had landed where it was aiming for, it probably would have excavated half my internal organs in a single blood-boltered moment. But Juliet plucked it out of the air and used its own momentum to slam it hard into the dirt again. Really hard. This time it was seeing stars, and a few seconds passed before it moved again. By that time, Juliet was kneeling beside it. She took the loup-garou in a tight embrace as it scrambled up and slowly, almost lovingly, bent it backward until its spine broke. It slid to the ground, its head twitching feebly, its body terribly still. Juliet raised one stilettoed foot, and I looked away. I just wished I'd thought to slam my hands over my ears, too, because the sound of a skull giving way under pressure is one that's kind of hard to forget once you've heard it.

"Bitch took me by surprise," Juliet growled, wiping blood away from her eyes—actually from her *eye,* because the other socket was empty. There was blood bubbling at her lips, too, and pretty much everywhere else. Her right shoulder was laid open to the bone. She walked across to the edge of the track and lowered herself carefully down onto a stump. "That was a neat trick with the stay-not," she muttered.

I looked at the ragged clump of greenery I was still clutching in my left hand. I opened my fingers and let it fall. "I got lucky," I said. "General rule is that anything that's flowering will do the job, but some herbs work better than others. I never did get the hang of sympathetic magic."

Hand clasped to her empty eye socket, Juliet flicked a meaningful glance at the only one of our erstwhile opponents who was both breathing and conscious. It was the man whose nose I'd broken.

"So who have we been fighting?" Juliet asked.

I walked over to the guy, knelt astride his chest, got a double handful of his lapels, and hauled him up onto his knees. He was in a lot of pain, and his eyes took a few seconds to get focused on me.

"Two words," I spat. "Who? Why? And make it convincing, or I'll feed you to the succubus."

"S-Sate—" he gurgled. "Sate—"

"Not getting it. Try harder."

"Satanist Church—of the—of the Amer—"

"Fuck!" I let him fall, and he hit the dirt again. "You're putting me on! Juliet, these guys are—"

"I heard." Her voice sounded strained. "Don't look around, Castor. I'm changing."

Once she'd said that, I had to fight the urge to sneak a sly peek. The van's side mirror had popped out when it went over and was lying in the roadway at my feet. All I had to do was lean forward and look down. But the indelible sound of that splintering skull was still reverberating inside my head. I didn't want an indelible sight to go with it.

The Satanist Church of the Americas. So these guys were nothing to do with Myriam Kale or our current fact-finding mission. They were Anton Fanke's boys and girls, another contingent of the same bunch of arseholes I'd rumbled with in West London the year before, when I was looking for the ghost of Abbie Torrington. They must have been following us all the way from the airport. But before that?

I gave the guy I was sitting on another shake. "You put a trace on my passport?" I demanded. "That's how you knew I was coming?"

He gave a twitch that looked as though it might have started out as an attempt to shake his head. "Told us," he slurred. His eyes were rolling on different orbits. He was probably in a worse way even than he looked.

"*Who* told you?"

"Friend. Friendly interest. Told us when. Where."

"Give me a name," I demanded.

"Don't—have—"

"Give me a name or I'll throw you to the succubus and let her finish you off."

He whimpered brokenly. "A-Ash! Said his name—was Ash!"

"Someone you've used before?"

Shake.

"Just a call out of the blue? Word to the wise?"

Nod.

"You can turn around now," Juliet said quietly from right behind me. I let the guy drop again, and he twisted away in terror just from the sound of her voice, but he was too weak to move very far.

I stood and looked Juliet up and down. She shot me a look as if challenging me to say something, so I bit back whatever profanity had come to my lips.

She'd done a good job, but it clearly hadn't come easy. Her eye was back in place in its socket, and through her ripped shirt, I could see that her shoulder was whole again: no telltale glint of bare bone. But she held herself stiffly, suggesting that she was still in pain, and she hadn't healed the rents in her clothes or removed the bloodstains. And that sense of fading I'd gotten when I looked at her on the plane was even stronger now. She looked like a watercolor picture of herself that had gotten rained on. She hadn't been strong enough yet to take in stride what she'd just done.

"Shall we move on?" she murmured.

"Sure," I said. "Give me a moment."

I knelt down beside Schnozzle Durante again and started going through his pockets. He was barely conscious and in no state to put up any kind of resistance. I found a mobile phone in his trousers, threw it down on the ground, and stamped it into shards.

"It would be easier to kill him," Juliet said at my shoulder.

"Why bother if there's no need?" I countered. "He's got no wheels, no phone, and he just screwed up what should have been a routine hit. Unless Uncle Sam's satanists are a lot more forgiving than the homegrown variety, he's going to want to go off the radar for a while. Either way, we'll be done before he gets his act together."

I walked on, forcing myself not to look back, tensed internally for the insinuatingly liquid smashed-skull noise I'd heard before. But either Juliet bought my reasoning or she couldn't be bothered to have an argument about it. She appeared at my elbow a moment later and walked on past me at a fast clip.

"You're too sentimental," she snapped back over her shoulder.

"I know. I'm all about puppy dogs and scented letters."

We got back into our spavined car, and I turned it around with difficulty. It was hard to control with two tires out, and the grinding noise I was hearing was probably the front axle doing something it shouldn't. But it stayed on the road, just about, and what the hell, it was all covered on the insurance.

We bumped and ground our way to the tiny hamlet of Caldwell, and out of it again on a road that made the previous dirt track look like a superhighway.

"Someone told those guys we were coming," I said to Juliet.

"I know."

"The same someone who put a tickler on my passport number. Our card's been marked. Not here, back in England."

She nodded without answering. She was looking out

the window at the rolling fields, her expression distant and cold.

The Seaforth farm was hard to tell at first from the surrounding woodland and scrub, because its fields were a dense tangle of weeds and young trees out of which an ancient, weathered scarecrow with a face made of sun-bleached sacking protruded like a shipwrecked sailor going down for the third time. But catching a glimpse of the farmhouse through a gap in the foliage, I wrestled the uncooperative car off the road and parked it a few yards away from an iron cattle gate whose white paint was two thirds flaked away.

"This must be the place," I said. "At least there's sod all else out here. Want to go take a look?"

Juliet glanced at me, her expression suggesting that wasn't a question in need of an answer. We got out and approached the gate. The heavy chain and rusting pad-lock made it clear that the gate wasn't in daily use. Juliet climbed over without preamble, and I followed more slowly, leaning out past the overgrown hedge to get a better look at the house.

It was in as bad a state of repair as the gate, the wood of the boards warped and dry, the shingled roof settled into a lazy concave bowl. An old mattress lay flopped over the porch rail like a heaving drunk, next to a wooden swing that looked as though it had seen better centuries. Hard to believe that anyone still lived here.

It was tough going through the shoulder-high weeds. Somewhere there had to be another gate and an actual driveway, but Juliet was already striding ahead, so I followed, letting her break the trail for me. That was a good idea, in theory, but Juliet seemed to walk around the brambles and devil's claw rather than through them, squeezing herself through gaps that were unfeasibly narrow for a grown woman. I still found myself struggling. By the time we got to the porch, I was torn and disheveled and in a fairly uneven temper.

There was no bell or knocker. I banged a tattoo on the screen door while Juliet turned 360 degrees, surveying the devastation. From here, no other man-made structure was visible. We might have dropped out of the sky, along with the farmhouse, into the merry, merry land of Oz.

I hit the screen door again, harder this time. There was no answer, and the echoes of the banging had that hollow finality that suggests an empty house. I was about to turn away, but then I caught a movement off on my left and turned.

It turned out the porch went around to the side of the house. At the far end of it, having just turned the corner and come into our line of sight, stood a very old woman dressed in a white dress whose hem was stained with dirt. Her face was almost as pale as Juliet's, but that was the only point of resemblance. Her hair was wispy silver, so thin that her scalp showed through. Her bare arms hung like lengths of string, her elbows awkward knots. Her feet were bare, too, and I noticed that one of them was turned at an odd angle so that she walked on its outer edge. She was carrying an orange plastic bowl, and she had a frown deeply etched into her face.

"Who are you people?" she said. Her voice had the broadest southern twang I'd heard since we touched down, but it was so quiet that a lot of the vivid effect was lost. It was barely louder than a sigh.

"Miss Seaforth?" I said, approaching her as slowly

and unthreateningly as I could. I held out my hand. "My name is Felix Castor, and this is Juliet Salazar. I'm sorry to barge in here like this, but we were hoping you might be prepared to talk to us about your sister."

I broke off. Ruth Seaforth's eyes had grown big and round. She sat down abruptly on the porch swing, making it shudder and creak.

"Oh Lord," she said, staring at me as though I were a telegram bearing a whole raft of politely coded bad news. "Oh…" Words seemed to fail her, although her mouth still worked, offering up speechless syllables.

Juliet went and sat down next to her. "We didn't mean to startle you," she said. The old woman was still staring at me, and I was finding that hollow, stunned, rabbit-in-the-headlights gaze pretty unsettling. Juliet put her hand on Ruth's and gave her a reassuring pat. That at least had the effect of making her finally take her eyes off me. "We've come from London," Juliet said. "A man was murdered there, in the way your sister, Myriam, used to murder people. That's why we've come."

Brutal honesty seemed to do the trick. Ruth visibly pulled herself together, moved her head in a tremulous nod, and with Juliet's gentle assistance, got to her feet again. She blinked three or four times. Probably not blinking away tears, but that was what it looked like.

"I haven't seen my sister since she died," she said. In other circumstances, it might have seemed an odd thing to announce, but as it was, I was grateful to have that clarified.

"We have," Juliet said. "We saw her and spoke to her only a few days ago." She was still holding the old woman's hand, and it was just as well, because at that point Ruth buckled and almost fell. Juliet had to put her other hand across Ruth's shoulders to support her until the moment passed.

"You saw her?"

"Yes," I confirmed. "We did. She—looked very different from the way she looked when she was alive, but it was her all the same."

Ruth Seaforth looked from me to Juliet and then back again. After a long, strained silence, she said, "Would you like some cookies and lemonade?"

The living room of the Seaforth farm was very wide and very low-ceilinged, an odd combination that, along with the fact that there were shutters up over most of the windows, made me feel like I'd descended into somebody's cellar. I'd been expecting the place to be as much of a ruin inside as out, but the room was very neat and tidy. The floorboards were warped and shrunken, as they were out on the porch, but a peach-colored rug disguised that fact fairly effectively except at the corners of the room, where it didn't stretch. There was a coffee table, only very slightly ring-stained at the edges, a three-piece suite and an upright piano, and three lovebirds gossiping softly in a cage hooked to a sturdy metal stand. On top of the piano was an old framed photograph of a family—presumably the Seaforths—posed awkwardly for a cameraman they clearly didn't know and who had done nothing to put them at their ease.

"Please sit down," Ruth Seaforth said, and she disappeared through another door. I crossed to the photo instead and examined it. If it was the Seaforths, the period had to be mid-1950s. Father and mother at the back, arm in arm but with no real suggestion of intimacy: the man smiling, although the look in his eyes was a little stern and serious.

Three teenage boys, then, forming the middle row. All much of a muchness, all broad, boisterous, manly self-satisfaction, looking as though they'd been caught in a rare moment of stillness and balance.

Then Ruth and Myriam, gazing solemnly up from where they sat in the front row. I was probably imagining things, but they didn't look happy. The expression in the eyes of the girl on the left, particularly, was like a message in a bottle: "Help, I am stranded on a desert island, and I need to be rescued." They were dressed in identical blue crinolines—Sunday best. They looked like dolls, and that wasn't a comparison I was happy with right then.

Juliet had sat down on the three piece's sofa. I went and joined her on it. "Feeling any better?" I asked.

She gave me a sour look. "Castor, the next time you ask me how I feel, I'm going to break the little finger on your right hand."

"I'm left-handed," I pointed out.

"I need to be able to escalate for repeat offenses."

Ruth Seaforth came in with a tray on which there were three glasses, a jug, a plate of biscuits, and a neatly folded stack of napkins. She set it down on the table in front of us, poured the lemonade, and then sat down in one of the chairs. "Help yourselves," she said, indicating the refreshments with a slightly trembling hand.

I picked up a biscuit, took a bite—it was about as tasty as dried Polyfilla—and washed it down with a sip of lemonade that was ice-cold and refreshing and so sour that my lips were sucked down into my throat.

Juliet ignored both food and drink. "It must have been devastating," she said, "when they returned the verdict on Myriam. The death sentence."

I winced at the bluntness, but Ruth took it on the chin. She nodded. "It was hardest for my father," she said. "He had to meet people every day, and he felt as though they were all looking at him differently, as though they saw Myriam when they spoke to him. He said"—she hesitated and shook her head as though denying the words even as she spoke them—"he said that it would have been better if she'd never been born."

"That's a terrible thing for a father to say," Juliet observed. I made a mental note to ask her in a calmer moment if she'd ever had one herself. After all, if she was somebody's sister, then presumably, she was somebody's daughter. A baby Juliet was a scary thing to contemplate.

"Yes," Ruth answered, still sounding calm and almost detached. "It was a terrible thing. But it was like him. My father was a very cold man."

I stepped in on cue. "Some men are cold to strangers, but to their family, they're entirely different."

Ruth smiled a pained smile. She bent down to pick up a biscuit, but her eyes remained locked on mine. "My father was very cordial with strangers," she said. "It was to his wife and his children that he was—hard."

"Does it hurt you to talk about this?" Juliet asked, as direct as ever.

Ruth shook her head. "Not anymore," she said. "No. It used to hurt when he and my brothers were still alive. Now that I'm the only one left—now that I know all of this is going to die with me—it doesn't seem to matter so much. I'd like to know, though, why you need to find out these things. And I'd like to know where you saw Myriam."

I told her the story of Doug and Janine Hunter, or at least the parts that were fit to print. I went very light on the forensic details. Ruth Seaforth sighed a lot as she listened and after I was done.

"It sounds like her," she said, seeming not the slightest bit surprised to hear about her sister's return from the dead. "I mean—the violence sounds like her. You have to understand, Mr.—I'm sorry, I can't remember your name."

"Castor. Felix Castor."

"Mr. Castor. I don't believe that violence was something she was born with. I think it was my father's gift to her." After a pause, she added, "To us all."

"You don't strike me as a violent woman, Miss Seaforth," I demurred.

"Don't I?" She dabbed her mouth on a lace-edged napkin. "No, maybe not. But that's mainly because I'm old, isn't it? Old people always seem harmless. I guess because they move slowly and look a little vague sometimes. It doesn't mean there's any less fire inside. It just means you don't get to do so much about it."

There was a bitterness in her voice that surprised me. I tried to get the conversation back on track. "So would it be fair to say that you and Myriam had an unhappy childhood?" I asked. "I mean, did you feel that—"

Juliet cut right through my measured and mealy-mouthed phrases. "Did your father abuse you?"

Ruth folded the napkin three times with excessive care before putting it back down on the plate. "Yes," she said. "He did."

"Sexually? Or did he just beat you?"

"The one shaded into the other. I was happy when he died, because he was the fountainhead of violence in this house. It all flowed from him. To our brothers, Zack, Paul, and Tyler. To Myriam. And to me."

"How did he die?" I asked.

Ruth seemed to consult her memory—or at least she paused, looking into the depths of her lemonade, before she answered. "Well," she said almost dreamily, "he slipped and fell off the roof of the barn when he was fixing it for winter. I wrote to Myriam to tell her, and she wrote back that she'd already heard. She said she was happy he hadn't died in his bed, but sorry it wasn't slower."

"And your brothers?" Juliet asked.

Another pause. "Tyler died first," Ruth said. "Some men from out of town came into the Pit Stop bar in Caldwell. A blond man in a white suit, they said, and two others. They picked a fight with him, and they took it outside. Beat him to death, more or less, though he lived a couple of days on a machine.

"Zack got himself drowned in some mud over by Caldwell Creek. There's a wallow there that's very deep, and he fell into it and didn't come out. Perhaps he was drunk. It's not that difficult to climb out if you're sober.

"And Paul died from a heroin overdose. That was a big scandal, as you can imagine. Nobody even knew you could get heroin around here back in those days. The doctor said it had to be the first time Paul had ever tried it, because there were no needle marks anywhere on his body. So I guess he didn't know how strong the dose was, and he took more than he could handle. I gather that's easy to do."

When she finished this litany of disasters, nobody spoke for a moment or two.

"How long ago did these things happen, exactly?" I asked, breaking the strained silence.

"A long time," said Ruth. She met my gaze and stared me out.

"While Myriam was still alive?"

"Yes. That long ago."

"So is it possible—" I left the question hanging. Ruth put her glass back down on the tray, hard. It hit the side of the jug, and the ringing sound hung in the air for a second. She tensed, seeming to be about to stand, but the impulse spent itself in a sort of tremor that passed through her. Still she didn't avoid our eyes. She seemed to me to have made a decision at some point in her life not to duck or flinch from anything.

"God works in mysterious ways," she said, her voice very low. "Or so we're told. But he doesn't have a monopoly on that, does he, Mr. Castor? It was an awful thing. Of course it was. But it spared me. All those deaths—spared me. I was twenty years old, and I was hoping to escape this house by getting married, but my father wouldn't let me out, and he wouldn't let any boys come by. He said he'd had one daughter go wild on him, and he wasn't going to have another go the same way. So I stayed here with him. And with my brothers. All the day and all the night." She looked at her hands, spreading the fingers slowly as if examining them for scars or imperfections. "Somebody had to come and save me. And somebody did."

She paused, but she didn't seem to have finished speaking, and neither I nor Juliet jumped into the gap. After a few moments Ruth took up again in a different tone, softer and more wistful. "She only came back to visit a couple of times, and it was always in secret, because she was afraid they'd hold her for Tucker's murder. But she used to write me letters. About Chicago. About the things she was doing there. They were full of lies—but nice lies. Lies that would make me happy for her. And it did make me happy to think that she was free of this place."

"Why do *you* stay here?" Juliet asked. There was no indication in her voice of what she was feeling, but I recognized the look on her face. All things considered, it was probably a lucky break for Lucas Seaforth and his three sons that they were dead already.

Ruth's eyebrows rose and fell again. "It's my home," she said. "It's the only place I know, really. And it's the only place she'd ever be able to find me if she wanted to come and see me again. And I'm too old to start over anywhere. I could move if I wanted to. Insurance paid off a lot when my father died, and it all came to me when there was no one else left to lay claim to it. But I don't really have any use for money. And I don't really have any use for travel. I'm happy where I am."

The last sentence was belied by the tears that sprang up in her eyes and overflowed down her cheeks. Water in a dry place. She blinked it away almost angrily, but it kept right on coming.

"You'll have to go now," she said, her voice perfectly clear despite the rain of tears.

"I'm sorry, Miss Seaforth," I said, meaning it. "We didn't want to upset you. But there's one more thing we'd really like to do while we're here. If you could just point us to where Myriam's grave is, with your permission, we'll visit it before we leave."

Ruth stood up and folded her arms with brittle ferocity. "No," she said.

"No?"

"No, you do not have my permission. Like I said, you have to go. I'm sorry, it's not because you've offended me in any way. I'm just very tired now, and I need to sleep. I hope you'll take account of my age and do as I ask."

"Of course." I stood up, and Juliet followed my lead. "Thanks for all your help, Miss Seaforth. And I'm sorry if we've trespassed on your time. We'll let ourselves out."

Ruth watched us all the way to the door, not moving an inch. I opened the door and stood aside for Juliet to go first, but she waved me through and then didn't follow. "I'll be a moment," she said.

I turned and stared at her. "What?"

"I'll be a moment, Castor. Wait on the porch." She took the door out of my hand and shut it in my face.

I think it was all that talk about abusive men that made her so brusque—and as symbolic humiliations went, it was one I could walk away from without a permanent limp, so on the whole, I was cool with it. I sat on the porch swing and waited for Juliet to finish whatever business she had with Ruth that required my not being there.

She came out about a quarter of an hour later, shot me a look in passing, and walked on down the steps back into the thick, encroaching undergrowth. I jumped to my feet, ran, and caught up with her.

"Is it this way?" I asked, falling in beside her.

She didn't look in my direction or slow down. "Is what this way?"

"Myriam's grave."

"No. It isn't."

"Then?"

"I'll tell you in the car."

We retraced our steps in silence, back to our blood-ied, bowed Cobalt, and I unlocked the doors. When we were inside, we sat in silence for a moment. Then, since Juliet didn't speak, I started the car and got us out onto the road. There was no way we'd make it all the way back to Birmingham in this undead heap, but we could drive into Brokenshire and then make some calls, see where we had to go to drop it off, and pick ourselves up another ride for the homeward leg of the journey. Best pick another road, though. The one we'd come on was probably still blocked.

～ Eighteen

THE WAITRESS at the Golden Café had clearly taken a fancy to Juliet. The fried-chicken platters she brought us were huge even by American standards, which meant that for a Brit like myself, with a delicate constitution, they were a little way short of a suicide note. I picked fastidiously while Juliet talked.

"The blond man from out of town," she said. "The one who killed Tyler Seaforth, the first brother."

"Yeah." I ran the conversation through in my mind, placed the reference. "The guy in the ice-cream suit. What about him?"

"He wasn't just from out of town. He was from England. London, in fact. That's why Ruth almost had a heart attack when she heard your accent."

That made a lot of sense, now I thought about it. I'd figured at the time that the mention of Myriam had made Ruth weak at the knees, but there couldn't be many other reasons *besides* Myriam why strangers would come calling, so that hadn't made a whole lot of sense. In a different way, though, this didn't, either.

"When she told that story," I said, picking over the logic in my mind, "she didn't give the impression that she was there when Tyler died. In fact, I'm pretty sure she said she was told about it afterward."

Juliet bit through a chicken leg, flesh and bone and all, and crunched down hard. She nodded, mouth full, but I had to wait for elaboration until she'd chewed and swallowed.

"She wasn't there," she said. "But she met this man later. He'd been sent to kill Tyler by Myriam, that's fairly obvious. Probably he arranged the other deaths, too—Lucas and the other two brothers. Ruth always knew she had a guardian angel, and she knew who it was. But there was no reason why Myriam couldn't work through proxies.

"The man came up to the farm on the day of Myriam's execution, and he introduced himself. Under the circumstances, which I'm sure I don't need to spell out for you, the fact that he'd helped to beat Tyler Seaforth to death wasn't much of a barrier to polite conversation. Ruth was much more inclined to kiss his hands than to call the police."

"What was his name?" I asked.

"The name he gave her was Bergson."

I almost laughed. "I think that's a pretty rarefied pun," I said. "Bergson was a French philosopher back in the thirties. I think he had some idea about a universe of pure spirit. Kind of like Plato, only with a more outrageous accent."

"Ruth didn't believe that was his real name. The point was that he told her—told her so she knew it was the truth—that he'd worked for Myriam or done favors for her in the past. And he said he was still working on her behalf. He insisted on that: All of this was for Myriam's sake.

"He gave Ruth the address and telephone number of the Illinois state penitentiary, and he told her everything she needed to know about claiming Myriam's body. Ruth had an absolute legal right, he said—all she had to do was exercise it. The body should be brought to the farm, and she should refuse all offers of help with the burial. If anyone asked, she was to say that it was all taken care of. And as soon as she was alone—as soon as the circus of cops and journalists and death junkies was off the premises—she was to call him on a number he gave her.

"Ruth had her doubts, but she also felt she had good reasons to trust this man. She argued it backward and forward with herself, but in the end, she did what she'd been told. She called him and told him when it was safe to come.

"He drove out in a flatbed truck with two other men. They loaded the casket onto the truck and tied it down. They covered it with a tarpaulin. Then, just before they left, Ruth screwed up her courage and asked the blond man where they were taking her dead sister. He didn't want to answer, but she burst into tears and begged him. She was going to be left alone, she told him. More alone than she'd ever been. She didn't miss her father or her brothers in the slightest, but now Myriam was gone, and Ruth didn't have anyone. The least he could do was tell her where he was taking her.

"And in the end he did. 'To the next life,' he said."

I let a forkful of mashed potato drop back into the

mountainous mass I'd scooped it from. "Fuck," I said blankly. It wasn't Oscar Wilde, but it expressed my feelings. "What are we talking about here? Gangsters raising gangsters from the dead? Why? Out of professional courtesy? And how could he promise that if he hadn't done it before? It's like some kind of fucking resurrectionist assembly line. Dead men pulling themselves up out of the grave by each other's bootstraps."

"You may be exaggerating the scale of this," Juliet told me coolly. "We still only know for sure about two cases. Kale and the man who was both Aaron Silver and then Les Lathwell."

She was right, but it didn't make me feel much better. "The scary thing is that fingerprint," I muttered, shoving my plate away still mostly full. "If they've found a way to cheat, Juliet—to steal the bodies of the living out from under them, the same way you and your brothers and sisters can— and if they can do it on the money, time after time..."

"Two big ifs," Juliet observed. I was barely listening. *The same ones as before,* John had said to me when I met him in my dream. *Always the same ones, again and again and again.*

Shying away from that unpleasant thought, I found another one that had been niggling at me while she spoke. "Did Mr. X say *why* he was doing all this?" I asked. "I mean, we know from all the available evidence that he wasn't sleeping with Myriam. He wouldn't have woken up again. So was he trying to recruit her? Did he owe her a favor? What was in it for him?"

Juliet impaled me on a cold stare. "Ruth thinks he loved Myriam. Passionately."

"Then why was he still alive?"

"Perhaps he never raped her."

"Alastair Barnard never raped her, either," I pointed out. "If anything, it was the other way around, but he's still dead. And not because he was an abuser of women. He was fucking gay."

"Married and gay."

"Juliet, this isn't about sexual etiquette. It's about recidivism. Kale is the worst kind of repeat offender: the kind who won't stop even when you put twelve thousand volts through them."

"And is that still what you want to do, Castor? Stop her?"

I blinked. "Is that a trick question? Yeah, of course I do."

"By exorcising her."

"Whatever it takes. I know it's a lot bigger than that now, but exorcising her is still on the program."

"Not for me."

The hush that descended over the café had nothing to do with what Juliet had just said. It was one of those statistical blips, the pauses in a couple of dozen conversations all falling at the same point. But it gave her words additional momentum as they sucker-punched me in the gut. And it made me lower my own voice when I answered, as though everyone in the room were listening. "Say how what now?"

Juliet twitched her shoulders in a chillingly offhand shrug. "Mallisham's account of Kale's life has made me see what she's doing in a different light. She only murders men. She was destroyed by men, and now she gives some of the pain back. I sympathize. More. I find a certain elegance in it."

I shook my head. "Well, I don't," I said. "Where's the

elegance in a random murder spree spanning half a century? Getting your own back on the men who abused you is one thing. Carving your way through the whole male gender is another."

I could see from Juliet's expression that this little speech hadn't made the slightest dent in her. With an unpleasant going-down-in-a-lift feeling in my stomach, I saw where this was going. If Juliet enlisted in Myriam Kale's cause, things could get messy. So messy I didn't want to think about it.

"What about your rep?" I asked her, changing tack. "You said it was a big thing to you to deliver as promised. Doug Hunter didn't kill Barnard. We know that now. He was possessed."

"It was his hand that held the hammer."

"But not his mind that decided to. Like you said, you were paid to uncover the truth about what happened in that hotel room. Are you going to stop halfway because you're suddenly a cheerleader for the real murderer? And what about the others, Mr. X and his friends? All the other fun-loving criminals who've been buried in coffins fitted with sliding doors? They're all men, apart from Myriam. They may have been using her in some game of their own. They've certainly left her to carry the can for this latest killing."

Juliet had gone back to eating. She was listening to me, but I wasn't having any impact. I was unnerved by the masklike impassivity in her face. Normally, Juliet didn't bother to disguise her feelings, because her feelings came out like water from a high-pressure hose. Right there and then I couldn't read her at all. And I had just the one shot left in my locker.

"You think she's happy?" I asked.

Juliet set down the nub end of bone that was all that was left of her chicken leg. Her eyes pierced mine. "What?"

"Kale. Do you think she's happy? Because she didn't look happy to me, staring out from behind Doug Hunter's face. One prison inside another prison, that's how I saw it. She looked like someone stuck in a bad dream that she couldn't wake up from. And Jan said she used to hear Doug crying at night for hours—"

"All right." Juliet's tone was cold, clipped. "So?"

"So carry on working with me. Let's at least find out what the fuck is really going on and where Myriam comes into it. Maybe find out what she really wants. What's keeping her walking, and killing, and raping forty years after she fried. Then you can decide what you want to do."

I looked up to find the waitress standing at my shoulder with the menus. She stared at me with big, startled eyes. She must have heard most of that last speech.

"Umm—you want any coffee or dessert?" she blurted. "Or should I just—?" She mimed turning around and walking away.

"I think we're good," I said. "Thanks. Just the bill."

The waitress fled, and Juliet stood, moving with a slight stiffness that suggested she still wasn't fully recovered from her earlier evisceration.

"I don't think so," she said. "But I take the point. Perhaps she isn't happy. And perhaps that *is* my responsibility, at least partly, since I provided some of the evidence that Coldwood used to arrest her."

Jumping up myself, I caught her wrist. "Juliet, no," I said, appalled. "I know what you're thinking, and that's not what Myriam needs at all. She's trapped in a loop.

She's still getting revenge for things that were done to her half a century ago. You're thinking of her as some kind of demon, but she's not. She's not like you. Alive or dead, she's human, and for humans, there's a law that always applies—action and reaction. What you do sticks to you and becomes a part of you. The more she kills, the more lost and fucked up she's going to get."

"Let go of my hand, Castor."

"Then tell me you're not going to go and bust Doug Hunter out of jail."

"I'll do what I think is best."

She was still staring at me. I did my best to lock on to those midnight-black eyes without falling into them and collapsing in a heap on the floor.

"I can't let you," I said simply. "Listen, when we met for the first time, when you seduced me and almost swallowed me whole, I was—imprinted. I heard you as a tune. I can't forget that music now, because I hear it every fucking day, whether you're with me or not. If you set Myriam Kale free, more people are going to die the way Barnard died, and it's a squalid, horrible way to die. I'm not going to let that happen. I'll play you out, Juliet. I'll do it. I'll exorcise you."

She didn't answer. For a moment we stood, my hand holding her wrist across the table, a frozen tableau.

Then she snatched her hand free, brought it up and around almost faster than I could see it, and slapped me hard across the face.

Actually, "hard" isn't an adequate word. I felt the impact and then heard the sound. The impact was something like crashing through your windscreen at fifty and hitting a brick wall—except that since it was the wall rather than me that was moving, I went pinwheeling backward through the air. The sound was like a gunshot, sharp and clear and very, very loud.

Nothing else was clear, though. All at once, for no very good reason that my dazed mind could grab hold of, I was on my back in the wreckage of someone else's table, splinters of wood and porcelain still falling in slow motion through the still air, and a ringing in my ears like a million Munchkins celebrating the demise of the Wicked Witch.

Equally abruptly, I was yanked to my feet again, and Juliet was holding me one-handed up close to her own lithe, unyielding body. It was somewhere I often fantasized about being, but the agonizing pain in my back and shoulders and the viselike grip of her fingers around my throat took an awful lot of the fun out of it.

"You'll have to bind me before you can break me," she said. "Let's see who's quicker, Castor. Because I'll hear the first note of that tune, however far away you are when you play it, and I'll rip your throat out before you get to the second."

This time the silence all around us was real—everyone frozen in unnatural, off-balance postures as though terrified of attracting Juliet's attention by a sound or a movement. I struggled to speak, managed to choke out a few words. "We—going Dutch—this time?"

With a wince of disgust, she let me drop. My legs wouldn't hold me, so I fell in a heap on the floor. Through eyes canted at ninety degrees to the vertical, I saw her turn and stalk out of the café. After a few seconds more of enjoying the luxury of breathing, I rolled over onto hands and knees and picked myself up.

Nobody approached me. They just watched expectantly with the rapt anticipation of people who'd just called the cops and were keen to see what happened when they arrived. I threw down a couple of twenties for the meal, nodded my thanks to the waitress, and limped out the door.

The Cobalt made it all the way back to Birmingham, raising sparks from the asphalt for the last ten miles or so. I was amazed not to be pulled over on the way, but by the time I climbed out of the car in the airport car park, I'd realized why that was. Juliet sucked in people's gazes and held them so completely that nobody in the Golden Café had registered me at all. When the cops finally arrived and took statements, I was willing to bet, most of the descriptions would include some variation on "just this guy."

There was paperwork to be filled out on the car, but surprisingly few recriminations. I invented a story about a collision with a concrete bollard. The clerk at the counter transcribed it faithfully and made me sign the form. There was an excess of a hundred dollars that I paid without a murmur. It seemed like the least I could do.

Then I was sitting in the departure lounge again, waiting for the next plane to Heathrow while the huge bruise on the right side of my face spread and deepened. I found myself wondering how Juliet was going to get back. I was pretty damn sure she wouldn't leave the ground, but I had no idea what she'd do instead. Or whether it would be faster or slower than a transatlantic flight.

By the time I landed at Heathrow, I was thinking straight again, so the first thing I did was to get to a phone and make the call I should have made from the States. It didn't do me a lot of good, though—at Pentonville, the highest I could get up the chain of command was the night duty officer, and something in his tone told me that he wasn't taking me seriously.

"A woman?" he kept on repeating every time I let him get a word in edgeways.

"No," I repeated with the brittle, strained patience you keep in reserve until you need it to deal with morons and Jehovah's Witnesses. "She looks like a woman. But she's actually a demon. A succubus."

"A demon. Right." I was getting the same strained patience bouncing right back at me, and I wasn't enjoying it much. "And who's she coming to visit again?"

"Doug Hunter. Only if she comes, it won't be to visit him. It'll be to break him out."

"Well, thanks for that little tip-off, sir. I'm sure we'll keep a lookout for her."

"You'll need to put up some wards," I said, persisting without much hope. "On the tops of the walls, as well as on the doors, because she doesn't have to use a door. And it's probably a good idea to have a priest handy if you've got one on staff. He can draw a line in holy water around the cell block, or bless the—"

"We'll keep a lookout for her," the duty officer repeated, and hung up.

I swore bitterly at the innocent phone receiver in my hand.

"Have a good trip, Castor?"

I turned in time to have a heavy briefcase shoved brusquely into my arms and into my stomach. Winded, I stared into the cold, hard glare of Nicky Heath. I took hold of the briefcase as he let go of it. Nicky examined my swollen, discolored face with something like satisfaction. He had a rolled-up newspaper in his hand, and he used it to point at my bruised cheek.

"No," he said. "I can see you had a bad one. Great! I'm really happy the suffering is being spread around. Where's the lap dancer from hell?"

"Flying under her own steam. Why? You got something for us, Nicky?"

The glare shot up the emotional register toward the hysterical. "Yeah, Castor, and what I got is a fucking news flash. You did it to me again, you bastard. Pulled me into your stupid grandstanding shit so people are knocking on *my* door because they want to cut pieces out of *you*. So this is the parting of the fucking ways. I just came over here to sign off on the job and tell you not to fucking bother to write."

I stared at him in numb perplexity. I was running on empty, and I didn't want to have to work out the translation for myself. "Someone tried to lean on you?" I asked.

"Someone tried to torch me. That someone is now dog meat. But they know where I live, so presumably, someone is gonna send someone else to finish the fucking job."

There was something surreal about the scene. Nicky was keeping his voice level and conversational so that people wouldn't look around and try to tune in to the conversation, but his teeth were bared in a snarl, and his pale, waxen face looked like the mask of an angry ghost in a Noh play.

"Okay," I said. "It's starting to look as though the

opposition is a bit better organized than I was expecting. I'm sorry. I'm really sorry."

"Yeah?" Nicky smiled grimly. "Well, save some of that sorry for when you hear the rest of the story, Castor. Get us a cab. I'll ride back into town with you and tell you what I got. After that, you're on your lonesome fucking own."

I raided a cashpoint machine, scraping the bottom of the hollow barrel that was my bank account. It was getting on for midnight, but there were a few taxis in the rank, and one of them crawled toward us as we came out from the terminal onto the pickup bay. Nicky looked at the driver, eyes narrowed, and his hand thumped into my chest as I stepped forward. "Not that one."

"What? Why?"

The taxi driver, a burly guy with way too much hair on his arms, was looking at us expectantly. "Roll on, motherfucker," Nicky told him.

The cabbie's face went blank with surprise and then livid. "Why, you fucking piece of—" He started to open his door, but a middle-aged couple came out of the terminal behind us, walked right past us, and got into the cab. The door closed again, and the cab rolled away, the driver shooting us a look of frustrated venom.

"Nicky," I said, "if you're going to pick fights with guys who are bigger than me, could you give me at least a couple of seconds' warning?"

"First cab could be a plant," Nicky said. "Second, too." He was already walking past the next cab in line as he spoke, and now he pulled open the door of the third.

"You've got to go from the front of the—" the driver began.

"Just drive," Nicky snapped. "I'm not paying you to fucking talk at me."

Nicky scooched over, and I climbed in beside him, putting the briefcase at my feet. This driver was—fortunately—older and less solidly built than the first. His balding head, his wispy hair clinging in loose tufts around his ears, and his bulbous nose made him look like a moonlighting circus clown. He turned a solemn gaze on Nicky, then on me, weighed dignity against discretion, and went for the easy option. We pulled away while the cabbie in front leaned on his horn in futile protest.

"Where to?" our driver demanded.

"Walthamstow," Nicky said. "Top end of Hoe Street. And turn your radio on."

The driver leaned forward. Tinny country-and-western music filled the cab.

"Louder," Nicky said. "All the way up."

I'd gotten to know Nicky's moods pretty well over the years, so the paranoia came as no surprise. His coming out to meet me, in spite of the fact that he saw me as the source of his troubles, was more revealing. Something heavy would have been needed to counterbalance his spectacularly overdeveloped survival instincts. The only thing I knew that was heavy enough was his spectacularly overdeveloped ego. He wanted—really wanted—to tell me what he'd found.

"So go ahead," I invited him as plunky guitar noises echoed around our ears.

"Make your day?"

"If you think you can, Nicky, yeah. Make my day. It's going to be a pretty tall order, though."

"How's this for starters?" He threw the newspaper in

my lap. *The Sun*. With the pressure of his hands removed, it started to unroll. I smoothed it out and read the headline. PREMIER MANAGER IN BUNGS SCANDAL. Okay, that was the sports page. I flipped it over. TWO DIE IN M1 INFERNO.

And a photo—an old photo, too flattering by about thirty pounds—of Gary Coldwood.

"Oh Jesus!" I muttered.

"Guy was a friend of yours, wasn't he, Castor? And it seems like only yesterday he was promising you 'something juicy.' I'm assuming that was work-related rather than some freaky outcrop of your love life. Then he jumps the barrier on the M1 northbound at one in the morning and hits a car coming the other way. Hundred-and-forty-mile-an-hour collision. Boom. Smoking spark plugs come down half a mile away. Two people in the other car, mother and ten-year-old daughter, both dead. Coldwood hauled out of the wreckage with both legs broken, stinking of booze. Funny how things work out."

I couldn't answer. I was still staring at the photo. Coldwood was wearing an expression I'd seen on his face at least a hundred times: a tough-guy cockiness that he'd copied from John Woo movies and never managed to get more than half right. He really wanted to be the scourge of evildoers. If he could have gotten away with wearing a cape and mask to work, he would have done it.

Nicky was still talking. "I checked this stuff out afterward, you understand. After I got broken into in the middle of the fucking night. Two guys, both carrying guns with no serial numbers on them. No ID, no pack drill. Deadfall trap got one of them, and the other died when I routed the main power through the lock he was trying to pick to get in to me. Coincidence? I asked myself. Old friends getting nostalgic? My fucking batshit family coming in for another pass? But no. After five minutes on the Internet, I turn up this Coldwood thing, and then I know it's you."

"Nicky—" I didn't even know what I was going to say. There was a tight, wound-up sensation in my chest that felt like it was climbing upward. This was my fault. John Gittings and Vince Chesney counted as negligent homicide, but this was worse somehow. I'd pushed Gary into the line of fire, and then I'd ducked.

"So now I'm interested," Nicky was saying. "Hey, pal, you want to turn that radio up? It's not reaching us in the back here. So now I'm looking for patterns. The first one I find is that Coldwood wasn't the only stubborn stain that got wiped out on this pass."

"There was someone else in the car with him?"

"Nope. But there were some other cops dying that night, and they were friends of his. A detective constable and a forensics guy named Marchioness. What kind of a name is that for a guy to wear? One of them jumped out of a window, the other was pushed in front of a train. Busy night for the Reaper, last night was. Unsociable hours, the whole fucking deal. He should talk to his union."

I turned to Nicky to tell him to get to the fucking point, but the dry black pebbles of his eyes met my stare with implacable calm.

"One more and then I'm done. You ever hear of a guy named Stuart Langley?"

"Of course," I said. "He's a ghostbreaker. Works out of Docklands." I suddenly remembered the story that Lou Beddows had told me on the day of John's funeral: the late-night call, the ambush, and the beating. *He lasted for a week, and then they turned the machine off...* "He was working with John," I said. "Wasn't he?"

"I don't know, Castor. J the G was going all around the houses looking for a partner to work his big case with him, so sure, maybe Stu Langley said yes. It might help to explain this other weird coincidence."

"What other—"

"The mother and daughter. In the car that hit Coldwood. Elspeth Langley and little Niamh Langley. Does it strike you that there's a pattern emerging here? I know I tend to see patterns where there aren't any: That's what paranoia is all about, right? But I trust I've set the scene for the big fucking revelations I'm about to lay on you?"

"Yeah," I said, the tightness coiling in my throat now. "You've set the scene."

"Right. You asked me to try to squeeze some sense out of the notes in John-boy's *A to Z...*"

It wasn't what I was expecting. "We're kind of past that," I reminded him curtly. "The latest thing I asked you to do was to find out where the bodies were buried."

Nicky nodded a little impatiently. "Yeah, and I put the feelers out. Nothing at first. A lot of nothing, because I put out a lot of feelers. So I went back to square one."

"The lists in John's book."

"Exactly. But this time I applied some fuzzy logic. Because it seemed to me that the key word was gonna be the one at the very end. After all, that's where Gittings finished up. If he was trying to solve a puzzle, then there's a good chance that last word was the answer: the output for all that fucking crazy input."

I thought back to the lists in the *A to Z*. The pages

and pages of clotted scribble, annotated and underlined almost to critical mass. "The last word was *smashna*," I said.

"Yeah," said Nicky. "Except it wasn't. John couldn't spell worth a flying fuck in English, and this wasn't English. So I fed it through some online translators, and I found the word he was really looking for." He looked at me, signaling that the punch line was coming and he didn't want to miss any detail of my reaction when I heard it. "It wasn't *smashna*—sweet, cool, great, fabuloso. It was *smashana*—the Hindi word for a cremation ground."

Obvious. So fucking obvious. Not the word, which I'd never heard before, but the payoff. Not a cemetery at all. John had tried the cemeteries and crossed them out one by one until he got to the truth. I smacked my forehead. It was a bad move, though, because it sent needles of pure agony through my bruised face and jarred neck.

"Thus forearmed," Nicky said, exuding grim smugness, "I narrowed my search fields and got much better results. All but a few of the badass dearly departed boys on Gittings's list—"

"—were cremated," I finished.

Nicky trumped my ace. "Were cremated in the same fucking place. Mount Grace. It's a private crematorium in East London. But you already know that, don't you, Fix? Because it's where John the Git was relocated when Carla decided to make light of grave matters."

Mount Grace. Yeah, it all fit, at least up to a point. "But then why would John..." I started, then I trailed off into silence. That wasn't the right question. We had at least two people verifiably risen from the dead. Les Lathwell's fingerprints on that bullet suggested that he'd returned in his own flesh, because he'd still had his own fingers, but Myriam Kale had possessed someone else's body, theoretically impossible though that was. Maybe John had been taken over, too. Maybe the weird things he'd done in the last weeks of his life had just been preparing the ground so that his suicide, when it came, would be taken at face value.

Or maybe I was being too subtle. Maybe John had finished his investigation by going native: switching horses in the middle of the River Styx. I could sort of see how that would work. If there was a gateway to immortality just off the Mile End Road, and if I knew exactly where it was, I might be tempted to stand in line and take my chances.

Because what Lathwell and his friends had, or seemed to have, was a lot better than the alternatives on offer. Ghosts could drink only the wine breath; zombies like Nicky had to stave off encroaching decay with fanatical care, or they'd quite literally fall to pieces; and loupgarous had all the disadvantages of trying to remain human while living in the skin of an animal, a battle that in the long run they all lost.

To come back as yourself—in living human flesh—was a sweet deal. And to come back again and again (because Les Lathwell's fingerprints were the same as Aaron Silver's), well, that was the cherry on top of the sempiternal trifle.

Either way, Mount Grace was the link. That was where the killers were buried. That was where John had gone after he'd engaged Todd to change his will. And I was willing to bet a rupee against a rollover lottery win that was where Myriam Kale had been taken after Ruth gave

up her sister's mortal remains to Mr. Bergson, the charm-
ing killer with the bleached blond hair.

"Thanks, Nicky," I said. "I owe you."

"Yeah," he confirmed. "You do. More than you can
pay. That briefcase is full of the Git's bits and pieces.
There's no way I'm gonna try and sell them now. I'm
going underground, and they're too fucking easy to track.
So you keep them to remember me by."

"Going underground?" I tried to read his expression.
"Do you mean that literally, or—"

"Ask me no questions, Castor, I'll tell you no fucking
lies."

I looked out the window. I had the sense of clocks tick-
ing and events accelerating past me, out of control. I'd
vaguely assumed that we'd be taking the North Circular,
and I could jump out at Wood Green on the way through
to Nicky's gaff in Walthamstow, but the cabbie had taken
the M25, and we were coming down on the A10 now,
through Enfield and Ponders End. A memory stirred in
my mind.

I looked at my watch. It was very late, but what the hell.
If nobody was home, I could always come back another
time. It felt like more than coincidence that I was passing
this close right after Nicky had dropped that bombshell
on me. Then again, that's how all the best coincidences
feel. First things first, though; too much unfinished business was pressing on me. If I could shunt some of it off,
I'd travel lighter.

"Can you get a message through to someone for me?"
I asked Nicky. "On your way to wherever it is you're
going?"

"Maybe," he allowed warily. "Who's the someone?"

"The governor of Pentonville."

He gave a sardonic laugh. "Fine. What do you want me to say? That you love him after all?"

"That a demon from hell is probably going to walk through his front door sometime in the next twenty-four hours, looking to let a murderer back out onto the street. A guy in the remand block. Douglas Hunter."

Nicky stared at me. "A demon from hell?"

"Yeah. Wearing human flesh. Answering to the description of a wet dream."

"Juliet?"

"Obviously."

"You're rolling over on Juliet?"

"I wish. Look, I don't think there's anyone in that place with the balls or the tradecraft to exorcise her. I just want them to keep her out. Otherwise—Well, a shitty situation gets one degree shittier."

Nicky considered. "I can drop him an e-mail through a blind proxy. That good enough?"

"That's perfect, Nicky. Thanks."

"You're very welcome. Where I'm going, even she won't find me, so what the fuck do I care?"

"Hey," I called to the cabbie, "can you fork a left at NagsHead Road?"

"I was going to anyway," he grunted.

"Great. You can drop me on the other side of the reservoir. That's Chingford Hatch, right?"

"Chingford Green. Chingford Hatch is a bit farther down."

"It'll be fine," I said. "Thanks."

"Who do you know all the way out here?" Nicky

demanded, genuinely curious. He is curious about everything, because he knows, deep down, that the huge global conspiracy of which we're all a part takes in every tiny detail. I think he even believes that one of the tiny details may turn out to be the clue that unlocks everything else.

"A guy who runs a crematorium," I said.

~ Nineteen

THE CAB ROLLED AWAY into the night, leaving me standing on a rain-slick pavement in the middle of a strangely lopsided street. In front of me was an unremarkable row of white-fronted semis. At my back was the Lea Valley reservoir, a broad slash of night-black nothingness barely contained behind a chain-link fence.

King's Head Hill lay to the north of me, most of the rest of Chingford to the south. Taking advantage of a streetlight, I fished out my wallet and rummaged through it until I found what I was looking for: the calling card that Peter Covington had given to Carla on the day her husband got cremated, and that Carla had passed on to me because she had nowhere to put it in her funereal glad rags. The address was off New Road, in Chingford Hatch, and it had a name instead of a number: the Maltings. Under a mile away, anyway, even if it was at the farther end of New Road, up by the golf course. I made a start.

As I walked, I mulled over what I knew and didn't

know. The crematorium was the center of some rein-carnation racket whose implications I couldn't get my head around yet. John Gittings had been investigating it when he died, and he'd known what was going down long before he knew where. He'd spent days and weeks going through every damn cemetery in London, crossing them off laboriously on his list before finally coming to the big revelation that it wasn't a cemetery he was looking for at all. *Smashana*. The lightbulb moment.

And what had he done after that? Two things I knew about already, and they didn't fit together all that well. He'd changed his will, insisting that he be burned at Mount Grace instead of being buried out at Waltham Cross. He'd done that even though he'd known by this time—or maybe from the start—that whatever the deal was at Mount Grace, it was by invitation only, with thugs, murderers, and former gangsters forming all or most of the clientele.

At the same time he'd planned an invasion. The let-ter I'd found inside his watch case, where he'd hidden it with such paranoid care, didn't bear any other interpreta-tion: *You'll just get the one pass, and it's got to be on INSCRIPTION night, so you can get them all together. Take backup; take lots of backup.*

So had he ever made that pass? Presumably not. He'd killed himself instead and given himself into the tender care of the born-again killers he'd been stalking. I couldn't see the logic, even for a man whose mind was crumbling away like a sandcastle at high tide. I just couldn't for the life of me see how that would work.

One thing I could see, though: Whatever was going on, Maynard Todd was at the heart of it. He'd said he handled most of Lionel Palance's business affairs, which meant he was de facto in charge of the crematorium if Palance didn't ask too many questions. He'd told me it was his suggestion that John Gittings should choose Mount Grace after he'd decided on cremation. Then he'd moved heaven and earth to make it happen, calming Carla's fears and bringing her on board with a tact and sensitivity that didn't go hand in hand with the word "lawyer" in my personal lexicon. And Gary Coldwood had had his accident—you can take the ironic emphasis for granted—after I'd pointed him toward Todd's office.

Okay, so Ruthven, Todd and Clay were next on the itinerary. But right now I had to keep my mind on the job at hand.

The Maltings wasn't a house at all, I realized as I reached the front gates. It was a mansion, set way back from the street behind a thick barricade of mature yew trees. The gates were electronic, as I could see by the thick hydraulic arms mounted at waist height across each one. There was a bell and a speaker grille, but I ignored them for the moment. There was plenty of more interesting stuff to look at.

It had crossed my mind as I walked that I might be wasting my time, that I'd find the house silent and dark, everyone safely tucked up in bed and sleeping the sleep of the more or less just. I needn't have worried. Every light was ablaze, and figures crossed and recrossed the lawn beyond the yew hedge, calling out to one another as they went. I couldn't hear what they were saying, but I could hear the urgency in their tones.

I rang the bell, waited, rang it again. Nobody answered. The crisis in the house, or rather on the house's grounds, hadn't left anybody free to deal with casual after-midnight callers. What the hell has happened to the social niceties these days?

Acting on the kind of impulse that had brought me up before unsympathetic magistrates more than once, I stowed my bags behind some bushes and shinnied up the gate. I'd already sized it up as an easy climb, and it didn't offer any unpleasant surprises at the top, where you sometimes find razor wire or bird lime. Within the space of about seven seconds, I was dropping down on the inside, on the margin of a flagstoned driveway that stretched off ahead of me to where it became a broad terrace in front of the distant, flamboyantly lit-up house.

The people weaving around on the big lawn seemed to be engaged in some kind of nocturnal hunt-meet. Some of them were beating the bushes, or rather combing them as though they hoped to find some shy woodland creatures nestled among the roots. Others were quartering the lawn itself, occasionally shining flashlights in one another's faces and then shouting apologies.

I walked into their midst, partly hoping to find Peter Covington and explain what the hell I was doing there, partly curious as to what it was they were looking for. Nobody accosted me or seemed to notice me at all. Once the beam of a flashlight picked me out, but it swung away as its owner discovered that I wasn't who he'd thought I was. "Sorry," came a muttered voice out of the darkness.

"No problem," I answered.

The grounds were bigger than I'd thought. There was an ornamental lake, a summerhouse, and a splodge of darkness that was probably some kind of arbor out in the middle of the lawn. Vague silhouettes circled around all three.

Three broad, shallow stone steps led up to the front door of the house, which was wide open. I walked inside and stood in the entrance hall at the foot of a flight of stairs that bifurcated at second-floor level, breaking away to left and right like an architectural cluster bomb.

"Anybody home?" I called. And then "Covington?" No answer.

Killing time, I looked at my surroundings in a "who lives in a house like this?" frame of mind. Someone with a shit lot of money to spend, that was for sure. The hall was bigger than Ropey's living room, and there was polished mahogany everywhere. Over my head hung a massive chandelier that was modern, asymmetrical, and ugly as sin. Money can buy you love at the market price, but good taste you've got to be born with. I counted my blessings and almost got to one.

A noise sounded from somewhere near at hand, once and then again: a muffled scuffling, like rats behind the skirting boards. I followed it to a cupboard under the stairs with a three-quarter-height door. The sort of place where, in a suburban semi, you might hide the Hoover and the dustpan. In this stately pile, it was probably the servants' quarters.

More scuffling. I opened the door and peered inside, seeing only a vertical stack of fuse boxes and some folding chairs. I smelled the acid reek of urine. Then I realized with a jolt that a pair of human eyes was peering out from behind the chairs. The cupboard was deeper than I'd thought, and someone was sitting back there in the dark. An old man with a slightly dazed, more than slightly sleepy look to him.

He didn't seem too alarmed at being found. He just

blinked and shielded his eyes as the light flooded into his bolt-hole. "Hide," he said. His voice thin and high, with a faint vibrato that sounded a little plaintive.

"Right," I agreed.

Then the lined face opened up in a disconcerting grin that looked as though it belonged somewhere else entirely. "Hide-and-seek."

A shiver went through me, but it came from a memory—John Gittings's last days as relayed to me by Carla—rather than from this harmless old man's crazy game, which at least gave the seemingly oversize staff something to do. "Maybe you should come out of there," I suggested as nonthreateningly as I could manage. "Do you want some help?"

He seemed to need a long time to think that through, but eventually, he said, "Ye-e-es," drawing the sound out into a querulous bleat.

I moved the chairs and helped him to his feet, taking care not to make him move any faster than he was comfortable with. He was so frail he looked as though he might break into pieces. He wore silk pajamas that were too big for him. There was a broad, dark stain spreading out and down from the crotch, which explained the gents' urinal smell.

I took a step backward, and then another, bending my head as I passed under the lintel. The old man shuffled out after me, not needing to bend because of his diminutive size and stooped shoulders.

As I was closing the cupboard door, I heard footsteps from behind me and turned my head with difficulty—the old man was still holding tight to my arm—to see who was coming. One of the search parties had come in out of the cold. At its head was a familiar face topped by a familiar shock of snow-white hair.

"Door was open, Mr. Covington," I said. "So I let myself in. Hope you don't mind."

He stared at me, then at the old man leaning against my arm, then back at me. "The door was open," he agreed, "but as I recall, the gate was locked. It still is. Do I know you? Your face is vaguely familiar."

"Felix Castor. We met at Mount Grace," I said. "On Wednesday, when John Gittings was cremated." By this time, two of the searchers—a man in an immaculate white shirt and gray suit trousers and a woman who was evidently a nurse—had gently and painstakingly prized the old man's fingers loose from my forearm and were leading him away, the woman murmuring reassuringly into his ear about getting cleaned up and having a nice cup of tea. I watched him out of sight, then turned back to Covington.

Covington nodded slowly, his expression still wary. "All right. Yes. I remember you. But what are you doing here now?"

"I was hoping to talk to Mr. Palance," I said. A presentiment hit me as soon as the words were out.

"Well," Covington said, nodding toward the door that the old man had disappeared through, "it looks as though you've already introduced yourself."

———————

"Mr. Palance—Lionel—had a stroke about ten years ago," Covington said, walking ahead of me along a corridor you could drive a truck down. It would have ruined the Persian carpet, though, and probably knocked one or two of the enormous Tiffany lamps off their wrought-iron brackets.

"A bad one?" I asked.

"No." Covington shook his head. His expression—what I could see of it—was closed, impossible to read. "Not a bad one. Not really. He was able to walk afterward, and his speech was back to normal after three months. But it came on the back of a lot of other problems. Most of them, I have to say, psychological. A nervous breakdown at the age of fifty-two that he never fully recovered from, and occasional bouts of dementia since.

"He'd had a very happy—almost blessed—life up until then, but it all came apart very quickly. That was when he first hired me to look after the day-to-day workings of the estate."

"Before the breakdown?" I asked. "Or after?"

The blond man looked over his shoulder at me, his eyes narrowing very slightly. "Before," he said. "A year or so before, I suppose. I was still relatively new when all that stuff happened. Why do you ask?"

I didn't even know myself. "Just wondering about the legal situation," I said glibly, remembering John Gittings's Alzheimer's and the doubts it might have cast on his changed will. "If he took you on when he wasn't in his right mind..."

Covington shrugged. "There's a trust," he said. "They're the real decision-makers as far as Lionel's investments are concerned. I'm just an administrator. And a sort of personal assistant. I deal with the running of the house, sort and answer the mail, liaise with the medical staff here. That sort of thing. The trustees manage the investment portfolio and pay my salary."

"Who looks after the crematorium?" I asked.

Covington held open an oak-paneled door, and I walked into what was evidently one of the family rooms. I smelled the smell of understated luxury: leather and fresh-cut flowers and old, old wood. A sixty-inch TV stood against one wall of the room and tried in vain to dominate it. The carpet underneath my shoes swallowed the sound of my footsteps. The curtains had a pattern of fleurs-de-lis, and you could have played a game of five-a-side football on the black leather settee. There was a bar, too, the full deal, with wall-mounted optics and a gleaming chrome soda siphon.

"Would you like a drink?" Covington asked, derailing the conversation. "Whiskey? Brandy?"

"Whiskey. Thanks."

"Straight or on the rocks?"

"Straight."

He went behind the bar and fixed the drinks, moving unhurriedly and with practiced ease, as though serving in a pub was where his real strengths lay, rather than managing an estate. The whiskey was Springbank Local Barley, 1966, which didn't surprise me in the least but did make my heart quicken just a little. Covington poured two generous measures and passed one across the bartop to me on a folded serviette. I took it up and swirled it in the glass, the rich aroma rising so that I breathed it in like an olfactory French kiss.

"The crematorium," I said again.

"Yes." Covington took a sip of his own drink, held it on his tongue for a second or two, and then swallowed. "Why do you want to know, Mr. Castor?"

Truth as far as it goes, the Galactic Girl Guides' ever serviceable motto.

"Because of John," I said. "He changed his will only a month or so before he died, and his widow, Carla, doesn't know why. I think it would help her to accept John's death if she were able to understand what changed his mind."

Covington strolled back around the bar, setting his drink down on the way, as though he were already tired of it. "And how does that translate into you coming here?" he demanded. He walked past me and sat down on the settee, waving me to a seat opposite him that was only big enough for a quick round of three-and-in. I took the seat because it gave me a few moments to think of an answer.

"I was just wondering if there was anything special—anything unique—about the site itself," I said. "Anything that might have attracted his attention in the first place. It's a long way from where he lived. If all he wanted was to be burned instead of buried, the Marylebone crematorium was a lot closer."

Covington nodded, but he was looking at me quizzically. "That's bullshit," he said at last.

His disarming directness caught me off balance. "In what sense of the word?" I asked, gamely but lamely.

"There's only one sense of the word, Mr. Castor. Bullshit is bullshit. Tell me what you really want to know."

Flushed out of cover, I weighed the possible outcomes of doing that. It was hard to read this man. Despite the harsh language, he didn't seem angry; only matter-of-fact and maybe slightly impatient at being snowed. Which could mean that he already knew more about this situation than I'd been assuming. Maybe more than I did myself. In spite of all my globe-trotting investigations, that wouldn't have been hard.

I hesitated long enough for him to notice, but he didn't

seem to be in any kind of a hurry. He waited in silence for me to make up my mind.

"Okay," I said at last, trying to find a way of putting it that got the essential point across without sounding ridiculously melodramatic. "There's something going on down there. Something really strange and really dangerous. Something illegal, maybe, but the laws don't cover this situation because it's stuff most people consider impossible. But everyone who gets close to it ends up dead."

That was enough to be going with. I'd tossed him a quid—let's see if he could offer me a quo.

Covington nodded, seeming to relax slightly. "Good," he said. "Then you know. I wouldn't have been able to explain it, but if you know, then that makes it a lot easier. Yes, you're right. There *is* something going on at Mount Grace. And I think your dead friend Mr. Gittings was investigating it when he died. In fact, I think that's why he died." He looked at me searchingly.

"John committed suicide," I pointed out, playing straight man and wondering if that objection sounded as fatuous to Covington as it did to me.

The blond man shrugged. "Yes," he agreed. "He did."

"In a locked room. With a shotgun."

Covington conceded those points, too, with a cold nod.

"Not an easy thing for someone to arrange," I hazarded.

"That depends, I suppose." Covington stood and crossed the room to close the door, which I'd left open. He locked it, turning the big, ornate key that had been left in the lock. Shutting me in or shutting someone else out? "For an outside job, yes, it would be difficult. For someone working from the inside—"

The glass was on the way to my mouth. I almost poured that precious liquid into my shirt collar as I suppressed a start of unwelcome surprise. "From the inside?" I repeated.

Covington stood over me, staring down. His hands were in his pockets, and I was getting the distinct impression that we might be on the same side, but I still had to fight the urge to jump up and take a defensive crouch. He was a formidable man, I realized, seeing him from this close up. There was a hard-edged definition to his muscles that suggested long hours on a bench press.

"Yes. You know what I mean, Mr. Castor. You've probably got your own reasons for pretending you don't, but you do. Another man's mind—another man's soul working from inside your friend's body—could do all the things that John Gittings was said to have done. Locked the door. Put the shotgun barrel in his mouth. Pulled the trigger. He'd know, wouldn't he, that his resurrection would follow in due course? So long as he could be sure that John's body was going back to Mount Grace."

I hadn't consciously reached that conclusion until he said it, but every word was like a reel clanking to a halt on an enormous slot machine: chunk chunk chunk chunk, followed by the tinny jingling of the jackpot.

"Why would he do it, though?" I asked. "If he—they—had already taken John over, then they didn't have to worry about the investigation anymore. If they did it to silence him, then the job was done. Why did they need to kill him?"

"You tell me," Covington suggested, still staring down at me.

"Because they don't go for broken-down old men," I

muttered. Chunk chunk chunk. "Because whoever got that gig—whoever possessed John—was only doing what had to be done to shut him up. Guided suicide. There was no need to stick around for the long term."

Covington nodded. "That's the way I read it," he said. "I'm sure when they're choosing their new wardrobe, they go for the young and healthy. John struck me as anything but."

Some of the reels were still spinning, still dropping into their final positions: a bell here, a lemon there. John's fragmented notes and the crazy paranoid dance he'd led me on proved that Carla had been right about him: His mind *was* starting to collapse in on itself. But some of the things she'd seen and described to me, she hadn't understood at all. How could she? When John went around the house writing messages to himself and hiding them, then went around again and burned them or ripped them up, that had looked like the purest insanity. But not if it was a game for two players; not if John was fighting back against the passenger riding inside his mind and soul and almost winning. But it wasn't a fair fight, of course. At least not after the other guy got the drop on him with a fucking shotgun.

I lurched to my feet. I couldn't keep sitting there anymore as my mind stripped its gears trying to accommodate these new facts.

"How do you know all this?" I asked, involuntarily shifting my weight and finding a good brace point, as though even now I was afraid that Covington might lean in and throw a punch at me.

"Until recently," Covington admitted, his expression turning a little grim, "I knew almost nothing. At least—I suspected that Mount Grace was a front for some kind of illegal activity. There were too many things that didn't add up. It was odd that the trust had kept an interest in Mount Grace at all, in a portfolio that was dominated by Pacific Rim venture stocks and West African gold. There wasn't any profit in it."

"Todd told me that Mr. Palance kept it on because it's a heritage site," I said.

Covington snorted. "Did he? Lionel never gave a damn about that stuff. And it's where they meet—the board, I mean; the trust's administrators—once a month, which meant it was certainly the center of something. But I naively assumed that the something was tied in with drugs or unlicensed gambling—a nest egg the trustees were building up with an eye to their retirement. And that didn't trouble my conscience very much at all. I've always believed that if you play your hand with a reasonable degree of skill, what you take proper care not to know can't hurt you."

"But then?"

"But then John Gittings came and told me some of what he'd found out about the place. That was in January. And I thought about a few things that I'd heard said at meetings of the board or seen referred to in old files. It all fell into place. I became aware that there was an organization underneath the one I knew: much older, completely invisible, with its own agenda."

He frowned and turned away. "I say it fell into place," he said. "But it didn't happen all at once. It took weeks, in fact. At the time I told Gittings he was insane and more or less threw him out of the place. Then I went away and thought, and realized that everything I'd been ignoring—it all came down to this. A reincarnation racket operating out of Mount Grace. Run not by the trustees but by the people whose ashes are kept there. It sounds insane when you put it like that, but that's what it is all the same."

"So what did you do?" I asked.

He looked at me as though I'd just done an impersonation of a duck singing the national anthem. "I didn't do anything," he said with an incredulous emphasis. "I still haven't done anything. I called Gittings to warn him off, but he was already dead by then. If I needed an illustration of the shit I was potentially in, there it was. These people can kill you and make it look—not even like an accident, like something you did to yourself. I kept my mouth shut and dug in."

He sighed. "And I made sure never to go into the crematorium itself from that moment on. I've been on the grounds, as you saw. I've unlocked the doors and locked them up again. But I haven't stepped inside the place itself, and I don't intend to. If that sounds irrational, you'll have to excuse me."

I said nothing. I was thinking of Doug Hunter and what he'd said when we met about his sprained ankle. That was how they'd gotten him. He'd sprained his ankle, and because there wasn't a first-aid kit, he'd gone into "the church next door." And when he'd came out, he'd been carrying a beast on his back that turned out to be Myriam Kale. I'd noticed the building site on Ropery Street. How could I not have made the connection?

No. Covington's precautions sounded anything but irrational. If anything, he was still taking unwarranted risks walking up to the door of the goddamn place.

Abruptly, Covington looked at his watch. "Listen, I

have to go and check on Lionel," he said. "Kim will have
him cleaned up now, and she'll probably be putting him
to bed. We have a routine, and he'll sleep better if he sees
me. You can wait if you want."

"Can I come along with you?" I asked on an impulse.

There was a definite frosty pause.

"He hasn't had anything to do with Mount Grace in
over a decade," the blond man said. "There's nothing he
can tell you."

"There may be things I can tell without talking to
him," I countered.

Covington looked unconvinced. "He's very frail. And he
needs his sleep. I don't want him upset any more tonight."

"I won't ask him any questions," I promised. "Or even
discuss any of this stuff while we're with him."

A brusque shrug. "All right. If you insist. Five minutes.
Then we'll leave so that Kim can settle him down. When
I tap you on the shoulder, we go, whether you're ready
or not."

"Sure," I agreed.

We walked along more miles of eight-lane corridor,
up a staircase that wasn't the one I'd seen in the front
hall, and into a bedroom that looked more like a hospital
ward. Mostly, that was the bed, which was one of those
electrically controlled multiposition efforts for people
with mobility problems. But I also noticed the pharmacopeia of pill packets and medicine bottles on a night table
next to the bed, the oxygen cylinder discreetly positioned
along one wall, and the flotilla of wheelchairs parked just
inside the door: motorized and manual, folding and solid,
solid steel and lightweight aluminum, something for
every occasion. In other respects, it resembled a child's

nursery. There were toys on the floor, including an ancient-looking Hornby train set with a perfect circle of track, and a bookcase full of very big books with very brightly colored spines.

Kim—the nurse I'd seen earlier—was adjusting the bed as we walked in. Lionel Palance was lying back on the high-banked pillows, breathing through a nebulizer that a male nurse held to his face. The old man's gaze rolled over me without seeming to see me, but his eyes focused on Covington and he smiled. Lionel's lips moved and made a muffled noise that might have been a greeting.

"Hello, Lionel," Covington said gently, sitting on the bed. "Taking your medicine. That's what I like to see."

The nurse took the nebulizer away and laid it down on the night table.

"Peter," the old man said in his high, fragile voice. And then, "Taking—my medicine."

Covington nodded, pantomiming approval. "Yeah, I saw. And Kim's going to read to you until you go to sleep. The *Just So Stories,* yeah? You're still on that one?"

"*Noddy,*" Kim murmured. "We're back to *Noddy.*"

Covington winced. "*Noddy's* too young for him," he said with an edge in his voice, as though they were parents disagreeing for the thousandth time about a child they had ambitions for.

Kim wasn't cowed. "But he likes it," she said. "It comforts him."

Covington raised his hands in surrender, I thought more because I was there than because he accepted the argument. "Anyway," he said, "you're going to have your story, and you're going to go to sleep, aren't you? You're going to be good now."

"All right, Peter," the old man agreed.

"Good night, Lionel. God bless. See you in the morning, please God." He recited this quickly, as though it were a formula.

"Good night, Peter," the old man fluted. "God bless. See you in the morning. Please God."

Covington stood up and made to move away, but the old man was still looking at him, still trying to speak, although he'd temporarily run out of breath. "We played hi—hide-and-seek."

The big blond hunk turned around and looked down at his nominal employer, dwarfed by the ultra-technological bed as he was by the ultra-luxurious house. Something in Covington's face changed, and for a moment he looked as though he'd taken a punch to the jaw. He blinked twice, the second longer than the first. When his eyes opened again, they were wet.

"Yeah," he said with an effort. "We did, Lionel. We played."

He walked out of the room quickly, without looking at me. I lingered, listening to the silence. Not really silence: Lionel Palance's breathing was hoarse and hesitant and clearly audible, and the two nurses were bustling off to one side of me, Kim stacking the medications back in the right places on the table while the male nurse bundled up the old man's soiled pajamas and put them in a plastic laundry bin. Something beeped in a vaguely emergency-room tone, but I couldn't see what or where it was.

Not really silence, but then I wasn't really listening, at least to any of that stuff. I was listening to Lionel—to the rhythm of his soul and self, the music I'd play if I ever wanted to summon him or send him away.

It was very faint, but it was there. More to the point, it was right: The key and the tone and the chords and the pace and the nuance all felt like they belonged there. He was himself, not a ghost riding flesh it had no claim to; not a demon playing with a meat puppet. Just a frail old man living out his last days in a second childhood, surrounded by all the luxuries that money could buy.

And yet he was part of all this, part of whatever was happening at Mount Grace. How could he not be when he was the owner of the place? Covington had said that Palance hadn't had anything to do with the crematorium for over a decade, but we were looking at events that had played out for over a century, so a few years more or less were no more than a drop in the ocean.

I couldn't question Palance, obviously, and it looked like I'd gotten all I was going to get from Covington. But I knew beyond any doubt that when I finally got the full story of Mount Grace and the born-again killers, it would turn out to be Palance's story, too. And—less than a conviction, but a very strong feeling—it was going to be a story lacking a happily-ever-after ending.

I backed quietly out of the room and rejoined Covington on the landing. There was nothing in his face or manner to indicate that he'd been moved or upset a few minutes earlier. He was cold and functional, almost brusque.

"What do you think you'll do?" he asked me as we walked back down the stairs. "I mean, you came here for a reason, didn't you? You're looking into this, and it's not just because you want John's widow to have closure."

"Yes," I admitted. "I came here for a reason. Too many people have died, Covington. Three more yesterday. I'm going to Mount Grace, and since I'm going to be outnumbered a hundred to one, I'm taking the reconnaissance pretty fucking seriously."

"It won't be enough," he said flatly. "Whatever you find out, and however you play it, you're not going to be able to do it alone."

"Are you offering to help?" I asked.

He laughed without the smallest trace of humor. "No. Absolutely not. I'm just saying, that's all. No point putting the gun in your mouth if suicide's not what you're after. Get yourself some backup—expert help. Maybe some other people in your profession."

"I'll take it under advisement," I muttered. "Is there anything you can do from this end? Get me a plan of the building, maybe. And a list of who's been cremated there over the past fifty or sixty years, say."

"It might be possible. But I'd have to ask Todd, and I doubt he'd cooperate. He doesn't like me very much."

"Todd the lawyer?"

"Todd the lawyer, Todd the son, and Todd the holy ghost. Todd the president of the board of trustees."

Chunk chunk chunk.

"Don't bother," I said. "I'll ask him myself."

———————

I walked down to the North Circular, hoping to catch another cab, but the night bus came along first, and I rode it around to New Southgate, all alone for most of the way but sharing it with a small crowd of friendly drunks on the last stretch. Their old man, anachronistically enough, said follow the van. I wanted to invite them to jump *under* a fucking van, but they were mostly big drunks, so I closed my eyes and let the crumbling brickwork of the wall of sound break over me.

Half past two in the morning. I walked down toward Wood Green with my head aching. Most of that was from where Juliet had done the laying on of hands, but some of it was from what Nicky and Covington had told me. I'd have to go to Mount Grace, but if I walked in off the street, I'd be outgunned and easy meat. After all, I had no idea what I'd be facing there or even if they'd know I was coming. I had to map the terrain, and I didn't know how.

I was bone-weary and not my usual happy-go-lucky self as I got back to the block and trudged up the endless stairs—lifts were all still out, inevitably—to Ropey's flat. Maybe the tiredness was why I didn't notice that the door unlocked on a single turn of the key, when I'd double-locked it on my way out, as I always did.

But as soon as I stepped over the threshold, I knew even in the pitch dark that I wasn't alone. My scalp prickled, and then the rest of me, too. I was being watched in the dark by something that was neither wholly alive nor wholly dead.

I stepped hastily away from the door so I wouldn't be silhouetted against the light from the corridor outside, but whatever was in here had dark-adapted eyes already, and it could pick me off at leisure if that was what it wanted. Slowly, silently, I snaked my hand into my coat and slid out the tin whistle. The silent presence had a distinct feel, and it was starting to resolve into notes—fragmented, for now, but the links would come if I could stay alive long enough.

"You might as well turn on the light," said a dry, brittle,

utterly inhuman voice. "If I was going to rip your throat out, I'd have done it as soon as you walked in."

I didn't need to turn on the light. That voice was imprinted on my mind almost as powerfully as Juliet's scent.

"Moloch," I snarled.

A faint snicker ratcheted out of the darkness like a rusty thumbscrew being laboriously turned.

"I thought it was time we pooled our resources," the demon said.

~ Twenty

I TURNED ON the light, shrugged off my coat, and threw it over the back of the sofa, then stepped out of my shoes as I advanced into the room. I managed to do all of this stuff fairly matter-of-factly. After all, like the fiend-in-the-shape-of-a-man said, he'd already had an open goal and refused to take the shot. Whatever this turned out to be, it wasn't a straightforward ambush.

"So how was your trip?" Moloch asked in the same tone of metal grinding against bone.

I made a so-so gesture. "Too many satanists," I said.

He nodded sympathetically, but his smile showed way too many teeth to be reassuring. "Our little fifth column. Yes. If it's any consolation, they all get eaten in the end."

He was sitting in the swivel chair, a seventies relic that was Ropey's most prized possession, after his music collection. Moloch was looking well: There was a ruddier tinge to his skin, and he'd even gained a little weight. His dress sense had improved, too. In place of the rags he'd been wearing when I first saw him outside the offices of Ruthven, Todd and Clay, he was dressed in black trousers, calf-length black boots, and a black granddad shirt with red jeweled studs at the neck and cuffs. He would have looked like some eighteenth-century priest playing a game of "my benefice is bigger than yours" if it weren't for the full-length leather coat. As it was, he looked like someone who'd taken *The Matrix* a little too seriously. The fingers of his two hands were cat's cradled around something small that gleamed white. He turned it slightly every now and then, the only move he made. When he saw that my gaze had turned to it, he opened his fingers and let me see what it was: a tiny skull, about the size of a human baby's but longer in the jaw, picked clean of flesh. I was willing to bet that it was a cat's skull.

"First things first," Moloch said briskly. "We don't want to be interrupted, so let's draw the curtains around our tent. Keep out the riffraff."

He spread his fingers with a flourish, letting the skull tumble off his palm. It made it most of the way to the floor, then it stopped in the air, six inches or so above the shag pile.

"Normal service will be resumed," Moloch murmured. "Eventually. Until then the walls will have no ears, and nobody can drop in on us unannounced."

Unable to take my eyes off the weirdly suspended skull, I sat at the farthest edge of the sofa, putting as much distance between me and the demon as I could—and keeping the whistle firmly gripped in my left hand, ready for use.

Moloch noticed and affected to be hurt. "I saved your life the other night," he reminded me reproachfully. "We're fighting the same fight, Felix."

"Are we?" I asked bluntly.

He gave me a slow, emphatic nod. "Oh, yes. Trust me on this."

"And who are we fighting *against*, exactly?"

"The immortals. The killers who found the exit door on the far side of hell. You remember I spoke to you about rhythm. Sequence. Cadence. I know the end of the story, and you know its start. Shall we embrace like brothers and share?"

"No," I suggested. "Let's not. Tell me what you want out of me and what you can give me, with no bullshit, and I'll tell you if I'm interested."

The demon pursed his lips. "I confess," he said, "I prefer a certain degree of commitment at the outset. A promise, at least. It doesn't need to be sealed in blood. If I tell you what I know, you'll use it to further my interests as well as your own. Just swear on something you care about. The formalities aren't important."

I stared him out.

"Felix." He made a sound like the desiccated, risen-from-the-tomb-unnaturally-alive mummy of a sigh. "We have to roll a boulder up a very large hill together. Without some basis of trust between us, it's going to be hard work."

I shrugged. "I don't even know what the boulder is," I pointed out. "I'm not likely to get my shoulder under it anytime soon—not on blind faith, anyway."

"Faith?" The demon made a terse, faintly obscene gesture. "No. I wouldn't advise you to deal with me on that basis. Did you mention me to the lady at all?"

"To Juliet? Yeah, I did."

"And how did she respond?"

I thought back. "She spat on the ground," I said.

He nodded with a certain satisfaction. "Immediately after she spoke my name, yes?"

"Yes."

"And you'll notice I haven't spoken hers. Only that of her brother, who is dead. These are useful precautions among our kind. Our names aren't given or chosen at random. They have unique properties, and to speak them casually, without due attention to"—he hesitated, visibly selecting the right word—"*prophylaxis* can lead to very serious consequences. And she has good reason both to hate and to fear me."

"I'll bet," I said, unimpressed. "And you know, I appreciate your frankness. I'd say it was a breath of fresh air except that the air stinks of rotten meat. This isn't getting us much further, is it?"

"No," Moloch agreed. "It isn't." He smiled nastily. "You're very amusing, Felix, do you know that? Your instinctive mistrust. The way you look for angles, for advantages, even when there aren't any. You see yourself as the finger in the dike, don't you? And me as the rising tide. But I promise you, very solemnly, in the bigger scheme of things, you're"—he touched the tips of his fingers together, opened them again, consigning me to oblivion—"insignificant."

"Can you have a rising tide of shit?" I asked politely. "I suppose technically, the answer's yes, but it's a disturbing image. I'd go for a different metaphor if I were you. Something more in a David and Goliath flavor. And you know, I'm like Avis rent-a-car: Because I'm insignificant, I try harder."

I was hoping to shake the aura of smugness he was

putting out, but his smile just broadened. "Do you even know, Castor, why the dead are rising? Why the order of things has reversed itself so that graves gape and give birth?"

In spite of myself, a tremor went through me. The demon must have seen it, because he smiled in modest gratification. "I think the answer is no," he murmured. "Poor little Dutch boy, laboring in the dark as the water rises around his ankles, then his knees, then—"

"Well, everyone's got a theory," I said, cutting across his chalk-on-blackboard eloquence. "Take a number and join the line."

Moloch shook his head. "I *don't* have a theory," he said, baring his teeth in what looked more like contempt than amusement. "I was there, human. I saw the damage done. The great project. Oh, yes. The *shedim* knew it for what it was."

The great project. Juliet had mentioned that, too, and then had pulled back from explaining what she meant. I felt a sudden brief wave of vertigo break over me, as though I'd been about to jump over a low wall but then discovered at the last moment that the far side gave onto a sheer drop.

"Whose project was it, then?" I asked, still in the same doubting Thomas voice. "Yours or someone else's?" What did it say about me that a scant couple of hours after hearing about Gary Coldwood's brush with the Reaper, I was shoving it to the back of my mind to play twenty questions with a demon? That I was so hungry for what he was about to tell me, I even put Mount Grace momentarily on the back burner of my mind?

Moloch stood up, his joints cracking alarmingly.

"Go on," I said.

The demon turned his eyes on me, and something happened in the air between us. It seemed to ripple and thicken, as though sour milk had been dropped into it and made it curdle. Suddenly, Moloch was gone from in front of me, and his hand clamped down on my left shoulder from behind. It took all my self-control not to dive off the sofa, hit the ground, and roll.

Twisting my head around, I met his unblinking eyes. As a show of strength, it did the job. My heart was racing and my throat was dry.

"I prefer not to," he growled. "I was only ... reminiscing. Thinking about the good old days. But they're gone now. The time is past when I could sit upon a chair made from my enemies' intestines and feast on your woeful kindred. That summer will not come again."

"It's a fucker," I agreed, trying to keep my voice level. "Where are the guts of yesteryear?"

"The lady," Moloch resumed, walking away from me again toward the window. "You know what she eats and how. Sexual desire is like a digestive enzyme for her—it lets her take spirit and flesh together. She inflames, and then she feeds. She can do it as well here as in the realms below, since all desire is ultimately in the mind."

He stared out into the night, ran his clawed fingertips absently down the pane. "My case isn't so fortunate. My meat is the souls of men who have killed other men, and women likewise. But the souls only, not the flesh. And even the souls I can only take, and feed on, and be nourished by, in certain very specific circumstances. The *shedim* are highly evolved, highly specialized. We have no mechanism for straining the life, the spirit, the *selfness* out of torn meat.

"So when hell changed—when the borders shifted—we began to starve. And there was no easy remedy. In the subtle realms we make..." He gestured vaguely. "I don't know the word...like small creatures that make traps and then wait for their prey to come to them instead of hunting. Traps that they weave out of their own bodies' mass."

"Webs," I suggested, my voice coming out cracked and strained because my throat was still painfully dry. "Spiderwebs."

"Exactly. In hell we make webs. But now the webs stood empty year after year. We became desperate, and we fought. Against the succubi. Against the bone-singers. Against each other. And the weaker we became, the more frenzied were these struggles. Like rats in a sack, we tore at each other and devoured each other's substance, even though it couldn't nourish us." Still staring out the window, he lapsed into silence.

"So you jumped ship?" I suggested, trying to keep him talking.

Moloch held up his hands in front of his own face, examining them with intense disfavor. "A chance conjuration allowed me to rise to Reth Adoma," he said. "Some necromancer who couldn't even frame a summoning, so that I rose out of the ground in a family burial plot in the middle of Essex. I looked for him—for the one who'd had the effrontery to summon me—but I never found him. A pity. I'd have liked to show my feelings on that score. Anyway, I wove myself a physical body so that I could stay here. Truly physical, I mean—not like the simulation of flesh that the lady wears. This body is real, and solid, and I live inside it as a hermit crab lives inside a borrowed shell. It took me many years to make out of pieces of flesh gleaned here and there. The alternative was to go home again and die."

He dropped his hands to his sides and turned his head to look at me again. "It was despair more than hope that kept me here," he said, the fires in his eyes flickering like distant beacons on the hills of another country. "My needs are not great, but as I said, they're very specialized. The nourishment I need lies in the souls of those of your kind who have killed many and taken pleasure in the killing. And whereas the succubus—your lady—is a hunter, I am a trapper. Traps for the soul are hard to build in the stunted, solid realms of Reth Adoma, squashed down by the hideous fist of gravity."

"Killers can't be that hard to find," I said with forced flippancy.

"No," the demon agreed. "They're not. I've found and eaten many, but it's like eating the dream of a meal and waking to find yourself still hungry. In hell"—his voice quivered with longing—"we used to let the souls lie for years on our terraces. Let them rot, and mature, and render down into their final form. And then, oh, then we feasted."

He laughed fondly at the memory. It was the kind of sound you really, really need to forget but know you never will. "Old souls, separated from flesh in a way that leaves no bruise on the tender spirit," he murmured. "That's what I hunger for. But here, in your thin, drab world, a meal like that is a great rarity.

"I've scraped up enough to survive through the decades. Barely. And you led me to two snacks that gave me some small nourishment. The were-thing that built its body out of cats...I closed with it twice, the first time when it was following you from the law office, the second when it tried to kill you at the laboratory. Both times I managed to ingest some of its essence while the soul was in transit and loosened from the flesh. Not perfect, but I was able to keep it down. It's made me stronger than I've been in many decades.

"But it's the mother lode I'm after, Castor. I want you to take me to the water hole where the great, ever-living killers come to drink, and drink again, of life and youth and strength. Take me there and turn me loose, and I'll eat them for you. After you've dressed and prepared the feast for me with your music."

He fell silent again, and the spell of his words was so strong that it was a few seconds before I realized that he was waiting for an answer. To be honest, it was an effort to focus my thoughts on what should have been the key issue: the born-again killers with their dead-men's-boots system of reincarnation. I wanted to grill this bastard about what he meant when he said that hell's borders had shifted, and what the great project had been.

But Moloch's expectant gaze was still fixed on me. With an effort, I stifled the questions jostling for position in my throat. He wanted me to give him an answer to his little proposition, but in true Castor style, I ducked. I was uncomfortably aware that he'd asked me for a promise. I didn't want to say anything to this creature that he might be able to hold me to later.

"By the mother lode," I said carefully, "you mean Mount Grace?"

"Of course."

"In that case, two further questions. Why do I need you? And why do you need me?"

Moloch's eyes narrowed slightly. "I've explained my position," he said, the ragged edges in his voice grinding against each other. "And so you're only asking these questions because you want to hold me at arm's length a little longer. There are two hundred souls behind the crematorium's walls. Souls that have learned the trick of invading living flesh. Could you exorcise them all before they took you down? I doubt it. They'd take you and possess you, and you'd be no more than another suit for them to wear. You need someone like me—someone who sits above them in the same food chain. Someone who was born and bred to prey on them."

I mulled that over, couldn't see any holes in it. But I didn't get to be as old as I was without reading the small print before signing. "There were two parts to the question," I reminded him, my tone and my face pure, cold deadpan.

The demon acknowledged the point with a curt nod. "Yes. Of course. I need you, Felix, to make me an entry point. With your whistle, with your lovely little party trick, you can make a hole in their defenses—bind them and distract them and make them stumble. They've held me at bay for more years than I care to count. There are a great many of them, as I said, and they're both old and strong. They've found ways to keep me from crossing that threshold, though I've tried a thousand times. Outside the crematorium, they move in flesh, and in flesh, I can't touch them. But pipe me in through the door, and you'll see the carnage a fox makes in a henhouse."

Silence fell once more. The burning eyes held me in place while Moloch waited for my binding word.

"It all sounds great," I said, tearing my own gaze away

from his with an effort. The effort was largely wasted. Magnetically, my head swiveled back around until the searchlight of his stare shone full on me again. It was like Juliet's hypnotic fascination but with no overlay of desire. It was naked coercion, the veils of seduction all stripped away. "But my music works on one ghost at a time. What you're asking me to do—it can't be done. I can't play two hundred tunes all at once."

Moloch hawked and spat with great deliberation. "Then do whatever needs to be done," he said. "Enlist yourself an army of exorcists—or dredge your own courage up from whatever cloaca you keep it in. Invite the lady to come with us, if she's still taking your calls. The details I'll leave to you. The offer is exactly as I've stated it. That we go to Mount Grace Crematorium, you and I. Together. In fact, you and I and the lady, because the odds will be against us even with her. Without her, we won't prevail. You will go to avenge your friend's death, which you're beginning to suspect—correctly—was actually two *separate* deaths. I will go to feed. The lady—Well, she'll go because you'll ask her to. Because she's trying to pretend to be human, and in some way, that makes her vulnerable to you even though she could kill you with a single flexing of her cunt.

"Say that all this will happen, and it will happen. Or say no, and I'll find somewhere else to eat. The meal you so kindly laid on for me has given me enough strength to wait a few centuries longer."

So this was it. The moment of truth. Maybe the demon was bluffing about going elsewhere. On the other hand, it was clear to see that he'd changed from the walking skeleton I'd met outside Todd's office. He probably could wait a little longer if he had to. Okay, he'd be as safe to be around as sweaty gelignite. But too many people had died already, and I couldn't see where a better offer was going to come from.

"All right," I said at last. "We'll go in there. Together. We'll wipe out the whole fucking nest of them."

"You swear this?"

"I swear it."

"On what do you swear it?"

"On myself, because I don't believe in any bastard else."

Moloch bowed with a faintly satirical emphasis. "Then it will be so," he said. He turned to the window again and opened it as far as it would go.

"Wait," I said. "There's something I need to do first. Before we tackle the ghosts. I want to go sweat the lawyer. Todd. He's in this up to his kishkas."

"Is he?" Moloch still had his back turned to me, so I couldn't see his face.

"Of course he is. He was the one working the angles to get John Gittings exhumed and trundled away to Mount Grace. He's handling the legal affairs of the Palance family, which means he's conducting the whole show. That's why you were hanging around outside his office. Because he's one of them—one of the killers whose scent you've been following. That's right, isn't it?"

"Possibly," Moloch said. "Again, you'll do as you see fit. I saved your life, and I gave you information you couldn't have obtained by any other means. At the moment you're heavily in my debt. So whatever you do on your own account, don't include me as a factor in your plans. All that's between us is the bargain, as we've already agreed it. When you're ready to make the journey to Mount Grace, just say my name—out in the open air, with silence all around, and preferably in darkness. I'll hear you."

I thought he was going to walk out the window into the night, but the night came to him instead. Blackness spilled into the room like a solid wave, washing over Moloch and swallowing him up. An instant later, it cleared, and he was gone.

There was a soft thump as the skull fell onto the carpet and rolled a few inches before rocking back and settling on its apex. The upside-down sockets stared vacantly at me, inviting me into the well within that used to be full to the brim with cat thoughts and now was full of nothing.

Normal service had resumed.

Almost in the same instant, the TV set gave an unsettlingly organic shudder, and the screen lit up like an eye opening in the dark corner of the room.

" don't even know where she came from," a man's voice said, sounding strained and almost tearful. The man on the screen was burly, middle-aged, dressed in what I took at first to be a police uniform. He didn't look prone to tears. "She walked right past the guard post, and we all—three of us—we all ran out after her. I was just thinking how did she get in, because there's a wall. It's twenty feet high, and then—there's an overhang with razor wire. You can't climb it. Nobody could climb it."

The image switched abruptly to an external shot of one of the five wings of Pentonville, and I realized that he wasn't a cop. He was a prison guard.

"Nobody else had any clearer explanations to give," said a news presenter's voice in public-solemnity mode, "for how a prisoner on remand for murder was able to walk out of one of London's highest-security prisons, in what was evidently a highly planned and meticulously executed raid. The mystery woman entered here—"

I shook my head to clear it, which turned out to be a mistake. The various dull aches in my neck and in the muscles of my face connected up into an all-singing, all-dancing multimedia extravaganza. On the screen, successive still photos of Pentonville were overlaid with computer graphics mapping a route through a gate, now hanging off its hinges, over an inner wall of impressive height and down through an interior space punctuated with inspection posts and barred, locked doors. The voice was still talking, but I was momentarily distracted by the pretty pictures.

Another talking head popped up, this one wearing a suit and batting for the home office. He denied allegations that staff cuts had played a part in these events. "There were plenty of guards on the scene. Three at the first guard post and three more in D wing itself. Two of them were very seriously assaulted—hospitalized. The rest seem to have been exposed to some sort of drug—a nerve gas or a hallucinogen—and are unable to give a clear account of what happened."

Cut away to some handheld footage of another uniformed guard sitting on the steps of an ambulance with a blanket over his shoulders. He was staring at nothing as cameras flashed all around him.

"She just looked at me," he said. "She just—and then—I was—I don't know. I don't know. I was so—" He hid his face in his hands, either trying to evade that remembered gaze or to relive it.

Cut to a still image of Doug Hunter, an archive shot of him walking into court, presumably on the day of his remand hearing. His face impassive, closed, giving nothing away.

"This is the man who walked out of the front gate of Pentonville this evening, leaving the prison and the system it represents in chaos—"

I'd found the remote by this time. Next I found the off switch. Moloch had made his point: Juliet was home, the fumets had hit the windmill, and if time had ever been on my side, then it sure as hell wasn't anymore.

I limped through into the bathroom, so overwhelmed with tiredness that I felt like my body was a puppet with some of the strings cut. I splashed cold water in my face, stripping one layer off the exhaustion and revealing a lot more layers underneath.

Try to forget about Juliet, at least for now. What she'd done, terrible though it was, was no surprise—and it was a big silver lining that she'd managed to do it without killing anyone. How long that would last was another question altogether. If she just let Myriam Kale walk away in Doug Hunter's body after the jailbreak, then it was only a matter of time before Kale met some guy who pushed all the wrong buttons for her. Then there'd be another Alastair Barnard lying in a hotel room somewhere for the maid to find when she came to change the sheets.

I couldn't do anything about that. I probably shouldn't even try; it would be like aiming the fire extinguisher at the flames, instead of at the base of the fire. Because Myriam Kale was a symptom of something bigger and older and a lot more terrifying.

Why had I agreed? Why had I decided to dance with

the devil? I'd known Asmodeus long enough to know what kind of moves demons favor and where I was likely to end up after the dance was done. But I didn't have any choice. Even if Juliet hadn't left me in the lurch, Moloch was right about the kind of help we needed: a specialist adapted to the terrain and the situation by whatever passed in hell for Darwinian pressures. The forces of supernature.

That left at least one question unanswered. How in the name of Christ and all his bloody saints was I going to hold up my end of the bargain? John Gittings had tried, and he seemed to have an informer on the inside—someone who was writing him briefing notes and giving him tips on strategy. *Take backup, take lots of backup, because youre certain to need it.* Exactly what Covington had advised me to do—and exactly what John had been calling me to arrange. Me and maybe Stu Langley, too. But I didn't pick up, Stu Langley got himself a fatal concussion, and John had to go in alone.

I stared at myself in the bathroom mirror, water pouring down my battered face and dripping onto my bloody, rumpled shirt. I was looking for cracks in the famous Castor facade, but I saw someone else's face staring back at me: John's face from my dream on the night before the cremation. What had he said to me? That he was supposed to give me something. And when I told him I'd already found the letter inside the pocket watch, he'd shaken his head as though that didn't matter at all.

Not the letter. The score. The final score, after the whistle blew.

The whistle?

Or the drums. I forget. It's like a skeleton, Fix. The skeleton of a song.

Maybe I had some backup already. Maybe John could pitch in for me in the way I'd refused to do for him.

Feeling slightly light-headed, I went back into the living room and rummaged around under the sofa cushions—my favored location for all flat valuables—until I found the sheet music I'd taken from the left-luggage locker at Victoria. I took it over to the table, laid it down, and smoothed out the worst of the creases.

The skeleton of a song. I hadn't even bothered to try to work out what that meant. Begging to differ from Sigmund, I'd never believed that dreams were the royal road to anywhere very much. But John was a drummer, and drummers are different from normal people. The skeleton of a song—not what was left when the substance of the song had rotted away, but the framework, the scaffolding, on which the rest of the song could be built.

That might be how a drummer felt about rhythm.

The notations on the sheet music were as opaque to me now as they had been when I first saw them: vertical flecks of ink densely but, as far as I could see, randomly spaced across the lines of the stave and the width of the page. Occasionally, a few marks interspersed that might have been letters or symbols: a vertical line with a horizontal slash near the top that could be a T or a plus sign; another that looked like a crude asterisk. Nothing to indicate how any of it fitted together or how it could be translated into sound.

Part of the problem was that I could never be arsed with reading sheet music even when I was trying to learn my own instrument. I picked out tunes in a rough and ready way, already listening more to whatever was going on in my head than anything else. So I didn't have much to compare this gibberish to.

If I was going to have a hope in hell of deciphering it, I'd need an expert.

I picked up the phone and dialed from memory. Got some irate old man out of bed because I was one step away from falling over and my thread-stripped brain had transposed two digits.

Tried again.

"Hello?" A woman's voice, fuzzy with sleep.

"Louise?" I said.

The same voice, a little sharper. "Yeah. Who's this?"

"Felix Castor."

"Fix. Fuck your mother, look at the goddamn time. Are you on something?"

"What's the name of your band, Lou?"

"My band?" she echoed with pained incomprehension.

"You still play, right?"

"Yeah."

"So what's the name of—"

"The Janitors of Anarchy. Fix, you didn't call me up in the middle of the night to ask—"

"No," I interrupted her, "I didn't. I just want to meet the drummer."

~ Twenty-one

HIS REAL NAME was Jamie Pomfret, Louise had said, but he played under the assumed splendor of Speedo Plank. I'd arranged to meet him at noon, allowing a generous seven hours for restorative unconsciousness. When I woke up, my head banging and my throat feeling like someone had tamped a couple of bagfuls of silica down into it, it was one-thirty. I called Louise again, getting a livelier and more varied torrent of abuse this time because she was properly awake. I apologized profusely, swore to God and a bunch of other guys that I'd never pull this shit on her again, and got her to call up Mr. Plank and reschedule.

Then I called Juliet's house, but it was Susan who picked up. She sounded cheerful enough until I told her where I was and asked if she'd heard from her other half. "But Jules is with you," Susan protested, confused.

"Not anymore," I admitted. I told her about my little difference of opinion with Juliet at the Golden Café in

Brokenshire, omitting some of the more colorful details, like Juliet kicking my arse around the room. Susan got more and more unhappy as she listened.

"But how will she get home?" she protested. "Felix, you shouldn't have left her there. She doesn't know how to behave without scaring or upsetting people. She's going to get into trouble."

The anxiety in her voice made me ashamed, even though there hadn't been any point in the proceedings where I'd felt like I had a choice. "She just walked out on me," I said, hearing the words as I said them and realizing how lame and evasive they sounded. "She was really angry, and she warned me not to follow her. Which I wasn't in any position to do, in any case. Long story, don't ask."

"But does she have her ticket? Her passport?"

"Susan," I said, trying to head off her alarm and anger, "she's back in the country already. She got back before I did. If she hasn't come home, that's because she's been . . . well, busy with other things. I was just hoping she might have gotten in touch with—"

"What kind of other things, Felix? What do you mean?"

I hedged. I didn't want to tell Susan Book that the woman [*sic*] she loved had been involved in a jailbreak—to free another woman (although one who was forty years dead and very convincingly disguised as a man) so that woman wouldn't have to stand trial for murder. It was probably a conversation that Juliet and Susan needed to have between themselves at some point, maybe over a glass of wine and a candlelit supper for two.

"It's something to do with the work she was doing for the Met," I said. Truth as far as it went. "I'm sure she's fine, but it was something she felt very strongly about, and she didn't want to wait. That's what I need to talk to her about, in fact. I've got some new information that I want to go over with her. If she comes home or gets in touch, could you tell her to call me?"

Susan said she'd pass the message along, but her tone was cold. She was blaming me for all this, in spite of my weasel words. As far as she was concerned, she'd invited me over for dinner, and I'd dragged a big bag of crap and chaos in with me and dumped it all over her floor. Even without knowing the whole story, she knew that much, and she was right.

I fixed myself a quick breakfast of toast and dry cereal, the milk in the fridge having transubstantiated into something green and malevolent. My neck and back ached so badly, I was moving like an arthritic granddad. The day was off to a great start.

Nicky had said they had Gary Coldwood in traction over at the Royal Free. A hop, a skip, and a jump, and I was treading the streets of Hampstead, a place where I've always felt as welcome as a slug in a salad. It didn't help that I'd forgotten to shave. Or maybe it did. At least people didn't seem inclined to intrude on my privacy.

There were two uniformed cops on duty outside the private ward where Coldwood was holed up, but they didn't stop me from going in or ask to take my name or anything. I wasn't sure whether they were there to stop Gary from leaving—in which case they probably should have had more faith in his broken legs—or if they'd been assigned to protect him from his screaming fans. Either way, they were earning their overtime fairly painlessly.

Coldwood wasn't feeling any pain, either, but that was

because he was doped up to the eyeballs and only about one tenth conscious. I sat there for ten minutes or so, wondering if he was going to surface far enough to realize that he wasn't alone. I wasn't even sure why I was here, or at least where the balance lay between apologizing and debriefing.

Eventually, I admitted defeat and got up to leave. Coldwood mumbled something, but it wasn't to me, and it wasn't intelligible. As I headed for the door, though, a nurse walked briskly in and cut off my escape. She was about forty and built like a Victorian wardrobe: a solid trapezoid with a single undifferentiated mound of breast like a continental shelf.

"Who are you?" she demanded brusquely.

"Friend of the family," I hedged.

"Well, you'll have to come back after I've given the sergeant his bed bath."

"I was hoping I could have a word with him about—"

"After his bed bath. Move along, please, or I'll do the both of you together."

I was about to protest at this ugly threat, but the noise of our voices made Coldwood stir and open his eyes, so we both shut up hurriedly.

"Fix," he mumbled. "Is that—Fuck, it is."

I hurried back to his bedside, ignoring the toxic glare of the nurse. "It's me, Gary," I said, kneeling down beside him in a posture familiar from a million tear-jerking scenes.

"Yeah." His voice was slurred and slow. "Thought I was just having a bad dream."

"You dream about me? Then what they're saying down at Uxbridge Road nick is true."

"Shut the—" He tailed off in the middle of the abuse,

his eyes defocusing. When his gaze found me again, he winced with the effort of concentration, obviously not sure what the hell I was doing there.

"Ruthven, Todd and Clay," I reminded him. "You had something juicy."

He nodded slowly. "Client base."

"Big-time gangsters?"

A shake of the head. "Judges. Politicos. Big businessmen. Ten pages of—fucking *Who's Who*."

"So?"

"So they meet once a month for a shindig at a fucking crematorium. Why'd you suppose that is?"

"They all went to the same school. Gary, once a calendar month, or—"

The nurse interrupted me, looming at my shoulder. "I think you're getting Sergeant Coldwood agitated," she chided me coldly.

"Lunar month," Coldwood mumbled. "Twenty-eight days. Every twenty-eight days. When it's—"

Dark of the moon.

Inscription night.

Its got to be on INSCRIPTION night, so you can get them all together.

I clapped Coldwood on the shoulder, even though he probably didn't feel it, and stood up. "Thanks, Gary," I said. "Feel better." When I left, the nurse was putting on rubber gloves. I wondered why people fetishized those things. They always scared the shit out of me.

I met Jamie/Speedo at the National Gallery, where, in his day job, he worked as a tour guide. That didn't seem to fit the profile, somehow, but maybe I stereotype drummers unfairly.

He was a bit of a letdown to look at as well. Very young, for one thing, and very shortsighted for another, wearing thick lenses of the kind that make you look not so much like an intellectual as some human-alien hybrid. His hair was short and neatly combed, with a faint sheen to it, as of gel or pomade. When he spoke in a quiet and diffident voice, I was inclined to think that I'd been put on a bum steer.

"You're a friend of Lou's," he said.

"Yeah."

"So what can I do for you? I can give you twenty minutes, then I've got to meet my next group."

We were in the gallery's main atrium, in between the cloakroom counter and the shop. Pomfret had been waiting at the desk when I arrived, visibly keen to get this over with, and he didn't seem any happier with me at first glance than I was with him. Then again, given the state of my face, I probably looked like a bare-knuckle fighter fallen on hard times.

I took the sheet music out of my pocket, unfolded it, and handed it to him. He scanned it with a critical eye. "What's the tune?" he asked at last.

"That's what I'm asking you," I answered. "Is there a tune in there? You're a drummer, so you'd know, right?"

He looked up from the music, shaking his head very emphatically. "No. I wouldn't. This is only a rhythm map. It's in hybrid notation, so it's not the easiest thing in the world to follow, but I've used both systems before, so I can roll with it. The thing is, it doesn't give you a tune. It only gives you the rhythms. And this one's really complicated. If I knew what the tune was, I'd be able to see how it all fits together."

"If I knew what the tune was, Speedo," I growled irritably, "I wouldn't be here. The tune's what I'm looking for."

Pomfret fired up all of a sudden, as though he had a reheat button and someone had just hit it. "Now, why are you pulling that crap on me?" he asked on a rising tone.

"What crap?" I asked, looking over my shoulder and then back at him, as if maybe he'd been hit by some crap flung by a chance passerby.

"Calling me Speedo. I'm Jamie here. Jamie Pomfret. My stage name's not a stick for you to poke me with, man. I don't want to hear it again in this conversation. Not if you expect me to do you a favor. I don't know you from a hole in the ground, and I don't have to put up with it. Okay?"

"Okay," I acknowledged, giving him a gesture that was halfway between a shrug and a hands-in-the-air surrender. "I'm sorry. I'm working in the dark on this, and it's putting me on edge. I didn't mean to sound like I'm taking the piss out of you."

Only partially mollified, Pomfret nodded. "Well, don't," he said. "Just don't, and we'll get along fine. I'll show you how the system works—what you can get out of this sheet and what you can't. And that's all I'll have time for, so you'll have to do the rest yourself. Let's go to the café."

The café was more or less deserted, which suited me fine. I bought a cappuccino for Pomfret and a double espresso for me, adding a packet of crisps as a token gesture toward lunch—or whatever meal my jet-lagged intestines were expecting to receive.

Pomfret took a sip of his coffee, wiped the foam from

his upper lip with the back of his thumb, and spread the sheet music out on the table. "Okay," he said. "Can you read ordinary sheet music?"

"Barely," I said. "I don't come across it that much, but I know what all the bits and pieces mean."

"Okay. So you're used to the idea of the stave as a way of indicating a sequence of notes, yeah?"

"Yeah."

"In drum music, they don't. Obviously. How could they? So when drum music is done like this, on standard-form music paper, it uses the stave to do something else. Each line stands for a voice—one of the drums in the rig. Top line is high hat. Middle line, or anywhere around it, is the snare drum. Bottom line is the bass. So each of these vertical strokes is a hit on one of the drums. Unless they're crossed, like this." He pointed to one crossed line, then another, then a third. "Those are probably cymbals."

I blinked. It wasn't that this was so hard to absorb; it was that I was already being taken in a direction I hadn't expected to go in. When John Gittings did an exorcism he used a little handheld tambour. Anything more than that tended to be a bit unwieldy in the field. "So this is scored for a whole drum kit?" I said.

Pomfret nodded. "Yeah, most likely. I mean, you can make the lines stand for any assortment of drums; doesn't have to be high-snare-bass-cymbal. But it usually is."

"Okay," I said, letting the point ride for now. "What about all these other marks? Are they letters? That one looks like a T, and that one could be a K. And we've got asterisks, Morse code dots and dashes..."

"That's frame notation," Pomfret said. "Different system altogether. Different letters stand for different sounds.

D is for 'doum': That's the bass sound. T and K—'tek' and 'ka'—both stand for the treble sound, depending on whether you're using the strong hand or the weak hand to make it. Asterisks or dashes stand for rests. The thing is, you'd normally use this system for a hand drum, not a full rig. It's a bit weird to see the two being thrown in together like this. It's like—" He hesitated, frowning, as though he weren't entirely happy with whatever he was about to say.

"Like what?" I demanded.

"It's like the drummer was scoring for different players—at least two, maybe three—but he wanted to plan it all out on the one sheet because that's how he was seeing it in his head. As one massively complicated rhythm made out of all these separate bits and pieces."

I stared at the sheet, trying to translate the dense, scribbled marks into sounds inside my mind. They still defeated me. "Show me," I said.

Pomfret sucked his teeth. "Easy to say. I need something to be the drums." He looked around the table. "Okay," he said, "let's give it a go." He took his empty coffee cup and turned it upside down in its saucer. "High hat," he said. Then he did the same with mine. "Snare." The sugar basin, a steel cylinder full of sealed packets, he dumped out on the table. The basin itself, upturned, was placed next to the coffee cups. "Bass." That left two spoons, which he put one inside the other, bowl end toward him. "Cymbals."

He demonstrated each item. Flicking the saucers made the coffee cups rattle briefly and hollowly. Thumping the sugar basin made a slightly deeper note. Tapping the spoons made them scrape against each other with a metallic ring. "This is how it starts," he muttered. Rattle rattle thump rattle rattle ring thump ring. "Then you get a backbeat coming in here like this—just the bass." Thump rest thump thump rest thump rest thump thump rest. "Okay, and now this. The hand drums. Beat then break. Beat then two breaks. You do that—on the edge of the table."

I gave it my best shot, unwillingly at first and feeling like an idiot. The waitress at the counter was looking over at us with something that was either concern or annoyance or maybe a mixture of both. But Pomfret didn't care—he was listening to some inner voice now, head tilted at a slight angle, gaze flicking from the sheet to empty space and then back again. The beat seemed to be accelerating, or at least Pomfret was playing it faster, his fingers flicking across the table so fast they almost became invisible.

Amazingly, something was starting to show through. As I whacked the table in crude synchrony with his skein of rattling, clanking sounds, there was a dim sense in my mind of random and disconnected things coming tight, coming together, and making meaning as they came—like the loose strings of a cat's cradle drawn taut between some child's fingers. Noise into signal.

Pomfret seemed less impressed. "No, that's shit," he grumbled, stopping abruptly. "The sounds are too similar." He rotated the bigger of the two coffee cups out of the lineup and replaced it with an empty Coke can from the next table. He tested it out, seemed satisfied with it, tried again and again, built up gradually from slow and steady to fast and furious, as if the rhythm had its own internal logic that dictated an accelerando tempo.

My rough-and-ready accompaniment became more

confident, even though I was reading the sheet music upside down. Actually, I was reading it less and less, because I was starting to see where the rhythm was going and could anticipate what shape my own part of it was meant to take. It was only a beginning, but it was strengthening with every moment that passed. Even though I was well outside my comfort zone, I was glimpsing the weave that John had made: the binding that was the first phase of an exorcism.

But Pomfret slowed down and stopped. "Look," he said, tapping the sheet. "He's adding in extra lines to the stave here. He's got to have three drummers now—one with a full kit and two with tablas or something. And it all goes crazy, because the new guy is half a beat out from the other two. He's just driving a bus through the rhythm."

"It closes the gap," I murmured, still hearing the beat inside my head. "It sneaks around behind them and closes the gap. This is incredible. Don't stop."

"I've only got two hands," Pomfret said. He looked at his watch. "And I've got to go, anyway. Look, whatever this stuff is, I wouldn't waste too much time on it if I were you. It's going to sound like shit, whatever it's played on. If it's something Lou put you on to, she's probably having a joke with you."

I came down reluctantly from the one-step-removed-from-reality zone I'd started to float away into. I stood up, gathering the sheet music with care. "It's no joke," I assured him. "Thanks for your help. When's your next gig?"

Pomfret blinked owlishly behind his oversize spectacles. "Tuesday," he said. "The Lock Tavern in Chalk Farm."

"I'll be there," I said. "I want to hear what you're like when you're Speedo Plank."

I checked out a couple of places where Juliet might have been; talked to a few people who might have seen her; got nowhere, not particularly fast.

The next few hours were going to be agony. I prowled around central London like a banished ghost looking for somewhere new to haunt. I felt angry and restless, a sour taste in my mouth because even now—having been told where my enemy lived, having had a loaded weapon placed in my hands—I couldn't act. Couldn't move until I'd filled in at least some of the blank spaces in my mental map: the spaces that currently read "here be monsters."

First and foremost, there was the question of what kind of odds I was facing. How many of the born-again killers would be at Mount Grace, and would I meet them in the flesh or in the spirit? It made a difference. John's symphony for drums might do what he'd obviously designed it to do, but if the souls of the dead were flying around loose when I walked in through the door, they could probably get to me before I got to them. If they were wearing other men's bodies, they'd put up a different kind of resistance, but at least I wouldn't have to worry about being possessed and turned into a meat robot, the way I suspected John had been.

Then there was the even spikier question of how far this network of the evil dead extended. They owned Mount Grace—owned the Palance estate, effectively, through the trustees who employed Peter Covington and ruled in the name of poor, senile old Lionel. They had their own law firm, for Christ's sake. There could be dozens or hundreds of them out in the field, wearing the bodies of the rich and famous and wielding their names. That would take a bigger nut than me to crack, if it could be cracked at all.

That was why I had to go through Ruthven, Todd and Clay before I went back out to Mount Grace. In some ways, it was a lousy idea, but I couldn't come up with a better one. I had to get hold of Maynard Todd's files. I had to know how big this was and how deep it went, or all I'd achieve by charging into Mount Grace would be to poke the nest and make sure the wasps came out good and angry.

So I had to go to Todd's office, and I couldn't make my move there until after they closed for the night. In the meantime, all I could do was wait—wondering what Juliet was up to and whether Myriam Kale had added any more notches to her garter belt.

I did have one more stop on my itinerary, though, and it was welcome in one respect only: because it had nothing at all to do with the mess I'd gotten myself into. It belonged to a different mess, older and, if anything, more intractable.

I could have taken a taxi to the Charles Stanger clinic, but my pockets were almost empty, and my bank balance was in the last stages of its historic decline. I had to husband my resources. So I took the tube to East Finchley and walked.

There was good news even before I went through the gates: The sound of rhythmic chanting reached me on Coppetts Road as I walked along the outer fence. I couldn't make out any words, but chants are chants. On marches and sit-ins and occupations, they all carry the same message, which is a variation on "You won't move us/stop us/intimidate us/make us cut our hair and wear suits." So the blockade was still in place, and morale was high. That meant, at the very least, that Jenna-Jane hadn't managed to get her hands on Rafi so far.

The Breath of Lifers were clearly there for the duration. They'd put up tents and benders, and they were ambling among them like early arrivals at a rock concert. Some of them were cooking on portable stoves or the little disposable barbecue sets they sell in Sainsbury's.

But when I finally located Pen among the happy campers, she looked so tired and so low that I was dismayed. She seemed to be equally shocked when she got her first look at me, but she didn't ask how my face came to look like a pound of raw chuck steak. The question would have carried too many messages she didn't want to send.

"So how's it all going?" I asked with forced lightness as we sat together on the crest of a tiny hill away from the main scrum of demonstrators.

Pen's shoulders twitched in the merest suggestion of a shrug. "We've managed to hold them off so far," she said. "They almost got him last night, because we weren't covering the kitchen entrance, where they take food deliveries. It's got its own car park, and it's way over on the other side of the building, and we just weren't thinking."

"But you've got it covered now?"

"Oh yeah. We were lucky that the driver was an idiot. He didn't think to switch off his headlights, so someone saw the van coming, and we got there in time to head them off." She tugged listlessly at the grass between her feet. "But it's only a matter of time. They've been trying to get a court order telling us to cease and desist. That magistrate up in Barnet—Runcie—he's bumped it up the docket somehow, and they're going to get a verdict tomorrow morning. Mulbridge must have slipped him a bribe or something."

"Not J-J's style," I observed. "She'd much rather put a knife to your windpipe than a tenner in your back pocket. It's all a matter of nuance."

Pen looked at me with glum resentment. "I'm not appreciating the nuances right now, Fix. In case you hadn't noticed, it's all I can do to keep up with the logistics. Can you spell me? I haven't slept since the last time I saw you."

"Sleep now," I suggested. "They're not going to try anything in broad daylight—especially not if they're expecting the courts to give them a thumbs-up to throw you out tomorrow."

She blinked in slow motion, her shadow-rimmed eyes not wanting to open again once she'd let them close. "But you'll stay," she pressed, the words forced out of her. "I can't sleep unless I know someone's watching. Someone who cares about him."

It wasn't what I wanted to do. I was thinking of the fight I had ahead of me: of Myriam Kale riding Doug Hunter back out into the world when I still hadn't made a single move against the real enemy—when I didn't even know who or how many they were, and I wouldn't begin to find out until I'd raided Maynard Todd's office and turned over his files. Time wasn't on my side. It was hard to sit here and feel the odds getting longer.

But I could see that Pen's natural resilience had reached its limits. She looked brittle, strained, liable to break in pieces at any moment.

"I'll stay," I said. "Put your head down. I'll wake you in an hour."

As things turned out, I gave her two and some odd minutes. The shadow of the Stanger clinic reached out toward us and then spilled over us while she slept. The Breathers ebbed and flowed, celebrating the oneness of all life on both sides of the grave, with chants and gestures of defiance that nobody except them was listening to.

"Soul and flesh are friends! Soul and flesh will mend! Death is not the end!"

I gave them one out of three.

While I was waiting, I killed the time by looking over the sheet music again, reading it as Jamie/Speedo had told me to, trying to sound the rhythms—the beats and the pauses, the overlaps and elisions—inside my head. I was imagining a tune that you could build to clothe that percussive skeleton; trying to translate a symphony for drums into something else. It was hard work, and it sucked me in hypnotically, taking me out of my flesh into the void where my weird talent operated. I was hardly aware of the passage of time, and it was only when Pen stirred on the grass beside me that I came to myself again—bringing back with me a few more crumbs of possibility, a few more twisted ribbons of not-quite-music. John's symphony, to a nondrummer, was like a five thousand–piece jigsaw where you had to put all the pieces in at once by pure guesswork and then see if what you got made any sense.

"What time is it?" Pen asked muzzily.

I looked at my watch. "After five," I said. "How are you feeling? A bit more human?"

"Like a limp biscuit," Pen muttered. She sat up and rubbed her eyes. "But go, if you need to. I'll manage."

I wasn't sure what cues I'd been giving off that told her how much of a hurry I was in to leave. We'd known each other long enough that stuff like that reached the level of telepathy. "Okay," I said, climbing to my feet. "Hold out for tonight. Tomorrow I'll be back in force."

She stared up at me, shielding her eyes against the setting sun that hung over my shoulder. "If you're back at all," she said.

"I didn't say that," I protested.

"Yes, you did." She stood up, too, and took a step toward me almost against her will. I thought that she might embrace me; she seemed to bring her arms up in synchrony but then stopped, retreated, folded them instead. "I'll never forgive you for what you did to Rafi," she said.

"I'm not looking for forgiveness, Pen. But if I do, I'll look elsewhere."

"But I don't want you to kill yourself working some stupid case. Werewolves can eat you. Demons can blind you and rape you and suck out your soul. Almost everything out there is faster than you, and all you've got is that stupid whistle. Whatever it is you've got it in your head to do, Fix, don't do it. I can see from here that you don't think it's going to work."

I mimed a dealer at a blackjack table. It's a gesture I've used on her a lot of times, when she seemed to be trying to give me a tarot reading without her deck in her hands. It always irritates her, and it always pushes her away—which was where I wanted her right then because she was way too close for comfort.

"Fine, then," she snapped. "Go and kill yourself. Don't worry about the shit you're leaving Rafi in. Let someone else pick up the bill. That's the default setting, isn't it?"

"Reckless hedonism," I agreed. "Devil take the hindmost."

"Which devil, Fix?"

"Next time I pass by, I'll bring you a catalog and some color swatches."

I walked away quickly, before she could get over the irritation and tackle me from a different direction. I didn't want to explain any more than I already had, and even more than that, I didn't want to go into this whole exercise with the feeling that there was another way I was too stupid to see. That just gets you second-guessing yourself, and that just gets you dead. I wanted to live.

But that's always been my problem. I set my sights way too high.

～ Twenty-two

STOKE NEWINGTON after dark: the Lubovich Hassidim and the scallies from Manor House wander the streets in feral packs, but I was in a bad enough mood by this time to take on anything I was likely to meet. God was in a bad mood, too—a strong wind was getting up, harrying plastic carrier bags and scraps of paper along the pavements, and the sky was filling up with pregnant clouds.

The offices of Ruthven, Todd and Clay were in reassuringly total darkness. I circled the outside of the building looking for the likeliest way in, deciding at last to go in from the back and on the first floor. I had my lockpicks with me and could have taken the street door inside of a New York minute, but there was too much chance of being seen by people walking past. I couldn't afford the time I'd lose in any brush with the forces of the law.

On the side street behind the office, there was a blind alley full of wheely bins and old fridges, the high walls topped with broken glass set in very old cement. The only door was bolted from the inside rather than locked, but the brickwork on either side of it was old and frost-pitted and offered pretty good purchase. I shinnied up the doorway itself, using footholds in the brickwork where I found them and bracing myself against either side where I didn't.

The top of the door was a couple of inches below the top of the frame. I stood on the door, wadded up my coat, and laid it down on the glass. I only had to stand on it for a moment, using it to step across to a shed roof. Then I leaned out and hooked the coat across after me, only a little worse for the wear.

The coat came into play again almost immediately. I wrapped it around my fist to break a single pane of the window at the other end of the shed and then—with gingerly care—to knock the broken glass out of the frame. It was handy that the building had never been double-glazed, although if it had, I could have dropped down into the yard and tried my luck with the back door. Safely out of view, I could have taken my time.

As it was, things seemed to be going my way. Even groping around in the dark and at an odd angle, kneeling because the pane was on a level with my knee, I found the window catch almost immediately and was able to lever it open. I slid the window up as far as it would go and climbed inside.

There was carpet under my feet, but it was too dark for me to see anything of the layout of the room I was in. Fighting the urge to blunder ahead and find my way by feel, I waited for my eyes to get a little more accustomed to the dark. It was just as well I did. As the space around me resolved itself slowly out of shadows into some degree of visibility, I realized that I wasn't in a room at all. I was in a turn of the stairwell, which was just as narrow as I remembered it. My first step would have pitched me down the stairs on my head.

Trying to remember the building from my one and only daytime visit, I went up rather than down. I had a rough sense where Todd's door would be in relation to the stairs, but not how far up it was. The first door opened when I tried the handle, but the layout within was wrong—the desk was over against the far wall instead of under the window. I pulled the door shut behind me and went on up.

On the next floor, the corresponding door seemed to be locked, but then I noticed with a faint stir of surprise that it was bolted from the outside. I undid the bolt and peered in.

This time the darkness was absolute, even when I pushed the door wide open. More unsettlingly, the room was emitting a soft bass rumble, almost more vibration than sound. Under the circumstances, there were close on a million good reasons for not turning the light on, but that was what I did. It was almost automatic—groping on the wall to my left to see if there was a switch there and, once I found it, flicking it on.

Outside of the movies, I'd never seen an assassin dismount and dismantle his sniper rifle and carefully put the pieces away in the sculpted foam receptacles of a sleek black suitcase. I assumed it happened, but with no personal experience to go on, I had to take it on trust. But I am now in a position to comment if I'm ever in a conversation about dismantled werewolves. When the light clicked on, that was what I was looking at.

The room was full of cats, and they were all asleep: on the floor, on the furniture, on the shelves, covering every surface in sight. The deep vibration was caused by their combined synchronous purring. I took an involuntary step backward, recoiling from the implications of what I was seeing. And in that queasy moment, as I hovered on the cusp of a decision, a cat in the center of the room, a big white-furred Persian lying on top of an antique rolltop escritoire, opened its eyes.

Then the cats around it did, too, and their neighbors and so forth, out from the center in a spreading wave, like one vast creature sending a single instruction via an old and creaky nervous system that took its own sweet time getting the message through.

A hundred or more cats stared at me, with ancient and inscrutable malevolence in their eyes. It was deeply, viscerally nasty, but there was worse to come. The Persian mewled on a rising tone, and the cats on either side of it pressed in and nuzzled its cheeks as if to comfort it. But that gentle contact became a firmer pressure, held for too long, and the flesh and fur of the three cats' faces started to run together into a repulsive, amorphous mass. The bodies followed, and more cats were crowding in, jumping down from dusty shelves full of old books of legal precedents or leaping up from the floor to join the press.

With a single muttered "Fuck!" I pulled my coat wide open and hooked my whistle out of the inside pocket. It occurred to me fleetingly to back out and bolt the door again, but what good would that do? When these cats coalesced into the creature they were going to become, doors weren't going to hold it.

The three cats in the center were gone now. The

spherical mound of pulpy flesh they'd become had a rudimentary face. The mound rose from the desk as more cats added themselves to the base of it, deliquescing more quickly all the time as though the process were gaining its own momentum. Working from memory, I found the stops and started to play.

I'd long ago forgotten the tune I'd composed to get the drop on Scrub the last time we'd met, and I couldn't be sure that this creature was the same loup-garou that had once worn the name and shape. Like Juliet said, if one werewolf could organize itself as a colony creature, then probably they all could if they got the inspiration.

I had one thing going for me, and one thing only. As the loup-garou in front of me assembled itself by inches and ounces, the sense of it grew stronger in my second sight, or rather my second hearing. The tune of the loup-garou strengthened and strengthened, became more vivid and inescapable from moment to moment. I let the plangent notes fill me, and then I let them ooze out of me through my lungs and my throat and my fingertips and the fragile piece of molded metal in my hands.

The coagulating mass in front of me roared in anger. It was much bigger already, and its disconcertingly liquid substance spilled down from the desk onto the floor, allowing the remaining cats a much bigger surface area to adhere to and be absorbed into. A stumpy appendage reached out toward me and developed blisters on its outer surface. The blisters grew into recognizable fingers that opened and closed spasmodically. Rapier claws grew out from the fingertips.

I was fighting panic now. I wanted to hurry, but the logic of the tune was pulling me in the opposite direction.

making me slow down, hold the notes as long as I could, and let them glide out into the room on a descending scale. The tower of matter quivered, ripples chasing one another across its surface. Each ripple was like the pass of a magician's hand, leaving behind first fur, then bare, disquietingly pink flesh, then fur again. The limbs were forced out from the main mass like meat from a mincing machine, and as soon as the legs were able to stand, they began to lurch toward me. The face rose and was extruded from the top of the tower like an obscene bubble, the flesh below it crimping and narrowing, creating a head and neck by default. It was all of a piece, the eyes the same color and texture as the flesh of the face, but they were starting to clear as I watched. The face leered, and my panic grew.

But the tune was right, and I was wrong. Slow and steady, note upon skirling note, it laid itself on the nascent thing in front of me like chains. It was working. The only question was whether it was working fast enough to keep me from being eaten alive. The loup-garou slowed, its back bent as though under a heavy weight, but it didn't stop. It took another step forward, the clutch of scimitars at the end of its arm flexing and clashing in front of my face. Its toothless mouth gaped open and grew fangs that solidified from doughy pink to gleaming white. I lurched back involuntarily, and the door frame banged my left elbow, almost knocking the whistle out of my hands. That would have been the end of the story, but I recovered with only a brief slur on one note of the tune.

A morbid paralysis was seizing the loup-garou, but it was coming from the feet on up. Its upper body still had a lot of flexibility, and it leaned forward, aiming a raking slash at my throat. I ducked back on my trailing foot, and the wicked claws turned the front of my coat into confetti. A sharp pain and a rush of warmth down my chest told me that at least one had drawn blood. Shuffling like a blind man, I backed out onto the landing an inch at a time until the wooden stair rail was pressing against the small of my back and I knew there was nowhere else to run. My options had narrowed to two: play or die.

I played, forcing the other option out of my mind. The loup-garou's legs buckled, and it crashed down onto its knees, but it was still trying to reach me. When the claws of the thing's outstretched arm slashed at my ankle, I ducked to the side and kicked it away. The loup-garou roared again, but the sound had a sloughing, sucking fall to it. It was the sound of something falling apart from the inside out.

The face, now fully formed, stared at me with indelible hatred. It was Scrub's face at first, then another wave crossed the surface of that flesh ocean, and it was the face of Leonard the copyboy. Struggling to form words, it spewed out blood and black bile. A few fragments of sound bubbled through the liquid decay. "C-Cas-Cast—"

The eyes became opaque again, and the fluid in the gaping mouth congealed all at once into something that looked as shiny and vitreous as setting tar. The loup-garou was probably dead by this point, but strange movements from this or that part of the massive, slumped body made me wary of stepping in close to check. I left it there, sprawled on the landing like something huge and unwanted left out for the dustman.

Maynard Todd's office was on the next turn of the stairs; I knew it when I saw the light already on. I didn't see anything particularly to be gained by subtlety. My fight with Scrub had made enough noise to wake the dead, assuming there were any more of them around, so anybody in there knew I was coming. I could always turn and walk away, but that didn't seem like an option. So I pushed the door wide and went on in.

Todd was sitting at his desk, the chair tilted back slightly so that he could lean on the shelves behind him. The gun in his hand was pointing at my chest, and his posture was completely relaxed.

"Mr. Castor," he said, pushing the chair on the client side of the desk out toward me with his foot. "How is it that you can never rely on religious cultists even to get a simple murder right? Take away their pentagrams and their mystic sigils, they're like little kids. I was very disappointed to hear that you'd survived your little trip to Alabama. But I try to treat every setback as an opportunity. Come on in and sit down."

I walked into the room, but I didn't take the chair. So long as I was standing, there was a chance I might get the drop on him at some point. Sitting down, I was dead meat. "Working late," I commented.

His gaze flicked the corner of the room. Looking in that direction myself, I saw a foldout bed. "I sleep here these days," Todd said, sounding a little flat and resigned. "Mrs. Todd has filed divorce papers. She says I'm not the man she married. And you know what? She has a point. I asked you to sit down, Mr. Castor. A bullet through your kneecap would force the issue."

I sat down. I wondered why he hadn't killed me already, if that was the plan. Maybe because he was worried about getting blood on the carpet. If that was it, his night was going to be ruined when he saw what was on the second-floor landing.

"You've come a long way in a short while," Todd went on. "That's a tribute to your detective skills."

"Thanks."

"Except that you're not a detective." Todd's tone hardened, and he gave me a look of actual dislike. "You're just a man who gets rid of unwanted ghosts. One step up from a backstreet abortionist. What they do at the start of the life cycle, you do at the end. And like them, you're doing it for the money. You don't have either the brains or the motivation to figure us out."

I didn't bother to give him an answer, because he didn't seem to need one. There was a photo of a beautiful if slightly austere-looking brunette on his desk. I picked it up and inspected it thoughtfully. "So who *did* Mrs. Todd marry?" I asked.

"An ambulance chaser with a death wish."

"Whereas you—?"

"I'm nobody you've heard of. The way I see it, if a criminal gets a name for himself, it's because he's stupid enough to get noticed. But this isn't a conversation we're having here, Mr. Castor. It may look like one, but that's only because it's hard to shake off the veneer of civilization. I'm a bit out of practice when it comes to actually hurting people. That was a conscious decision on our part—switching over to legitimate enterprises as far as possible—but it's got its drawbacks. You lose the professional edge." He leaned forward, putting the front legs of his chair back on the carpet, and stood up. "To tell you the truth," he said, coming around the desk, "back in Mile End, I always preferred a knife to a gun. So I'll probably start with a knife, if that's all right with you. Just while I'm easing myself back in. You get more control that way, too. It would annoy me if you bled to death or went into shock before you tell me what I need to know."

Aha. So that was how it was. I tensed as he approached, looking for a window of opportunity into which I could shove a low blow or a kick to the balls. But he stayed carefully out of my reach as he rummaged in his pocket. I expected his hand to come out with a knife in it, but it didn't. He was holding a sturdy, slightly scuffed pair of police handcuffs. That was worse news, in a way.

"Pass your hands through the bars of the chairback," Todd ordered me.

"Tell me what you need to know," I temporized, meeting his cold, stern gaze. "Maybe we can do this the easy way."

Todd shook his head. "The hard way is the way I know," he said. "And I tend to rely on the product more if I've squeezed it out myself, so to speak. Last time of asking, Mr. Castor."

I hesitated. There were ways of slipping out of handcuffs, but it helped if the guy putting them on you was a bit of a dim bulb. Play along or lose a kneecap? I made the call and did as I was told, not liking it much. Unfortunately, Todd was skilled and careful. He pressed hard, closing the cuffs as far as the ratchets would let him, and even though I clenched my fists and tensed the muscles of my forearms in the best traditions of Ian Fleming, I could feel that there was no leeway. I was firmly attached to the chair, and the only ways out were springing the lock on the cuffs—possible only with a pick—or smashing the chair to kindling. It didn't seem that likely that Todd would sit still for either.

"Okay," he said, straightening only after he'd tugged on each of my arms and satisfied himself that my hands didn't have enough free play to reach my coat or trouser pockets. He didn't bother to search me. Probably he surmised, rightly, that there was nothing I was carrying that could trump a .38.

He went back around the desk, opened the top drawer, and took out a very serious piece of ironmongery. The blade was only four or five inches long, but it was curiously shaped, with a slight thickening an inch below the point and an asymmetrical profile. The grip was of black polymerized rubber. This was a knife designed for lethal use in difficult circumstances: a weapon of very intimate and individual destruction.

"You've come a long way from Mile End," I said, for something to say.

"Oh, yes," Todd agreed, testing the edge of the blade on the ball of his thumb. "But it's an easy commute. You're about to find out how easy."

"You think I was stupid enough to walk in here alone?"

"Well, you arrived alone, so yes. That's exactly what I think. If I'm wrong, I may end up being seriously embarrassed. But let's look on the bright side: I'm not wrong, and that's not going to happen." He ambled back around to my side of the desk, where he half sat, half leaned against it. The posture of a man settling in for the long haul. "So who are you working for?" he asked.

I wasn't interested in misdirection or strategy. I just wanted to find an answer that would keep me from getting carved up for as long as possible. The longer I stalled, the better the chance that something might come up that I could use against Todd. Okay, I was clutching at straws. I knew how bad the situation was, but hope—even pathetic, bargain-basement hope—springs eternal.

"A woman named Janine Hunter," I said. "Her old man's up on a murder charge, and she—"

The tip of the knife dipped, flicked across my cheek. Something warm and wet spilled down over my face, and I was tasting my own blood.

"Janine," Todd said. "Yes. We know about Janine." He sounded so detached, I thought he might be on the verge of wandering away and finding something better to do with his time. "She works reasonably well as a cover story. Full marks for effort there. But what I want to know, obviously, is who told you about us. About Mount Grace, and Lionel Palance, and the whole operation. The way we come back. We saw it happen with Gittings, and then we saw it again with you. A little bit of fumbling around for effect, and then you go right to where the answers are. Because someone's driving from the backseat. That's the name I need, Mr. Castor. Confession is going to be good for your soul. And for—let's say—your left eye." To add emphasis to the words, he held the knife in front of my eyes and showed me my own blood on the blade. "Then your right, after a very short interval for reflection."

So the truth wouldn't do, I thought. I'd have to fall back on bullshit. "I don't know his name," I said. "We only talked over the phone."

"Then how did he pay you? I've checked your bank account. There's even less action going on there than in your love life. So there must have been a meeting. Describe him for me."

It's meant to be harder to lie to someone if you're

making eye contact with him. I made myself stare Todd straight in the face, so he didn't run away with any ideas about my reliability as an informant.

"He'll kill me," I said.

Todd shook his head. "No," he reassured me. "He won't. I'll kill you as soon as I've got all the details straight. So don't worry about him. Worry about me and about how messy this will get if you start being coy. What does he look like, our man? Details. As many as you can give me."

I bowed my head as if I was giving in to the inevitable. "Tall," I said. "Taller than me. About my age, maybe a little older. Wore a suit even more expensive than yours. Had a beard. Not full—trimmed. A guy who cares about his appearance."

"Eyes?"

"Didn't notice."

"Hair?"

"Blond."

I could see only the lower half of Todd's body from this position, but even so, he couldn't mask a slight stiffening in his posture—a coming to attention. Either he hadn't been expecting that, or it had confirmed his worst fears.

"Build?" he said. He was trying to sound as bored and disengaged as he was before, but it rang false now. Interesting. It would be nice to live long enough to find out what that meant.

"He was heavyset," I said. "A bit of a brawler. But an upper-class brawler, obviously. None of your street trash."

"Look at me," Todd snapped. I raised my head again. Todd pointed the knife at my left eye. "I was there when you—" he started to say, but then he obviously had second thoughts. "Accent?" he demanded brusquely.

"Like yours. Cultured, you know, but only the one coat of paint. Something else showing through."

"Is that right?" He smiled the way a shark smiles. "You saw through me, did you, Castor? Right, right. You're way too sharp for the likes of me."

The knife snaked in a second time, and I yelled in pain and fear. But when Todd straightened again, I was still seeing out of both eyes. It was my ear he'd cut, the knife blade coming away on a rising trajectory as though he'd drawn a tick. Cheekbone: check. Ear: check.

"What did you call him?" he asked in the same conversational tone. "This cultured prizefighter?"

My mind was full of dancing devils, for some reason. "Louie," I said, thinking of Louis Cyphre in the movie *Angel Heart*. What a crock of shit that was. You sort of hope that if the devil's into wordplay, he'll show a little more class. "Louie...Rourke."

"And how did he contact you?"

I shrugged, trying not to let my relief show on my face. If he'd swallow Louie Rourke without blinking, there was hope for me yet. "I told you—by phone. He said he wanted to hire me to do an exorcism. A really big one. He said it might be dangerous, but nothing a good ghost-breaker wouldn't be able to handle. The money would be good—really good—and he'd give me all the information I needed to pull it off safely."

Todd wiped the blade on his own palm, inspected the smear of blood it left there. Then he looked at me again. "Congratulations," he said. "You just bought yourself another five minutes of life. Tell me about that. About how this...Rourke prepped you. What he already knew about us."

"Why do you care?" I demanded. A dangerous light flared behind Todd's eyes. It was a calculated risk. I needed a few seconds to think through the moves I'd made along the way and to scrape together an answer that might convince him. Well, I got the few seconds, but it was like they say: There's no such thing as a free lunch. Todd swung the knife a little more recklessly, and blood poured down from my forehead into my eyes. There are a lot of blood vessels in your forehead, and they bleed promiscuously. My eyes were glued shut in an instant. Todd opened them again with his thumbs on my eyelids. I blinked through the blood, up into his wide eyes.

"I care, you fucking imbecile, because it's him I want to get my hands on," he snarled. "Not you. What the fuck do you matter? You're dead already. You tell me enough to get my hands on this guy who's calling himself Rourke, and you get to die a little bit cleaner, that's all. That's what your life has come down to, Castor. You probably should have been a watchmaker."

"All right," I muttered thickly. "All right, just don't hurt me anymore."

It was kind of an embarrassing line, but it did the job. Todd sat back down on the edge of the desk and waved his interrogation tool expansively. "Then talk," he suggested.

"He—he told me about the inscription," I said, and I saw Todd's shoulders stiffen as he tried to avoid giving away anything on his face. Overfinessed, you bastard. Hunter had said three days. I did the mental arithmetic. "It's tonight, isn't it? He said it was going to be tonight."

Todd didn't bother to answer. "Go on."

"He told me there were about two hundred of you," I said, quoting the figure that Moloch had given me. "And that the operation had been going on for a good few years now. Since"—I tried to elide over the slight hesitation so Todd wouldn't notice it—"Aaron Silver's time. He said Silver was the founding member."

"Did he?"

I kept my eyes on his. "Was he wrong?"

"The man with the knife asks the questions, Castor. Keep talking until I tell you to stop."

"He knew about Silver and Les Lathwell being the same man. I guess that's what he meant, you know? That the guy had always been there, overseeing the whole operation." Todd's lips curled back in a sneer. He didn't like that form of words at all. Something else occurred to me: Hadn't Nicky told me that Silver's real name was Berg? Les Lathwell had been out in America in the sixties, learning the gangster game from the Chicago Mobs, and from Berg to Bergson wasn't a big jump at all. I chanced my arm. "It was Silver—I mean Les Lathwell—who brought in Myriam Kale, wasn't it? So there he is, taking the lead again. Actively recruiting for the cause. I bet a real psycho killer was a feather in your caps."

Todd raised the knife in his clenched fist but then thought better of it and gave me an openhanded smack across the face instead. "Are you really that fucking stupid?" he demanded. "Or are you trying to make me kill you before you talk? Kale was a goddamn disaster right from the start. I told him: She's sick in the head. For the rest of us, killing's a means to an end. For her, it's an addiction. A disease. She's never gonna stop, and she's always gonna draw the wrong kind of attention. She's the last thing in the world we want. Someone who shits in the nest because she doesn't know any better and you can't teach her any better. Fucking—madwoman!'"

Todd had been right about the veneer of civilization. Something earthy, East End, and broad was creeping into his accent as his emotions got the better of him. I decided to encourage it. If he was angry, then he was off balance and not thinking straight, and you never knew what kind of options might open themselves up.

"But it was Silver's choice," I said, "because it was his game. Mr. Rourke said if I could take Silver out, then everything else would fall apart of its own accord."

Todd laughed incredulously, shaking his head. "Take Silver out? Fuck, if I'd known that was on your agenda, I'd have waited and let you take a shot. We'd do it ourselves, except he's too cagey to give us an opening. Him and his American whore have fucking ruined us. Made us visible again after we worked for years to cover our tracks. Live forever. Live like *kings* forever. Build up an empire, stronger and safer than anything we had when we were alive. That was what was in the prospectus—and it was his own fucking prospectus! 'We can own this city.' And we do! We do own it! We take our cut, and we take our pleasure, and nobody even knows—or if they find out, they die, and their wives and kids die, and their gardens are sown with fucking salt. We've got it all. But you know what they say about love being blind. He wouldn't listen to reason. From the moment he met her, he was a changed man. Take Silver out?" He laughed again, but there was a bitter, choking sound in it. "You should have fucking said."

"Yeah," I agreed, "Kale was your weak spot all along. Every time you gave her a new body, she'd kill again..."

Todd was nodding, so I went on. All I was doing was what mediums do: using the stooge's feedback to refine the guesswork, zeroing in on the truth so it looks like you've known it all along. "The old psychosis showing itself again, every time. But you couldn't just stop. Couldn't just leave her in the ground. Silver wouldn't let you. So I guess Mr. Rourke was right about the pecking order."

"We're a collective," Todd growled. "Democratic and egalitarian. Everything is fair, and everything is set out nice and clear in the rules. You spend a year up on top, riding one of the bodies with the influence and the power and the celebrity lifestyle—then you spend a year as one of the grunts, earning your keep, minding the shop. We don't trust anyone else to maintain the crematorium or to guard it. We keep it all in the family.

"But that cuntbubble is as strong as the rest of us put together. He started to write his *own* rules. And because he's the oldest, we've got to go carefully. Time isn't just money, it's power, too. We don't know what kind of safeguards he put in place for himself back when he was the only one. Just in case of emergencies. He's never going to let himself be caught with his pants down. If we did kill him..." He didn't finish the sentence, but his shrug conveyed his meaning: that killing Aaron Silver, in flesh or spirit or both, would be the start of something, not the end of it. "So that was your brief," he said, coming back to the point. "Not the rest of us. Just Silver. That's why you went out to Alabama? Tracing his steps?"

"Looking for information about Kale. She seems to be his weak spot."

Todd nodded. "Yeah, you're right there. But the paraphernalia you collected from Chesney—most of that wasn't anything to do with Silver. So what was the deal there?"

"I didn't know what Chesney had," I temporized. "I had to take a look."

Todd looked surprised at that—and suspicious. "Then you weren't working with Gittings?"

I had the feeling of thin ice starting to crack under me. "Not directly," I said. "Gittings and Langley were the first string. I was the second. Rourke didn't activate me until they crashed and burned. And obviously, the first thing I had to do was to find out how far they'd gotten."

Todd was staring at me hard. Whatever was going on behind that stare, it wasn't looking good. "Then how come you spent so long sniffing around Gittings's widow?" he demanded.

I pretended to look uncomfortable and abashed. "Me and Carla are old friends," I said. "Kind of—more than friends once upon a time. I thought—you know, there wouldn't be any harm in reminding her of that."

Todd relaxed slightly, giving me a contemptuous grin. "That's actually funny, Castor. Groves was stuck inside the house right there with you, and all you were thinking about was getting your leg over?"

"I know," I said, adopting a tone of bitter, naked resentment. "I figured it out later. Groves was the one who possessed John, right?"

"Possessed him, realized the guy's brain was turning to cheese, shot himself. That was a hairy moment. If you're in someone else's body and he goes into the whole second-childhood thing, what happens to you? Groves didn't want to stick around and find out. And he thought he was safe because of the will. Return to sender. But he forgot about the wards on Gittings's door, too strong for him. He couldn't get out of the house. He had to pull that tantrum to get you interested. I wasn't sure what to make of you right then. I thought either you'd be useful or we'd end up having to kill you. But it turned out it wasn't an either-or kind of proposition."

"I thought John knew too much about your operation to walk into a trap," I said, trying to push his expansive mood as far as I could. "How did you get him?"

Todd seemed to have momentarily forgotten his rule about the man with the knife. He shrugged. "The actual recipe is a trade secret," he said. "But we got him the same way we get everyone. He came onto the premises, and we got the drop on him. That's what we had in mind for you, of course, on the day we burned Gittings. But your demon bitch walked in, and we had to abort the mission. We weren't sure we could take her down, and we didn't want yet another loose end floating around. That's the only reason you walked out of Mount Grace under your own steam. Best-laid plans.

"Listen, this has been illuminating, but I don't want to draw it out any longer. You want to buy some more time, or are you all out of revelations?"

He stood up and moved around to one side of me, knife in hand at the level of his waist. I could more or less see the angle he'd decided to use: an upthrust, probably to my throat, from behind and off to the side to minimize the amount of blood he got on himself.

"Rourke isn't alone," I said quickly. "There are two other guys. De Niro and Rampling—"

"Don't fight it, Castor. Under the circumstances, things could be a fuck of a sight worse."

I was already moving as his hand flashed up. I kicked with my legs, not against him—he hadn't been stupid enough to bring himself into range—but against the desk. I pitched out and down as the blade sliced shallowly across my shoulder.

I was hoping the impact would smash the back of the chair. It didn't. Desperately, I swung myself to the left and then to the right, sawing with the handcuff chain against the unyielding bars of the chairback. With a muffled exclamation, Todd leaned in over me, but the bars gave way, and I rolled aside as he reached for me, kicking out again in a one-two bicycling movement and missing him by a mile but fending him off long enough for me to swivel, get my knees on the ground, and lurch/stumble back up onto my feet. My hands were still cuffed behind my back, but at least I was in with a chance now.

Or I would have if Todd hadn't kept the gun in his pocket when he switched to the knife. He stepped back, the gun once again in his hand. He looked annoyed. "What the fuck did that achieve?" he demanded.

Was it a trick of the light, or was something moving behind him, outside the window? I took a step toward the door, and he moved in to block, which conveniently blindsided him as far as the window was concerned.

"You're not going to kill me," I said, playing for seconds.

"No?" Todd raised a mildly skeptical eyebrow. "How come?"

"The noise," I said. "Someone will hear. And you'll have a roomful of dead cats to explain as well as me."

He aimed at my head, thought better of it, lowered the gun to point it at my stomach: messier and more painful but a safer shot. "Silencer," he explained, and pulled the trigger. I was watching his hand, and I dropped as his index finger squeezed, but he still would have hit me. Even with gravity on my side, I couldn't outrace a bullet.

But the window exploded inward, and a human figure danced in a blur out of the unfolding storm of broken glass, limbs scything so quickly that they left stroboscopic afterimages on the air. There was a wet, insinuating crack, and Todd's arm folded backward at a point where the human body doesn't actually have a moving joint. The figure landed and turned without any sense of haste or even intention. It was like watching someone practice the steps of a dance. The figure kicked Todd in the stomach; the sound this time was more muffled, but the damage seemed as profound. Todd slid sideways against the desk, crumpling inward like a flower closing for the night, and then slowly sank down onto his knees.

Moloch straightened his cuffs like a dandy after a duel, staring down with cold amusement at the man he had just crippled. I gawped at him, confused and uncomprehending.

"Not the savior you were expecting?" the demon demanded, giving me a glance of cold, sardonic amusement. Todd was curled up almost into a fetal crouch on the floor, absolutely silent, absolutely still. He could even have been dead. The kick to the stomach was easily hard enough to have ruptured some vital organ.

I struggled up on one knee but then took a breather, my legs trembling. "Not exactly," I admitted hoarsely. "You told me you'd had enough of saving my life. I think you said it was my turn to scratch your back, or something to that effect."

"Yes. That's what I said. And that's what you did, Castor. That sad wreckage downstairs"—he kissed his fingers—"perfectly aged. The spirit filleted and pared from the flesh with great delicacy. I can't remember when I last ate so well."

I fought the urge to throw up. Moloch had walked around behind me and was busying himself with the handcuffs. I heard the links part with a loud, grating clank of metal against metal. Flexing my arms, I discovered that they were free to move, although the cuffs still hung around my wrists like bracelets, and my right shoulder throbbed agonizingly where Todd's knife had stabbed deep into the fleshy part of it.

I stood up a little shakily. "It's all part of the service," I said. "At least it is now. I didn't plan it this way."

"No," Moloch agreed. "But I've found you to be worth following. Serendipity is your whore. And I thought you'd work a little harder if you felt you were working without a safety net."

"Pick him up," I said, pointing at Todd. "Put him in the chair." Moloch nodded amiably, bent down, and hauled the lawyer to his feet. Todd wasn't dead; he wasn't even unconscious. But his face was deathly pale, and he screamed when Moloch lifted him, flailing with his good arm as his bad one dangled loosely at an impossible angle.

Moloch dropped Todd into the chair, then looked inquiringly at me. I'd crossed to the shattered window, and I was drinking in great gulps of the clean night air. I'd supped full with horrors, but it wasn't even midnight yet, and I had darker work still to do.

"See if you can find some rope," I muttered without

looking round. "He probably won't stay upright any other way."

———————————

The sheet music had taken a bit of damage when Scrub-slash-Leonard took that last wild swipe at my chest and almost laid my insides open to the world. Nothing that wouldn't heal, though. I laid it out on the desk and smoothed it down with the flat of my hand. Todd watched me with a shell-shocked lack of curiosity, his injured arm lashed across his chest, the other tied behind him. It turned out that the room where Scrub had been stowed contained a builder's drum of rope—about two hundred feet, unstarted. Moloch had used all of it to secure Todd to the chair, virtually weaving a cocoon around him and leaving very little of him still in view, apart from his pale face.

I sat myself on the desk, more or less where Todd had been sitting during my interrogation. Moloch stood over by the window with his back to us, letting me make my play with no interruptions. Maybe he just wasn't interested in this side of things.

"You started a sentence earlier," I reminded Todd. "You were there when I something-or-other. How was that going to end?"

"I forget," Todd said with a sneer that sounded convincing despite the slight slur in his voice. He had to be in a lot of pain. And it was going to get worse before it got better.

"Okay. Doesn't matter," I reassured him. "Todd, I broke in here tonight to look through your files and get the lowdown on the Mount Grace posse. But since you're here in the flesh—even if it isn't exactly your flesh—there's another favor you can do me. It's going to be ugly, and it's going to be messy, and at the end of it, I don't know what kind of shape you'll be in, but it won't be good. To tell you the truth, it makes me a little bit sick just thinking about it, but I'll do it if I have to. Because if it works, it could save my life later tonight. So I figure I'll cut you a deal. Tell me about the setup at the crematorium. About inscription night. How many people are going to be there. What sort of defenses they'll have laid on. When it will all get started and when's the best time to go in. Tell me what to expect and I'll leave it at that. I'll walk out the door, and the cleaners will find you in the morning."

Todd glanced up at me again from under half-lidded eyes. The pain of his injured arm seemed to have driven him into mild shock; either that or he was controlling it with some kind of meditation technique, because there was something otherworldly about his calm. He breathed out through his nostrils, conveying a world of contempt. "You bluff badly, Castor," he murmured. "I'm a dead man already, so death doesn't scare me. And I've got powerful friends. Torture me and kill me, I'll just come back."

"If you're dead, I can send you on your way," I countered. "That's what I do." Moloch perked up at that and looked around at me with a feral smile. The idea of catching Todd's soul on the wing seemed to be a turn-on for him.

"You," I said, pointing a finger at Moloch, "stay out of this or our deal's canceled. Try to take this one soul now, and you'll lose your chance of eating all the others. You understand me?"

Moloch's answer came from between bared teeth. "Yes."

"Okay, then." I turned to Todd again. "You know what I'm talking about," I said. "Don't you. I'm an exorcist. I have the power to bind and break you."

This time he managed a faint, sickly smile. "Do you?"

"Funny you should ask," I said deadpan. "Normally, if I'm this close to a ghost, no matter what it's wearing, I get a ping on my radar. When I met you and Scrub—sorry, I mean Leonard—downstairs here, I got nothing. And every time I've seen you outside this building, nothing all over again. You've got good camouflage, I have to say. I'd love to know how it's done. But then I guess you've been in the game long enough to have figured out a lot of the angles."

Todd didn't answer, but there was a glint in his eye as he looked at me—a hint of challenge or mockery. Looking down at the music, fixing the opening beats in my mind, I slid my whistle out of my inside pocket and shipped it into the operating position.

"But here's the bad news," I said. "John Gittings *did* manage to get a fix on you. I don't know where he was standing or what sort of tricks he used. He wasn't a particularly smart guy, in my opinion, but he did it anyway. He nailed you and got you down on paper." I cleared my throat, spat on the floor. "And that's what I'm going to play for you this evening," I muttered, not looking at Todd. I put the whistle to my lips, tried to find the sense. I took one deep breath, held it for a second, then another second, until the seconds became beats and the music invited me in.

Open with a hot trill like manic birdsong, but the bird's a dive-bomber, and it crashes down hard through the scale to level out a full octave lower in a welter of hard, pugnacious chords. Bail out into C and hold it for a full four beats before dropping even farther. It was all guesswork—and I was trying to cover both parts of John's wacky notation, playing two voices on the same instrument. Todd looked at me with blank puzzlement, but beyond that, he didn't respond.

Change the key, change the time, start again. Still no reaction from Todd. When I got to the hard part, where Jamie Pomfret had told me a third drummer was meant to come in, I started to tap my heel against the desk in crude counterpoint to the music. It was hard not to tap on the beat, but John's music was quite clear that the new voice should be at odds with the rest of the rhythm. I kept it up until the weird lack of synchronization made me stumble, lose my sense of direction, and stop dead in the middle of a bar.

"What's the point of this?" Moloch demanded.

"Shut up," I said, trying to think my way through the sequence that had just tripped me.

Again from the top, and faster now because the sense was growing inside me again: the sense that was my knack, my stock in trade, and that had started to kick in back at the National Gallery café when Pomfret was playing the cruet set for all he was worth. My fingers were finding the right stops almost without being told to, and the atonal skirl leaked out into the air like toxic waste.

Todd winced, which was encouraging. I had to hope it didn't only mean he was a music lover.

I skated up to the crux again, started to kick with one heel and then with both. The wailing voice of the whistle and the hollow thudding rhythm clashed and fought. Moloch shook his head and scowled, but Todd was starting to look a little afraid. "Castor—" he whispered. I couldn't hear the word under the music, but I saw his lips move and read it there. Another chord change brought a flicker of real pain, making him screw his eyes tight shut. John's evil medicine was working. A symphony for drums, played blind and fumbling on a tin whistle. But if it works, don't knock it.

"Castor!" Todd said again, louder. There was a catch in his voice, and his eyes rolled. I carried on playing. Deep in the logic of the scribbled score, it would have been almost impossible to stop. I'd given him a choice, but now there were no choices left. A single phrase from the David Bowie song "Sound and Vision" formed in the music and then dissolved, a surprise visitor from another dimension. Flying on autopilot, I was more surprised to see it there than anyone.

The music rushed to its climax, the backbeat limping along behind in a slow-quick-slow. Todd was yelling, tears coursing down his cheeks. "Ash! It's the ash! The ash is our physical focus, and we feed it to the people we want to take. Then we all invade them together, subdue them together, and a single spirit stays inside. Please, Castor! That's the truth. Inscription stops the host soul from reasserting itself. It's still there, but it's too weak to fight us. We reinscribe once a month, to make sure—Don't! Don't!"

He carried on babbling, but the words were lost to me in the drumming of my own blood. Drumming. Yes. This symphony needed percussion—demanded it. I jumped down off the desk and started stamping on the floor with my left foot. It turned into a clumsy dance. I was staggering around like a drunk, the sounds rising through me and making me move whichever way they needed me to move. Downstairs I'd played for my life, cold and focused, pulling every note out of my mind and out of the darkness by will alone. What was welling up inside me now was different, and will had very little part to play in it. The closing notes seemed almost to tear the back of my throat, and when they faded, I found that I was down on my knees on the floor beside Todd's chair.

Groggily, I straightened and stood. I stared down at the lawyer in his hemp cocoon. His head lolled at an angle, his glazed eyes staring at nothing. A string of spittle trailed from the corner of his mouth onto the collar of his shirt. I thought he was dead, but I realized after a few moments that his tongue was moving inside his mouth. He was trying to form words.

I bent down, put my ear to his mouth, and listened. Nothing intelligible, although there was a faint rise and fall of sound like the half-heard voices in between radio stations that you can never focus into audibility.

"You drove the possessing spirit out," Moloch said, at my elbow.

"Yeah, I did," I said, the words hurting my tender throat. "And look—someone else is still home."

"The original owner of this flesh," Moloch confirmed. "He seems—disoriented."

"He seems pretty much catatonic," I muttered, looking away. "Did you catch Todd on the wing?"

"*This* is Todd. The soul that animates this meat now. What fled is not Todd but someone else who lived in his body and stole his name. But no, I didn't eat it. You told me not to. I let it leave unmolested."

I nodded. I had to sit down. That performance had left

me feeling as hollow as a cored piece of fruit. A dull ache
was starting inside my head. I stumbled across to a vacant
chair and sank into it. My breath was coming as rough
and ragged as if I'd just swum the Channel, and panic was
settling on my mind like a physical weight.

The thing that had been Todd looked past me with its
eyes focused on nothing very much.

"What did he say?" I asked the demon. "He was shouting toward the end, but I couldn't stop to listen or I would
have lost the tune. Lost the sense of it."

He summarized with crisp precision, turning away
from the shell of Maynard Todd as though it held no further interest for him. "That they use the ash of their cremation as a physical vessel for the possession of new host
bodies. The host is tricked or forced into eating the ash.
Then all the souls in this—cabal—invade the intended
host at once, subduing his soul so that one of their number
can possess his body."

"I caught that much," I said. "I thought there was
more."

Moloch nodded. "He said they tried to do this to you
when you went to Mount Grace to burn John Gittings. Todd
gave you a drink of brandy from a hip flask. The ash was
dispersed in the liquor. But the succubus came before they
could complete the possession, and they had to stop."

I remembered the sudden terrible sickness that had
come over me as John's casket rolled through the furnace
doors. Not like me at all, and now I knew why. It *wasn't*
me at all.

"He also said that the procedure—the possession—is
only temporary. The soul of the possessed tries to reassert itself—tries to break free from their control. It gets

stronger again over time, however hard they whip it into submission. They have to meet at Mount Grace once a month to repeat the ritual, for want of a better word, and reassert their control. They do this at the dark of the moon, and they call it—"

"Inscription."

"Yes." He stared at me with a hungry intensity. "Castor, he answered your question, finally, when he was desperate and trying to make you spare him. But in any case, you'd only have to look out the window. The dark of the moon is tonight."

"I know."

"We have them. We can take them all."

I nodded slowly. "Yeah."

Maybe the feeling of foreboding I was experiencing was paranoia. I'd just performed a full exorcism—or something that felt like one. The ghost that had flown out from this room either should have vanished into the ether or should be heading for hell at a good cruising speed. That was where the smart money was lying.

But what was the worst-case scenario? That the tough old soul had been cast out but had the strength to resist utter dissolution. That it knew where it was going and had the strength to get there. Sure, the thing inside John Gittings had needed to be taken to Mount Grace and burned there again—but then John's house had more wards and fendings on it than Pentonville had bars. They were designed to keep the dead out, but they cut both ways. That was why the mad, desperate ghost had gone geist. But here at Todd's offices, as I'd noticed when I first came in, there wasn't anything to keep the evil dead from coming and going as they pleased.

So I'd had my rehearsal for the big show, and that was good, but it was more than possible I'd told the bastards I was coming. They'd have all the time in the world to prepare us a really nasty welcome.

"We've got to go now," I said.

Moloch gave me a look of ruthless, detached appraisal. "You think you can walk?" he asked.

I nodded again. "Yeah," I said from a fog of exhaustion and pain. "Just getting my second wind."

"We can't go now," he reminded me in the same cold tone. "We need the lady."

I climbed unwillingly to my feet. "I know," I muttered. "Can you find her?"

I didn't answer, because I didn't know. There was only one place I'd thought of that was worth looking, and I knew for a fact I wasn't going to be welcome there. I trudged down the stairs. I couldn't hear Moloch's footfalls, but the prickle on the back of my neck told me that he was following.

The night loomed ahead of us like a mountain. Only idiots climb mountains in the dark.

∼ Twenty-three

I HADN'T EXPECTED to be back in Royal Oak so soon, and Susan Book wasn't expecting to see me there. In the four or five seconds between "Jerusalem" sounding and the door opening, I braced myself for storms.

But Susan wasn't in the mood to give me a hard time. Her eyes looked swollen with unshed tears, or maybe with sleep. Everything about her posture suggested misery and a preemptive surrender to despair. Juliet's absence was obviously hitting her very hard. Given that even looking at Juliet felt a little bit like taking a hit of some illicit drug, to be withdrawn from her so suddenly must be like going into the instant, unwelcome free fall of cold turkey.

Susan stared at me. "I told you she wasn't here," she mumbled tonelessly.

"I know," I agreed. "I'm thinking that maybe I know a way to bring her back. Can I come in and explain?"

I hunched my shoulders against the gathering wind, playing the pity card to give myself an additional argument if my words didn't work. Beside me, Moloch tilted his head back, sniffed the air, and growled. "This hovel stinks of the lady," he said, in his car-wreck-in-slow-motion voice. Susan swiveled her head to stare at him, her eyes widening. She hadn't noticed him until he spoke.

Maybe after living with Juliet for so long, she could tell what he was by looking. That would explain the fear that crossed her face. But even if you didn't know, he was an intimidating presence, and he was glaring at her with an unreadable emotion in his dark eyes. Susan gripped the edge of the door in both hands, as though preparing to close it in our faces, but she hesitated, caught in a cross fire between her survival instinct and her good breeding.

I wasn't sure how to make the introduction, so I didn't try. Instead, I turned to Moloch as the more immediate problem. "Juliet lives here," I said to him. "But she's not here now. She hasn't made contact with anyone since she got back from the States. Well, apart from Doug Hunter, of course, and that's no use to us." I turned back to Susan. "Or has she called you?" I asked.

Susan's anxious gaze flicked back and forth between the two of us. "No," she said. "Not a word. I'm just— sitting here by the phone."

"She's probably lying," Moloch said, his tone detached and thoughtful. "You could hurt her and make sure, one way or the other. You clearly have impressive skills in that area."

Susan gave a yelp, like a dog that's had its tail trodden on, and tried to slam the door. Moloch held it open with one negligent, unhurried hand. I knocked the hand away, and he gave me a look of politely mystified inquiry as the door slammed in our faces.

"Nobody," I said with slow, heavy emphasis, "is hurting anyone. In fact, you're not even coming in here."

"No?" Moloch's voice was mild, but there was an edge of amusement to it.

"No. You're going to wait on the other side of the street, under that lamp." I pointed. "And you're not going to come near this door, or this house, until I come out."

"And why am I going to do that?"

"Because if you don't, the poor doggy isn't going to get so much as a bone to gnaw on. If you want to eat tonight, you'll do this my way."

He stared at me in silence for the space of two or three heartbeats. It felt like a lot longer.

"If she offers you tea," he said at last with a nasty grin, "decline it. Time is short enough as it is." He turned his back on me and walked away.

I knocked again and waited. After a minute or so, I rang the bell.

Eventually, the door opened a crack, and Susan stared out. The tears had been shed in the meantime. Her cheeks were wet, and her face, as she glowered up at me, was full of terrible pain. "You should go away now, Fix," she said, her voice surprisingly strong, as though crying had bled some poison out of her. "It's not right for you to be talking to me after what you did to Jules. You should have been a better friend to her."

I opened my mouth to say that it was Juliet who'd broken a table across my back, rather than the other way around, but this wasn't the time for scoring cheap points. "I think I can bring her back," I said again. "If I can come in for a minute, I'll explain what I want to do. If you say no, I'll leave."

"No. I don't want you to come in here. Not while I'm alone."

"Then let me explain out here," I suggested.

"I don't want to hear what you've got to say."

"Susan," I said, making my last pitch, "this is something she needs to know about. She's done something that might make it...hard for her to stay here on earth. Or at least here in London. Something that puts her way, way over on the wrong side of the law. She's made a choice, and in my opinion, it was the wrong one. It will hurt her."

"Nothing can hurt her," Susan said, shaking her head again. I wasn't sure if it was a boast or a lament.

"Losing you would hurt her, I think. And if she has to do a moonlight flit—if all the exorcists the Met can lay their hands on are sharpening their knives for her, and she makes the city too hot to hold her—she'll leave you behind." I paused to let that idea sink in, then went in for the kill. "Or do you think you can go and live with her folks for a while?"

A whole cavalcade of emotions crossed Susan's face. I wanted to look away. Moloch's words about my having a gift for hurting people were still hanging in the air. This wouldn't count as torture at Abu Ghraib, but standing on a doorstep in West London in the arse end of winter with the rising wind carving sharper edges on my face, that was exactly what it felt like.

Susan was looking at me, shaking her head, rejecting the picture I'd painted, or maybe rejecting me, seeing through my sullied flesh to my shabby heart and saying no. She stood aside wordlessly and let me come in, then closed the door, locked it, and bolted it top and bottom. I waited until she was done and let her lead the way into the living room. It was a gesture, a pretense that she was in control of what was happening. I thought about the aborted dinner party and everything that had happened since, and I had to struggle against a feeling of shame. Susan was right in spite of everything. I should have been a better friend.

She waved me to a chair with a visible lack of enthusiasm. I stayed standing. I didn't feel like I had a right to any hospitality. She sat down herself in one of the armchairs. It was a surprise, and not a happy one, to see a half-empty whiskey bottle and a half-full glass on the occasional table next to her.

"What I wanted to do," I explained, "was play the first few notes of an exorcism—an exorcism for Juliet." Susan's eyes went big and wide, and she started to speak, but I hurried on, talking over her. "Not the binding or the sending, Sue—just the summoning. Juliet said she'd hear that wherever I played it, and come and—" "Rip your throat out" had been her actual words; I groped for a mealymouthed substitute. "—stop me from finishing."

Susan glared at me in deep, almost speechless outrage. She was trembling now. "Oh, she'd stop you," she assured me.

"Believe me, Sue, I'm not underestimating her. I'm hoping I can explain why I've come before she cuts in and does something irrevocable to me. That's why I want to do it here. I'm thinking maybe she'll hesitate before doing something really violent in front of you. She wouldn't want to hurt or scare you."

That didn't seem to make Susan any happier. Exhausted as I was, and desperate as I was to be moving on and doing what had to be done before I fell down and passed out and deflated like a punctured balloon, I tried to explain. "There's a woman," I said. "Someone she met. Not—romantically. Met in the line of duty. And this woman needs help, that's the plain truth. Which is what Juliet is trying to do. But I don't think the help that Juliet is giving this woman is what she needs. This is what we argued about back in Alabama. There's more to it, but I'm hoping that Juliet will accept a compromise solution if I offer one." I shrugged. "That's it," I said. "The whole thing. So it's up to you. I'm going to do this anyway, but if you tell me not to do it here, I'll go someplace else."

Susan picked up her whiskey glass, but she didn't drink from it. She turned it in her hands and stared into the shallows of the half-finished drink.

"This woman..." she said. "It's the woman you were talking about before you went away? The killer?"

Warily, I nodded.

"Who did she kill?"

"Most recently, a middle-aged gay guy who was looking for a bit of rough trade. Before that"—I picked my words with care—"a lot of people, but mostly people who'd hurt her. Or people she thought might hurt her. She's ill. Killing is one of the symptoms of her illness."

Susan put the glass to her lips and emptied it. She made a sour face. "I'm not good at this," she said. I was surprised I hadn't noticed the slur in her voice at the door. "I don't even like the taste. I think I'm going to get sick before I get drunk."

"Susan—" I began.

She shook her head impatiently. "Play your tune. I want this to be over. I don't want it in my life anymore."

I nodded. For the third time tonight, I unshipped my

whistle and held it in my hands, ready to play. My mind was fogged by exhaustion, though, and although I knew the notes I had to play—the notes of a summoning that would have Juliet's name written all over it—I couldn't get my mind into the place where it needed to be. I felt like someone trying to fit his eye to the lens of a telescope, and screwing up the angle so that all he could see was the magnified reflection of the blood vessels inside his own eyeball.

I played a note, more or less at random, hoping my sixth sense would kick in and the music would start to flow. It didn't. Nothing at all came into my mind, not even a note that would connect to this one in a way that made sense.

I lowered the whistle and stared at it, blinking my eyes back into focus. It was strange, and it was frightening. I'd had good days and bad days, but I'd never had my knack desert me quite so suddenly and completely. All I wanted to do was the summoning. It was the easiest part of an exorcism: It made a path, a line of least resistance for the spirit you were looking for to move through. It was usually easiest if you were close to the spirit, harder the farther away you got, but the only reason it wouldn't work at all, wouldn't even stay in my head long enough to suggest the beginnings of a tune, was if—

"She's already here," I said. "Isn't she?"

"She's upstairs," Susan muttered, pointing. "In our bedroom. Or it *was* our bedroom. I don't know what it is now." Slowly, deliberately, but still spilling a little on the table, she poured herself another drink.

I walked past her, wanting to offer some kind of solace but not sure what form it ought to take. Bad friend

Felix was on the prowl again. Good news wasn't on the agenda.

The main bedroom was dead ahead. Juliet was sitting on the windowsill, legs hugged to her chest, both feet off the ground. In a way, it was a curiously little-girlish pose. Doug Hunter was tied to the bed by an ad hoc but formidable assemblage of rope and old leather belts. He seemed calm enough, but it was a bleak, frazzled calm: the calm of someone who'd already tested himself—or herself, arguably—against the ropes extensively and lost every time. Myriam Kale looked out at me from behind those bland, pale blue eyes and smiled asymmetrically.

I stopped in the doorway. "Permission to approach," I said.

Juliet gave me what, in a human woman, would have been an old-fashioned look. "You can come in, Castor," she said. "I'm not going to attack you. I'm not going to hold it against you that you were right—or at least not to that extent."

I walked in, skirting the bed, and stood beside Juliet, looking out through the window. Under the streetlamp opposite, a dark form waited with its head bowed, endlessly patient—waiting for a banquet that would make up for a century of starvation.

"So how'd you get home?" I asked Juliet, knowing that the one thing I wouldn't get out of her would be the truth. "Transatlantic cable? Fishing coracle? Back of a whale? What?"

"The scenic route," she said. "It's another one of those things that you wouldn't understand."

"Right, right." I was too tired to rise to the bait. "I've been talking to that friend of yours some more. You know, the one from the old neighborhood." I nodded at the window, but she didn't bother to look.

"I smelled him," she said. "You should be more careful around demons, Castor. It's only safe so long as they need you."

"Now you tell me." I turned to look at the figure on the bed. Doug Hunter grinned and thrust his hips toward me in a suggestive mime. "So how's Myriam?" I asked.

"She's falling apart. She always does, apparently. She begged them not to bring her back after the last time, but they did anyway. But this time they gave her a man's body because they thought it might help her control the urges."

"They being ...?"

Juliet shrugged, shook her head. "She's not rational for very long at a time now. That's more or less all I got. She talks about Lesley, mainly. Lesley Lathwell. And *to* him some of the time. She tells him that she loves him. That she'll kill him. That she wants him to kill her. She talks about something called inscription a lot, too. She doesn't want it, she won't accept it, she didn't mean to miss it. And then she cries. Or swears. Or bites her tongue and spits blood over the sheets."

"Back in the remand wing," I said, "they had Doug on antipsychotics. A mild prescription to keep him stabilized. I don't suppose you brought any out with you?" Juliet looked at me. "No. I know. Not the way your mind works. And I never thought to mention it to you when you were flinging me around the diner. Pity. It actually would have been a better line than 'I'll hunt you down and kill you like a dog.' That seemed to upset you."

"Can we get some more of the medicine from a doctor?"

"Not without taking Doug to *see* a doctor. And if we do that, we're all ending up in Pentonville."

"I'm not going home," Myriam Kale said from the bed, speaking out of Doug Hunter's throat as though from the bottom of a deep pit. Her voice sounded hoarse and agonized. "You can't make me go home. He'll come and get me. He'll take me out of there. He's my home now. I walked in the quiet night on the side of the road, and I came back, and it was all still there. The blood on the seats. It still smells of it."

"Then what?" Juliet said. "I thought of calling Coldwood, but I don't want to get Susan in trouble. If Hunter is found in her house—"

"It's not just Susan," I pointed out, fighting the urge to look at my watch. Time was against us. We had to move. But Juliet could only be invited, not coerced. "It's you, too. You busted Hunter out of jail. You never walked in front of a camera, but there aren't that many people around who could have done what you did. The only thing that's saved you so far is that Gary Coldwood is in the hospital, and he's the one who knows where you live."

She seemed surprised at this news. "In the hospital? What happened to him?"

"I set him on this thing after someone tried to kill me. I thought maybe he could shake the tree better than I could, but they just trashed his career and broke his legs instead. Juliet, we have to sort this out. Not only Myriam Kale but all of it. Mount Grace, the reincarnation racket, the whole thing."

"Let me go," Myriam Kale suggested from the bed, staring at me with wide, insane eyes. "I'll blow you, mister. I'll blow you and I'll swallow. Best you've ever had."

Juliet frowned. "Mount Grace? The crematorium? How is any of this connected to Mount Grace?"

I brought her up to speed as quickly as I could, starting with John's funeral and covering all the main fixtures since. When I got to Moloch's part in recent events, she drew back her teeth in a snarl. And when I suggested that she might want to come along with us for a little breaking and entering and wholesale slaughter, she shook her head in somber wonder. "Fight alongside the demon?" she demanded.

"Essentially, yeah," I said, trying not to sound defensive. "If you've got a rodent problem, you need a terrier. Best estimate, there are around two hundred of these bastards. Could you take them all by yourself?"

"No. The ones in the flesh would be easy meat for me. The ghosts...I don't believe they'd respond to me in the necessary way."

"Right. And I could exorcise the ghosts, but it's murderously hard. I already played that tune once tonight, and it was like taking a beating from a bunch of guys with baseball bats. The chances are that it wouldn't be enough, not by itself. These guys are tough. Some of them have cheated the grave for a hundred years. I think I could punch their spirits out of the bodies they've borrowed, but I seriously doubt I could push them all the way off the mortal plane. They'd still be around, and they'd still be dangerous—they'd be gunning for me, and it's odds on they'd get me. But Moloch is a specialized predator. He'd be there with his knife and fork to finish the job. See, the three of us together can—"

"Castor, what do we stand to gain from this? Spell it out for me."

I paused. I'd hoped she might get absorbed in the logistics and not ask any of the really tough questions. "Revenge?" I ventured.

She seemed genuinely surprised. "For Coldwood?"

"Yeah."

A long pause.

"I don't think so," said Juliet. "This isn't my fight. Less now than before, in fact. Nobody's paying. Nobody will care when we're done. Revenge isn't enough."

I let out a long breath. "Well, okay...I could appeal to your sense of civic duty, but I hate it when you laugh at me. At my end, it's become kind of a life-and-death thing. They know I've found out about them, and they're not going to let it drop." I hesitated. "As for you, what you stand to gain, obviously, is—from a global perspective— when all's said and done—"

"You get to stay with me," said Susan from the doorway.

We both turned to stare at her in perfect comedic sync.

"Sue," Juliet said, the tone softer than the words. "Wait downstairs. This isn't something that concerns you."

Susan came in, closed the door behind her, and folded her arms. The expression on her flushed face was one I'd never seen there before. She cast one nervous glance at the bound figure on the bed, then she directed her full attention at Juliet.

"You brought an escaped murderer into my house, Jules," she said in a tone that had something of a taut string about it. "And I let you do it because I thought you wouldn't have done it unless you had to. But if it's just because she's a woman who kills men and that used to be your—your *thing,* too, then that's not good enough. And

Felix is right about one thing. If you don't fix this, you'll have to go away. I'll lose you. I'm not going to lose you because of something like this."

Juliet couldn't have been more nonplussed if a cavalcade of tap-dancing mice had sung the words at her. She blinked, visibly thinking her way around the situation. "If I have to leave," she said, "I'll come back to you. They can't keep me away."

The taut string snapped.

"They can send you home!" Susan shouted, advancing with her hands clenched into fists as though she were going to hit Juliet. She was crying again, but she didn't wipe away the tears on her cheeks or even seem to notice them; she was incandescent enough that I was surprised they didn't evaporate. "They can trap you and send you back down to hell, no matter how strong you are. You'd be down there in the dark, and you'd have to wait until someone called you back up again. Except that they'd call you as a slave, the way you were before. Or else I'd have to find a way to summon you up myself, and then what? Then you'd be *my* slave! We'd—we wouldn't be us anymore. We'd be a stupid, sick joke. It's got to stop, Jules. You've got to stop it, and then you've got to explain and say you're sorry."

From about halfway through this speech, she'd been screaming the words rather than yelling them. Her fists were trembling like tuning forks. Juliet caught them in her hands, pushed them down to Susan's sides, and then embraced her. Susan slumped in her arms, all the fight abruptly gone from her.

"You've got to," she mumbled almost inaudibly, her head pressed to Juliet's breast. "Please. For me."

Juliet stared at me over Susan's head. She looked unhappy. No, more than that. She looked afraid—and it wasn't of the Mount Grace ghosts.

"Is that the plan, then?" she demanded, her face a somber deadpan. "We go to the crematorium. We break in. And I keep the three of us alive long enough for you to play your tune and for Moloch to feast?"

I was a bit taken aback by how quickly the tide had turned. I realized, much to my own surprise, that I hadn't been expecting to win this one. "There's a little more to it than that," I said lamely, "but yeah, that's the basic scheme."

"It's absurd. We don't know their strength or their numbers."

Juliet kissed Susan gently on the cheek, held on to her for a moment longer, and then set her to one side very firmly. Susan took all this with great stoicism.

I delved into my pocket and brought out my ace in the hole. It was the torn fragment of notepaper that I'd found in John Gittings's pocket watch. When you looked at it, he really had gone out of his way to make sure I'd have everything I needed. In fact, he'd been shrewder when his brain was disintegrating than he'd been at any time in his life before.

"John was there before us," I said.

"Isn't that why he died?"

"Yeah, but he left us some notes. It's pretty vague on their strengths, but it drops some succulent hints about their weaknesses."

"And you," Juliet said, giving me a cold, hard stare. "You said this tune was hard to play—that it drains you. Do you think you've got the energy to play it again tonight?

Please don't take this personally, but you look as though you'd have a hard time blowing up a child's balloon."

I'd been thinking the same thing, but since I didn't see any other choice, I shrugged the question off. "I'll be fine," I said. "I always am on the night."

Juliet's expression didn't change. "If you can't do it," she said, "you'd better tell me now. There's no point in going into a fight with a plan that can't work."

"All right," I admitted. "Right now I don't think I could do it. But it's going to take us at least an hour to get over there. I'm hoping that'll give me the time I need to get match-fit again."

She nodded. "We'll see," she said with grim promise.

I left the two of them alone for a minute or two to say their goodbyes. When Juliet came down from the bedroom, I shot her a look of inquiry. She walked right past me, her face unreadable but her shoulders hunched in a tension I'd never seen in her. Juliet normally uses her body language to draw people in; it's second nature to her, because it's part of the way she feeds. For her to lose control of it, even around the edges, was a surprising and, in some ways, disturbing thing to see.

Moloch smiled as he saw us coming and gave Juliet an ironic bow. "The sister of Baphomet," he grated. "I'm honored above all of my kindred. Never would I have imagined my lowly station would permit—"

Juliet's ringing smack knocked him back on his heels, his head thrown sideways by the force of the blow. "You should have stayed in your lowly station," she snarled, her gaze skewering him. "It's grotesque to see you crawling on the face of the earth. One word, Moloch. One word more will use up all that's left of my slender fucking patience."

A demon's face isn't that much harder to read than a human one. I could see in his narrowed eyes and tight smile that he'd already thought of a cool comeback—and that he didn't quite have the balls to try to deliver it.

"Are we good?" I asked, breaking the tense silence.

They both nodded unconvincingly.

"Then let's go commit some atrocities."

~ Twenty-four

WHEN YOU'RE CLIMBING a mountain, the first thing you do is set up a base camp. In our case, it was the building site at the bottom of Ropery Street, right next door to the crematorium and facing it across a no-man's-land of churned mud. Okay, there was also a tall fence separating us from the landscaped grounds, but our line of sight was clear. Clear enough to see the car head-lights coming up the curve of the drive in twos and threes, the lights slowing and stopping and then winking out as the drivers headed into the building. The inscription had begun, or else it would begin soon. Either way, we had all our enemies, living and dead, in the same spot. Lucky us.

We stood close to the top of the tower of scaffolding that surrounded the shell of a building yet to be. Moloch and Juliet stared intently into the darkness, which held no secrets from them. For my part, I couldn't see a blind fucking thing. It was dark of the moon, and the sky above us was a curdled mass of black on black. This high up, the wind was a constant barrage of sucker punches. But the storm was holding off, maybe waiting for a more dramatic moment.

"There are armed men," Juliet said. "A lot of them. Some of them at the gate, some in front of the doors. More of them are taking up positions on the grounds. They seem to know what they're doing. Two or three men in a group, each group in line of sight of at least two others."

"Hired security," I said. "Probably black market, if they're carrying guns."

"They're carrying rifles," Moloch murmured. "They have guns in their belts. Also grenades."

I shrugged as nonchalantly as I could. "It makes sense," I said. "This is when our dead-guy mafia are at their weakest—individually and as a group."

"In what way?" Juliet demanded.

"They all need to tie up and gag their inner hostages again, so I'd guess at least some of their strength has to be taken up in keeping a tight hold on the bodies they're wearing. After the ritual, they're okay for the next month. They're also vulnerable because they're all here together. They know damn well that if anyone wants to take them out, this is the best time to do it. Hence the paranoid security. We should be encouraged by it, really. It shows that they're scared."

"It also shows that they're neither stupid nor blind," Juliet pointed out. "We'd have a lot more chance of success if they were both."

I didn't answer. I was looking down at the wooden planks of the scaffolding beneath my feet, which had shifted in the wind. This was where Doug Hunter's life had taken a turn for the worse, I now knew. I'd called Jan to check the hypothesis, but I'd already known what her answer would be. This was the last place he'd worked, and on the day he sprained his ankle, he'd walked next door to the crematorium to see if he could beg, borrow, or requisition a first-aid kit. And that was the last thing he'd done as himself.

It felt like a bad omen to be launching our own attack from a place with a history like that. I wanted to get out of here and make a start, because the sooner we made a start, the sooner the whole thing would be over.

But as I took a step toward the ladder, Juliet put out a hand and clamped it down on my shoulder, stopping me in my tracks.

"Castor," she said. "There's something you still need to do up here. You"—this was to Moloch—"go down and wait for us at the bottom. We'll join you in about five minutes."

Moloch bared his teeth. "There shouldn't be any secrets between allies," he said. "Whatever you've got to say, we should all hear."

"I don't have anything to say," Juliet told him. "As far as that goes, I'm sure your ears are keen enough to pick up everything that goes on up here. But you don't get to watch."

Moloch said nothing. With visible reluctance, he put his feet on the ladder and started to descend.

I stared at Juliet. She stared back. The elevator in my stomach slipped its cables and plunged precipitately to the bottom of its shaft.

"You're still weak," Juliet said.

"Yeah," I said, my voice sounding slightly strangled and strained in my own ears. "I've been better."

"You may not know this, Castor, but I can give as well as take."

I just kept staring. I was rummaging in my head for words. There were no words left. "You can—"

"When I feed, I take the strength, the life, and the soul from the men I fuck. I started to do it to you once, so I'm sure you remember."

I nodded. Waking in the dark, sweat cold on my face and chest, heart hammering an overclocked suburban mambo, I remembered most nights.

"I'm not going to make love with you. It would hurt Susan if she knew, and I prefer not to lie to her. But I *am* going to lend you some strength to work with. It might make the difference between you living and dying tonight."

Two steps brought her up close to me, and her eyes were staring directly into mine. Point-blank. Point-singularity, her pupils two black holes that dragged me in not against my will but using my will to fuel their own local gravity.

She put one hand on the back of my neck, drawing me close. Our lips met.

At least I assume they met. If hypnotherapy were guaranteed to help me to remember, I'd sign up for a course today and happily pay whatever it cost up to and including my right arm. But while I can summon up without even trying every agonizing detail of the night when Juliet tried to rape and devour me, the only thing I remember about that kiss is a sensation like the whole of my body being melted, rendered like tallow, blasted into steam, and then falling like molten rain back into the same place I'd been standing. I don't even know how long it took; it wasn't the sort of thing that had a time signature on it. It was there,

it was everywhere, and then it was over. Juliet was stepping away from me toward the ladder, and I was standing
there alone, each cell of my body separately and searingly
aware of the cold night air touching it.

"That should be enough," said Juliet's voice from some
unfathomable distance. "Use it wisely."

With enormous reluctance, coming down from a height
that was already fading out of my mind and leaving no
traces, I turned to follow her. A brittle heat filled me, and
it was as dry as the air in a furnace. Otherwise, I might
have cried.

"And now," said Moloch with ironic emphasis when
we reached the bottom of the ladder, "if you've adjusted
your dress—" Juliet's warning glare silenced him.

"We're the point men," I said to him. "We're going in
from the front. Juliet's going to join us when she's done
what needs to be done here."

He bowed, gesturing for me to take the lead. I looked
around at Juliet one more time. "Luck," I said, for want of
anything better to say.

"There's no such thing," she told me dispassionately,
already walking away. "Trust in luck and you'll die
tonight."

I headed for the entrance to the yard. The gate had been
closed with a padlock when we turned up, but Moloch
had twisted the lock between finger and thumb, and it had
snapped off clean. Then he'd tossed it negligently over
his shoulder. There was nothing to slow us down as we
walked back out onto the street.

The front gates of the crematorium were a much heftier
proposition. They were off on our left, fifty yards away at
most. I hadn't taken the time to admire them on the day

of John's cremation, but I could see that they were built to withstand a serious siege. Where they touched, they wore a massive chain and a clutch of padlocks like a giant's charm bracelet.

We took our time, not wanting to get there too early. The impassive men inside stared out at us through the bars as we approached. There were three of them, all dressed in the sober black uniforms of priests or security guards, though most priests don't have that kind of physique. I stared back. No sign of small arms—only sidewinder nightsticks in holsters at their waists. But then they wouldn't want a chance passerby to notice anything odd and dial 999. The rifles would put in an appearance soon enough if we gave them any excuse.

"Evening, gents," I said, coming to a halt right in front of the gates. Juliet's arcane energies were burning inside me. I felt slightly hysterical; it was hard not to laugh out loud.

The guy in the middle gave me a bored, neutral look. "Anything we can do for you?" he asked in a tone that emphatically didn't expect a yes and wouldn't be happy to hear one.

"Yeah," I said equably. "We've come to see Uncle George. He's in the memorial garden, right next to the stone cherub with the fascist graffiti on its arse. George Armstrong Castor. He was in the cavalry."

The guard didn't answer me right away. He gave us both a harder look, his eyebrows inverting themselves into a dark V of stony disapproval. "The memorial garden is closed," he said. "You'll have to come back tomorrow morning."

I shook my head firmly. "Tomorrow morning is no

use," I said. "We're grieving now. By tomorrow we could be feeling cynical and self-sufficient again. So would you mind opening up before I lose my temper?"

The words hung in the air. I was smiling as I said them, a slightly crazed smile that did nothing to take away the edge of threat. But the guard's pained expression as he scratched his ear and squared his shoulders said very eloquently that the threat wasn't a credible one, and that he'd had more than enough of being polite.

"Fuck off out of it, pally," he said. "I've told you we're closed."

Moloch stepped past me and took a two-handed grip on the bars, arms at full stretch. He shook the gates on their hinges, testing their weight and heft. One of the guards on the flank gave a jeering laugh. But the guy in charge wasn't seeing the funny side. He took a step toward the gate, his hand going to the grip of his nightstick. And that, by a happy chance, was when the fun started. There was a rending crash from our right. The three guards, taken by surprise, all turned their heads to see what the noise was. We'd known it was coming, so we didn't.

Todd had said that the Mount Grace collective liked to keep things in the family, so what happened next was no more than the pirate souls in possession of these men deserved. I couldn't help remembering, though, that the flesh still belonged to someone else—that each of these human bodies had a prisoner locked in an oubliette somewhere, screaming to be released. Moloch granted them their wish in a particularly hideous way.

He pushed the gates up and in, the hinges breaking open with sharp, metallic cracks like the blows of a hammer on an anvil. Then he swung them like a giant flyswatter and brought them down on the three men, crushing them to the ground.

I looked away as I stepped across the ad hoc drawbridge, trying not to see the red ruin of blood and bone under my feet. I told myself we had no choice. I thought about John Gittings, and Vince Chesney, and Gary Coldwood. It didn't help: Nothing was ever going to make these scales balance.

Moloch was striding on ahead, not bothering to look back and see whether I was following. I took out my whistle and put it to my lips.

The wall isnt a wall, John's letter had said. In other words, the ghosts of Mount Grace weren't constrained by physical barriers, and anyone who thought he could hold his fire until he got to the front door or the furnace room or wherever he reckoned ground zero might be probably wasn't going to make it.

I started to play. There was no fumbling or feeling my way into it this time, partly because the music was still fresh in my mind from when I'd wielded it like a scalpel to slice spirit from flesh back in Maynard Todd's office, but mainly because whatever juice Juliet had charged me up with when we kissed was fizzing and burning through my blood. It didn't feel like a current running through me; it was more visceral than that. It was as though *I* were current, running through the world.

Another crash, and as we rounded the long curve of the driveway, I saw the earthmover breaking cover a hundred yards ahead. Juliet's driving skills hadn't improved, but a bulldozer is a simple enough thing to control so long as you don't care what you hit. The first avalanche of sound—the one that had distracted the guards at the gate—had been when she rammed the fence and broke through from the building site into the crematorium ground. Now she was cutting diagonally across the path ahead of us, leaving in her wake a ruin of desecrated urns and mangled fence posts. Running men took potshots at her while trying to keep from falling under the massive Caterpillar treads that bore her on. She ignored the shots, both the ones that missed and the occasional ones that found their mark.

And she drew the pursuit away from us, into and through the decorative hedge of privet on the far side of the drive, bending before her in a wind that was one notch down from a hurricane, and still there hadn't been a single drop of rain. Moloch and I walked on, more or less unmolested, and the doors of the building loomed ahead of us.

The doors weren't going to be fun, though. The black-uniformed men stationed on the steps had seen us coming, and they were already kneeling to take aim. Moloch took off toward them at a run, and I veered off the path into the trees, not even missing a note, part of my mind working out the likely trajectories of any bullets that might miss him and find their way to me.

I circled wide, hearing the impact of flesh on flesh and the choked-off screams of the men on the steps as the demon landed among them, undeterred by their bullets and so eager for the feast still to come that even sadism had temporarily lost its charm. By the time I came out of the stand of trees, he was already turning to look for me, rigid with impatience, his fists clenching and unclenching at his sides. Men lay around him like fallen leaves, unconscious or dead.

I was still playing, and by now the music had taken on

its own momentum, as it had in Todd's office. It was playing itself through me, so I felt like all I had to do was keep the whistle to my lips and let myself be a conduit for it. Otherwise, the buildup of pressure would probably burst my brain like a big, overfilled water balloon.

I crossed the drive and ascended the steps, my feet thumping arrhythmically on the ground to create the complex, out-of-phase backbeat the music needed to do its stuff. I was aware of resistance, but it wasn't coming in the form I'd expected. I'd thought the evil dead would try to possess me and that I'd feel the same dizziness and weakness I'd experienced on the day of John's cremation. But it wasn't like that at all, not at first. It began as a sense of drag, as though I were up to my thighs in cold water and had to push myself through it, my steps slowing involuntarily.

Moloch turned as I joined him, squared his shoulders, and kicked the doors wide open, then strode across the threshold without looking back. Two more guards were waiting just inside, and they shot him in the chest and head. He picked up one of the two—left hand on the throat, right gripping the crotch—and swung him in a tight semicircle so that his skull met the other man's with appalling, unstoppable force. It was a single movement, a single missed beat, and then Moloch was walking on, leaving the bodies slumped together under the angel of Saint Matthew, whose robes were stained with their blood and brains.

I followed along behind, but even though we were out of the wind, the going was getting harder. The feeling of resistance was growing now that we were inside the building. The cold water was up above my waist, and it was congealing into ice, counteracting the fever heat that Juliet had gifted me with. Without knowing exactly when it had started, I became aware of a noise almost beyond the limits of hearing: an atonal skirl that was picking at the stitches of my skein of music, undoing the spell I was trying to weave by infinitesimal increments.

The last time I'd walked down this hall, it had seemed barely twenty paces long. It seemed a lot longer now, and every step added to the distance rather than taking away from it. One. Two. Three. Perspective bowed and buckled, space surrendered, hemorrhaged. I raised my left foot and felt the agonized pause, the gap in time before it fell again, as a hole in the music through which my own mind was starting to bleed out. Seven. Eight. I was trudging along a subway tunnel, the air closing in, the ground pulling away and away into unfathomable distance.

Nine.

The mosquito whine of unheard voices enfolded me. I knew them for what they were: the unsepulchered dead, defending their inner sanctum with the single-minded viciousness that had been their hallmark in life. I could even distinguish the different voices in the insect chorus as my death sense kicked in like passive radar, analyzing and identifying the cold, cruel intelligences that were bent on killing me.

Up ahead of me, Moloch stumbled, but my perceptions were so attenuated that he seemed to do it in slow motion. Another security guard was standing at the doors of the chapel, a handgun in his fist aimed at Moloch's torso, his finger pumping the trigger. Ragged holes blossomed in the taut black leather stretched across Moloch's back, and green ichor flowed from them like tears: incidental details, both to me and to him. But the air was thickening and curdling around the demon's head and shoulders, the evil dead rallying to keep him out. He slowed, his head bowing under an invisible weight.

I felt that weight, too. The tenth step was going to be my last. My foot was coming down as heavy as a sack full of spanners, and I doubted I'd have the strength to lift it up again. And even if I did, what then? Another step, and another, like Sisyphus's boulder, with nothing more to show for it than another yard gained—a slight shift in position that would be more than offset by the endless organic growth of the hallway. Better to stop and rest and see what came next. Maybe nothing. Nothing would be good.

Moloch was reaching out with both hands toward the man who was shooting him, again and again, in the chest, but he was groping like a blind man, and like mine, his feet were rooted to the spot. I understood the blindness, dimly. Something foul was silting in my head, too, swallowing up my faltering concentration in its feculent, liquid depositions, piling up behind my eyes like mud on a riverbed.

I found myself drawing the note that was in my mouth into a sighing-out breath that had nowhere to go but down. I had no idea what would follow it. It was hard even to care. My mind was a slender filament of light and the filament was flickering, stuttering, stop start stop.

Juliet saved me—Juliet and our rough-and-ready timing. There was another apocalyptic crash from outside that shook the foundations of the building, and simultaneously, my consciousness bobbed to the surface again, yawing and pitching so that the world lurched drunkenly around me and I almost fell to my knees. The hypersonic whine in my ears dropped a notch and became a hollow, keening moan.

Moloch laughed, harsh and triumphant.

Outside, although I couldn't see it, I knew that Juliet had just piloted the bulldozer, blade lowered and ready, through the picturesque glades and paths of the garden of remembrance. Funereal urns were exploding like ripe fruit under the Caterpillar tracks, spilling dry and ancient dust into the hungry wind. And feeling their earthly tabernacles defiled, feeling the other wind that blew from eternity plucking at them million-fingered, the dead men were afraid. They faltered in their attack, because they hadn't expected to be counterattacked in such a viciously intimate way. It was the advice that John had passed on to me inside the case of the pocket watch, as it had been passed on to him by his mysterious informant. *Remember you can still threaten them. Physically, I mean. If you pull your foot back to kick, a man is going to cover his balls.* I hadn't realized what that meant until Todd had told me that he and his dead pals used their own ashes as the medium of transference when they leapfrogged into new bodies. That was when I saw the rough outline of what we'd have to do. And when we got to the building site, and Moloch found the keys to the bulldozer in the site hut inside a safe whose walls were barely three inches thick . . . well, it seemed like destiny.

The lull was already over. The dead men renewed their assault on us, although no doubt another contingent had peeled off to find Juliet and deliver unto her the verdict and the sentence of their time-distilled hatred. In all, we'd had maybe five seconds of respite.

It was all I needed. In crowding me so closely, the dead

men had done me a big favor: They'd imprinted their essence on my death sense so vividly I could have played it in the dark with gloves on. I started to play again, and the tune writhed in the air like a living thing, closed and locked onto the rabid spirits even as they swooped back in for a second pass. They were expecting easy meat: They ran full speed into a moving avalanche.

Moloch stretched, and because most of my attention was elsewhere, I thought the sound I heard was the crack of one of his bones. It wasn't: It was the hollow report of the guard's gun as the firing pin fell on an empty chamber. He stared at it in numb dismay, then his hand started to move toward his belt where he probably had a spare clip. Moloch's punch demolished most of his face, so the movement was never completed. He thudded backward into the doors of the chapel and slithered to the floor. Moloch pushed the doors open and stepped over the dying man into the room.

I followed, pouring out sweet music like a ninja throws shurikens.

The chapel was full of roiling ghosts, made visible by the tune that anchored them against their will to this spot. They were like some sort of complex, ever moving cat's cradle, gliding past and through one another without ever seeming to touch. Faces and limbs and various misplaced or truncated echoes of human form appeared within the mass and then vanished back into it.

Moloch shot me a look. "Allegro," he growled. "And if you can manage it, *al pepe*."

He went down on one knee and bent his head. For a moment, grotesquely, he looked as though he were paying his respects to the enemies he was about to devour. But it wasn't anything like that at all. It was something a whole lot more disgusting.

He'd told me he'd made this body for himself, slowly and painstakingly. If I'd given any thought to what that meant, I'd have imagined some process like the knitting of a sweater. But I'd picked the wrong metaphor, clearly. The black leather of Moloch's coat parted vertically as the flesh within knotted and burgeoned. Suddenly, there was a broadening split in the coat through which something red and churning could be seen, as though Moloch's insides were molten liquid.

Out of that cauldron something rose like steam, then solidified in the air into a shape that made my stomach clench and sour bile rise in my throat. It had a lot of limbs and a lot of mouths. The limbs threshed the air, passing through the turbulent mass of spirits that hovered there in a complex repeating pattern. They lost their coherence, emulsified into something that quickly lost any residue of humanity. Then the mouths opened, and Moloch began to drink.

It took a long time. I looked away, concentrating on the music and trying to shut out the sounds of the demon's banquet. But that left me looking at the guard with the ruined face, so in the end, I closed my eyes and played for a few minutes more in the dark, in a sort of abstract trance.

A hand on my shoulder brought me out of it, and when I opened my eyes, Juliet was at my side. She was boltered with blood from hairline to boots. I wondered if any of the men she'd killed had died with hard-ons. Probably not. She would have been moving too fast, working too hard, to be able to linger and bring her lethal charm to bear on them. For some reason that I couldn't explain, I felt relieved by that.

The room was silent. Most of the ghosts were gone. The bloated ectoplasmic hulk of Moloch hovered and pulsated in the air above us like some blasphemous Goodyear blimp, peristaltic ripples passing across its surface as its myriad appendages Hoovered the air.

"Great stuff," I said hoarsely. "Only next time, you want to go into second gear when you're up past ten miles an hour. I meant to tell you that when you gave me a lift in your Maserati the other day."

Juliet didn't seem to be in the mood for banter. "We need to leave," she murmured, staring up at the terrible spectral mass. The tentacles were moving more sluggishly, and the mouths were closing one by one. If there were such a thing as the ghost of a wafer-thin mint, the demon had reached the stage of the meal where it might be offered to him.

I saw Juliet's point and headed for the door, but it was already too late.

"Ah!" Moloch exclaimed oleaginously, in a voice that seemed to reach us by making the bones of our skull vibrate directly, cutting out the etheric middle man. "The sister of Baphomet. Did I ever tell you how I killed him?"

Juliet looked up at the obscene, sated thing with its dozens of grinning mouths. "From behind," she said.

The physical body that the demon had abandoned in order to feed raised its head abruptly and stood. "And shall I tell you how I'm going to kill you?" he asked.

Juliet raised an eyebrow, its perfect line spoiled by a piece of human tissue plastered to her forehead with human blood. *"Shedim ere'fa minur,"* she said. *"Ehad iniru, ke rekol ha dith gerainou."*

Both Molochs—the blimp and the one that looked like a man—roared in response. Both went for Juliet at the same time.

Juliet met the man head-on and stopped him dead in his tracks. They both moved so fast that there was almost no sense of movement; they seemed to flick between static postures like a slide show. Moloch was trying the shock-and-awe tactics he'd used against the loup-garou, throwing punches and kicks like confetti at a wedding. Juliet blocked every one and even got in a couple of her own so that Moloch was giving ground, parrying rather than hitting out.

But then the tentacles of the blimp-thing drifted through her head and shoulders and chest. She froze in place for a fraction of a heartbeat. Moloch saw the window, and he was there, his right hand raised above his head, clawed fingers spread. The smack of impact came a second later. Juliet flew backward through the air and hit the wall with a sack-of-meat thud.

"Oh, those are just stories," Moloch snarled. "I'm not even sure I could get it up with a raddled piece of flesh like you."

Juliet gathered herself and stood with a visible effort. Three livid wounds marred her face, running diagonally in parallel from her left temple. Blood was already welling up from them in vigorous arterial gouts. But it wasn't the wound that was giving her trouble, nor the blood; it was the puppet strings dangling down from the blimp monster, attaching themselves in thicker and thicker profusion to her forehead, her arms, her back and chest. She took a step forward, gathering herself to spring, but she was too slow by some huge, wasteful portion of a second. Moloch's foot slammed into her stomach, and she folded. Then he swiveled like a dervish dancing, and his second kick, rising into her downturned face, lifted her off her feet. This time she hit the wall hard enough to leave a skull-shaped indent in one of the wooden panels.

I fitted the whistle to my lips again, sick horror making my movements clumsy, my mind empty and unresponsive. Moloch didn't even look at me; he just gestured. One of the trailing tentacles of the blimp-thing drifted lazily across my throat, which constricted in sudden agony. I made a grunting wheeze of protest—the only sound that I could force out of my mouth. Another tendril rippled through my chest, and my legs buckled under me, sending me crashing down onto my knees.

"A hundred years," Moloch remarked conversationally. "That's a long time to go between meals. No doubt it was good for my figure, but still. Not pleasant. Not pleasant at all." Levering herself up on hands and knees, Juliet reached blindly for his ankle, maybe intending to trip him. He stepped on her wrist, twisting as he brought his weight down. There was an audible crack.

"The great project," he snarled, standing over her. "The *shedim* will piss on the rubble of your great project and bury your children in the wastelands where it stood." He lifted her one-handed, looked into her face almost tenderly. "And the woman you live with," he said. "I'll keep her as a pet for a little while. Until she starts to bore me. Then I'll eat her over some long and leisurely period of time. *Meiden agon,* sister of Baphomet. All things in moderation."

He raised her above his head, held her there for a

second, and then brought her down so that her back broke across his raised knee. Juliet gave a grunt of pain. It was so unexpected, and so wrong, that my system flooded with adrenaline. Nothing could hurt Juliet. Nothing could shake her poise. That was part of what made her what she was.

My brain kicking sluggishly back into gear, I started to beat out a tattoo with my palms on the cold stones of the floor. The sound was faint, and it hardly carried above the butcher-shop noises of what Moloch was doing to Juliet. But it was a rhythm—and a rhythm, as John Gittings had taught me, is the skeleton of a song.

Moloch didn't notice at first. He was still delivering his gloating monologue, drawing out the pain and the humiliation of Juliet's death so that it would measure up to the happy fantasies he'd been living on for the last century. He was working on her face with both hands, talking in a low intimate murmur so that his words didn't reach me. The blimp was above and behind him, its tentacles stretching down through his chest and into hers. Of course. If murderers had a patron saint, it would be Juliet. This must be the best part of the meal.

A naked rhythm is slyer and more slippery than a whistled tune. It's like the narrow blade of a shank slipped in between your ribs: It doesn't even hurt until it moves and starts to make a broader incision. I let it go in deep, deeper, deeper still. My hoarse, hissing breath was a part of the pattern now, and the sounds my wrists made against the cuffs of my shirt, and the creak of my shoes as I shifted my weight, coming up on one knee. All of it, all the negligible, tiny, repeated, inscaped sounds were converging into something impossibly subtle, impossibly slender and sharp. The effort of keeping it so tightly focused was like a physical ache in my gut. I held it as long as I could.

Then let the rhythm blade unfold like the spokes of an umbrella inside the demon's rancid, pulpy heart.

Moloch stiffened, turned to stare at me in wide-eyed astonishment.

"Three—three most useless things in the world," I croaked, forcing the sounds out of my lacerated throat. I could taste the blood that came with them.

"Castor—" he muttered, unbelieving, uncomprehending.

"A nun's tits—the pope's balls—and a round of applause for the band."

The blimp exploded with a wet, flaccid, whimpering belch. Moloch's chest exploded, too, where the tentacles were routed through it. Ribs showed like jagged teeth through his ruined flesh. His human form toppled over like a tree and fell full-length on the floor, unmoving, a greenish-black stain spreading lazily out from underneath it.

It felt like an impossible task to get back on my feet, but I knew I had to try. The gunfire, the wanton destruction wrought by the bulldozer, and the screams of the dying wouldn't have gone unnoticed. After all, this wasn't Kilburn. It wouldn't be too long before the bright-eyed boys in blue came around to see what the trouble was, and it was probably a good idea if they didn't find us here.

Juliet was a mess. I knew rationally that any damage she survived, she could repair. This body was just something that she wore when she was in town. All the same, it hurt to look at her, and my hands shook as I picked her up. She was a lot lighter than she looked, as I'd discovered on an earlier occasion. She hung limp in my arms. Her lips moved, but no sound came out.

"I'm going to have to carry you," I told her. "I know your back's broken, but I can't think of any other way of doing this. I hope it doesn't hurt too much."

Finding the last remnants of the strength she'd lent to me, I carried her to the door, down the hallway, and out into the chill night air.

This wasn't over yet. There was still one more man I had to visit tonight: visit and maybe kill. Again.

The wind was as strong as ever; and now at last the rain began to fall, with perfect timing, like the tears of two hundred funerals saved up and shed at once.

Twenty-five

THE BIG ADVANTAGE of Juliet's Maserati was its acceleration: It had warp engines as well as impulse power. When I got onto the North Circular—which at three in the morning was mercifully deserted and put my foot down on the pedal, six or seven cartloads of bullying g-force pressed me back into the hand-stitched leather, and the streetlights blue-shifted. I got to Chingford Hatch in what felt like a minute and a half.

The gates of the Maltings were wide open, and so was the front door. Just like the last time I'd been here, all the lights were on; but this time there was a general absence of people running around like headless chickens. I parked and glanced at Juliet lying across the backseat, absolutely still.

It was too dark to tell whether the healing process had already begun. If she were conscious, I could ask her how she was feeling, and if she broke my little finger, as she'd threatened to do back in Alabama, it would be a sign that she was starting to rally. In any case, I couldn't take her with me where I was going.

I got out of the car and walked across the stone flags to the door. I still didn't see a soul, and dead silence met me in the hallway. I wandered from room to room, expecting an ambush at first and looking behind every door, but you can't keep those hair-trigger reflexes honed forever. After a while it became more of a tense stroll.

I found Covington in Lionel Palance's bedroom. He was sitting in a steel-framed chair next to Palance's bed, reading the old man a bedtime story—and it wasn't *Noddy*. I guess he must have put his foot down about that. I walked into the room, making as little noise as I could, and stood behind him while he read. He did the voices pretty convincingly.

"'What have you been doing, Taffy?' said Tegumai. He had mended his spear and was carefully waving it to and fro.

"'It's a little berangement of my own, Daddy dear,' said Taffy. 'If you won't ask me questions, you'll know all about it in a little time, and you'll be surprised. You don't know how surprised you'll be, Daddy! Promise you'll be surprised.'

"'Very well,' said Tegumai, and went on fishing."

Covington glanced across at his audience of one. Palance was already asleep, his chest rising and falling without sound.

Covington closed the book and put it on the bedside table in the midst of all the medicines. His movements were a little jerky, so one or two of them fell off onto the floor. He picked them up and put them back in their places. He leaned forward, kissed Palance on the forehead without waking him, and then straightened again, squaring his shoulders as though for some ordeal.

"Castor," he said, turning for the first time to acknowledge me. He looked impossibly tired. "How did it go?"

"Pretty well, Aaron, all things considered."

"Meaning?"

"Meaning that if you went to Mount Grace right now, you'd find it looking like a morgue."

"Well—good. That's good. At least I presume it's good. And you and your—team all came out of it okay?"

I made a palm-wobbling so-so gesture. "We had one fatality. Fortunately."

He stood, looked calmly into my eyes. "And now you've come for me."

"Pretty much."

"Fancy a whiskey?"

"Pretty much."

He led the way down the stairs to the same room we'd used the night before. It felt like another lifetime. He picked up the Springbank, but I put my hand on his arm and shook my head. "Something rougher," I said. "Please. Rotgut, if you've got any."

He found some blended Scotch with a name I didn't recognize, held it up for my approval. I nodded.

"'Bartender, give me two fingers of red-eye,'" he quoted. He mimed the ancient joke, poking his fingers toward but not into my eyes. I didn't laugh. I wasn't in the mood, somehow.

He set out two glasses, poured a generous measure into one. Then he looked at the bottle, thought better of it, and took that, leaving the other glass empty on the bar. "Shall we sit down?" he asked, gesturing.

"Whatever." I followed him across to the leather three piece. He sprawled on the sofa, and I took one of the chairs. He chinked the bottle to my glass and then took a deep swallow of the whiskey. He didn't even shudder, although God knew it wasn't smooth.

"You called me Aaron," he observed, running his tongue across his lips.

"You'd prefer I called you Peter?"

He thought about that. "No, not really," he admitted. "Actually—in a strange way—there's a rightness to it. I made up Silver for myself, but Aaron was the name I was born with. What goes around, comes around. How did you know?"

I let my eyebrows rise and fall. "You weren't particularly trying to hide."

He acknowledged the point with a shrug. "Still. John Gittings never saw through me. Or did he? Was my name in his notes?"

"No." I swirled the whiskey in the glass, watching the filaments roll in the liquor like the ghosts of worms. I thought back, trying to get the sequence straight in my own mind because the conviction had crept over me by slow degrees; there hadn't been any one moment when the lightbulb had lit up above my head. "John didn't work it out. But the letter you sent him was a part of it, I suppose. You told him to take backup, and you told me the same thing when I came to see you. I guess that struck a chord. What was with the spelling, by the way? Just your instinct for camouflage kicking in?"

Covington made a slightly rueful face. "I can't spell," he said. "There's probably a name for this now—or there will be soon. Aaron Silver leaned English late in life, and he never got his head around the orthography. Now I find that every new body I live in has the same limitations as the original. It's possible to change, but it's hard. And it doesn't last. Old habits keep reasserting themselves. The past is—more present than the now. It's easier for me to write like that than it is to look up the correct spellings. Was that all? Just that one coincidence? Me saying the same thing to you that I wrote to Gittings?"

"No."

"Then—"

"You really want me to run through all the loose change you were dropping?"

"If you don't mind, yes. I still find it hard to believe that I've developed a death wish after working so hard for so long to stay alive. Indulge me."

I delved into my scattered thoughts again. "I was actually looking for you," I said. "Or at least—not for you, specifically, but for someone behind the scenes who was making things happen. You had to be there. Someone hired John and gave him a small fortune to spend on those death-row trinkets. Someone told him about the setup at Mount Grace but for some reason let him grope around in the dark for weeks on end, checking out cemeteries rather than just giving him the address. Someone playing games, in other words. Feeding him crumbs to keep him moving, but not wanting to show his hand. Maybe because if John went directly to Mount Grace, all your dead friends would know who sent him."

Covington smiled coldly—maybe at the word "friends." "Go on."

"Jan Hunter had a mysterious benefactor, too—someone who called her up claiming to be Paul Sumner, but

Paul Sumner was already dead. You again, I'm guessing, trying to keep the momentum going in spite of John's death—and maybe also looking for a way to stop Doug Hunter from going down for a murder he didn't commit. Strings were being pulled all the way down the line. Did you summon Moloch, too?" Covington nodded without speaking. "Yeah, I thought so. Big coincidence otherwise—that a demon with those dietary needs happened to be raised from hell where he'd catch the scent of the Mount Grace permanent floating barbecue. But there weren't any coincidences operating here. It was all part of the master plan." I took a long swig on the whiskey. It burned pleasantly in my mouth.

"So that was the main thing," I said. "The strings. You don't get all those strings without someone to pull on them. How did I know it was you? Just lots of little things. Your real name—Aaron Silver's real name, I mean—was Berg, and the name you gave to Ruth Kale was Bergson." He opened his mouth to speak, and I anticipated his objection. "No, you're right. I wouldn't have picked up on that if I didn't already know. It was the Paragon, Silver. You let yourself get seen by two people there."

He looked surprised. "I know. But I had my collar drawn up, and I was moving fast. I didn't think either of them got a good look at me."

"They didn't. But their different descriptions got me thinking. The desk clerk, Merrill—he said you were an old man. But Onugeta jostled against you in the hallway and felt how solidly muscled you were; he knew you had to be a young, fit guy. So why would Merrill think you were old?"

"I don't know, Castor. Why would he?"

I pointed at his head. "Your snow-white locks. You walked past his desk with your head down and your collar up, and all he saw of you was your hair. And I dunno, maybe there's something about how you walk: another echo. Something that goes with being a century and a half old. Either way, the paradox got my mind working. And once it was working, I saw that the little question—who was that masked man?—was the same as the big question. Why were you there at all? Why did you take the hammer away with you? Locking the stable door after the horse had bolted, even though Doug Hunter—with Myriam Kale inside him—was going to be arrested anyway."

Covington shook his head slowly. "You really thought this through, didn't you? Why did I?"

"Because flesh is clay. When a human soul possesses an animal body, it bends it as far as it can into a human shape. Sometimes the animal soul pushes back, and you can get some really interesting—not to say nasty—results as the seesaw tips. The same thing happens to you and your friends, doesn't it? The longer you stay inside a body that isn't yours, the more it adjusts to having you there. The more it slides into the shape and form you remember having in your old body. That's why you're snow-white blond as Peter Covington, and why you were snow-white blond as Les Lathwell—because Aaron Silver's soul remembered having snow-white hair. And that hammer, gripped in Doug Hunter's hand as Myriam Kale came bubbling up out of his soul and into the driver's seat—"

"—had Myriam Kale's fingerprints on it. Right. The hammer is behind the bar, by the way. I assume you'll be wanting to take it with you when you go. And it won't make any difference to me or to Mimi after tonight. Can I refresh your drink, Castor?"

I looked at my empty glass. "Probably better not," I said. "I need a clear head if I'm going to play you out."

"You don't need to worry. I won't make it hard for you. But I'm in the mood to confess before I die. I've got a favor to ask you, too. Have another drink with me."

Fuck it. Why not? It was his house and his booze. I held out the glass, and he filled it from the bottle he'd been drinking from. Well, alcohol is meant to be a good disinfectant.

"How long has it been since your last confession?" I asked him.

He laughed. "A hundred and some years. And I'm Jewish, not Catholic. Born Jewish, anyway. Religion never meant very much to me, which is why I had myself burned rather than buried. I didn't believe in the bodily resurrection. All my life I just did what I had to do to get by, and that never seemed to leave much room for thinking about God. The last time I went to shul was on my bar mitzvah. Three years after that, I killed my first man. Probably the one thing had as much to do with growing up as the other did."

Suddenly, the prospect of hearing all this seemed a lot less attractive. "So you were a bad man," I said. "We can take that as read, if you like. Move on to the atonement and the absolution."

"I've been handling the atonement in my own sweet way, Castor. And for your information, I haven't started telling you my sins yet. I don't think any of the men I killed back when I was Aaron Silver had any reason to complain. They would have done the same to me if I'd given them an opening. One of them did in the end. Henry Meyer-Lindeman got the drop on me in a whorehouse in Streatham. Actually on the job. Shot me and shot a lady by the name of Ginny Tester under me. We both died instantly."

"And in your end was your beginning."

Covington grimaced. "Not right away. It was a shock, waking after my own death and finding that I was trapped in Mount Grace. Tied to my own ashes. You never really are, of course. The trap consists of your own habits. Your own ways of thinking. But it felt real. It felt as though I'd be spending eternity on that one little plot of ground, and eternity would be a long time passing.

"But a year later, Stephen Kesel died, and he felt the same way about burial that I did. And four years after, it was Rudolf Gough's turn. And that was critical mass. There was an old janitor who used to live on the site. We took him one night while he was asleep—the three of us working together. Then we took turns to ride him. We were back in business.

"The first thing I did was to visit Meyer-Lindeman and pay him back with interest. I liked Ginny Tester a lot; she deserved better than to die in that undignified way. Steve and Rudy had similar visits to make—good ones and bad ones.

"But we realized pretty quickly that this went beyond dealing with unfinished business. We also figured out that it wasn't possible for one of us to betray the others. Steve tried to take off on his own, but he came limping back three days later. The janitor was fighting back, and it took the three of us to whip him into line again.

"So there we were. We were immortal, but only so long as we stuck together. An immortality collective. Till death us do part, only it never could, whether we wanted it to or not.

"All the rules and refinements came over the next twenty years or so—the years of throwing things against the wall to see whether they stuck. Experimentation and refinement. We discovered that the ashes made everything ten times easier, and they made the possession stick longer. We discovered that night was better than day, particularly for the initial breaking in of a new body, and that the dark of the moon was the best time of all. We turned it into a very streamlined process. Tried and tested. It helped that nobody believed what we were doing was even possible. That meant nobody was on their guard."

"What about Myriam Kale?" I asked. "Where does she come in?"

For a moment I thought Covington hadn't heard me. He was looking up at the ceiling, his posture one of acute attention. "Did you hear Lionel crying?" he demanded.

"I didn't hear a thing."

He relaxed a little. "Okay. Just the wind, I guess. I picked this room because it's right under his. If he stirs, we'll hear him. You'll notice I sent the nurses away, so I'm . . . on duty tonight. Myriam, right. Myriam was Yoko Ono. The femme fatale who gets the blame for breaking up the band."

He took another long swig of whiskey. He'd been drinking pretty regularly and pretty determinedly at every pause in the conversation, and the bottle was mostly empty. He was nerving himself up for something, but I wondered whether he might already have missed his stop.

"By the sixties," Covington said, "I was in my eighth body, if you can believe that. We wore them out pretty quickly: The psychic punishment is reflected in premature aging. Our numbers were up to two hundred, which is where they've stayed ever since, and we'd already had the idea of moving out of organized crime into legitimate business—things that would make us just as rich but at the same time lessen the chance of any police investigation finding us by accident.

"For me, it was getting...claustrophobic. I wasn't enjoying the company of my peers much at all. And I'd been practicing meditation techniques. I found that if I was really disciplined, I could maintain control of the body I was in more or less indefinitely, without reinscription.

"I went to the States intending to take a good long holiday—to stay away from Mount Grace for as long as possible. But I needed an excuse, and so I made up this bullshit story about making contact with the American mobs. Then to make it look like I was doing that, I spent some time with the Chicago families. That's how I met Myriam.

"I think I loved her because she was the opposite of everything I'd become. Okay, she was a killer; to that extent, we were the same. But there was no calculation in anything she did. She was spontaneous, following her instincts all the time, whether they were bad or good. Whereas at Mount Grace, calculation was our heart and soul. We'd become parts of a machine, and the machine ground on. And she was vulnerable and damaged, where we were immortal and beyond all harm. I don't know. I can't psychoanalyze myself. I was drawn to her. I wanted to help her. Probably the love came later, and it was never consummated. The closest we came to having actual sex was me masturbating her once while we were at a drive-in movie. She cried when she came, cried buckets. Like she couldn't bear it. God, what had been done to her! She was still strong, but...broken. Broken way past mending.

"But like I said, this was a holiday. I came home and threw myself back into the day-to-day, life-to-life stuff. The Krays, who were never part of our little clique, were arrested and carted off to Broadmoor, and we had the whole of the East End to ourselves. Then I read about Myriam being caught and convicted, and I made up my mind right then to bring her in."

"Are we up to the sins yet?" I asked.

He smiled humorlessly. "Almost. The rest of the committee was against it from the start. They could see all kinds of trouble arising from having an actual psychopath in our club—and they were right, obviously. I saw most of the potential problems myself, but I didn't care. I was determined to try. I felt...responsible for her somehow. And I hoped against all the evidence that in a new body, she might recover. Get over her madness and become what she was meant to be before all the rapes and the beatings.

"It didn't work. And yeah, now we're up to the sins. I feel sorry, and I feel ashamed when I think of the men she murdered. I never did acquire much of a taste for torture—and for personal reasons, I hate it when violence and sex get mixed up together. It always makes me think of poor Ginny.

"But the harm was done. The committee was terrified that Myriam would draw unwanted attention. They even paid to have that poor bastard Sumner—the hack writer—bumped off because he wrote a book about her. It got harder and harder to convince them to give her another chance—and last year, when I suggested giving her a man's body as a way of jolting her out of her old behavior patterns, they told me it was the last time. That meeting got kind of heated. I told them they were pathetic little echoes of what they'd been when they were alive, so scared of losing their creature comforts that they weren't really living at all anymore. They accused me of being too big for my boots, trying to run Mount Grace as though it were my personal empire. They threatened to expel me, and I told them they couldn't. Not anymore. I didn't need them to keep my hold on this body, and I could take another one anytime I wanted to, without their help. That was probably an unwise thing to say. When they realized how strong I was, they broke with me completely. By that time, it came as something of a relief. Because by that time I had something else eating at me. Worse even than Myriam."

"Palance," I guessed.

"Yeah," Covington whispered. "Lionel." He emptied the bottle in one final three-glug swallow.

"Who is he, Covington?"

"He's my son."

In the dead silence that followed this flat assertion, I did the math and failed to make it come out even close. Covington read the calculation and the outcome in my face and made a sweeping gesture with his hand to head off any objection. "I didn't father him as Aaron Silver," he said. "I was in one of the other bodies. I can't even remember which one; they all merge together now. They all ended up *looking* exactly the same after I'd been wearing them for a year or so, anyway.

"You see, Castor, once we'd gotten the mechanics of possession all worked out, the only problems we had left were the legal ones. We had a lot of property that we had to pass on from one generation to the next—from one *body* to the next—and we wanted to do it in ways that didn't look odd to someone looking in from outside. Some of us had trained as lawyers, which meant that as far as contracts went, we could nail down any arrangement we liked. But it had to look right. Right enough to keep anybody from wanting to look any deeper.

"So Seb Driscoll—the guy you met as Todd—he had a brilliant idea. We have kids. Doesn't have to be a church-wedding, house-in-the-suburbs kind of deal. We knock up some woman every now and then, so we've got biological children of our own. Because if you've got a kid—certifiably, genetically yours—everything becomes really easy. When the time comes to take a new body, you leave everything to the kid. You top yourself. You jump. Now *you're* the kid, and you've got the fortune, and nobody is going to ask any questions. You just look like a mensch, like a stand-up guy who saw his duty right at the end of his life and did it. End of story." Covington stood up slowly and carefully. To judge from the look on his face and the slight jerkiness in his movements, the booze was starting to kick in.

"So what went wrong?" I asked.

"Nothing." His voice dripped with bitterness. "Except—human nature, maybe. You could forgive me for thinking I didn't have any by this time, couldn't you? After all the things I'd done. All the mayhem, the killings, down through the years. Life is cheap, right? But not your own. And your kids are a little bit of your own life growing in someone else."

He didn't seem to know what to do with himself now that he was up on his feet again. He tried pacing, but that didn't seem to work. He'd stop after every few steps as though trying to remember a specific sequence of movements and it kept escaping from him, forcing him to break off and start again.

"There were problems with Lionel," he said, staring at the floor. "We needed to make a certain land transfer at an awkward time—when he was only two years old. We went ahead and did it because there wasn't any other choice. Then the woman who was Lionel's mother started making difficulties—trying to spend our money—and Driscoll ordered a hit on her. But it was botched, and she went public, and it wasn't easy after that to get close to her. Or rather, it wasn't easy in any of the regular ways.

"But Driscoll saw a way of squaring the circle. He possessed Lionel, and we got Lionel to kill her."

In spite of everything I'd already seen and done that night, I felt an uncomfortable movement in my stomach. "His own mother?"

"Yeah. When he was three months past his second birthday. Cute, huh? That train set upstairs—I don't know if you saw it—that was what I sent him. Stupid gift for a two-year-old. He couldn't even put the fucking track together. But it didn't matter, because he wouldn't get to play with it.

"Driscoll thought it was funny. He'd worn a lot of bodies by that time, but he'd never tried wearing a kid. So he stayed there for a few months. Made quite a joke out of it, turning up for the monthly inscription with a—with a sharp-tailored suit, and looking at me out of my own son's—Do you mind? I need some fresh air."

He took aim with the bottle and hurled it against the picture window. The bottle shattered. The window fractured across but stayed whole. Frustrated, Covington crossed to the bar, picked up a heavy glass ashtray, and slung it like a discus. That did the job: It went pinwheeling through the window, which shattered spectacularly, and impacted on the stone flags outside in a fountain of shards that winked and sparkled briefly in the glare of one of the security lights. As though it hadn't happened, Covington turned to me again. His eyes were dry, but his cheeks were flushed, and a terrible strain twisted his mouth, making his handsome face a thing you wanted to look away from.

"So anyway, that started a whole craze. Driscoll talked it up so much, everyone had to try. Between his second and tenth birthdays, I'd estimate that Lionel had forty or fifty different passengers. And I let it happen. I stood by, and I—did nothing. Didn't think about it. Didn't care. Told myself I didn't care, anyway. Life is cheap, and the rest is—sentiment. Which is even cheaper.

"At ten Lionel was left to himself for a while. They lost interest. But it was too late by then. The cognitive centers in the brain—I don't know. I've heard it explained in four or five different ways. At the crucial points in his brain development, he'd been—asleep. A prisoner in his own body, bludgeoned into eight years of unconsciousness. He was never going to be normal. It turned out that you couldn't put those years back."

He took a deep, ragged breath. "So we had a hard

choice," he said. "Lionel was still the legal possessor of a lot of land—a big chunk of our assets. He was a ward of the court, in my legal custody, but there'd be problems if I administered his property as though it were mine. That would look like malfeasance. It was exactly what we wanted to avoid.

"We took the low road instead. Carried on possessing Lionel, carried on using him as our puppet, working on a strictly enforced rota, because the novelty had worn off by this stage and nobody was very keen to go through puberty again. We kept up the whole routine until he came of age. After that, he was as viable a suit to wear as anybody else, and it didn't matter so much. The job was done.

"But so was the damage. Now that it was too late, I could see—could really see for the first time—how monstrous a thing we were doing. How big an obscenity we were.

"I couldn't save Lionel. I'd even been part of what was done to him. What I could do was decide that there wouldn't be any more Lionels. That the operation would finally be shut down. And when they lost interest in him— when he got too old and they let him go at last—I brought him here. I've tried to make him comfortable, at least. I was trying for happy, but most of the time, comfortable is what we can manage. He doesn't remember much, but he has nightmares, and he's always confused. Always a little bit panicky, as though he's forgotten something important and something awful is about to happen and it'll be his fault.

"So you see, it wasn't Myriam. They all think it was, and maybe for them, that was the real crisis. For me—the camel's back was already well and truly fucked. Whatever they let me do for Myriam, or tried to stop me from doing, I was done. I was all done."

He looked at me bleakly. "Another drink?"

"No."

"No. Not for me, either, I guess. I can see the way you're looking at me, Castor. I would have killed you for that once."

"It's your party, Aaron. It's been your party all along."

He nodded. "Yeah, it has. What time is it?"

"About five-thirty."

"The next shift of nurses comes in at six. I need to make sure they all clock in. If someone doesn't make it, I have to call the service. After that, I'm yours. We'll go where Myriam is. We'll sort this out."

"Fine." I pulled myself wearily to my feet. Covington could have saved his effort. Breaking the window hadn't done anything to clear the air. I crossed to the bar, found the hammer wrapped in bubble plastic behind it, and hefted it onto my shoulder. "I'll wait for you in the car. Come on out whenever you're ready."

Retracing my steps through the maze, I came out onto the driveway and climbed into the car. The form-fitted leather was way too comfortable, and I dozed off into uneasy dreams. John Gittings was in them; so was Gary Coldwood. When a hand on my shoulder—the one that Todd had stabbed me in earlier that evening—woke me back into the world, cold sweat slicked my body from head to foot.

It was Covington, and he was already in the passenger seat. "Nice car," he said without much enthusiasm. "Did it belong to the dead woman in the backseat?"

"Demon," I corrected him. "Yeah, it's hers. And the rumors of her death are usually exaggerated."

"Whenever you're ready, Castor."

I turned the key in the ignition. I didn't think I'd ever be ready. But even in the cold, damp, misty predawn after a night of bloodletting and pain, you can always rely on Italian engineering. The Maserati started the first time, and I eased her out through the gates.

∽ Twenty-six

Sᴜᴇ ʙᴏᴏᴋ ɢʀᴇᴇᴛᴇᴅ the sight of her fallen lover with a wail of anguish, then she wrested Juliet's body out of my hands and took her away from me into another room—even Sue could carry Juliet's negligible bulk without strain—and kicked the door shut behind her. I took that to mean that if we wanted tea and biscuits, we'd have to rustle them up for ourselves.

But Covington was hungry for something else entirely, and he wasn't in the mood for delayed gratification. "Where is she?" he demanded, looking peremptorily around the small hall. "Is she here?"

"Up the stairs," I said, and he was taking them three at a time almost before the word was out of my mouth. I didn't follow straightaway. The energy Juliet had lent me had all drained away, and the events of the last few hours were taking their inevitable toll. I felt like a piece of windblown crud that had fetched up out of the night at the foot of these stairs and couldn't be expected to go any farther. Windblown crud doesn't defy gravity. It knows its place.

But eventually, I summoned the willpower from somewhere and started to climb. From the bedroom facing me, I heard Covington's murmured voice and then a crazed laugh from Doug Hunter's throat.

I hesitated on the top step, not sure whether this was a private party. Covington's "We'll sort this out" gave me no clue at all as to what he had planned, or even whom the "we" referred to.

Leaning my back against the wall, I enjoyed the momentary sensation of weightlessness that comes with having carried something very heavy for a long time and finally been allowed to set it down. Tomorrow there was more shit still to come, but tomorrow was another day—technically, anyway, even though it was probably less than half an hour to sunup.

The weightlessness passed, but I still felt curiously detached from my own emotions. The guilt that had bitten into me when I heard about Gary Coldwood's death was mercifully dulled, but there was no sense of triumph or satisfaction in having dealt with his would-be killers. If anything, Covington's account had left me feeling as though there was mourning still to be done; but I couldn't make a start on it yet.

Covington's voice rose and fell in the bedroom, his words never quite becoming audible. I could hear Kale's replies, though.

"No. I didn't see you. I looked for you and didn't see you. You left me!"

Murmuring from Covington.

"Oh, that's fine! That's wonderful! Whatever you want

to call it. Fucking—cocks! Cocks talking, calling themselves men! Love me? Oh yeah, I'll bet you do. I'll bet
you do!"

Murmur.

"Well, this is me now. It's not him anymore, it's me."

Murmur.

"I don't even know the way. But if I knew the way, I
couldn't do it. Not on my own, Les! Not—not all that way
on my own. Don't make me. Don't ask me to."

Murmur.

"No."

Murmur.

"You can't. Don't lie to me! I won't even have a fucking hand to hold."

Murmur.

Long silence.

Kale laughed, and the laugh turned into a sob. "Don't
leave me. Don't leave me, Les. I'm so scared."

For the first time I heard him answer her. "I'm going,
Mimi. I've made up my mind. And you can't keep a hold
on this body anymore without me and the others to help
you. Come now, with me, or come later, on your own.
That's the only choice you've got."

Another long silence.

Covington appeared in the doorway. "We need you,"
he said.

———————————

At any other time, I might have balked at the thought
of playing two souls at the same time, but I'd just played
two hundred and come out of it with my mind intact, so
this didn't feel too hard. And Covington didn't want a full

exorcism, only an unbinding. Something that would lift them both out of their flesh and leave them free to move.

Embarrassingly, though, it was a while before the music would come. I'd flogged my talent pretty hard that night, and the sense of dissociation still hung around me like the wooziness after anesthesia. Covington had untied Kale's arms and upper body, and they sat together on the bed, his arms around her—or rather, Doug's—shoulders protectively. She clung to him so hard that I could see the whitening of her knuckles. The two of them stared at me wordlessly, like already condemned prisoners waiting to hear the outcome of some last appeal.

At last I ventured a note, and I knew when I heard it that it wasn't right. I held it anyway, then modulated down the scale until I locked in to something that felt like it was alive and moving. I let it find its own way out through the bore, almost unstopped, using breath control alone to shape it. It wasn't a tune; it was an incoherent wail pretending to be music.

Covington kissed Myriam Kale on Doug Hunter's forehead, whispered something that I couldn't hear over the sound of the whistle, and then slid sideways off the bed. Kale lasted a few moments longer before slumping back onto the pillow, her eyes glazing over before they closed.

Covington's ghost was a smudgy blur hovering over his body. Maybe that was a side effect of the protective camouflage that the risen dead of Mount Grace had used in the days of their ascendancy—or maybe it was a side effect of being so damn old and having slid and glided through so many different flesh houses over the last hundred years. Maybe he'd distilled down into this minimal placeholder for a human shape.

But Kale was magnificent. I saw then, for the first time, what the photos had failed to capture: the energy and the feral grace that had drawn in so many men and made the great Aaron Silver linger and be lost.

The two spirits—the one so painfully vivid, the other so nearly not there—came together in the air over the bed and then started to waver as though in some kind of heat haze. It was something I'd never seen before: self-exorcism, a willed and wanted abdication. She smiled as she faded, but then apes smile when they're afraid, and there was something of blind terror about her eyes. Still, she was looking at him—at the man who'd been born Aaron Berg and then worn so many other names—and I thought the expression was softening into something else as it sublimed out of my visible spectrum altogether.

Doug Hunter came around after only a few minutes. I was afraid he might draw entirely the wrong conclusion from finding himself tied to a bed in a room in a strange house with a guy he didn't recognize sitting on a chair next to the bed, but that was one complication I didn't have to worry about. He was too weak and too sick to care much about where he was, and his memories came back with his strength.

Peter Covington—assuming that was the blond man's original name—wasn't so lucky. Like Maynard Todd, he'd been ridden for much longer by the Mount Grace dead, and it had damaged him more deeply. He lay on the floor, conscious but unable or unwilling to stir, his lips moving silently.

I helped Doug to untie himself, and then I helped him to stand. "Where's—Jan?" he slurred.

"Waiting for you at home," I told him. "You want to go there now?"

He tried to speak but couldn't get the word out. He nodded instead.

"You're still wanted for murder, Doug. You probably want to give yourself up rather than let them catch you and bring you in."

He nodded again. "To-tomorrow."

Yeah. There's always tomorrow.

~ Twenty-seven

THE WORLD TURNED under me, and I turned with it.

These things harrowed me with fear and wonder at the time, but you know how it is. With the endless repetitions of memory, they lost a lot of their impact. You've probably had similar weeks yourself.

With Sue Book guarding her lover like a tenderhearted rottweiler, Juliet recovered almost 100 percent in the space of a couple of weeks—but there's a world of meaning in that "almost." Moloch had wounded her on a level deeper than flesh, and there was only so much that flesh could do to mend it. She refused to talk about the details, and when I kept pressing anyway, prurient bastard that I am, she handed me an invitation in a dinky, girly little envelope with a silver border. I stopped when I got to the line that read CEREMONY OF CIVIL UNION. I'm still hoping that the names, when I get to them, will be those of two people I don't know from Eve.

Gary Coldwood recovered, too. He endured six months' suspension from duty, but he was reinstated at his original rank when the evidence of a fit-up piled up so high it was in danger of toppling over and hurting someone. The engine block of his car had been tampered with, and likewise the brakes. There were rope burns on his hands, and his upper lip had been split wide open by whoever force-fed him the booze; they even found some broken glass from a Bacardi bottle in his upper palate. He used his half a year of enforced leisure to finish his forensics course, and now you can't have a conversation with him without coagulation, postmortem artifacts, or stellate wound patterns getting a mention. But he's got the limp, and he's got the scar, and there's an unspoken something in the air whenever we meet. He doesn't expect me to apologize; it wouldn't help if I did. Maybe we'll meet less and less often until either the something or the friendship goes away.

Jan Hunter came and found me at my office in Harlesden one bleak Tuesday afternoon shelving dangerously into evening. She tried to pay me the rest of the money we'd agreed on when she hired me. I kept my hands in my pockets.

"I do read the papers, Jan," I said. "Doug got off on the murder charge because they finally decided to allow that hammer in as evidence. But he still got three years for the jailbreak. You don't owe me a thing."

"You know exactly what I owe you, Mr. Castor," she insisted. "Whoever did the crime, it's my husband who's going to serve that sentence, and it's my husband who'll come out—next year, if he keeps his nose clean—to find me waiting for him. If it wasn't for you, I might never have seen him again."

I knew that was a lie, but it was a hard one to explain. Alone, without the Mount Grace trust to carry out the monthly reinscription, Myriam Kale would have found herself expelled from Doug's body sooner or later. And if the way we'd done it had eased the trauma and lessened the damage, the thanks probably belonged to the man who'd died a second time to make it happen. I told Jan to put the money toward a second honeymoon. If she invests it wisely, it might pay for a dirty weekend in Clacton.

It took me a long time to go through the files I took from Maynard Todd's office, but the preliminary sweep of the names was quick and easy—although some of them made my eyebrows skitter across the top of my head and come to rest behind my ears. There were a couple of cabinet ministers in there for starters, along with a Radio 4 presenter, the head of a major union, and the CEOs of three companies even I've heard of.

But the biggest surprise wasn't any of those. It was another name that sent me on my travels to the top end of the Northern Line, five days after all this shit had hit the fan and when the echoes had already started to fade.

Court number one at Barnet had a full docket that morning: I didn't bother to look at the details, but summary justice was scheduled to be meted out to an impressive number of people. Never mind the quality, as the saying goes. Feel the burn.

I sat at the back of the court, making myself as inconspicuous as I could, but something was throwing the honorable Mr. Montague Runcie off his honorable stride. He wasn't looking in the peak of condition, for one thing:

His face was pale, and there was a sheen of sweat on his forehead, as though he were hunkered down under about five degrees of fever. And he kept looking over at me in the back row center, getting more and more rattled each time. He fought his way manfully through the first case (a persistent burglar going down for a three-stretch), but he lost the thread of things a bit in the second (nonpayment of council tax) and got downright tetchy in the third (bad debt). Finally, he called a recess of half an hour and stormed off the bench so quickly that we didn't have time to stand up and sit down again when the door slammed behind him.

A minute or so after that, the court clerk picked his way casually to the back row and asked me if I'd mind attending His Honor in his chambers. I said I'd be delighted, and asked whether I could bring my bronze funerary urn with me. It held the mortal remains of my uncle George, and it was hard for me to be parted from them.

Runcie favored me with a berserker glare as I walked in, but he had enough presence of mind to dismiss the clerk before he started in on me. I took the opportunity to sit down on the far side of the dignified mahogany barricade that was his desk. Runcie was standing, so rigid with indignation that he was vibrating slightly, like a tuning fork. He really looked unwell, the pallor going beyond ashen into waxy.

"How dare you bring that—thing into my courtroom?" he demanded, waving a finger at the urn, as soon as we were alone. "What's the meaning of it?"

I gave the urn a wipe, because the bronze was a bit tarnished here and there. "Well," I explained, "it's a mark of respect for the dead, primarily, but it also gives the living a focus for their grief. Otherwise you could just flush your ashes down the khazi and use the money for—"

"Don't give me all that—nonsense," Runcie interrupted me, forcing the words past clenched teeth. "Why did you bring it here? Why are you showing it to me?"

"Ah!" I said, shaking my head ruefully at my own misunderstanding. "Yeah, I get you now. Not so much 'What the hell is that?' as 'What the hell is that doing in my courtroom?' Well, Mr. R., it's a great, huge, festering, bloated bastard of a memento mori. Which, if your Latin isn't up to it, means—"

"I know what it means."

"—a reminder of death; a vivid or stirring testimony to human mort—"

"I know what it means!" Runcie screamed. "Get it out of my courtroom or I'll find you in contempt! You'll do thirty days, you understand me?"

I massaged my nose thoughtfully. "Thirty days is a long time," I observed.

Runcie shook his head, his eyes a little wild. "Oh, no. Thirty days is my opening bid, Mr.—whatever your name is. Carson? Carter? I know you. I know what you're aiming to do here. You can't intimidate a magistrate. But you can get yourself into a lot of trouble trying."

I didn't bother to answer. I turned the urn to face him. The name on it wasn't Runcie, but it made him moan and fall backward into his chair, all the fight knocked out of him in a second.

"Now," I said easily, "we know where we stand. You on that road with all the paving slabs made out of good intentions you never cashed in. And me on your balls."

Runcie said something. It wasn't that easy to hear, but

the name on the urn was in there, along with some protest or disclaimer or denial. I turned the slightly dented
bronze vessel around again and examined the name.
"John Colmore," I read. "Aka Jack Spot, the king of Ald-
gate. That's you, isn't it? You would have been one of the
early ones, I'm guessing. And far from the worst. I gather
you charged the Jewish businesses around Mile End a lot
of money for 'protection'—but then when the blackshirts
rolled up, you actually weighed in and provided some,
which is something of a novelty. And you've improved
yourself since then, obviously. Aaron Silver told me some
of you had trained as lawyers for tactical reasons, but
bloody hell, eh? A beak. You *can* take the boy out of the
gutter."

Runcie gave me a look that was pure poison, but I for-
gave him because he had nothing at all to back it up.

"So don't get me wrong, Jack," I concluded. "I've got
nothing against you personally. But I've got to look out
for me and mine, and right now, from where I'm sitting,
you're part of the problem. So here's how it's going to
go. You're going to serve an injunction against Jenna-Jane
Mulbridge, immediately restraining her against taking
Rafi Ditko out of the Stanger clinic. You'll also rule yourself *ultra vires* on the power-of-attorney thing and bump
it up to one of your mates in the court of appeal with a
quiet nudge and a wink to decide in Pen Bruckner's favor.
These things you will do now, while I watch. And then
you might want to clock off early and have a G and T,
because you'll have earned it."

Runcie was still glaring at me like I'd trodden dog shit
into his Persian carpet. "The law can't be bought, Mr.
Castor."

"I wouldn't dream of trying," I protested, throwing out my arms in injured innocence. "Although I suspect Jenna-Jane did. But this—this is extortion, not bribery."

"You can't threaten me."

"Can't I? Let me paint you a picture, then. You're a ghost sitting in a body, which, if I'm any judge—pardon the pun—is already starting to reject you. Your friends aren't around anymore to help you get the whip hand again. No more inscriptions, now or ever, so there's no going back. Which leaves you with three options. Sing along if you know the words." I counted them off on my fingers. "One. You hold on for dear life and savor every last second of your fleshly existence until, finally, the last one of your fingernails is prized loose and you go sailing off into eternity like a balloon with its string cut.

"Two—and this is a risky one—you let go. Leave now, while you're still strong, instead of wearing yourself out with a fight you can't win. Find yourself a fresh corpse to nest in or a dog to redecorate. Come back as a zombie or a loup-garou and live to fight another day. If you opt for two, I can even give you some pointers. I've been around the track a few times when it comes to borrowed flesh.

"But then there's three. Are you ready for three?"

Runcie had his head buried in his hands and didn't give any sign of hearing me, but I knew he was listening.

"Three is this. You piss me off, and I play you a short, merry tune. And then it's all over, Jack. Right here and right now. Because I'm the bingo caller from hell, and I've got your number. And some of my friends are dead because some of your friends liked to shoot first before anyone could ask any questions, so I don't owe you a single fucking favor in the whole wide world."

I stood up. "Your choice. And because I'm in a bright, bubbly, expansive mood today, I'm going to give you until I reach the door."

∽ Twenty-eight

THAT COUNTED AS a happy ending, in my book. It was a case I was able to walk away from, which put me among the front runners if you look at the statistics. Rafi was safe from Jenna-Jane's scientific curiosity, for the moment, at least. He could relax and unpack in his padded cell made for two. And that, in turn, put me back in good with Pen, to the point where she could actually bear to talk to me for whole minutes at a time. I even had grounds for hope that she might break down and let me come and live in her attic again when Ropey Doyle came back from Ireland with a snow-white tan and a broader accent.

The righteous will get their reward in the kingdom of heaven. The rest of us poor sons of bitches have to content ourselves with what we can scrape together here on earth.

I think back, in idle moments, to when I was a kid in Walton, Liverpool. Sometimes in summer, on really hot days, we'd go down to a place called the Sisters. It was a series of bomb craters on a huge expanse of waste ground next to a closed-down railway track. The bigger craters had filled up with water over time and become ponds.

Even on the hottest day, the water would be freezing cold. You'd stick your foot in, then swear a lot and back off, and get jeered at both by kids who'd already gone in and by kids who had no intention of trying. So you'd wade in a bit deeper, and a bit deeper—foot, to calf, to knee, to hip—and the cold would be biting into your legs, and it would be agony. Then it was lapping at your stomach and it was worse. You kept hoping you'd acclimatize, but the more you drew it out, the more it hurt. Until, suddenly, you were in over your shoulders and—just like that—it was absolutely fine. Cool, refreshing, the best thing ever. Best of all, you got to laugh at all the other poor bastards who were still at the toe-dipping stage.

I always envied the few hardy souls who took a running jump, hit the water all curled up into a ball, and then opened up, laughing, already there: the whole incremental ordeal bypassed in a single moment of raw courage.

So what I'm getting at is this. Okay, maybe it's cold in the grave. Maybe you come out of the light and think, Fuck your mother, this is bad. This is worse than anything I would have guessed. But the trick is to clench your teeth, get a running start, and dive.

When I hit that other country from whose bourne no traveler backpedals, I'm going to be moving fast. I'm gambling the first ten seconds or so will be the worst.

VISIT US ONLINE

@ WWW.HACHETTEBOOKGROUP.COM.

AT THE HACHETTE BOOK GROUP WEB SITE YOU'LL FIND:

CHAPTER EXCERPTS FROM SELECTED
NEW RELEASES
•
ORIGINAL AUTHOR AND EDITOR ARTICLES
•
AUDIO EXCERPTS
•
BESTSELLER NEWS
•
ELECTRONIC NEWSLETTERS
•
AUTHOR TOUR INFORMATION
•
CONTESTS, QUIZZES, AND POLLS
•
FUN, QUIRKY RECOMMENDATION CENTER
•
PLUS MUCH MORE!

BOOKMARK HACHETTE BOOK GROUP
@ WWW.HACHETTEBOOKGROUP.COM.